Fire and Ice

ALSO BY J. A. JANCE

Joanna Brady Mysteries

Desert Heat

Tombstone Courage

Shoot/Don't Shoot

Dead to Rights

Skeleton Canyon

Rattlesnake Crossing

Outlaw Mountain

Devil's Claw

Paradise Lost

Partner in Crime

Exit Wounds

Dead Wrong

Damage Control

J. P. Beaumont Mysteries

Until Proven Guilty

Injustice for All

Trial by Fury

Taking the Fifth

Improbable Cause

A More Perfect Union

Dismissed with Prejudice

Minor in Possession

Payment in Kind

Without Due Process

Failure to Appear

Lying in Wait

Name Withheld

Breach of Duty

Birds of Prey

Partner in Crime

Long Time Gone

Justice Denied

and

Hour of the Hunter

Kiss of the Bees

Day of the Dead

Edge of Evil

Web of Evil

Hand of Evil

Cruel Intent

Fire and Ice

J. A. Jance

This book is a work of fiction. The characters, incidents, and dialogue are drawn from the author's imagination and are not to be construed as real. Any resemblance to actual events or persons, living or dead, is entirely coincidental.

HarperCollins books may be purchased for educational, business, or sales promotional use. For information please write: Special Markets Department, HarperCollins Publishers, 10 East 53rd Street, New York, NY 10022.

FIRST HARPERLUXE EDITION

HarperLuxe™ is a trademark of HarperCollins Publishers

Library of Congress Cataloging-in-Publication Data is available upon request.

ISBN: 978-0-06-177477-5

09 10 11 12 13 ID/RRD 10 9 8 7 6 5 4 3 2 1

For Larry Dever and Ken Wallentine,
the real deals

And for Hal Witter,
the real deal, too

Fire and Ice

Prologue

November

Driving east on I-90, Tomas Rivera was surprised to see the snow spinning down out of a darkened sky in huge fat flakes that threatened to overwhelm the puny efforts of the 4-Runner's hardworking windshield wipers. It was only the sixth of November. Snow this heavy didn't often come to the Cascades so early in the season. Beyond Eastgate and North Bend electronic signs flashed a warning that traction devices were required in the pass.

The signaled warnings didn't concern Tomas all that much. He was sure the stolen SUV's four-wheel drive would get him through any snow on the roadway. Overworked cops would be so busy dealing with multiple fender-benders that he doubted they'd be on the lookout for stolen vehicles. It also seemed likely that it was too soon for the Department of Transportation to be doing avalanche control, but what if they were? What if he got stopped at the pass and had to wait for snowplows or ended up being stuck at the chain-up area for an hour or two? What if the girl on the floor in the far back of the SUV woke up suddenly and started making noises—thumping, bumping, or groaning? If people were standing around outside in the waiting area, he worried they might hear her or see her or start asking questions.

Despite the cold, Tomas found he was sweating. His armpits were soaked, and so were his hands inside the gloves, but he didn't dare take them off.

"Wear gloves," Miguel had warned him. "Whatever you do, wear gloves."

Since it wasn't a good idea to cross Miguel, Tomas wore gloves.

The poor woman had already been bound, presumably gagged, wrapped loosely in a tarp and dumped in the back of the 4-Runner when Miguel delivered the vehicle to him. Miguel didn't say where she was from or why she was there, and Tomas didn't ask. The less he knew about her, the better.

"Take her out in the woods and get rid of her," Miguel had said. "There's a full gas can in the back. Use that. Throw her out, pull her teeth, douse her with gasoline, and light a match. When you're done, ditch the car somewhere far away. Understand?"

Tomas had nodded. He understood all right. And he understood what would happen if he didn't. Tomas also understood Miguel and the men he worked with. They were rich and powerful, dangerous and ruthless. They were the kind of men who would kill you in a heartbeat, not with their two hands, of course, but they would have somebody around willing to do the dirty work. They'd hand it off to some poor dope who owed them and owed big; or to someone like Tomas who didn't dare step out of line for fear of what would happen to him—or to his family.

Yes, Tomas thought. Someone just like me.

He understood what it meant to commit a mortal sin. If he didn't get to confession and died, he'd go straight to hell. And if he didn't do what he'd been told, he'd be living in hell. In a way, he already was. He had paid good money—money earned doing backbreaking, dangerous delimbing work out in the woods—to have Lupe and the boys smuggled across the border and brought north. But having paid a small fortune to Miguel's coyotes didn't mean Tomas and Lupe were home free. Miguel had made it clear that if Tomas didn't do what was required of him, what might happen to Little Tomas and Alfonso would be worse than death. For the thousandth time Tomas wished he had left well enough alone. Things weren't necessarily pleasant or comfortable in the little tin-roofed shack where Lupe and the boys had lived in Cuidad Obregon. But he'd had no idea about the real price of bringing his little family to the United States of America.

So Tomas kept driving. He turned off the freeway at Cabin Creek Road and headed off into the maze of National Forest roads that carried loggers and logging equipment off into the wilderness. That's why Miguel had come looking for him to do this particular job. Tomas knew all those roads like the back of his hand—because he had driven them himself, ferrying crews in and out of the woods. With severe winter weather setting in, the logging crews were out of the picture for the time being—until the snow melted in the spring. Or summer.

Even though it made it hard to see, Tomas was grateful for the deepening snow. There would be no tire tracks left for the cops to trace. And no footprints, either. By morning, all tracks would be nothing more than slight dents. And in weather like this, no one would be out there watching, either. Only the dumbest of cross-country skiers would venture this far off the main roads.

As Tomas drove, he wondered what the woman had done that merited this death sentence, but he didn't wonder too hard. That was Miguel's business, not his.

Tomas stopped the SUV a mile or so short of Lake Kachess at a spot where yet another road wandered away from the one he was on. The intersection created a small clearing that was barely big enough for him to swing the 4-Runner in a tight circle without running the risk of getting stuck. When he turned off the engine, he was dismayed to realize that his prisoner was awake and moaning. Miguel had told him she was out for good, but clearly that wasn't true.

Shaking his head, Tomas punched the button that unlocked the hatch, then got out and walked through swirling snow to the back of the vehicle. Opening the cargo bay, he reached in and grabbed the tarp-wrapped bundle. As he pulled it toward him, the woman inside struggled and tried to roll away. Grabbing for her a second time, his hand caught on what was evidently a cowboy boot, one that came off in his hand. It surprised him and bothered him somehow. He didn't want to know she wore cowboy boots. He didn't want to know anything about her at all.

When he finally had her free of the floorboard, he let her drop to the ground. The force of the fall knocked the breath out of her. For a brief moment she was quiet, then she started moving and struggling once more. The mewling sounds coming from under the tarp were aimed at him in a wordless plea that was clear enough.

"Please don't do this. Please. Please. Please."

Tomas didn't want to do it, either. But it was too late to stop; too late to turn back. Tomas knew that if he failed or wavered, Lupe and the boys would become Miguel's next target.

Tugging at the end of the tarp, he dragged her away from the road and into the shelter of a second growth tree. Then he went back for the tire iron. Several blows to the head from that rendered the woman senseless. He knew what he was supposed to do then. Tomas had the needle-nose pliers there in his pocket. But he also knew, as Miguel did not, that pulling her teeth was something Tomas could not do.

When his boys had lost their baby teeth—their loose baby teeth—Lupe had been the one who did the honors. The very idea of removing hers . . . Instead, he went back to the car and retrieved the gas can, poured the liquid over the now still tarp, and lit the match. He had to light more than one because it took more than one before the fumes finally ignited.

When they did, he moved back out of reach, crossing himself and uttering a quick prayer as the flames roared skyward through the swirling snow. In the flickering firelight, he looked down and noticed that while he was wrestling her out of the SUV, the cowboy boot had come to rest in the snow near the back bumper. Reaching down, Tomas picked it up and was about to toss it into the raging fire when he noticed that something had been taped to the instep. Peeling off the tape, he pulled out a small rectangular piece of stiff paper. It was blank on one side, but the other side revealed the smiling photo—a school photo, no doubt—of a dark-haired boy not that much older than his own sons.

Tomas looked back through the eddying snow. The tarp was fully engulfed now. So was the woman. The odor of burning gasoline was giving way to something else. He quickly tossed the boot into the flames, but for some reason he couldn't bring himself to part with the photo. Slipping that into the pocket of his shirt, he turned and clambered back into the SUV.

As Tomas drove away, he wondered where and how he'd get rid of the 4-Runner. It had to be somewhere far away from surveillance cameras. He couldn't afford to be seen anywhere near it, and not just because it was a stolen vehicle.

Now it was a matter of life and death—his as well as hers.

March

LAKE KACHESS

Ken Leggett wasn't what you could call a warm and fuzzy guy. For one thing, he didn't like people much. It wasn't that he was a bigot. Not at all. It wasn't a matter of his not liking blacks or Hispanics or Chinese—he disliked them all, whites included. He was your basic all-inclusive disliker.

Which was why this solitary job as a heavy-equipment operator was the best one he'd ever had—or kept. In the spring he spent eight to ten hours a day riding a snowplow and uncovering mile after mile of forest road that logging companies used to harvest their treasure troves of wood from one clear-cut section of the Cascades after another.

Once the existing roads were cleared, he traded the snowplow for either a road grader, which he used to carve even more roads, or a front-end loader, which could be used to accumulate slash—the brush and branches left behind after the logs had been cut down, graded, and hauled away.

As long as he was riding his machinery, Ken didn't have to listen to anyone else talk. He could be alone with his thoughts, which ranged from the profound to the mundane. Just being out in the woods made it pretty clear that God existed, and knowing his ex-mother-in-law, to say nothing of his ex-wife, made it clear that the devil and hell were real entities as well. Given all that, then, it made perfect sense that the world should be so screwed up—that the Washington Redskins would probably never win the Super Bowl and that the Seattle Mariners would never win the World Series, either.

The fact that Ken liked the Mariners was pretty self-explanatory. After all, he lived in North Bend—outside North Bend, really—and Seattle was just a few miles down the road. As for why he loved the Redskins? He'd never been to Washington—D.C., that is. In fact, the only time he'd ever ventured out of Washington State had been back in the 1980s, when his then-wife had dragged him up to Vancouver, B.C., for something called Expo. He had hated it. It had rained like crazy, and most of the exhibits were stupid. If he wanted to be wet and miserable, all he had to do was go to work.

He sure as hell didn't have to pay good money for the privilege.

As for the Redskins? What he liked about them most was that they hadn't bowed to public opinion and changed their name to something more politically palatable. And when he was watching football games in the Beaver Bar in North Bend, he loved shouting out "Go, Redskins!" and waiting to see if anyone had balls enough to give him any grief over it. When it came to barroom fights, Little Kenny Leggett, as he was sometimes called despite the fact that he was a bruising six-five, knew how to handle himself—and a broken beer bottle.

So here he was sending a spray of snow flying off the road and thinking about the fact that he was glad to be going back to work. Early. A whole month earlier than anyone had expected. When winter had landed with a knock-out punch early in November, everybody figured snow was going to bury the Cascades with record-shattering intensity. The ski resorts had all hoped for a memorable season, and that turned out to be true for the wrong reason—way too little snow rather than too much.

That first heavy snowfall got washed away by equally record-shattering rains a few days later. For the rest of the winter the snow never quite got its groove back and had proved to be unusually mild. It snowed some, but not enough for skiers really to get out there. And not enough for the bureaucrats to stop whining about it, either. In fact, just that morning, on his way to work, Ken had heard some jerk from the water department complaining that the lack of snowfall and runoff might well lead to water rationing in the Pacific Northwest before the end of summer.

Yeah, Ken thought. Right. That makes sense, especially in Washington, where it rains constantly, ten months out of twelve.

Ken glanced at his watch. The switch to daylight saving time made for longer afternoons, but it was nearing quitting time, and that meant he was also nearing the end of that day's run. His boss wasn't keen on paying overtime, and Ken wasn't interested in working for free, so he needed to be back at the equipment shed by the time he was supposed to be off duty.

It was a long way back—a long slow way—and the thermos of coffee he had drunk with his lunch had run through the system. After turning the plow around in a small clearing, he set the brake. Then, shutting off the engine, he clambered down and went to make some yellow snow.

After the steady roar of equipment, the sudden stillness was a shock to his system. He knew that old saying about if a tree falls in the forest and nobody hears it . . . He wondered sometimes about what happened if you took a leak in the woods and no one heard you or saw you, did it exist? Chuckling at that private joke, he headed for a tree that was a few feet off the road to do his business. Better here where there was little chance of being seen. Close to civilization, somebody might be out there. Ken didn't exactly think of himself as shy, but still . . .

Spring was coming. The snow had melted away completely in some spots, but under the trees it was still thick enough. Once he was out of sight of the road, he spotted what appeared to be a small boulder sticking up out of the snow. He unzipped and took aim at that. As the stream of steaming yellow urine hit the rock, the remaining snow melted away and a series of odd cracks became visible in the rock's surface. Squinting, Ken bent to take a closer look. Only after a long moment did what he was seeing finally register. When it did, the horrible realization hit him like the surge of a powerful electric shock. That boulder wasn't a boulder at all. It was a skull, a gaping human skull, sitting at an angle, half in and half out of a batch of melting yellow snow.

Staring at the awful visage in astonishment, Ken staggered backward, all the while trying desperately to zip up his pants as he went. Unaware of where he was going, he stumbled over something—a root, he hoped—and fell to the ground. But when he looked back to see what had tripped him, he realized that it wasn't a root at all. He had stumbled over a length of bone that his fleeing footsteps had dislodged from a thin layer of melting snow.

That was when he lost it. With a groan he ducked his head and was very, very sick. At last, when there was nothing left to heave, Ken Leggett wiped his mouth on his sleeve and lurched to his feet. With a ground speed that would have astonished his old high school football coach, Ken headed for the safety of his snowplow. Once inside, he locked both doors and then leaned against the steering wheel, shaking from head to toe and gasping for breath.

His first thought was that he'd just forget about it and let someone else find it later—much later. Ken didn't like cops. He wasn't good with cops. And if he reported finding a body, what if they thought he was somehow responsible? But then he managed to pull himself together.

What if this was my brother or my son? Or my sister or daughter? he thought. I wouldn't want whoever found them to walk away and leave them. Straighten up, he told himself. Have some balls for once and do the right thing.

He reached over to the stack of orange construction cones he kept on the snowplow's muddied floorboard.

He pulled one of those loose and then, after opening the window, dropped it outside. It landed right in the middle of the footprints he'd left in the snow as he leaped back into the vehicle. At least this way he'd be able to find the spot again; he'd be able to bring someone here.

Steeling himself for that ordeal, Ken made himself a promise. Once he got through with the cops, he would hit the Beaver Bar and stay there until he was good and drunk. The best thing about the Beave was that he could walk home from there. Ken Leggett already had a lifetime's worth of DUIs. He had paid all those off now, and he sure as hell didn't need another one.

He started the snowplow then and put it in gear. Halfway back to the equipment shed, he stopped and checked to see if he had a signal on his cell phone—only half a bar but enough. His hands still shook as he dialed the number.

"Washington State Patrol," the 911 operator answered. "What are you reporting?"

"A body," Ken replied. His voice was shaking, too, right along with his hands. "I just found a dead body out here in the woods."

"You're certain this person is deceased?" the operator asked.

"He's dead, all right," Ken answered. "As far as I can see, all that's left of him is bones."

Chapter 1

March

I am not a wimp. Maybe that sounds too much like Richard Nixon's "I am not a crook," but it's true. I'm not. With twenty-plus years at Seattle PD, most of it on the Homicide Squad, and with several more years of laboring in the Washington State Attorney General's Special Homicide Investigation Team, I think I can make that statement with some confidence. Usually. Most of the time. Right up until I got on the Mad Hatter's Tea Party ride at Disneyland with my six-year-old granddaughter, Karen Louise, aka Kayla.

She had been in charge of the spinning. She loved it. I did not. When the ride ended, she went skipping away as happy as can be toward her waiting parents while I staggered along after her. Over her shoulder I heard her say, "Can we go again?" Then, stopping to look at me, she added, "Gramps, how come your face is so green?"

Good question.

When Kayla was younger, she used to call me Gumpa, which I liked. Now I've been demoted or promoted, I'm not sure which, to Gramps, which I don't like. It's better, however, than what she calls Dave Livingston, my first wife's second husband and official widower. (Karen, Kayla's biological grandmother, has been dead for a long time now, but Dave is still a permanent part of all our lives.) Kayla stuck him with the handle of Poppa. As far as I'm concerned, that's a lot worse than Gramps.

But back to my face. It really was green. I was having a tough time standing upright, and believe me, I hadn't had a drop to drink, either. By then, though, Mel figured out that I was in trouble.

Melissa Majors Soames is my third wife. That seems like a bit of a misnomer, since my second wife, Anne Corley, was married to me for less than twenty-four hours. Our time together was, as they say, short but brief, ending in what is often referred to as "suicide by cop." It bothered me that Anne preferred being dead to being married to me, and it gave me something of a complex—I believe shrinks call it a fear of commitment—that made it difficult for me to move on. Mel Soames was the one who finally changed all that.

She and I met while working for the S.H.I.T. squad. (Yes, I agree, it's an unfortunate name, but we're stuck with it.) Originally we just worked together, then it evolved into something else. Mel is someone who is absolutely cool in the face of trouble, and she's watched my back on more than one occasion. And since this whole idea of having a "three-day family-bonding vacation at Disneyland" had been her bright idea, it was only fair that she should watch my back now.

She didn't come racing up to see if I was all right because she could see perfectly well that I wasn't. Instead, she went looking for help in the guise of a uniformed park employee, who dropped the broom he was wielding and led me to the first-aid station. It seems to me that it would have made sense to have a branch office of that a lot closer to the damned teacups.

So I went to the infirmary. Mel stayed long enough to be sure I was in good hands, then bustled off to "let everyone know what's happening." I stayed where I was, spending a good part of day three of our three-day ticket pass flat on my back on an ER-style cot with a very officious nurse taking my pulse and asking me questions.

"Ever been seasick?" she wanted to know.

"Several times," I told her. I could have added every time I get near a boat, but I didn't.

"Do you have any Antivert with you?" she asked.

"I beg your pardon?"

"Antivert. Meclizine. If you're prone to seasickness, you should probably carry some with you. Without it, I can't imagine what you were thinking. Why did you go on that ride?"

"My granddaughter wanted me to."

She gave me a bemused look and shook her head. "That's what they all say. You'd think grown men would have better sense."

She was right about that. I should have had better sense, but of course I didn't say so.

"We don't hand out medication here," she said. "Why don't you just lie there for a while with your eyes closed. That may help."

When she finally left me alone, I must have fallen asleep. I woke up when my phone rang.

"Beau," Ross Alan Connors said. "Where are you?"

Connors has been the Washington State Attorney General for quite some time now, and he was the one who had plucked me from my post-retirement doldrums after leaving Seattle PD and installed me in his then relatively new Special Homicide Investigation Team. The previous fall's election cycle had seen him fend off hotly contested attacks in both the primary and general elections. With campaigning out of the way for now, he seemed to be focusing on the job, enough so that he was calling me on Sunday afternoon when I was supposedly on vacation.

"California," I told him. "Disneyland, actually."

I didn't mention the infirmary part. That was none of his business.

"Harry tells me you're due back tomorrow."

Harry was my boss, Harry Ignatius Ball, known to friend and foe alike as Harry I. Ball. People who hear his name and think that gives them a license to write him off as some kind of joke are making a big mistake. He's like a crocodile lurking in the water with just his eyes showing. The teeth are there, just under the surface, ready and waiting to nail the unwary.

"Yes," I told him. "Our plane leaves here bright and early. We should be at our desks by one."

When Mel had broached the Disneyland idea, she had wanted us to pull off this major family-style event while, at the same time, having as little impact as possible—one and a half day's worth—on our accumulated vacation time. We had flown down on Thursday after work and were due back Monday at one.

On my own, I've never been big on vacations of any kind. Unused vacation days have slipped through my fingers time and again without my really noticing or caring, but Mel Soames is another kind of person altogether. She has her heart set on our taking a road trip this summer. She wants to cross the border into BC, head east over the Canadian Rockies and then come back to Seattle by way of Yellowstone and Glacier. This sounds like way too much scenery for me, but she's the woman in my life and I want to keep her happy, so a-driving we will go.

"Mel can go to the office," Ross said, "but not you. I want you in Ellensburg at the earliest possible moment."

If you leave the Seattle area driving east on I-90, Ellensburg is the second stopping-off place after you cross the Cascades. First there's Cle Elum and next Ellensburg. Neither of them strikes me as much of a garden spot.

"Why would I want to go to Ellensburg?" I asked.

"To be there when the Kittitas M.E. does an autopsy. Friday afternoon some heavy-equipment operator was out snowplowing a national forest road over by Lake Kachess where he ended up digging up more than he bargained for. This is number six."

I didn't have to ask number six what—I already knew. For the past two months S.H.I.T. had been working on the murders of several young Hispanic women whose charred remains had been found at various dump sites scattered all over western Washington. So far none of them had been identified. As far as we could tell, none of our victims had been reported missing. We'd pretty well decided that our dead girls were probably involved in prostitution, but until we managed to identify one of them and could start making connections, it was going to be damnably difficult to figure out who had killed them.

These days it's routine for the dental records of missing persons to be entered into a national missing persons database. That wasn't possible with our current set of victims. None of them had teeth. None of them! And the teeth in question hadn't been lost to poor dental hygiene, either. They had been forcibly removed. As in yanked out by the roots!

"Same MO?" I asked.

"Pretty much except for the fact that this one seems to have her teeth," Ross said. "So either we have a different doer or the guy ran out of time. This victim was wrapped in a tarp and set on fire just like the others. The body was found late Friday afternoon. It took until Saturday morning for the Kittitas County Sheriff's Department to retrieve the remains. Unfortunately, their M.E. has been out of town at a conference, so that has slowed down the process. They put the remains on ice until she returns and expect the autopsy to happen sometime tomorrow afternoon. That's where you come in. I want you there when it happens in case there's some detail that we know about that the locals might miss."

"Our plane's due to depart at ten-twenty," I told him.

"That'll be cutting it close then," Ross said. "God only knows how long it'll take for you to get your luggage once you get here."

Thanks to a legacy from Anne Corley, Mel and I had flown down to California on a private jet. All we'd have to do was step off the plane and wait for the luggage to be loaded into our waiting car before we drove it off the tarmac, but rubbing my boss's nose in that seemed like a bad idea.

"I'll make it," I said. "I'll drop Mel off at the condo to pick up the other car and then I'll head out."

"All right," Ross said. "Be there as soon as you can."

"Do you have a number for the Kittitas M.E.'s office?" I asked.

"Sure. Can you take it down?"

I had no intention of telling him that I was flat on my back in the first-aid station and I wasn't about to ask the nurse to lend me a pen or pencil.

"Can you text it to me?" I asked.

This was something coming from someone who had come to twenty-first-century technology kicking and screaming all the way. I'm surprised I wasn't struck by lightning on the spot, but that's what comes of having Generation X progeny. I had learned about text messaging the hard way—because my kids, Kelly and Scott, had insisted on it.

"Sure," Ross said. "I'll have Katie send it over to you."

Katie Dunn was Ross's Gen X secretary. Knowing Ross is even more of a wireless troglodyte than I am made me feel some better—more with it, as we used to say back in the day.

I had just stuffed the phone back into my pocket when the nurse led Kelly into the room.

"How are you?" she asked, concern written on her face. "Mel told us what happened and that you needed to take it easy for a while. Are you feeling any better?"

I swung my feet off the side of the bed and sat up slowly.

"Take it easy," the nurse advised.

But the nap had done the trick. I was definitely feeling better. "I'm fine," I said. "One hundred percent."

"Mel went with Jeremy. He's taking the kids back to the hotel," Kelly explained. "She'll help get them fed and make sure the babysitter arrangements hold up. If you're still feeling up to having that dinner, that is."

That was what Mel had told Kelly, of course. And that's what she was doing, but only up to a point. The reasons she was doing those things were a whole lot murkier—to Kelly, at least, if not to me.

Kelly and I haven't always been on the best of terms. In fact, we've usually not been on the best of terms. She had run away from home prior to high school graduation and managed to get herself knocked up. Her shotgun wedding had ended up being unavoidably delayed, so Kayla had arrived on the scene before her parents had ever tied the knot. I have always thought most of this Kelly-based uproar is deliberate.

Mel takes the position that it's more complex than that—both conscious and not. She thinks Kelly's ongoing rebellion has been a way for her to get back at her parents—at both Karen and me. Although I didn't know about it at the time, Kelly was mad as hell at her mother for coming down with cancer and dying while Kelly was still in her teens, and she was mad as hell at me for having been drunk most of the time while she was growing up. And now she's apparently mad at me for not being drunk. When it comes to kids, sometimes you just can't win.

So Mel had designed this whole Disneyland adventure, complete with inviting my son and daughter-in-law, Scott and Cherisse, along for the ride, for no other reason than to see if she could help smooth out some of the emotional wrinkles between Kelly and me. So far so good. As far as I could tell, everyone seemed to be having a good time. There had been no cross words, at least none I had heard. And I suspected that was also why Mel had sent Kelly to drag me out of the infirmary.

"I should have gone on the teacups with her," Kelly said as we walked toward the monorail. "Jeremy won't set foot on one of those on a bet, but rides like that don't bother me. They never have. And Kayla loves them so much. She rode the teacups three more times after you left. She didn't want to ride on anything else."

I stopped cold. Kelly turned back to look at me. "Are you all right?" she asked.

It took me a minute to figure out what to say. I now knew something about Kelly and her mother and her daughter, and it was something she didn't know about me. As I said already, I was mostly AWOL when Kelly and Scott were little—drinking and/or working. Karen was the one who took them to soccer and T-ball and movies. She was also the one who "did the Puyallup" with them each fall. When it's time for the Western Washington State Fair each September, that's what they used to call it—"doing the Puyallup." It was Karen instead of me who walked them through the displays of farm animals and baked goods; who taught them to love eating cotton candy and elephant ears; and who took them for rides on the midway.

"You're just like your mother," I said, over the lump that rose suddenly in my throat and made it difficult to speak. "And Kayla's just like you."

"What's that supposed to mean?" Kelly asked. She sounded angry and defensive. It was so like her to take offense and to assume that whatever I said was somehow an underhanded criticism.

"Did your mother ever tell you about the first time I took her to the Puyallup?"

"No," Kelly said. "She never did. Why?"

"She wanted to ride the Tilt-a-Whirl, and I knew if I did that, I'd be sick. Rides like that always make me sick. So I bought the tickets. Your mother and I stood in line, but when it came time to get on, I couldn't do it. She ended up having to go on the ride with the people who were standing in line behind us. Here I was, supposedly this hotshot young guy with the beautiful girl on his arm, and all I could do was stand there like an idiot and wait for the ride to end and for her to get off. It was one of the most humiliating moments of my life. We never talked about it again afterward, but she never asked me to get on one of those rides again, either."

Kelly was staring up into my face. She looked so much like her mother right then—was so much like her mother—that it was downright spooky. It turns out DNA is pretty amazing stuff.

"So why did you do it?" she asked.

Now I was lost. Yes, I had been telling Kelly the story, but her question caught me off guard. I didn't know what "it" she was asking about.

"Do what?" I asked.

"If you already knew it would make you sick, why on earth did you get on the Mad Hatter's Tea Party with Kayla?"

"I thought maybe I'd grown out of it?" I asked lamely.

Kelly shook her head as if to say I hadn't yet stumbled on the right answer. "And?" she prompted.

"Because my granddaughter wanted me to?" I added.

The storm clouds that had washed across Kelly's face vanished. She reached up, grabbed me around the neck, and kissed my cheek.

"Oh, Daddy," she said with a laugh. "You're such a dope, but I love you."

See what I mean about Mel Soames? The woman is a genius.

Chapter 2

The call came in just after the morning briefing ended and as Sheriff Joanna Brady was about to tackle that day's bushel basketful of paperwork.

"Sorry to disturb you," Larry Kendrick, her lead dispatcher, had said. "We've had a call about a possible homicide north of Bowie at a place called Action Trail Adventures."

"Never heard of it," Joanna said.

"I'm not surprised. It's an all-terrain vehicle hot spot. They keep a fairly low profile, probably to avoid coming up against planning and zoning restrictions. I've dispatched Detectives Carpenter and Howell to the scene, and I've asked Jeannine to send out an Animal Control officer. She has Natalie Wilson coming over from Willcox. She should be on the scene within the next twenty minutes or so."

Ernie Carpenter was Joanna's senior homicide detective, a guy who had put in his twenty years and was verging on being ready to pull the plug and put himself out to pasture. Debra Howell had been working homicide for the better part of two years, partnering with Ernie as often as possible as she gradually learned the ropes. Jeannine Phillips, on the other hand, was Joanna's head of Animal Control. Animal Control had been stuffed into Joanna's area of responsibility years earlier, supposedly on a temporary basis, which had now turned permanent. Natalie Wilson was Jeannine's new hire.

"What's going on?" Joanna asked. "Why an ACO?"

"A concerned citizen called it in. He was out on his ATV when he saw buzzards circling overhead. He went there and saw what he thinks is a body, but he can't get close enough to tell for sure. There's a dog there with the victim, and he's fierce as hell. The dog is keeping the vultures away, but he's doing the same thing to everyone else, acting like he's ready to tear them limb from limb. With the dog there, no one has been able to get close enough to the victim to check on him. He looks dead, but maybe he's not."

"Any idea what happened to him?" Joanna asked.

"The guy who called it in on his cell phone says it looks like he was run over by something. It could be an accident, but it could be something else, too."

Five years earlier, when Joanna Brady had first run for office as sheriff of Cochise County, it had been in the aftermath of her first husband's death. Deputy Andrew Roy Brady had been gunned down by a drug trafficker's hit man while he himself had been standing for election. People had encouraged Joanna to run in Andy's place. When she was elected, many people had assumed it was a gesture of sympathy more than anything else. She may have been the daughter of one law enforcement officer and the widow of another, but she had never been a cop herself, and no one really expected that she would be.

Once she took office, Joanna had assumed the administrative duties that came with the office, but she had also set herself the task of becoming a real cop. She had enrolled in and graduated from the same police academy course of training that was required of all her new recruits. She did enough range work to keep her weapons skills at proper levels, and rather than hiding out in her office and behind her desk, she had insisted on going to the scene of every homicide that had occurred on her watch and in her jurisdiction. If this possible homicide turned into a real one, Joanna knew she would go there as well.

"Thanks for keeping me posted, Larry," she told him. "When you know more details, let me know or tell Ernie to call me."

As soon as Joanna put down the telephone, she returned to the stack of paperwork—the never-ending stack of paperwork—that was the bane of her existence. It had always been bad, but now it was worse. Her longtime chief deputy and second in command, Frank Montoya, had been wooed away from her department when he was offered the chief of police job in the nearby city of Sierra Vista. She missed him more than she could say.

Frank had been one of her opponents in her original race for sheriff. After winning the election, she had chosen him to serve as one of her two chief deputies. Turning a major opponent into a loyal ally had been a stroke of genius on Joanna's part. Frank's attention to detail had been a major asset to her. He had kept an eagle eye on budgetary issues and had handled the complex job of shift scheduling with a casual flair that had made it seem easy. He had also been at the forefront of bringing Joanna's department into the world of twenty-first-century information/technology.

Joanna had decided against turning the chief deputy search over to a head-hunting search firm. Instead, after several months of deliberation, she had promoted from within. Tom Hadlock, her jail commander, who had a master's degree in public administration, had seemed a reasonable choice. Two months into his new and greatly expanded role, however, Tom was still struggling, and so was Joanna. Tom may have had a university degree to his credit, but on the job he was stiff and inexperienced and lacking the easygoing confidence and competence that had made working with Frank such a pleasure.

Staring at a paper copy of the next month's shift schedule that had finally made it to Joanna's desk a day later than it should have been, she shook her head regretfully and recalled the words to that old Bob Dylan song: "You don't know what you've got 'til it's gone."

Of course, Frank wasn't completely gone. He had asked her to stand up with him and be his "best man"—Joanna liked to think of it as "best person"—at the wedding that was scheduled to happen on Saturday morning of this very week. Joanna had been honored to accept, but the hoopla surrounding the wedding and Joanna's expected participation in all of it added more complications to a week that was already busy even before Larry Kendrick's Monday morning phone call.

Joanna signed off on the scheduling paperwork and had started making progress on her mound of correspondence when her direct line rang again. This time the caller was Ernie.

"Sorry to bother you, boss," Ernie said. "Natalie finally corralled the dog—a Doberman-looking mutt—

and hauled him out of the way so someone could check on the guy. He's dead, all right. Looks to me like he's been that way for some time—several hours at least."

"Have you called the M.E.?" Joanna asked.

"You know Dr. Machett," Ernie said sourly. "Remember? We're not allowed to call him directly. I talked to Madge Livingston. She said she'd send him a text message and that he'd call when he can. I guess she's not allowed to call him directly, either. Makes me miss the hell out of Doc Winfield."

Joanna missed him, too. Dr. George Winfield, the previous Cochise County medical examiner and, coincidentally, Joanna's stepfather, had announced his retirement at almost the same time Frank Montoya had given Joanna his notice. Giddy as a pair of teenagers, George and her mother, Eleanor, had headed off on their first snowbird adventure in a newly purchased but used motor home. They were currently gearing up for their second summer's worth of RVing. In the meantime, Joanna couldn't help feeling that she had been left holding the bag.

Losing two valued members of her team—George Winfield and Frank Montoya—at once had come as a severe body blow to Joanna's administration, and the constant readjustment uproar inside her department since then had left her reeling. For months, Joanna's officers had been plagued by having to work with a series of contract M.E.s who had filled in on a temporary basis. A month earlier, the Board of Supervisors had finally gotten around to hiring George's permanent replacement. They had given the M.E. nod to Dr. Guy Machett, a newcomer to Cochise County, and to Arizona as well, who had earned both his medical degree and his pathology specialty from Johns Hopkins University.

Dr. Machett was energetic and smart, but he seemed overly impressed with himself along with his high-blown credentials. He often prefaced derogatory remarks about southeastern Arizona with the words "Where I come from . . .," to which Joanna often wanted to reply, "So why don't you go back there?"

Two weeks earlier, in the aftermath of a tragic automobile accident, Joanna had seen Dr. Machett interact with grieving family members of a young man who had died as a result of a single-vehicle rollover. In dealing with the parents, Machett had exhibited zero amounts of charm and even less empathy. As Joanna had told her husband, Butch, after that uncomfortable encounter, "Guy Machett has the bedside manner of your basic bullfrog." Butch had laughed off her comment, but as far as Joanna was concerned, the situation with Dr. Machett was no laughing matter.

For one thing, he had insisted on establishing an official "chain of command" style of operation. When George Winfield had been running the show, Joanna's detectives had been allowed unlimited access to him. They had been encouraged to contact the M.E. directly whenever they judged that the situation warranted his involvement. Not so with Dr. Machett. As far as he was concerned, lowly homicide detectives, people Machett deemed to be somehow beneath him, had to "go through channels"—which is to say through Joanna or through his office—in order to contact him or summon him to a crime scene. And he had made it clear that no one, under any circumstances, was to refer to him as Doc. He was Dr. Machett, thank you very much.

Despite his apparent arrogance, Joanna couldn't help but wonder if it was possible that he was putting on a front. For one thing, although he was several years older than Joanna, he was relatively new and untried as far as doing the job was concerned. And he didn't have the foggiest idea about the importance of winning friends and influencing people. In fact, in the course of a few short weeks, he had managed to create a whole cheering section of people who were actively rooting for the man to fall flat on his face.

"But Machett is on his way to the crime scene?" Joanna asked.

"Beats the hell out of me," Ernie replied. "According to Madge, he'll get back to me. I take that to mean he'll get back to me eventually—when he's damned good and ready."

"What do you think we have?" Joanna asked, changing the subject away from Dr. Machett's all-too-obvious shortcomings and back to the victim.

"The guy who called it in thought it was an ATV accident. Now that I've seen it, I'd have to say from the tracks that it looks more like a hit-and-run," Ernie said. "Or else maybe a hit, hit, hit-and-run. I think the dead guy was run down deliberately, and whoever did it is long gone. It looks to me like he was run over several different times by the same vehicle, or maybe once each by several separate vehicles."

"ATVs?" Joanna asked.

"I'd say we're looking for something bigger than that," Ernie replied. "And I don't know how many. One for sure, but maybe more."

"What about having CSI make casts of the tracks?" she asked. "Surely you'd be able to tell the number of vehicles from the number of tracks."

"Sorry, boss, no can do," Ernie said. "These are sand dunes."

"Sand dunes?" Joanna repeated. Driving to California, she remembered being impressed by the glorious red sand dunes west of Yuma along I-8. She had lived in Cochise County all her life. The idea that there might be sand dunes much closer to home came as something of a shock. "I didn't know we had any of those," she said.

"You do now," Ernie told her. "And believe me, tracks that are left in sand like what's here aren't remotely castable."

"What about identification?"

"None on the body," he said, "at least none that we've found so far."

"What about the dog? Does it have tags?"

"Maybe so. He was wearing a collar and it looks like he has tags, but no one can get close enough to read them. Natalie's working on him now, trying to get him into her truck. Once she does that, maybe she'll be able to tell us something. When I get off the phone with you, I'll ask her."

"All right then," Joanna said. "I'm on my way."

"Good," Ernie said. "I'm glad to hear it. Dave Hollicker is headed here as well."

Most of the time, Joanna's CSI unit was a two-person team made up of Dave and Casey Ledford, Joanna's latent fingerprint tech. Unfortunately, Casey was currently out of town attending a training conference on the latest upgrades in AFIS—the nationwide

Automated Fingerprint Identification System. With Casey unavailable, Dave Hollicker was reduced to being a one-man show.

Joanna put down her phone and donned her Kevlar vest, then opened the door to her office and spoke to her secretary, Kristin Gregovich.

"How long will you be gone?" Kristin wanted to know.

"It's a crime scene," Joanna told her. "I'll be back eventually; I just don't know when."

Relieved to have an excuse to leave her paperwork jungle behind, Joanna hurried out her private back entrance and into her Crown Victoria parked a few steps from her door. A few minutes later, she was driving east on U.S. Highway 80, heading for Double Adobe, Elfrida, and ultimately Bowie.

Joanna's jurisdiction, Cochise County, was an eighty-square-mile block of territory as large as Rhode Island and Connecticut combined. On the south it was bordered by Mexico and on the east by New Mexico. Her office in the Justice Center was in the lower right-hand corner of the county. The crime scene was seventy miles straight north of there—except she couldn't drive straight north. The roads didn't run that way.

Along the highway, she was glad to see the signs of spring—the bright greens of newly leafed mesquite and the carpet of bright yellow flowers that lined either side of the roadway. Lost in thought, she had driven only a few miles when her phone rang.

"Sheriff Brady here," she said.

"I found Bowie on my GPS," Guy Machett said without preamble or greeting. "I can make it there just fine, but where the hell is the crime scene?"

His attitude grated on Joanna as much as his words did. He pronounced Bowie the outlander way, Bowie as in bow tie as opposed to the approved southeastern Arizona pronunciation.

"It's pronounced boo-ee," she told him.

"That's not how it's spelled in my BlackBerry," he returned.

And obviously your BlackBerry couldn't be wrong, Joanna thought to herself. "But it is how people around here say it," she told him. And it's how you'll pronounce it, too, if you don't want the locals laughing at you.

"The crime scene is northeast of there," she said. "Some GPS receivers don't cover those rural roads and areas very well."

"I was scheduled to be at a continuing ed conference in Tucson all day today," Machett said. "It bugs the hell out of me to miss it, but I'll be there as soon as I can."

"If you're leaving Tucson now, you should arrive in about an hour then," Joanna said. "That's about the time I'll get there as well. Call me. I'll help guide you in."

"Make that three hours," Machett grumbled. "They can't expect me to drive around in that god-awful van wherever I go. I had to drive to Tucson in my personal vehicle. That means I'll have to drive all the way back to Bisbee and pick up the van before I come to the crime scene."

George didn't mind driving around in the M.E.'s van, Joanna thought.

"What about Bobby?" she asked. "Couldn't he drive the van over and meet you there?"

Bobby Short had spent the last two years working as George Winfield's full-time assistant.

"Bobby quit," Machett said, sounding offended. "Just like that. He came into my office last Friday morning. He told me he had two weeks of vacation coming. Said he was taking them both and that he wouldn't be back. More's the pity. He wasn't a trained M.E. tech by any means, but I could have used him for some of the heavy lifting. The one I'd really like to see quit is Madge Living-ston. She's a joke."

Bobby Short hadn't been particularly long in the brains department, but he had been a cheerful, willing worker in a difficult job. Joanna had no idea what

Machett had said or done that had provoked Bobby enough to quit his job, but apparently he had. Madge, the M.E. office's other full-time employee, who served as both secretary and clerk, had been a fixture in the Cochise County administrative staff hierarchy for as long as Joanna could remember. She was an opinionated peroxide blonde who smoked unfiltered Camels out by the morgue's Dumpsters and rode her Harley to work. George Winfield had gotten along with her just fine, but then George could get along with almost anyone, including Joanna Brady's difficult mother, Eleanor.

Joanna understood that Madge wasn't everyone's cup of tea, but she was anything but a joke. If Guy Machett went after her, he would do so at his own peril—sort of like moving a big rock and uncovering a nest of baby rattlesnakes hidden underneath.

Joanna could have warned him about all that, but she didn't. "I'll see you at the crime scene then," she said. "Whenever you get there."

"Why are you going?" Machett asked.

She understood the implication. What he meant was that, as sheriff, she was far too important to show up at a run-of-the-mill crime scene.

I do it because it's part of my job, Joanna thought. "It's a possible homicide," she explained.

"Don't you trust your detectives to handle it?" he asked.

"I trust my detectives implicitly," she returned. "But we do the job together."

"That may be fine as far as you're concerned," he said. "If you've got nothing better to do and don't mind showing up in person, bully for you. It's a waste of valuable time and training for me to be expected to make a personal appearance whenever some hick from Cochise County decides to croak out in the middle of nowhere. I fully intend to get myself some decent help to handle situations like this, and it won't be some untrained gofer, either."

For years now, Joanna's department's hiring practices had suffered under the county's notorious cost-containment policy of NNP—no new personnel—and it was still very much in effect. It was only through using one of Frank Montoya's creative budgetary sleights of hand that she'd been able to add on Natalie Wilson as her new Animal Control officer. NNP allowed for replacement of lost employees. That meant Guy Machett would be able to hire someone to take over Bobby Short's position, but she doubted he'd be able to add anyone else. Picking a fight with Madge Livingston was one thing. Taking on the Board of Supervisors over hiring issues would be downright foolhardy.

Good luck with that, Joanna thought.

"See you when you get there then. As I said, when you get as far as Bowie," she added, forcefully pronouncing the word in the manner she regarded as the right way, "call me again. Either I'll guide you from there or one of my deputies will." With that, she ended the call.

Rolling north through the Sulphur Springs Valley toward Willcox, Joanna was left thinking about what an overbearing jerk Machett was and about how much she missed working with George Winfield on a day-to-day basis. They had been thrown together as M.E. and sheriff long before George had married Joanna's mother, and afterward as well. Rather than appreciating George's close working relationship with her daughter, Eleanor Lathrop had been jealous of it, but she'd been even more jealous of George's job itself. Now that he was retired, the two of them were able to spend time off by themselves, traveling in the used Newell Coach they'd purchased. It was clear enough that this new Eleanor was happier and more contented than the mother Joanna had known all her life. It didn't seem fair, however, that Eleanor's new-found happiness came with the unfortunate trade-off that left Joanna working with Dr. Guy Machett.

Despite Joanna's confidence about her own ability to locate the crime scene, she was forced to make two false starts after leaving Bowie before she finally pulled up at the wrought-iron gate that marked the main entrance to Action Trail Adventures. She stopped her Crown Victoria and rolled down her window. The entry gate was wide open. Just beyond her window stood a post equipped with both a telephone receiver and a keypad. On the first section of barbed-wire fence to the right of the gate was a hand-painted sign that read PRIVATE PROPERTY. AUTHORIZED PERSONNEL ONLY. CALL FOR ADMITTANCE. The fence post nearest the gate held the tangled remains of what might have been a surveillance camera. Fifty yards or so away from the gate sat a decrepit, dusty Airstream trailer with an equally disreputable F-150 pickup parked nearby.

"Looks like somebody tore that camera out by its roots," someone said.

Joanna turned away from the trailer in time to see Natalie Wilson walking toward her. The ACO wasn't any bigger than Joanna's own five-foot-one frame, but she was tough as nails. Natalie had spent a couple of years on the professional rodeo circuit and had applied to work for Animal Control after turning in her spurs and saddle. Next to her, walking docilely on a leash, was an enormous dog—a Doberman, apparently. Once they were within a few feet of the car, the dog spotted Joanna through the window. He lunged at her, barking. Remembering what Ernie had said about the dead man's vicious dog keeping investigators at bay, Joanna drew back in alarm.

"Quiet, Miller," Natalie ordered, yanking back on the leash. "Sit!"

Without a moment's hesitation the dog complied. He stopped barking and sat, still keeping a close eye on Joanna. It was enough of a threat that she made no move to open the door.

"This is the dead guy's dog?" she asked.

Natalie nodded. "That's right."

"Ernie told me he's dangerous. What's he doing out of your truck? Shouldn't he be on his way to the pound?"

"I called Jeannine and asked about that," Natalie answered. "She checked. Miller's not a stray. His tags and shots are all current and in order, and this is where he lives. Since he hasn't set foot outside the property line, we've got no call to take him into custody. Jeannine said for me to stay here with him. We're hoping one of the dead guy's relatives will come forward and take him."

"But Ernie said—"

"That Miller was vicious?" Natalie asked. "That's a laugh. The poor thing was scared to death. He was also hungry and thirsty. Not only that, someone had killed his owner and taken a potshot at him as well. Fortunately the bullet only grazed the top of his shoulder. He should probably see a vet, but Jeannine is hoping that whoever takes him will handle that."

Looking closer, Joanna could see a bloody mark that sliced across the top of the dog's back. And she had to agree that right that moment, the dog didn't seem the least bit vicious.

"That's his name?" Joanna asked. "Miller?"

Natalie nodded. "Funny name for a dog, but he was wearing a name tag along with his dog tag. He's a two-year-old Doberman mix. And he's not vicious. All he was doing was trying to protect his owner. If that had happened to me, I'd probably turn vicious, too. You're a good dog, aren't you, Miller," Natalie added gently, speaking to the dog. "You're a very good boy."

Miller responded by looking at her and wagging his stub of a tail the tiniest bit.

Joanna had learned that in the topsy-turvy world of Animal Control, the animals' names often took precedence over those of any humans involved.

"If we know the dog's name," Joanna said, "and if you've seen his tags, does that mean we know the victim's name as well?"

"Attwood," Natalie answered. "Lester Attwood. At least that's what Jeannine says anyway, and the address Attwood listed as his home address in our records matches up to this one."

"You called that over to Detective Carpenter?"

"Just a few minutes ago," Natalie agreed with a nod. "He said he's on his way. For me to wait here."

Looking off to the east, Joanna saw a cloud of light tan dust billowing skyward. A few minutes later, Ernie arrived, driving the new four-wheel-drive Yukon that had finally replaced the aging Econoline van her detectives had used for years. Ernie parked next to Joanna's patrol car, then rolled down his window and glared out through it first at the dog and then at Natalie.

"What the hell?" he muttered. "That dog is a holy terror. Why'd you let him out?"

Miller, who seemed to be as happy to see Ernie as Ernie was to see him, made a very believable lunge at the idling SUV.

"No!" Natalie ordered. "Leave it. Sit."

Once again Miller obeyed Natalie's command. He sat while Natalie returned Ernie's look, glare for glare. "Just because he doesn't like you," she told the detective, "doesn't mean the dog is vicious. Maybe he's got good sense."

"Just keep him away from me," Ernie said. "I don't trust him." With that, he turned to Joanna. "Want to go see the crime scene?"

Joanna nodded. "Should I follow you?"

Ernie shook his head. "Not unless you want that Crown Vic of yours to be stuck up to its hubcaps. We're talking world-class sand here, boss."

A new Yukon was on order for Joanna as well and was due to be delivered in two weeks, but that wouldn't help today. Without a word Joanna exited her vehicle.

"What about the dog?" Natalie asked. "Have you done anything about finding out who's going to take him?"

That was always an ACO's straightforward concern—what would become of the animal? As a homicide detective, Ernie's concerns and possible courses of action were far more complicated.

"Thanks to you, we may finally have a lead on our victim's ID, and I appreciate that," he said, "I really do. Now that we think we know the man's name, our next job is to verify that—to find someone who can identify the body. After that we have to locate and notify his next of kin. That's a lot to worry about without even thinking about that dog. Got it?"

"Got it." Natalie's brisk reply hinted that she wasn't backing down. "Got it loud and clear." With that, she tugged on Miller's leash. "Come on, boy," she told the dog. "Let's go for a walk." She didn't say "far away from this jerk," but she might as well have. Her meaning was abundantly clear.

Natalie Wilson turned on her heel and marched away with Miller walking placidly beside her.

"Where on earth did Jeannine Phillips find that piece of work?" Ernie Carpenter wanted to know.

"I believe she fell off the rodeo circuit," Joanna replied. "She used to be a barrel racer."

"Figures," Ernie said disapprovingly. "Women like that are always a handful."

That parting remark might have been a lot funnier if Joanna hadn't taken it so personally. Not only did she suspect it was absolutely true, there was something else that bothered her. Her very own daughter, fourteen-year-old Jenny, had her own heart set on the world of rodeo. Being sheriff was hard work, but it was easier for Joanna to discuss murder and mayhem than it was to consider her daughter's plans for the future.

"Come on," Joanna said, climbing into the Yukon's passenger seat, where she immediately fastened her seat belt. "Let's go take a look at that dead body."

Chapter 3

As they drove away from the gate, Joanna was still thinking about Jenny and her rodeo-riding ambitions when Ernie brought her back to the case.

"I left Deb with the witness," Ernie said.

"What witness?" Joanna asked. "The man who found the body?"

"Seems like a pretty squared-away guy. His name's Maury Robbins. He's a 911 operator from Tucson, and he's also an all-terrain vehicle enthusiast. He comes down here on his days off whenever he can. What he told me is that he drove down late last night after his shift ended. He got here about three A.M. The gate was open, but he didn't think that much about it. He drove on in, set up his Jayco—"

"His what?" Joanna asked.

"His Jayco. It's one of those little pop-up camper things. He carries his ATV in the bed of his pickup truck and drags the camper along behind."

"So there's an actual campsite here?"

"Yes, but it's pretty primitive," Ernie replied. "No concrete pads, no running water. People have to haul in their own water and the only facilities turn out to be a few strategically located Porta Pottis. Maury's camper has its own facilities. News to me. The Jayco I had years ago sure as hell didn't."

Joanna smiled to herself. When she had first arrived on the scene, Ernie had apologized whenever he used a bad word around her. She liked the fact that they had both moved beyond that. And right now, Joanna wasn't especially interested in either Ernie's language or his old camper.

"So this is private property?" she asked. "Action Trail Adventures isn't situated on state or federally owned land?"

"Yes," Ernie said. "That's my understanding. It's privately owned. Robbins told me he pays an annual fee that gives him access through a card-activated gate. That way he can let himself in or out as needed. There's also a keypad where you can punch in an entry code to open the gate."

"Anyway," Ernie continued, "Robbins got in last night. This morning, when he took his ATV out for a ride, he found the body lying facedown in the sand with the dog standing guard over it. Once we finally managed to drag the dog away, Robbins was able to take a closer look at the victim and give us a tentative ID. He says the guy's first name is Lester. He had no idea about his last name, or any next of kin, either."

"Lester's last name is Attwood," Joanna said, but she was thinking about the number of times so-called good citizens calling in reports of a homicide turned out to be perpetrators.

"Do you think Mr. Robbins might be involved in whatever happened here?" she asked.

Ernie shook his head. "Not to my way of thinking. At any rate, as you said, the name we got back from Animal Control on the dog's license is Lester Attwood. According to Records, Attwood's driver's license is suspended. His rap sheet shows six DUIs, two criminal assaults, two driving without a license."

"So we've got a photo then?"

"On the computer," Ernie said. "Not one I can print right now. Any idea when Dr. Machett will bother getting his butt out here?"

"All I can tell you is that he's on his way," Joanna said.

"I'm not holding my breath," Ernie grumbled. "He always takes his own sweet time about getting to a crime scene, and we're left standing with one foot in the air until he does."

Following a fairly smooth gravel road, the Yukon wound down into a steep wash. When they roared up the far side, they came out on the boundary of a breathtaking landscape. Even though Joanna had been warned about them in advance, seeing the tawny-colored dunes in person took her by surprise. Starting with a line of demarcation just to the left of the gravel, the dunes stretched off into the distance in a series of rounded hills. Here and there the rippled surface of the sand was marred by a series of tire tracks.

Gripping the steering wheel with both hands, Ernie swung the Yukon off the road and into the dunes along a course that included several of those tracks. Even with four-wheel drive, he had to maintain a fair amount of speed to keep from getting bogged down.

As they jolted along, Joanna checked her seat belt and then held on to her armrest. "How can this be?" she said over the laboring sound of the engine. "I've lived here all my life and never knew these dunes were here!"

"Think about Kartchner Caverns," Ernie replied. "Lots of people knew about that before it ever came out in public. This is all on private property. As far as I know, it's only been open to ATVers in the last few years. Now that I think about it, I think some environmental group or other was trying to buy it up a few years back, but the owner wouldn't sell."

Kartchner Caverns, a series of limestone caverns on the far side of Benson, was Cochise County's most recent tourism hot spot. The caves had been discovered in the late seventies by a pair of hikers who had been exploring the countryside at the base of the Whetstone Mountains. When they had first located and started exploring the caverns, they were located on private land owned by a family named Kartchner. It had taken another ten years to make arrangements to transfer the property to the state of Arizona and turn it into a state park people could actually come visit. Now Kartchner Caverns is a genuine tourist home run. Joanna wondered if something similar was going on with Action Trail Adventures. People in the ATV community seemed to know all about it. No one else did.

Is that what this murder is all about? Joanna wondered. Have we wandered into some kind of environmental range war?

The Yukon crested a dune. In the cleft between that dune and the next, Joanna caught sight of the crime scene. The debris field included an upright ATV as well as a second one that had been tipped over onto its side. Yards away from the vehicles in a tangle of tire tracks lay something that, from this distance, might have been a pile of loose laundry.

The victim, Joanna thought. "Stop for a minute, please," she said to Ernie. "Let me take a look from here."

Ernie stopped abruptly, allowing a towering plume of dust to blow past them. When it cleared, Joanna could see the victim again. He looked like a crumpled rag doll, lying facedown in sand. Around him ranged a complex scribble of vehicle tracks that resembled the Etch-a-Sketch doodlings of some giant-sized child.

Joanna glanced at her detective. "So what do you think happened?" she asked.

Ernie shrugged. "I don't know," he said. "It looks to me like several vehicles were involved."

"And several people?"

Ernie nodded. "We've got tracks of that one wrecked ATV and at least two others, four-wheel-drive pickups, most likely, one with dual rear tires. I'm guessing the dead guy rode up on the wrecked ATV right through there."

Ernie pointed casually off to his left, where a pair of tracks emerged from the cleft between the dunes and then disappeared into the tumult of disturbed sand.

"Once he got here, I'm guessing there was an altercation of some kind. There may have been some gunfire."

"What makes you say that?"

"For one thing, somebody evidently took a shot at the dog. There's an empty scabbard on the ATV. I doubt the owner would have shot his own dog. But if there are weapons or shell casings out here, we'll need metal detectors to find them."

"Okay, so all these guys meet up. What do you think happened next?"

"At some point, I think, our victim, the guy on the ATV, may have tried to leave. One of the larger vehicles T-boned him and knocked him ass over teakettle. Once the victim was on foot, the other guys ran him down. Not just once, either—several times over."

"Sounds cold-blooded," Joanna said.

Ernie nodded. "It was cold-blooded. I suspect he died from internal injuries. Machett should be able to tell us for sure, if and when he bothers to show up."

Despite being in agreement with Ernie's disparaging remark about Dr. Machett, Joanna let it pass. "What about that single track?" she asked, pointing to a track in the sand that disappeared over the top of the next dune. "The one that leads off to the right from the body?"

"Looks to me like the dog made that one, either going or coming or maybe both," Ernie said. "The bad guys probably ran him off, but he came back as soon as the coast was clear. I have to give the damned dog credit," the detective added grudgingly. "Even though he'd been shot, he was downright fierce about not letting any of us near that body. After he offered to tear me limb from limb, I was a little surprised to see Natalie Wilson with him on a leash, walking around just as nice as you please."

Which is why you work homicide and she's animal control, Joanna thought.

She studied the expanse of disrupted sand around the body. "You said you thought one of the vehicles had dual tires. How do you know that?"

"This isn't the shortest way to and from the gate, but it's the most passable. If you look carefully, you can see the dips left in the sand by the dual wheels even though you can't make out the treads on the tire."

Joanna looked down and saw that he was right. The tracks were there, but the fine grade of the sand left behind no visible tread.

"The victim didn't bother following the road when he came here, and he didn't take a direct route from the gate, either," Ernie said. "It looks to me like he approached the scene by zigzagging in and out between the dunes."

"Trying to stay out of sight, maybe?" Joanna asked.

Ernie nodded. "Could be," he said.

"In other words," Joanna said, "it's possible the victim realized something was amiss and came out to investigate."

"Maybe," Ernie agreed.

"What about the trailer back by the gate?" Joanna asked. "Any sign of breaking and entering?"

"Lots," Ernie said. "The front door is smashed and the inside is a mess. No way to tell from looking at it if anything was taken. We'll need to dust it for prints, but with Casey away at that conference, that's problematic. Jaime said he can collect the prints, but we won't be able to run them through AFIS until Casey gets back."

Jaime Carbajal was Joanna's third homicide detective. It was unusual to have Joanna's entire homicide unit focused on only one case, but for right now she was glad that was possible.

"By the way, where is Jaime?" Joanna wanted to know.

"I asked him to stop off and pick up a search warrant for the trailer."

"But the guy who lived there is dead . . ." Joanna began.

"I know, I know," Ernie replied. "But what if he isn't the owner? What if the trailer actually belongs to Action Trail? The owners of that might have an objection."

"What are you thinking?" Joanna asked.

"Look," Ernie said, "I know this is all supposition on my part, but what if Action Trail Adventures is being used as a cover for a drug-smuggling operation? Maybe the victim was in on it; maybe he wasn't. But supposing we end up finding out that the owners of Action Trail Adventures are somehow involved in what went on.We'd better be damned sure we have a valid search warrant in hand before we ever set foot inside that trailer. Otherwise, whatever we find there could end up being ruled as inadmissable."

"Good point," Joanna said.

"And I noticed what looked like the remains of a surveillance camera near the gate," Ernie added. "The killers probably took that down as they were leaving."

"Makes sense to me," Joanna said. "But if there's a camera, there's probably also a tape. We need to find that, too."

"Yes, we do," Ernie asked. "Seen enough?"

"I think so," Joanna said. "Let's go talk with your witness."

I'm just an ordinary guy, and it's taken me a lifetime to learn that we all exist in a world of unintended consequences. For me that's more than just a slogan. It's life itself. My unmarried mother had no intention of getting pregnant with me, but she did. And when her fiancé, my father, died in a motorcycle accident prior to my birth, my mother had choices. Even though abortions were illegal back then, she could probably have found a way to make one happen, but she didn't. And she could have given me up for adoption, but she didn't do that, either. In spite of her family's opposition, she had me and raised me and, if you ask me, she did a damned fine job of it, too.

I lost Karen, my first wife, twice. The first time was as a result of the divorce and that was an unintended consequence of my years of drinking. I usually claim it was caused by working and drinking, but you need to consider the source. That's how alcoholics work. Even when we finally sober up, we try to rationalize things away and minimize the impact our love affair with the bottle had on ourselves and the people around us. When I lost Karen the second time, it was to cancer. Not my fault. I didn't cause it, and I like to think that, before she died, I managed to make amends for some of the heartache I caused her, and I'm very fortunate to have lived long enough to have a chance to get back in my kids' lives.

And then there's Anne Corley, my second wife. When I think of Anne now, I can still see her, striding purposefully through that cemetery on Queen Anne Hill in her bright red dress. And that's pretty much all I remember, and maybe it's better that way. Of course, I was still drinking then, so a lot of my forgetfulness may be due to booze, but there's no arguing with the fact that what happened between us in the course of those next few dizzying days was astonishing—both astonishingly good and astonishingly bad. Thrown together, we were a fire that burned too hot and bright to last—like the brilliant flash from a dying lightbulb just before it goes black.

What I do know about those few interim days was that we didn't talk about money. We never talked about money. We had far more important things to think about and do, but the money was there all the time. The fact that Anne had plenty of money was plain to see in everything about her: in the car she drove—a Porsche 928; in the hotel where she stayed—the Four Seasons Olympic in those days; in the clothing she wore; in the way she carried herself.

At the time I was far too wrapped up in being with her to wonder what she could possibly see in a hard-drinking homicide cop. And once she was gone, I was too devastated by losing her to have any grasp on what she had given me. It turned out I wasn't so much a fortune hunter as I was a fortune finder. The money she gave me was there, but for a long time I didn't pay much attention to it. (Thank God, Anne also left me under the wing of her very capable attorney, Ralph Ames, who was paying attention to it. He's also the one who finally helped force me into treatment, but that's another story.)

Over the years I didn't talk about the money with anyone other than Ralph Ames and with Ron Peters, my best friend on the force. Make that my best friend, period. Ron knew all about it. He was there in my apartment on that awful afternoon after Anne Corley died and he did me the enormous favor of running what remained of our wedding cake down the garbage disposal. I suppose there was some talk around the department when I moved from the Royal Crest to Belltown Terrace, but since I didn't make a big deal of it, neither did my coworkers at Seattle PD or at the Special Homicide Investigation Team. And since I kept coming into the office just like any other poor working stiff and since I didn't make a fuss about my financial situation, neither did anyone else. The subject of money seldom came up.

Until recently, and that brings me to yet another unintended consequence, Mel, my third wife, and the light of my life. At the time I met Melissa Soames, I wasn't at all interested in having either another partner or another wife. Despite both our efforts to the contrary, she became both. Once she showed up to work at S.H.I.T. and once I laid eyes on her, I should have known she was trouble, but I didn't, and by the time I figured it out, it was too late. The wheels were off the bus. J. P. Beaumont was a goner.

When Mel and I were courting, we didn't talk about money any more than Anne Corley and I had. Mel's first husband had been pretty well fixed as far as finances were concerned, but he was also a jerk who made sure she didn't make off with much. Once Mel and I were married and had to file our first set of income taxes, things changed and suddenly money was an issue.

"What the hell's the matter with you?" Mel had demanded, hands on her hips. "Why on earth do you think Anne Corley gave you all that money in the first place?"

It's funny that's how Mel and I both talk about her—Anne Corley, with both names. It's almost as though I never lasted long enough to be on a first-name basis with the woman. Mel has copied that peculiarity.

"Because she liked me?" I asked lamely.

I have to admit, I had never given that question all that much thought or even any thought. Why would I?

"Because she wanted you to have fun with it," Mel told me. "Because she figured out the moment she met you that you worked too hard—that you were too serious and too driven. She wanted to lighten your load. Instead, you've kept right on working too hard and amassing a fortune. It's time that changed. You can either sit around like some modern King Midas, or you can get off your dead butt (she didn't say butt, actually) and have some fun with that gift while you're still young enough to enjoy it. I don't need to be a rich widow. We're both alive and healthy. Let's have fun now!"

Our trip to Disneyland was a direct result of that conversation. The only bad unintended consequence of that, of course, had been my ride on the teacups.

It turns out that Mel has lots of good ideas for spending my money. Sometime earlier, Mel had become involved with a group of high-flying Seattle-area women who had introduced her to the miracle of private jets, or "Business Aviation," as they call it in the literature. It turned out that the women had been up to no good, but the private-jet lesson had stuck.

Mel liked using them, and now so do I. It's nice to travel on your own schedule and to get off and on planes with your luggage and dignity intact. It's slick that you don't have to remove your belt or your shoes or your jacket. All you have to do is show your ID, get on the plane, and off you go. If you want to take along a brand-new ten-ounce container of toothpaste? Fine. If you want to take along a twelve-ounce container of mouthwash or baby formula? That's fine, too. And if you happen to carry a stray 9-mm with you? That's not a problem, either. You don't have to walk through any metal detectors. You show the pilots your government-issue ID and away you go.

Being able to do all these things doesn't come cheap, as I had learned when I flew all my nearest and dearest to Las Vegas for Mel's and my wedding. It was expensive but a fun first crack at flying private aircraft. Once I actually tried it and found out "how the other half lived," I had zero interest in ever getting back into one of those slow-moving TSA security check lines at Sea-Tac airport. And that's how Mel and I had flown to Anaheim, on board a Hawker 400XP. And that's how we were flying home as well.

When Ross Connors had talked about the chances of my being able to get my luggage back in time to make it over to Ellensburg for the Jane Doe autopsy, I didn't come right out and say that I knew good and well that getting my luggage wasn't going to be a problem. And so, although I didn't mention any of that to Ross, I did place a call to Owners' Services and let them know that we'd like to leave an hour earlier than our originally scheduled departure time of 10:30 A.M.

"So what do you think?" Mel asked, once we were buckled into our seats and drinking our coffee while we taxied to the end of the runway. "Was it a success?"

I reached across the aisle, took her hand, and kissed the back of it. "Unqualified," I told her. "Everybody had fun. There were no major blow-ups. Kelly was on speaking terms with me the whole time. It doesn't get any better than that."

Mel, whose relationship with her own father isn't exactly trouble-free, has been more of a help in decoding my daughter than she could have imagined.

"Jeremy's an interesting guy," she said. "The more I'm around him, the more I like him."

Which was my opinion, too. He deals with Kelly's periodic outbursts with a quiet reserve that is calming without being patronizing. He's good with the kids, goes to work every day, carries his weight around the house, and loves my daughter to distraction. What more could a father-in-law want?

"I'm glad they'll be spending some of Kayla's spring break with Dave."

Mel's easy acceptance of everyone's ongoing relationship with my first wife's second husband was another thing that made her easy to love. She had come into our family, lumps and all, and figured out a way to make it work. After three days of nonstop grandkids, though, I was glad to share the wealth and the work with someone else. I was more than ready to let their "other" grandpa have a crack at them.

"Me, too," I said, and meant it.

I dozed as we flew north. It was bumpy as we did our approach to Boeing Field, circling over Puget Sound, and coming down just to the west of downtown Seattle and our Belltown Terrace condo. It had been sunny in southern California. It was raining in Seattle. My car was sitting waiting for us on the tarmac. Four minutes after landing, our bags had been transferred to the car and we headed north. I dropped Mel and the luggage off with the doorman at Belltown Terrace and went east on the 520 Bridge.

After a winter of hardly any snow, it was snowing some as I headed across Snoqualmie Pass—not enough to require chains, but enough to make for slow going in the pass. I shouldn't have bothered. When I reached the Kittitas County M.E.'s office, I was stopped by a square-jawed receptionist named Connie Whitman who gave me the third degree. Who was I? What did I want? Did I have an appointment? Et cetera, et cetera, et cetera. I'm not sure why it is that gatekeepers always get my hackles up, but they generally do. And it was only after I had been grilled three ways to Sunday that I was finally given the information that Dr. Laura Hopewell was on her way back from a conference and had been unavoidably delayed by low-lying fog at SFO.

"Any idea when she'll arrive then?" I asked.

Ms. Whitman gave me what I regard as the receptionist's signature cold-eyed stare. "No idea," she said. "She'll get here when she gets here."

Steamed but knowing better than to mention it, I left the office. I put as much distance as possible between the receptionist and myself. I made my way back out to the freeway and grabbed some lunch at Dinah's Diner.

While I waited for my "Cascade Burger," I called into the office and talked to Harry. "So you lucked out, drew the latest honey crisp, and ended up in Ellensburg?" he asked. "When do you think you'll be back?"

Harry I. Ball is a good guy in a man's man sort of way, but don't expect him to toe the PC line when it comes to talking the talk. That's one of the reasons he ended up in charge of S.H.I.T.—he flunked out of his local department's diversity training. I think Ross Connors took pity on him and gave him a job because he's a great cop who knows how to get the job done, and that was more important than his being unfailingly politically incorrect.

When he made that comment about "honey crisp," I knew he was talking about our series of dead females and not some new kind of whole-grain breakfast cereal.

"You might not want to use that particular term with Mel or Barbara," I advised.

Barbara Galvin is our secretary. Mel and Barbara live in a post-feminist world. I doubt either one of them ever burned a bra, but if the two of them took a notion to clean Harry's clock, I wouldn't have bet money on Harry.

"Right," he said. "Sorry."

"The Kittitas M.E.'s plane got delayed in San Francisco," I told him. "I don't know when she'll get around to doing the autopsy, and I won't be back until after she does. Is there anything in particular you can tell me about this case?"

"The guy who found the bones last Friday is named Kenneth Leggett. He's a heavy-equipment operator who lives on North First Street in North Bend. So far he's been interviewed by the locals but not by anyone from our office. Do you have your computer with you?"

"Yes," I said. Astonishingly enough, after years of resisting computers, I now seldom leave home without one, usually air-card equipped. I'm a new man as far as telecommunications are concerned. Harry isn't. He's glad computers work as long as he doesn't have to use them himself.

"Good," he said. "I'll have Barbara send over one of those PFDs of the crime scene report."

"You mean a PDF?" I asked.

"Whatever," Harry replied. "You know what I mean, and when you get a look at the report, you'll see. The tarp business pretty well corks it."

"The tags are clipped off?" I asked.

"You got it," Harry said.

In each of the previous five cases, the victim had been wrapped in a tarp before being set on fire. In each instance one corner of the tarp that had served as a shroud had been cut off—not torn off, but carefully clipped off. Not surprisingly, those missing corners happened to be the ones that would have held the manufacturing tags along with identifying information that might have led us back both to the original manufacturer and to possible local retail outlets. Not having the tags made it infinitely more difficult to get a line on the ultimate purchaser. Ross Connors had crime lab folks doing chemical analyses of each tarp fragment we'd found in hopes of narrowing where the tarps might have come from, but so far that wasn't leading us where we needed to go.

"Personal effects?" I asked.

"She was wearing boots, snakeskin Tony Lamas, and what looks like an engagement ring on one of her fingers. No wedding band, though," Harry said. "The M.E. may find more on the corpse itself."

That had been the situation in two of the other cases, where personal items had come to light only in the course of the autopsy.

Just then a smiling waitress came to my table to deliver what turned out to be a gigantic hamburger. Early in my career as a homicide detective, the grisly discussion at hand might well have wrecked my appetite. I'm beyond that now. Lunch is lunch, whatever the topic of conversation.

"All right," I said to Harry. "My food's here. Have to go. Have Barbara send me the info."

As soon as I finished my lunch, I paid the tab and headed back over to the M.E.'s office. I wanted to be there, Johnny-on-the-spot, when Dr. Laura Hopewell was ready to rumble. Over the years I've learned that most medical examiners have one thing in common with a live theater performance: Don't show up after the opening curtain and expect the usher to hand you a program and show you to your seat.

It isn't going to happen.

Chapter 4

Joanna arrived in time to be in on part of Detective Howell's interview with Mr. Maury Robbins. Clearly much of it was a repeat of what Ernie had already asked him. But that was standard in a homicide investigation—to ask the same questions several different times to see if there were any discrepancies.

"Like I told that Detective Carpenter," Robbins said. "When I come here after work, I usually arrive somewhere between two and three in the morning."

"And the gate was open when you got here?" Deb asked.

"Right," Maury said, "wide open. At the time I thought, why bother buying a season pass when anyone who wanted to could just drive right in?"

"Besides the gate, did you notice anything else that was out of the ordinary?"

"The dog," Maury said. "Lester's dog usually raises hell. I forget what his name is, something that starts with an *M*, I think. I always hear him barking when I roll down the window to open the gate. Last night he didn't make a peep."

"Can you tell me anything in particular about Lester Attwood?"

"That's his last name, Attwood?"

Debra nodded.

"Not much," Maury said. "I mean, I knew him. Everybody who comes here knows Les. I'm here a couple of times a month. He'd usually meander around the place a couple of times a day, to make sure everything was okay. Sometimes people would get stuck, and he'd help drag 'em out. Sometimes we'd talk. He struck me as a good enough guy, but one who'd put in some hard miles. I asked him once how many times he'd had his nose broken. Said he couldn't remember."

"So he was a fighter, then?" Debra asked. "A brawler?"

"Probably, but by the time I met Les, he seemed to have put his demons behind him and had his life back on track."

"About last night," Debra said. "Aside from the open gate and missing dog, did you notice anything else amiss?"

"Nope," Robbins answered. "That about covers it."

"Tell me about this morning," Deb asked.

"I got up, made some breakfast, unloaded Moxie—that's what I call my ATV. It was while I was doing that that I heard the dog barking. I looked off in that direction, and that's when I first saw the buzzards circling overhead. They were gliding around and around, just like they do in cartoons. I'm sure now the poor dog was barking his head off trying to keep them away. But seeing the birds made me curious. A little later, when I was ready to take my first ride, the dog was still barking, so I headed here to check it out."

"You suspected something was dead?" Joanna asked, inserting her own question into the conversation.

"Yeah," Maury said. "I figured it would turn out to be a cow or a coyote or a jackrabbit. There are a lot of those around here. I sure as hell didn't expect it to be a person."

"When you realized the victim was a person, did you recognize him?"

"Are you kidding? That dog wouldn't let me close enough to see anything, much less touch him."

Dave Hollicker arrived on the scene. After surveying the situation, he dragged something that looked like a stack of plastic pavers out of the back of his van. The twenty-by-twenty-inch grid pieces can be clicked together and used to create temporary parking. In this case Dave laid them out across the debris field where they formed a two-inch-thick firm pathway that investigators could use to come and go from the body without further disturbing the field of churned sand that surrounded the victim.

"Is that all then?" Robbins asked, glancing first at the two detectives and then at Joanna. "No more questions?"

"Not right now," Deb said.

"If you don't mind, then," Maury said, "I'll pack up and head out. I was looking forward to having some quiet time to myself to relax. I wasn't planning on finding a homicide victim. Detective Howell has all my numbers. I'm not due back at work until Wednesday afternoon, though," he added. "I work four P.M. to midnight. If you need anything at all, feel free to give me a call."

His last comment seemed to be aimed directly at Detective Howell rather than anyone else. The way he said it made Joanna think he wasn't just wanting to talk about the case.

"Good," Deb told him. "We'll be in touch."

"I saw the way he was looking at you," Ernie said to Deb as Robbins sped away on his ATV. "I think you made yourself a conquest." Joanna suppressed a smile when she realized Ernie had shared that same impression.

"Leave me alone," Debra said impatiently. "All I did was interview the man. I was just doing my job."

"Sure you were," Ernie said, "but he sounded like he was more interested in you than he was in answering your questions."

There was a squawk from the radio in Ernie's Yukon. He was still talking on the radio when Joanna heard the sound of another approaching vehicle. Ernie reemerged, waving in the direction of the new arrival. "Victim's sister is on her way," he called to Joanna. "Natalie tried to give us a heads-up, but it took this long to relay the message."

When Animal Control had been folded into Joanna's department on a "temporary" basis, she had soon discovered that the two radio systems involved were incompatible. Requests to replace Animal Control's system with new and compatible equipment had been disallowed on the grounds that the situation was "temporary." Permanently temporary. Relaying messages back and forth was cumbersome, time-consuming, and, in this case, pointless. By the time Joanna knew someone was coming, she was pretty much there.

The three officers watched as an antique jeep careened over the top of the dune behind them. Ernie moved forward to flag down the vehicle. For a time it appeared that the jeep was going to plow right into him. The female driver stopped only a couple of feet from where Ernie was standing. The woman, tanned and weather-beaten, wore a man's Western shirt and a faded baseball cap. A foot-long gray ponytail stuck out through the hole in the back of the cap. Looking at her, Joanna estimated the woman to be in her late sixties or early seventies. There was no need to guess about her state of mind. She was mad as hell.

"Where's my brother?" she demanded. "What's happened and what have you done with him? That's Lester's ATV over there. It looks like it's been wrecked." She pointed at the fallen ATV. "Is he all right? And who the hell are all of you?"

Since Ernie was right in front of the bumper, he was closer to the newly arrived vehicle than anyone else. Producing his badge and ID wallet, he held them up. "I'm Detective Ernie Carpenter with the Cochise County Sheriff's Department. That's Sheriff Brady and Detective Howell," he added, pointing in their direction. "I'm afraid there's been an accident."

"I can see that!" the woman snapped. "What do you think I am, blind or something? Now get the hell out of my way."

The engine was still idling. She gunned it determinedly, as though she fully intended to hit the gas and barge right past him. Or over him.

"You can't go there, miss," he insisted. "It's a crime scene."

"Don't you 'miss' me . . ." she began, but before she could pull away, Ernie reached across her, switched off the ignition on the steering column, and took possession of the keys. In the momentary quiet, the woman gave Ernie a piercing look.

"Wait a minute. Did you say crime scene?" she asked. It seemed as though she had only then internalized his words.

Ernie nodded again. "Yes, ma'am," he said. "It's a possible homicide."

A shocked expression flitted across the woman's face. "You're saying someone's dead—that they've been murdered?" she asked.

"There's been a fatality," the detective told her, keeping his voice neutral. "We don't know yet if it's a homicide. That's what we're investigating right now."

"My brother lives out here," the woman said forcefully. "Tell me who's dead. Where?"

In answer Ernie nodded slightly in Dave Hollicker's direction. Before anyone could stop her, the woman bolted from the jeep. With an unexpected burst of speed she dodged past Ernie and sprinted toward Dave, heading straight off across the sand. Without pausing to confer, Joanna and Deb Howell leaped forward to head the woman off. Each of them managed to lay hands on an arm and together they jerked the woman to a stop.

"Let me go," she shouted, trying to extricate herself. "What if that's my brother over there? I saw Lester's dog back at the gate with another cop. She wouldn't tell me what was going on, either, but Miller wouldn't have left Les's side unless something was terribly wrong."

"Our victim may very well be your brother," Joanna agreed calmly, trying to reason with the still struggling woman. "But you can't go there. As Detective Carpenter told you, this is a crime scene. We need to preserve it. We have to keep it the way it is in hopes of figuring out what happened."

"Let me go!"

"No!" Joanna told her. "Not until you calm down. You can't just go tearing off across the sand. What if the victim does turn out to be your brother? The only way we'll be able to find out what really happened to him is by examining every detail of the crime scene so we can figure out what went on."

As suddenly as the struggle had started, it ended. The woman dropped her arms and stopped pulling. "Okay," she said. "Okay."

Joanna let go of the arm she was holding. As a precaution, Debra continued to hold on to hers.

"Who are you?" Joanna asked. "What's your name?"

The woman took a deep breath. "Margie," she said. "My name's Margie Savage."

"You said you think this man—the victim—may be your brother?" Joanna asked.

"My baby brother," Margie answered. "His name is Lester—Lester Attwood. He lives in that camper back by the gate. His truck's there, but he's not. I was afraid something bad had happened to him."

"What made you think that?" Joanna asked. "Is that why you came here today?"

Margie nodded. "I work at the post office in Bowie. One of the neighbors from up the road stopped by a little while ago and told me something strange was going on up here. He said he'd seen an Animal Control truck turn in here and a cop car, too, one that took off over the dunes. I couldn't figure out why Animal Control would be here. I know Miller's licensed. I took care of that myself. So I headed out here on my lunch hour to see what happened. I followed the tracks and they led me right here. So what did happen? Did he come down that dune too fast and take a spill? I kept telling him to stay off that ATV, that the damned thing would be the death of him."

That jeep doesn't look much safer, Joanna thought, but what she said was "We don't think what happened was an accident. That's why Detectives Carpenter and Howell are here. They're homicide detectives, and that man you see working over there . . ." She pointed at Dave. "He's my crime scene investigator. That's why we're trying to preserve the crime scene—so we can examine it for clues."

"You're saying Lester's been murdered?" Margie repeated the words as if she couldn't quite believe them.

"We think murder is a distinct possibility," Joanna answered. "As to whether or not the victim is your brother . . ."

Margie squared her shoulders and raised her chin. "Show him to me," she said. "Let me see for myself. I'm not going to faint or anything. I'm a hell of a lot tougher than that."

"You're sure?"

"I'm sure."

"All right, then," Joanna said. "Follow me. If you don't mind, please stay on the pathway."

Margie nodded. "I will," she said.

With Joanna leading the way, they started off across the intervening sand by following the plastic-grid path Dave Hollicker had laid down. A full ten yards from the half-buried body, Margie came to an abrupt stop. Ernie, following behind, almost ran into her.

"It's him," Margie said. "That's my brother."

Joanna stopped, too. From where she stood, all that was visible of the body was the back of the man's head and neck, as well as the top of his shirt collar. What looked like an ugly bruise covered the back of his neck from the top of his shirt to the bottom of his hairline.

Joanna was surprised by the certainty in Margie's voice. "Are you sure?" Joanna asked. "You can identify him from all the way back here?"

"It's the birthmark," Margie said. "The one on the back of his neck."

Joanna looked again at what she had assumed to be a recent injury. "That's a birthmark instead of a bruise?" she asked.

Margie nodded. "The whole time we were growing up I was forever having to beat the crap out of asshole kids who teased him about it. They'd torment him and tell him the discoloration on his neck was really the mark of the devil. By the time I finished blackening their eyes, they knew all about the mark of the devil."

She paused and gave a small snort. "When I was younger, I used to have a pretty mean left hook. I busted out Tommy Leroy's right front tooth when I was sixteen, and it wasn't no baby tooth, either. He was only fourteen, but he was also a good five inches taller than me. I thought his mother was gonna kill me when she found out about it, but then someone told her what he'd been doing—that Tommy and some friends of his had been picking on Lester—she changed her mind. She lit into Tommy herself and gave him a whuppin', too. Not that any of that ever helped poor Les," she added sadly.

For a long moment, she stood staring across the expanse of sand toward her brother's still form. "It's like the guy never had a chance at a decent life," she said finally. "The cards were so stacked against him from the start that you could hardly blame him for drowning his sorrows in booze."

With that, she turned and walked back the way they had come, deftly slipping past Ernie without once venturing off Dave Hollicker's plastic-grid trail. By the time Margie reached the side of her jeep, she sank down on her knees next to it, buried her face in her hands, and wept. Joanna realized then that Margie Savage had put on a good front of being tough, but it was only that—a front. Joanna caught up with her in time to hear her sob, "I'm sorry, Mama," she said. "I'm so, so sorry."

"None of this is your fault," Joanna said consolingly, "unless you did this. Did you?"

Margie shook her head. "But I promised our mama that I'd look after him, that I'd keep him safe. Once he sobered up, I helped him get this caretaker's job so's I could keep an eye on him. Now he's dead."

She pulled a red hankie out of the pocket of her jeans and blew her nose into it. Then she straightened her shoulders and looked back at the ATV. "They ran him down, didn't they?" she said.

"That's what it looks like," Joanna agreed. "We won't know for sure until we finish our investigation."

"And who did it?"

"We don't know that, either. Is there a chance your brother got involved with some unsavory characters?"

"Les has been involved with 'unsavory characters' all his life," Margie replied. "He didn't hardly know any other kind. I thought he'd left all that behind him—those kinds of friends, but maybe he had a slip."

"A slip," Ernie said, latching on to the sobriety lingo. "Are you saying he'd been through drug or alcohol treatment?"

"Alcohol," Margie answered. "Three times, to be exact, but this last time it finally took. Les had been sober for a little over a year. Fourteen months, to be exact. Said the only kind of booze he still had around the house was Miller."

"Miller High Life?" Ernie asked. "You mean he still drank beer?"

"Not that kind of Miller," Margie said. "His dog. Les was still drinking two years ago when somebody dumped an almost dead puppy out by the garbage cans at the trailer court in Tucson where Les used to live. The puppy was a tiny little thing. To begin with, Les fed him with an eyedropper and later with a toy baby bottle. He finally managed to nurse him back to health. Les named the dog after his favorite beer—Miller—and even taught him to bring him a cold one from the fridge. He thought that was funnier 'an a rubber crutch. 'Hey, Miller,' he'd say, 'bring me a Miller.' And that dog would do it just as cute as can be. Truth be told, Les let that dog drink some of his beer as well. But finally Lester went through treatment and sobered up. It turns out that when Les stopped drinking, so did Miller. But when Les wanted a soda from the fridge, he'd still say the same thing—for Miller to bring him a beer. Les told me it was just too much trouble to try teaching that dog a new command. Besides, Les liked it. He said asking the dog to bring him a soda didn't have quite the same ring to it; wasn't as funny."

Margie paused and looked around. "Les loved that dog to distraction," she added. "What's going to happen to him now?"

Joanna had learned over time that dealing with pets left behind by homicide victims was often a tough call. Sometimes any number of people—friends and relatives—came forward to lay claim to the suddenly orphaned animal. Other times no one did and the unwanted dog or cat or gerbil ended up being hauled away to the pound. As head of Animal Control, Jeannine Phillips was a tiger about finding homes for abandoned animals, but sometimes even she came up empty.

"Miller loved Lester, but ever since he stopped being a puppy, I've been half scared of him," Margie admitted. "And after getting used to living out here with all this room to run around, I think he'd be too much dog for me and my little single-wide. I doubt he'd get along with my pug, Miss Priss, either."

Joanna had learned enough about animal control to see that sending Miller to live with someone who was scared of him was an invitation to disaster—for Marge Savage, for her little pug, and for Miller as well. A second choice would be to send Miller to live with some other relative so the dog wouldn't be shipped off either to the pound or to live with complete strangers.

"Is there anyone else who's familiar with the dog?" Joanna asked.

"My stepsons know him, of course," Margie said.

"Could one of them take him?" Joanna asked.

The woman shook her head. "They both have little kids," she said. "Miller's a Doberman, after all—part Doberman, anyway. He's used to being around grown-ups."

Joanna sighed. "All right, then," she said. "You have enough on your plate right now to worry about the dog, but we certainly can't leave the poor thing here. I'll have my ACO take Miller back to the pound in Bisbee."

"You won't let them put him down, will you?" Margie asked. "I mean, none of this is Miller's fault."

That was certainly true.

"I can't promise," Joanna said, knowing how often her pound filled up with unwanted animals. "We'll do our best to find a place for him, but if you happen to think of anyone else who might want him . . ."

The sentence was interrupted by the ringing of Joanna's cell phone. "I'm here," Guy Machett announced in her ear. "At least I think I'm here. I'm at a place where the sign on the gate says 'Action Trail Adventures.' This is where the guy at the post office told me to come. There's an Animal Control truck parked out on the shoulder of the road. I don't see anyone in it."

"You asked for directions from the post office?" Joanna asked.

"Yeah, right here in Bowie," the M.E. replied. "Why not? Those people have to know where to find people."

Joanna noticed the man was still using the bow-and-arrow pronunciation of Bowie. He had also disregarded her advice about calling her for directions. She knew that his driving up to Bowie's post office in a vehicle marked COCHISE COUNTY MEDICAL EXAMINER would have caused a firestorm of small-town interest even it hadn't been Margie Savage's place of employment.

"The crime scene is out here in the dunes," she told him. "If you like, I could send Ernie or Debra to come guide you in."

"I don't need a babysitter," he said. "I'm perfectly capable of getting there myself. Just tell me where you are."

Joanna turned to Ernie. "How far is it from the gate to where we turned off?"

"Three-quarters of a mile," he said. "Give or take."

Joanna returned to the phone. "All right," she said. "Turn right on the gravel road and follow that for three-quarters of a mile. You'll see where the tracks lead off to the left into the dunes."

Joanna ended the call. "The M.E.," she replied in answer to Ernie's quizzical look. "He's coming."

For the next several minutes she took a backseat to her detectives while Debra and Ernie plied Margie for information about her brother. "How long did Les work here?" Ernie asked.

"Since he got out of treatment," Margie said. "A little over a year. My two stepsons own the place, and they hired him as a favor to me. The ranch has been in the family—their mother's family—for generations, and they inherited it after Monty died. Monty was my husband, you see. Third husband. The boys—Arnie and Chuck—have wanted to turn it into an ATV playground for years. Monty was against it, but once it belonged to them, they went ahead and did what they wanted."

"Is there any bad blood between your stepsons and your brother?" Debra Howell asked.

"Between Les and the boys? Good heavens, no!" Margie exclaimed, rolling her eyes. "They've been good as gold to him, and to me, too. Just as Les was getting out of treatment, their previous caretaker quit. I asked them if they'd mind hiring him. He'd had to move out of his other place when he went in for treatment, and I knew the job here came with a place to live. I sure as hell didn't want Les and his dog living with me.

"It was a huge relief for me when they hired him. That way I knew Les had a roof over his head, and he made a little money, too, enough to supplement his Social Security and keep him and Miller in food. Chuck and Arnie let him have that old pickup truck and the ATV to drive around here and use for chores, but the rule was, Les wasn't allowed to take either one of them off the property or onto the highway. With all those DUIs on his record, he'd lost his driver's license and couldn't have gotten insurance on a bet. So I'd take him into town if he needed groceries and dog food. Or one of my daughters-in-law would. Like I said, Chuck and Arnie and their families were all as good to him as they could be, even if they did it because they were doing me a favor. They're nice people."

"Did Les have a girlfriend?" Deb asked.

Margie snorted at the very idea. "Not a girlfriend," she said. "More like a drinking buddy."

"Does she have a name?"

"LaVerne," Margie said.

"Last name?"

"LaVerne," Margie replied. "I believe her last name's Hartley and I think she lives in Benson, but once Les sobered up, Old LaVerne gave him the brush-off. My reading is that if he was off the sauce, she didn't want anything to do with him. Besides, she didn't like Miller, and Miller didn't like her. 'Les,' I told him more than once, 'when it comes to women, that dog of yours has got way better sense than you do.' "

"Do you happen to have LaVerne's phone number?"

"No. It's probably in the phone book, but I doubt this has anything to do with her."

Deb jotted a note, and Joanna knew that one of her detectives would be calling on LaVerne Hartley soon to verify whether or not that was the case.

"What about drugs?" Debra asked. "Was your brother mixed up with any of that?"

"I already told you. As far as Les was concerned, alcohol was his drug of choice—his only drug of choice. He wasn't into meth or coke or pot or even cigarettes. Just booze."

Joanna's phone rang. "I'm stuck," Guy Machett said when Joanna answered.

He sounded aggrieved—as though the fact that he'd gotten his vehicle mired down in sand was all Joanna's fault. She turned and looked back over the path she and Ernie had used to drive from the gravel road to the crime scene. Debra had come in that same way, and so had Margie Savage. There was, however, no sign of the M.E.'s van.

"Stuck where?" Joanna asked.

"In the sand," he snapped irritably. "Where do you think?"

Joanna covered the mouthpiece. "The M.E.," she told the others. "He's stuck." Removing her hand, she spoke into the phone. "I'm looking back toward the road," she said. "I don't see any sign of you."

"I didn't bother with the road," Machett said. "I ran into that woman from the truck—the one from the dog pound. She told me you were out this way. I didn't see any point in following the road when the shortest distance between two points is a straight line."

Not when you're driving through sand, you jerk, Joanna thought. It turned out Guy Machett did need a babysitter.

"Where are you exactly?" she asked.

"Somewhere between the gate and where you are," he said. "Can you come pull me out or send someone who can?"

"You need a tow truck," Joanna said.

"Then call one for me," Machett replied.

Months earlier, Joanna's department had been forced to eat a five-thousand-dollar towing bill when a murder victim's vehicle had crashed through a guardrail and come to rest on a steep mountainside. She didn't want to fall into a similar trap. She suspected that if she or someone from her department called for the tow, Guy

Machett would somehow find a way to have the costs come out of her budget instead of his.

"I'll get you a number and call you back."

"Come on," Machett said. "That homicide cop of yours has four-wheel drive. I've seen it. Couldn't you just send him over here with a tow chain?"

And get Ernie stuck, too? Joanna thought. Not on your life.

"He's interviewing a witness right now," she said. "And I don't think our insurance covers DIY towing. If something happened to your vehicle or ours, the damage wouldn't be covered."

"Have a heart, Sheriff Brady," he wheedled. "Help me out here."

But on this matter, Joanna's mind was made up. "I'll get you the number," she said.

She called Dispatch, got the names and numbers of several towing companies, and relayed them back to Guy Machett. Then Joanna called in to Animal Control and spoke to Jeannine Phillips. It was easier and faster to call on the phone than to work with the nonworking radio system.

"Have Officer Wilson take the homicide victim's dog into custody and bring him back to Bisbee."

"To the pound?" Jeannine asked. "Does that mean none of the relatives want him?"

"Not so far."

"Natalie already asked me about this," Jeannine said. "According to her, Miller seems to be a great dog. He's been neutered, has all his shots, and is properly licensed. Instead of bringing him to the pound, she was wondering if she could foster him until we find out if the relatives give a final yea or nay. If they don't want him, Natalie might take him permanently."

Joanna felt a slight lightening in her chest. In the course of that tough afternoon, not having to lock up a grieving dog seemed like a good thing—a small but good thing.

"Great," she said. "If you don't have a problem with that arrangement, far be it from me to interfere."

Call waiting buzzed, and Joanna switched over to another call. "I just talked to towing company number three," Guy Machett complained. "They can't be here in anything less than an hour. What the hell am I supposed to do in the meantime—waste my whole day?"

Of course Guy Machett wasn't the only one wasting time. Until he made his appearance to examine the victim, Joanna's detectives were also stuck in a holding pattern.

Joanna covered the mouthpiece with her hand. "The tow truck's at least an hour away," Joanna told Ernie. "Want to try pulling him out with the Yukon?"

"What's the matter?" Margie interrupted before Ernie had a chance to answer. "Who's stuck?"

"The medical examiner," Joanna said. "He's bogged down in the sand somewhere between here and the gate."

"Oh, for Pete's sake," Margie Savage said. "Why don't I just go get him? I've been driving these dunes most of my life. I've got a tow chain right here on my jeep, and I know how to use it."

"You wouldn't mind?" Joanna asked.

"Hell, no," Margie said. "Why would I mind?"

With that, she headed for her jeep. Ernie moved as if to stop her, but Joanna held up her hand.

"Let her go," she said. "There's nothing Dr. Machett will hate more than being rescued by an old lady."

And nothing I'll like better.

Chapter 5

By the time I got back to the Kittitas County complex, I had no intention of going another few rounds with the receptionist. Instead, I prowled the parking lot. You've heard the old adage: Rank hath its privilege? In the world of bureaucrats, no privilege counts for quite as much as having your very own reserved parking place. It didn't take long to find the spot that was marked: RESERVED MEDICAL EXAMINER.

I kept circling the parking lot until someone finally left a parking place that gave me a clear view of the M.E.'s precious spot. That way, when she finally showed up, I'd be the first to know. I put the seat all the way back, opened my computer, logged on, and indulged myself. For a long time, I had resisted doing online crossword puzzles. Doing them on a computer rather than in a banged-up folded newspaper had seemed sacrilegious somehow.

But I'm over it. That was another change Mel had instituted in my life. Despite her love of fast, powerful cars—she adores the Porsche Cayman I gave her as a wedding present—she's a greenie at heart. She has managed to convince me to give up on newsprint altogether, including crosswords, which were the only thing I thought papers were good for to begin with.

Just because it was raining in Seattle and snowing in Snoqualmie Pass didn't mean it was raining or snowing here. Ellensburg is right at the edge of Washington State's unexpected stretch of desert. So I sat in the clear cold sunlight, squinting at my dim computer screen, and worked the *New York Times* puzzle. In a little over five minutes. That's the problem with Monday and Tuesday puzzles these days. Most of the time they're way too easy.

A few minutes later and an hour and a half after the receptionist had given me the brush-off, a bright red Prius pulled into the M.E.'s reserved spot. A young woman with long dark hair and wearing an enormous pair of sunglasses got out of the car and then turned to retrieve a briefcase. I put down the computer and scrambled to intercept her.

"Dr. Hopewell?" I asked tentatively.

Peeling off the glasses, she swung around and faced me. I was surprised to see a pair of almond-shaped dark eyes, angry dark eyes, staring back at me. "Yes," she said. "I'm Dr. Hopewell. That was certainly quick. Where is it?"

Excuse me? She seemed to be in the middle of a conversation I hadn't yet started.

"Where's what?" I asked.

"My suitcase. The airline called while I was still in the pass. They said they had found the missing luggage and they were dispatching someone to deliver it to me. I thought maybe the airline finally got around to doing something right for a change."

That seemed unlikely, but rather than telling her so, I managed to fumble my ID out of my pocket and hand it over. "Sorry," I said. "Special Investigator J. P. Beaumont. I'm here for the autopsy."

"Oh," she said. She glanced at my ID and handed it back. "Sorry about that," she said. "As you can see, there's been a slight delay. Come on in. I've been out of town. I've heard about the case, but so far I haven't seen anything about it. As soon as I get suited up, we can start. You can wait in my office if you like."

She led me through the lobby. I waltzed past the evil-eyed receptionist without being hit by any incoming missiles and hurried on into the relative safety of the morgue's nonpublic areas. The first office beyond the swinging doors was labeled DR. HOPEWELL. She ushered me into that and offered me one of two visitors' chairs. Then she set the briefcase down behind a suspiciously clean and orderly desk.

"Wait here," she instructed. "I'll be right back."

I find that women in positions of authority have a tendency to be at one extreme or the other. Either they're comfortable with themselves and easy to get along with—like Mel, for instance—or they can be a royal pain in the butt. I had no idea where Dr. Hopewell would stand on the particular dividing line. To be on the safe side, I did exactly as I'd been told and sat where she'd left me.

While I waited, I examined her small but exceptionally neat office in some detail. Eventually my eyes were drawn to a framed photo on the wall—a graduation photo with a smiling cap-and-gown-clad Laura Hopewell standing between a very non-Asian middle-aged couple, a man and a woman. I was still studying the photo when Dr. Hopewell returned.

"Those are my parents," she said. "They adopted me from China when I was three."

"They look like nice people," I said.

She nodded. "They are."

"And you must make them very proud."

She shrugged and sighed. "Maybe not so much," she said. "My mother would rather I was curing cancer or delivering babies instead of solving murders."

That made me laugh. "Some things never change," I said. "When I told my mother I was going to be a cop, she felt the same way."

That broke the ice. "Come on," Dr. Hopewell said. "Let's go get this done."

Which we did.

Standing in on autopsies is tough, but it's part of my job. Bereaved family members go to funerals. They remember the dearly departed in eulogies and they start the process of saying good-bye. For homicide cops, autopsies are a way of saying hello. What the M.E. uncovers in an autopsy is usually a starting point. By learning everything we can about the victims at the moment of death, we begin trying to find out what happened to them and why. And with unidentified victims, it's even more basic than that. Before we can find out who killed them, we have to know who they are. And in this case, once we established the victim's identity, we needed to ascertain if her death was related to the others we were investigating.

"All right, Mr. Craft," she called to her assistant. "Let's get started."

The assistant rolled out a gurney. Rather than a sheet-draped body, the gurney held a sheet-draped box. Inside was what looked like a haphazard collection of bones. This would be an autopsy with some assembly required. One by one, Dr. Hopewell began removing bones from the box, examining the charred and chewed remains as she brought them out, and then laying them out in a rough approximation of a human form.

As I watched this painstaking process I was reminded of something I hadn't thought about in years. As a high school sophomore, I had used my own hard-earned cash to buy myself a motorcycle at a garage sale. I had dragged it home in pieces, with the frame and tires in one section and with all the smaller parts stashed in an old wooden laundry basket. I had used all the mechanical skill my high school auto-shop teacher had been able to instill in me into trying to put the pieces back together.

My father died in a motorcycle accident months before I was born. Taking that part of my history into consideration, you could say that my mother wasn't overjoyed at the prospect of my having a motorcycle of my own. She didn't come right out and actually forbid me to do it, but she watched the piece-by-piece reconstruction process with an undisguised lack of enthusiasm.

I'm a lot older now than I was then, and I also have a far greater understanding of what women will and won't do in order to get their way. Standing in the Kittitas County morgue and watching the bones being laid out on the examining table, I wondered if it was possible that my mother had sabotaged the whole process. Once I finally got the bike back together, I never did make it work. Had my mother somehow managed to remove the one critical part that made it so I couldn't get the engine to turn over? However it happened, I never managed a single ride.

Something similar seemed to be going on here. Dr. Hopewell could put the pieces back in some semblance of the right order, but no one was going to be able to breathe life back into that body. Whoever was dead was going to stay that way.

"Our victim is a female," Dr. Hopewell intoned early in the process. "Late twenties to early thirties."

"Wait a minute," I objected. "I thought we already knew that. Isn't that why I'm here?"

Dr. Hopewell gave me what my son-in-law calls "the stink eye" over the top of her surgical mask. "I believe the CSI people made their initial assessment regarding the victim's gender based on other evidence found at the scene," she said. "There was an engagement ring, a woman's boot, and some odd fragments of clothing. But just because someone dresses like a woman doesn't make her a woman. The bones do."

I homed in on the engagement ring. That was strikingly different from our other victims, where no identifiable jewelry or clothing had been found.

"No robbery then?" I asked.

Dr. Hopewell shrugged, reached into the box, and removed the skull. As soon as she did so, I saw the other huge difference Ross Connors had already mentioned. This skull still had teeth. The teeth of all the other victims had been removed, if not prior to death, then at least prior to the time the corpse had been set on fire.

Dr. Hopewell examined the skull for a long time before she spoke again. "Lots of signs of blunt trauma here," she said. "It looks like any number of them could have been fatal."

"What about strangulation?" I asked. "Any sign of that?"

Dr. Hopewell shook her head. "None," she said.

That was a point this victim had in common with the others. They hadn't been strangled, either.

"Look at this," Dr. Hopewell said. She used a hemostat to pluck a long strand of blackened material out of the box and held it up to the light.

"Rope, maybe?" I asked.

She nodded. "Restraints. Bag, please, Mr. Craft."

Her assistant stepped forward with an open evidence bag and she dropped the strand of burned rope into it.

"What about hair?" I asked.

"Some," she said.

"Enough for DNA testing?"

Dr. Hopewell's eyes met mine. "We don't do DNA testing," she said. "And we don't order it, either. Too expensive. My office can't afford it."

"Mine can," I said with some confidence. It was reassuring to know that I worked for a guy who would spare no expense when it came to doing the job. "Forward what you have to the Washington State Patrol Crime lab. Tell them it's a Ross Connors case."

Dr. Hopewell nodded again and returned to her work and her narrative. "The victim was evidently lying on her back when she was set on fire. You'll notice that the charring is far more pronounced on the top portions of the body than it is on the bottom," she continued. "I would assume that whoever did this probably expected that the body would burn down to mere ashes, thus erasing all trace evidence. Unfortunately for him, the fire went out prematurely."

"Due to weather conditions?" I asked. In the Cascades in November, it's either raining or snowing.

"The weather could be partly responsible in putting the fire out," Dr. Hopewell conceded. "But remember, most of the people who turn to crime do so because they don't have many other career options. They aren't smart and didn't pay attention in school. The guy who did this—and I'm pretty sure it was a guy—obviously had no idea that the human body is more than fifty percent water. He may have poured on all the gasoline he had, but it wasn't nearly enough to do the job completely. Unfortunately for us, when the fire was out, there was still enough flesh on the bones to attract carrion eaters. That's why the bones were scattered around the way they were."

Suddenly the door to the morgue swung open. A woman who appeared to be in her mid-to-late-thirties strode into the room. She was five-six or -seven and solidly built. She looked tough enough that I wouldn't have been surprised if she could take me in a fair fight.

"How come you started already?" she demanded of the M.E. "Connie was supposed to call and let me know when you got back. I wanted to be here for this. I was supposed to be here." Noticing me, the woman stopped short in mid-tirade and stared at me. "Who the hell is this guy?" she added pointedly. "What's he doing here?"

"His name is J. P. Beaumont," Dr. Hopewell said. "He's an investigator with the AG's office, and this is

Detective Lucinda Caldwell, Kittitas County Sheriff's Department."

"Homicide," Detective Caldwell added unnecessarily, since I'd already figured out that much on my own.

It struck me that if Detective Caldwell thought the lady in the outside office was going to lift a hand to help her or anyone else, she was a lot more naive than your run-of-the-mill homicide cop ought to be.

"Glad to meet you," I said. I wasn't particularly glad to meet her, but I'm old enough to know that a certain amount of insincerity is necessary to get along in this world. "People call me Beau," I said. "Or else J.P."

"I don't give a damn what people call you," she said. "I'm going to call you gone. This is my case. What are you doing here?"

Ross Connors had sent in Special Homicide because of the possible connection between this victim and the five other cases we were already working. But the truth was, the body had been found in Kittitas County, and their homicide folks should have been primary. Until Detective Caldwell's abrupt arrival, the local constabulary had been notable in their absence.

My initial instinct was to take offense at Detective Caldwell's proprietary approach. I started to object but then thought better of it. I happened to remember how I used to feel back in the old days at Seattle PD when some arrogant piece of brass would deign to come down from on high and venture onto the fifth floor to tell me and the other lowly homicide cops how to do our jobs. Or the time when some twit of an FBI agent ended up being parachuted into the middle of one of my cases and took it upon himself to rub my nose in the concept that he was smart and I was stupid. Given all that, it made sense that Detective Caldwell might be territorial about her case. What I had to do was find a way to work with her.

"My boss, Attorney General Ross Connors, believes this case might be related to several other ones we've been working."

"I don't care who you are or where you're from," Detective Caldwell declared. "You've got no business horning in on my—"

"Play nice, you two," Dr. Hopewell ordered. "I happen to be doing an autopsy here. How about if you cool it, Lucy? You can sort out all the jurisdictional wrangling later on. In the meantime, you need to know that our victim is female. Probably late twenties, early thirties. She's had at least one child, and she died on or around November eighth."

That caught my attention, and Detective Caldwell's, too. "You can tell that from looking at this pile of bones?" Lucy Caldwell asked.

"I can tell that from looking at her watch," Dr. Hopewell said, holding up the charred remains of a watch. "It was still on her wrist, and that's the day it stopped running."

Detective Caldwell nudged Bob Craft, the M.E.'s assistant, out of the way and bullied herself directly between me and the M.E. Even so, I managed to step around the detective's stolid body long enough to take a closer look at the damaged watch.

Getting older is an interesting process. My eyesight isn't what it used to be. I'm annoyed at times when, if I don't want to resort to reading glasses, I have to hold menus as far away as my arms will reach. That's the only way to make them readable. In this case, however, that peculiarity served me in good stead. It allowed me to see that although the crystal covering was broken and the strap had been burned away, the numbers across the bottom, the ones showing the date, were still clearly visible.

My first impression was that this was a reasonably expensive watch that might very well be traceable. The same thing could also be true of the ring, which had already been taken into evidence. Before I could say anything to that effect, however, Lucinda Caldwell produced an evidence bag of her own.

"I'll take that," she said. "Put it in here."

And Dr. Hopewell did. By then the body was pretty much put back together except for some bits that had probably been carried off by marauding carnivores. Those pieces would most likely never be found.

Dr. Hopewell stepped back from the examining table, snapped off her gloves, and nodded to her assistant. "You can switch off the camera, Mr. Craft," she said. As he hurried to do her bidding, she turned to Detective Caldwell and added, "I'll have my diener make copies of the tape."

"Diener" happens to be a highfalutin name for plain old ordinary morgue assistant. It annoyed me that the M.E. found it necessary to play that kind of cop-talk one-upmanship. I prefer using ordinary English to law enforcement jargon.

"Please give Ms. Whitman your e-mail information," Hopewell said. "That way we can send you each a copy of my final report."

Looking up, I noticed for the first time that an overhead camera had silently recorded all the proceedings. That was a new one to me. I wasn't sure I wanted to live in a world where autopsies were routinely recorded in HD color and then sent out over the Internet. How long would it be before some ghoulish entrepreneur set up an Autopsies-R-Us Web site and started letting viewers log on at will? It would probably mean an end to the macabre black humor comments cops and M.E.s have long used as a coping mechanism to see their way through the routine, mind-numbing horror of human dissections.

"You'll get her dental information entered into the Missing Person database?" I asked.

Dr. Hopewell nodded. "Once we have the X rays, Mr. Craft will see to that as well."

With Detective Caldwell leading the way, we started down the hallway toward the lobby. It depressed me to think that the receptionist in the outer office would be in charge of distribution. It occurred to me that Detective Caldwell and I would both probably end up waiting for that e-mail for a very long time, probably about as long as . . . well, as long as Detective Caldwell had waited for Connie Whitman's call to let her know the M.E. had returned to her office. I had an idea that Ms. Whitman's receptionist's passive-aggressive behavior wouldn't be limited to her gatekeeping responsibilities. I also doubted she would favor one law enforcement entity over any other.

Detective Caldwell must have arrived at the same conclusion. She didn't say a word to me until after we had stopped off at Connie's desk and given her our e-mail information. Once we were outside, however, it was a different story.

While we had been involved with the autopsy, the coming storm had blown over the Cascades and was making its presence known. Clear skies had been replaced by lowering clouds. It was cold as hell and spitting a combination of snow and sleet. None of that did anything to cool Detective Lucinda Caldwell's temper.

"So," she said, turning on me, "I suppose since you work for the attorney general, you think you're some kind of big deal?"

I had already figured out that when genes were being passed out, Detective Caldwell had missed out entirely on having a sense of humor. In our kind of work, however, that can leave you at a distinct disadvantage.

"I'm no kind of big deal," I replied earnestly. "I actually work for S.H.I.T."

I deliberately didn't spell it out, and Detective Caldwell's resulting confusion was a delight to see. She hadn't been paying attention before and she was clearly unfamiliar with the bureaucratic faux pas that had resulted from calling our unit the Special Homicide Investigation Team. And the way she rose to the bait was gratifying. It wasn't easy to keep a straight face, but I managed.

"I'll have you know," she said, "I won't be spoken to that way. I want the name of your immediate supervisor."

That was almost too good. Hilarious, even. "That would be Harry I. Ball," I said in all seriousness. "Would you like his number?"

She flushed with anger. "Go to hell," she said, and stalked away.

I hurried after her. "That's Harry Ignatius Ball," I told her. "He's the commander of the attorney general's Special Homicide Investigation Team's second unit. We're based in Bellevue, and we're investigating a series of homicides that are similar to this one, deaths that may or may not be related."

Detective Caldwell may not have had a sense of humor, but she was listening. It finally dawned on her that there might be something more to what I was saying—that I wasn't just giving her a hard time, although I have to confess that I had enjoyed that part of our conversation immensely.

She stopped and turned back to face me. "What homicides?" she demanded.

Detective Caldwell had me there. This was a simple question that I didn't much want to answer. I felt like a politician who thinks he can get away with saying something in one part of the country without having it go over like a pregnant pole-vaulter everywhere else. The cases in question had come from several different jurisdictions, and Ross Connors had been trying to keep our involvement under the media radar. I understood that. By keeping us out of it, we left the locals to take most of the media heat. Come to think of it, a little heat would have been welcome right about then.

"How about we go by your office and discuss it."

"You're not going anywhere near my office," she returned.

My Mercedes was parked right there in the front row. "How about if we go sit in my car, then?" I suggested. "Let's at least get in out of the cold."

I clicked open the door to let her in, and as soon as we settled inside, I knew that was a tactical blunder on my part.

"Since when does an employee of the state go cruising around in a Mercedes-Benz?"

When he started S.H.I.T., Ross Connors had made an executive decision that the organization would dispense with company cars. Having lived through Seattle PD's brief and poorly thought-out romance with K-cars back in the eighties, I was more than happy to be able to use my own wheels. Keeping dutiful track of the mileage and turning in the resulting expense reports on time can be a pain, but it certainly beats the alternative. I'll choose riding in my used Mercedes over being stuck in a brand-new Crown Victoria any day of the week.

"Forget about the car," I said. "Let's talk about cases."

"Yes, let's," she said. "Which cases?"

And so I told her. Most of it, anyway, but not all the telling details. I didn't know this woman and I didn't really trust her to keep things quiet. What if she went running off at the mouth to some local newspaper reporter, or, even worse, to some visiting newsie from Seattle? So I made no mention of the victims' missing teeth in the five previous cases. That was an official holdback in our investigation and I decided to keep it that way. I settled, instead, for focusing on the tarps that had been used to wrap the various bodies and on the fact that the manufacturer tags on those had all been systematically removed in what appeared to be a very similar fashion.

Despite Detective Caldwell's previous display of attitude, she now appeared to be paying close attention. "I was there when our CSI tech found that piece of tarp," she said. "And I was there when he put it into the evidence log. We both noticed that missing tag. What I want to know is how you found out about it."

I didn't know for sure how that had happened, but I had my suspicions.

"Ross Connors is a very smart man," I said. "I would imagine that a discreet inquiry has gone out to

CSI units all over Washington State and beyond asking for information on any incidents in which blue construction tarps or parts thereof were found at crime scenes."

That statement was followed by a brief silence. I figured Detective Caldwell was about to give me another blast of temper. Instead she issued a resigned sigh. "All right, then," she said, reaching for the door handle. "I've still got what's left of the watch. I need to get it into the evidence log along with the engagement ring and the toe ring."

"What toe ring?" I asked.

"It was in the boot," she said. "A snakeskin cowboy boot that didn't quite burn."

"One boot but not two?"

"Only one," Detective Caldwell said. "Let's go. How about if you follow me back to the department. I'll give you a look at what else we have. Who knows? Maybe you'll come up with an idea or two."

Her grudging acceptance wasn't exactly a heartfelt apology, but it was as close to one as I was going to get.

"Great," I said, turning on the ignition. "Lead the way."

As far as Joanna was concerned, sending Margie Savage to rescue Guy Machett from the sand was well worth the price of admission. He had been ripped before. He arrived at the crime scene in a state of high dudgeon and without Margie Savage, who had pulled him out and then gone on her way. Considering the M.E.'s state of mind, that was probably a good thing.

"That woman's a nutcase," he complained as he opened the cargo door and hauled out a bag of equipment. "She absolutely floored it. She yanked me out of the sand like it was some kind of grudge match. It's a wonder I don't have whiplash, and look at what she did to my bumper."

Machett was right. The minivan's front bumper had been mangled beyond all recognition. What was left of it was rubbing up against the right front tire and would most likely have to be removed before the vehicle could be driven back to town.

"No doubt she thought you were in a hurry," Joanna said. Just beyond Guy Machett and outside his vision, Ernie Carpenter favored Joanna with a wink and a very small grin.

"Now where the hell's this damn body?" Machett continued.

"Out there," she said, pointing. "Dave Hollicker laid down a trail of click-together pavers to make it easier to walk out to the body while preserving the crime scene as much as possible."

Machett gave Dave's plastic path a disparaging look. "You expect me to run a gurney across that?"

As a matter of fact I do, Joanna thought, but she was done. She'd had enough of Guy Machett's temper tantrums for one day, and she didn't need any more.

"You do whatever you need to do," she said. "I'm sure you and Dave will be able to work it out. In the meantime, Detective Carpenter, how about if you give me a ride back out to my vehicle. I'll leave the rest of you to it."

"That guy's no Doc Winfield," Ernie said, once they had climbed into the Yukon and driven out of earshot.

The understated elegance in Ernie's comment was enough to make Joanna smile. "No, he's not," she agreed.

"And he's not going to last," Ernie added.

That unequivocal statement was enough to make Joanna sit up and take notice. Maybe something was going on that she hadn't heard about.

"What makes you say that?" she asked.

"Because he's a balloon full of hot air and somebody needs to pop it—somebody who's got his twenty years in and doesn't have anything to lose."

Joanna knew Ernie wanted to be the one doing the popping, but he was now one of the grand old men of her department. Having already lost the services of Frank Montoya and the good counsel of Dr. George Winfield, she couldn't afford to be without Ernie's time and experience.

"Ignore him," she said. "I need you around far more than I need Machett to be taken down a peg."

When they arrived back at the gate, Natalie Wilson's dog pound vehicle was gone and Miller was as well. A second Crown Victoria was parked next to Joanna's. That Crown Vic, which had once been driven primarily by Frank Montoya, had now been passed down to her three-man homicide team. Detective Jaime Carbajal was inside it, talking on the phone. When Joanna approached the vehicle, he rolled down the window and waved a piece of paper.

"The search warrant?" she asked.

He nodded. "Be right with you." When he stepped out of the car and slammed the door shut a few moments later, the thunderous appearance on his face told Joanna something was wrong.

"What's the matter?" she asked.

He let out a long breath. It sounded like air being released from an overloaded tire. "That was Debra Highsmith," he said. "Luis got in another fight today. He's being suspended. She's of the opinion that whatever's wrong with Luis is all my fault, and she wanted me to come get him. I told her I can't. Delcia's going instead."

Luis Andrade was Jaime's nephew, the son of Marcella Andrade, Jaime's ne'er-do-well sister, a sometime prostitute who had abandoned her progeny the previous summer. Despite having a son of their own, Jaime and his wife had gone to court and petitioned for custody, which had been granted. At the time taking their nephew in seemed like a no-brainer. Luis had come across as a good, self-motivated kid who had looked after his mother more than she had looked after him. At first Luis had convinced everyone, including himself, that his mother's disappearance was temporary. As the months went by and the loss of his mother seemed more and more permanent, he had started getting into trouble. His grades had fallen. He'd lost interest in sports. And Joanna knew that this was the third time in as many weeks that he'd been in trouble at school for fighting.

As for Debra Highsmith, the high school principal? Joanna had done a few rounds with the woman herself. Two years earlier, one of the high school counselors had suggested that Joanna, as sheriff of Cochise County, be invited to speak to the students at a career day assembly. Joanna had been pleased to accept until she'd been told that due to the school's zero-tolerance weapons policy, she would have to check her weapons at the door. She had complied that one time, but since then, in the aftermath of a rash of school shooting fatalities around the country, that rule had been quietly rescinded. Zero tolerance of weapons no longer applied to those carried by trained police officers. The last time Joanna had addressed a school audience, she had done so in her uniform, and no mention had been made of the fact that she'd been armed with both a Taser and a firearm.

"Is Luis all right?" Joanna asked.

"He's not all right," Jaime said. "He's a long way from all right. Marcella has wrecked everything she ever touched. Why should her son be any different?"

"Anything I can do to help?"

Jaime shook his head. "Ernie and I will execute this warrant," he said. "At least it'll give me something to think about besides going home and trying to knock some sense into Luis's head."

"Don't do that," Joanna said. "He's been through a lot. He'll come around eventually."

"I hope so," Jaime said, but he didn't sound convinced.

Joanna was tempted to hang around while they searched for clues in Lester Attwood's Airstream. That sounded far more interesting than going back to her office and facing down a snarl of administrative nitty-gritty. Unfortunately, without Frank Montoya there to handle some of those issues, she had to focus more and more of her energy on day-to-day departmental issues. She knew that if she ever fell behind, she'd never catch up.

"Okay," she said. "Good luck. I'll head back to the office and leave you and Ernie to it."

Chapter 6

Lucy Caldwell left me sitting in a grim little cubicle with the murder book while she went to get the evidence box. I scanned through what was there. The skull and bones had been found on Friday afternoon by a road worker of some kind, a guy named Ken Leggett. I made a note of his name, address, and phone number.

Lucy returned, dragging another cop with her. “This is Gary Fields,” she said. “He’s my partner.” Gary dropped an evidence box on the desk, gave me a look, and rolled his eyes.

“Anything else?” he wanted to know. “I need a smoke.”

“Knock yourself out,” Lucy told him.

When you’re a cop, partners are important. Knowing what to expect from the officer next to you sometimes means the difference between life or death. Clearly the partnership between Detectives Caldwell and Fields wasn't a match made in heaven. And the fact that Gary preferred going out for a cigarette to discussing a current investigation didn't speak well for him. This was a homicide—his homicide—and he should have exhibited a little more interest. At least I thought he should have.

"What's his problem?" I asked.

Lucy shrugged. "He thinks a woman's place is in the home and not in homicide."

Truth be known, not too long ago that used to be my attitude as well. Once upon a time, the fifth floor at Seattle PD was an all-boys club, one with no girls allowed right up until Sue Danielson arrived on the scene. Since then, I had changed my mind about all that, and I thought the rest of the world had changed right along with me. But maybe not some of the "good old boys" in Kittitas County. And if Detective Caldwell was being treated as a pariah by her homicide detective colleagues, that could go a long way in explaining her pissed-off attitude toward me.

"Remind me to introduce Detective Fields to my wife," I said. "She'll clean his clock."

Lucy Caldwell responded to that with a thin smile. Then she opened the box and pulled out a video—good old-fashioned VHS. The local M.E. might have gone high tech and high def, but the sheriff's department was still stuck in the twentieth century.

"Here's the interview we did with Leggett, the guy who found the body. Want to see it?"

I knew that watching the actual interview would take hours—as many hours as the interview itself. No instant replays. No commercial interruptions, and no TiVoed highlights. Besides, since it looked as though I was going to be working with Detective Caldwell, it seemed to me that a show of mutual respect might help us along.

"What about him?" I asked. "Do you think he might have had something to do with it?"

"I came to Homicide from Sexual Assault," Lucy said. "I've interviewed a few scumbags in my time. Leggett is divorced. He drinks too much; he's had several DUIs and several run-ins with the King County cops over in North Bend where he lives. He's the guy who found the body, but in my estimation, he didn't do this. When we interviewed him, he was beyond upset. He saw what he thought was a rock and took a leak on it. But being upset doesn't make him a killer. I would have been upset, too."

I read between the lines. "But somebody around here does think he's the doer," I ventured. "Who would that be?"

"Gary," Lucy answered. "My partner."

"Based on what evidence?" I asked.

"On what he likes to call gut instinct," Lucy answered.

"His gut instinct but not yours, I take it?"

"Mine doesn't count."

Generally speaking, getting caught in the cross fire between feuding partners is a very bad idea. It's true in domestic-violence situations, and it's also true when the dueling partners happen to be cops. So I backed off. I made a mental note to stop off and visit with Mr. Leggett on my own. That way I'd be able to form my own opinions about his possible involvement and about his guilt or innocence.

While we talked, Lucy had removed the cardboard lid to the box. As soon as she did so, the room filled with the odor of dead smoke, and not just plain smoke, either. There was something else under the smoke, an ugly aftertaste that lingered on the back of my tongue. I recognized it but didn't want to acknowledge what it was.

For a few minutes, Lucy busied herself with logging in the item we'd brought back from the M.E.'s office—the broken watch—into the evidence log. The shattered watch was a Timex—relatively cheap but reliable. It wasn't still ticking as the ads say, but the fact that the date was still visible gave us an invaluable piece of information.

"What else do you have in there?" I asked.

"Exhibit number one," she said, handing me a small glassine bag. Inside it was what looked like a misshapen hunk of gold with a small emerald-cut stone.

"An engagement ring?" I asked.

Lucy nodded.

"Including a real diamond?" I asked.

Lucy nodded again. "My guess is that the heat of the fire was enough to melt the gold. But the diamond is real enough—three quarters of a carat, and it looks like good quality to me.

"So robbery definitely wasn't part of the motivation here."

Nodding again, Lucy reached into the box and pulled out a large paper bag. "This is exhibit number two," she said. "A buckskin jacket, complete with fringe."

Instead of handing it to me, she set that one down and pulled out another bag. "Cowboy boot," she said. "Tony Lama. Snakeskin. Size seven. This is a man's size seven, by the way, so I'm guessing the victim probably wore a woman's size eight. That's what I wear. If news about the boot and the jacket ever gets out, I imagine they'll stop calling our victim the Lake Kachess Jane Doe and start calling her the Annie Oakley Jane Doe."

Once again, Lucy set down the bag without letting me touch it. Then she opened the third bag for me. Inside I saw what looked like the remains of a belt.

"Our CSI guy says that the burn patterns on the belt are consistent with its being used as a restraint."

"In other words, it wasn't around her waist at the time of the fire."

Lucy nodded and produced yet another bag. That one contained a collection of charred remains that were evidently the remnants of the tarp, and some frayed pieces of rope.

"We went out to the crime scene on Saturday morning," Lucy explained. "We took along a generator and a commercial carpet dryer so we could melt the snow. The M.E.'s assistant gathered up the bones. We took everything else. The problem is, what do we do with it now?"

"What's all this doing here?" I asked. " Why isn't it at the crime lab?"

"What crime lab?" Lucy returned. "We don't have a crime lab."

"But you have a state-of-the-art M.E. . . ." I began.

"That's because someone gave us a grant," Lucy said. "Paid for the physical plant on condition that we staff it with an M.E. and an assistant. So now there's a big budget shortfall for everything else. I've been trying all week to get Gary off the dime, asking him to send this batch of evidence out to the state patrol crime lab for examination. He's been dragging his feet, though. Doesn't want to have his name on the request that will put our department that much more in the red."

"Wait a minute," I said. "You've got to be kidding me. He's stalling on examining the evidence in a homicide investigation because he doesn't want to sign off on a crime lab invoice? That's ridiculous. There could be important evidence here."

Lucy Caldwell nodded. "Yes," she agreed. "There could be."

Which meant that the bottom line here was . . . well, the bottom line. I understood that what looked like general ineptitude and stupidity was really a symptom of something else—that old bugaboo, interdepartmental fiscal warfare. I would guess that almost every big-city cop has a hopeless daydream of someday ending up working in a sleepy little hamlet somewhere—a magical place where everything is all sweetness and light and where dirty interdepartmental infighting or personality-based political agendas would be forever banished. Right. Sure they will. That'll happen about the time pigs fly.

"So what are you saying?" I asked.

Lucy Caldwell gave me a scathing look as if I just wasn't getting it. "You work for the AG's office, right?" she asked.

I nodded.

"Doesn't that mean you could get this stuff into the Washington State Patrol crime lab for analysis?"

"I'm reasonably sure I could do just that."

Just then Gary sauntered back into the room, bringing with him a cloud of leftover cigarette smoke. Lucy's reaction to his return was not only immediate, it was downright riveting.

"You have a hell of a lot of nerve, Beaumont!" she barked at me, slamming the palm of her hand hard on the surface of the desk. "So does your boss. What makes him think he can send his lackey over here to demand we turn over our evidence to him? That sucks, and you can tell your boss I said so."

Her performance amounted to a remarkable imitation of Dr. Jekyll turning into Mr. Hyde. And since I'd made no such demands regarding their evidence, I was pretty much left staring at her in openmouthed amazement. I wasn't sure why Detective Caldwell had suddenly decided to make me the bad guy here. For the sake of argument, however, I decided to play along, dropping names as I went.

"As I told you earlier, Attorney General Ross Connors is very interested in your case and its possible connection to several other cases we've been investigating. And I have an idea, when it comes to storing, examining, and identifying trace evidence on this kind of material . . ." I waved vaguely at the collection of sacks. "In instances like this, we have far more assets at our disposal than you have here."

This was pure BS, of course. Lucy had already told me that they had no assets—as in zero, but Gary was enjoying hell out of the performance. He looked from Lucy to me and then back to Lucy with a slow grin spreading across his face.

"What's all this about?" he wanted to know. "And what's all this about Ross Connors?"

"Mr. Beaumont here is a hotshot who works for the Attorney General's Office," Lucy said. She spoke calmly enough, but she looked like she was still ready to tear people apart. "He came here today expecting to lord it over us and make a grab for our Lake Kachess Jane Doe evidence. I told him no way. This is our case, Gary. We're primary. They've got no right to interfere."

Gary's grin widened. He was so thrilled to have a chance to rub his underling's nose in it that he didn't realize he was being suckered by the tired old good cop/bad cop ruse.

"Now, listen here, Lucy," Gary interrupted. "If the attorney general says jump, we'd by God better jump."

His tone was so patronizing I was surprised Lucy didn't haul off and slap him upside the head. I would have, but she didn't. She let him get away with it.

"But, Gary . . ." she began earnestly.

Detective Fields dismissed her objection with a wave of his hand. "Let's just be sure that when we check things out to him, we do it the right way. We'll sign off on all the paperwork, preserve the chain of evidence, and all that. As long as we cross all the t's and dot all the i's, it won't come back and bite us in the butt. So go get me the damned forms."

After giving Gary one final look that should have turned him into a pillar of salt, Lucy marched out of the cubicle.

"Just ignore her," Gary advised me with a grin. "She's a little more emotional than usual. It's probably that time of month."

In the world of Seattle PD, where political correctness is the name of the game, a sexist comment like that would probably have been enough for Detective Fields to find himself brought up on charges of creating a hostile work environment. The social culture here was evidently a little different.

Lucy returned, bringing with her a set of forms that would release the evidence to my care and keeping. She slapped it down on the table.

"You fill it out then," she told Gary. "I'm not going to."

She left again. Gary turned his hand to the paperwork with an amazingly cheerful attitude. "There you go," he said at last, signing off on the bottom of the last form with a considerable flourish. "It's all yours," he said. "Let us know what you find out, as I'm sure you will."

"Yes, I will," I agreed. "Absolutely."

Of course, Fields hadn't mentioned the budget problem to me or that his department was operating in a world of hurt. How could he? I'm a fellow officer and a guy. And of course he signed off on the request. It was his way of throwing his weight around and showing me that he was the big bad boss and poor little Detective Caldwell had to do things his way. Right. Of course she did.

I took charge of both the paperwork and the evidence box. As I emerged from the cubicle, Lucy Caldwell was waiting just outside. She stood with her arms crossed, her eyes shooting daggers at me and at her partner as well. She didn't crack a smile, and neither did I, but we both knew she'd won.

Detective Fields had been screwed—without a kiss—and he didn't even know it; didn't have a clue.

Which, if you ask me, was exactly what he deserved.

Leaving the crime scene, Joanna headed back to the department. Her mind was still grappling with the apparent murder of Lester Attwood when her phone rang.

"Hey, Joey," Butch said. "How's it going?"

This is the kind of question spouses ask each other all the time. It's usually on a par with "How's the weather?" and doesn't generally require a complicated answer. Unless what you're doing right then is driving away from the scene of a homicide.

When Joanna was first elected sheriff, she was still a relatively new widow, a single mother of a single child. She had not anticipated remarrying, but that was before Butch Dixon appeared in her life and refused to take no for an answer. Now, sometime later, she was still sheriff. She was also the married mother of a usually cooperative teenager, fourteen-year-old Jenny, who would turn fifteen in a little over a week, and an almost never cooperative son, Dennis, who was just a little beyond his first birthday and more than slightly opinionated for his age, something his doting grandmother chalked up to his bright red hair.

"Fine," Joanna said, editing out any number of things she might have said. "How's it going for you?"

"I'm still home."

Joanna knew that Butch had been planning a quick trip to Tucson that day to pick up steaks for the Texas Hold'Em bachelor party they would be hosting for Frank Montoya on Thursday night.

"I thought you were leaving a lot earlier than this," Joanna said.

Butch sighed. "So did I, but the appliance repairman who was supposed to be here bright and early this morning didn't come until just a few minutes ago."

Their relatively new front-loading, water-saving washer had come to grief a week earlier, and it had taken almost that long to get worked into the repair schedule. Joanna was worried the machine had died for good. She envisioned being told that the washer, now minutes beyond the expiration of its warranty, would have to be hauled off to the junkyard.

"What's the bad news on that?"

"Socks," Butch said.

For a second Joanna thought that her Bluetooth earpiece might have cut out on her. "What?"

"Socks," Butch repeated. "Dennis's socks—several of them—were stuck in the drain. He says we're supposed to use a lingerie sack when we wash them. Do we even have a lingerie sack?"

"I used to have one, years ago," Joanna said. "My mother thought I needed one. Jenny used it to carry some baby chicks around once. I don't think it ever came back inside the house."

"I'll put that on my Tucson shopping list," Butch said. "But now that I'm getting such a late start, I was wondering if you'd like to go along. Carol says it's fine with her. If it looks like we'll be getting home too late, she'll just plan on having the kids stay over at her place until morning."

Carol Sunderson was a widow whose disabled husband had died in an electrical fire that had destroyed their rented mobile home the previous November. Left homeless, she and her two grandsons and black-and-white Sheltie, Scamp, had taken up residence in Joanna's old house on High Lonesome Ranch. Carol paid rent for the privilege of living there, but Joanna and Butch paid her a salary for her invaluable service as a live-out housekeeper and nanny.

It was Carol's calming presence that kept Joanna's and Butch's busy lives organized. Her cooking and cleaning and child-caring made Butch's at-home writing a whole lot easier. While their washing machine had been down for the count, Carol had taken their necessary laundry home and had done it there. And although at almost fifteen, Jenny could conceivably have stayed on her own, Joanna and Butch thought it was best not to leave her on her own with the baby. Jenny was a teenager, as Joanna's mother Eleanor had pointed out on more than one occasion. Although Jenny doted on her baby brother, it wasn't fair to give her too much responsibility for the little one.

Bless Carol, Joanna thought.

"Well," Butch said. "Will you come with me or not?"

Joanna glanced at her watch. It was a little past three. Working as sheriff, she certainly wasn't required to punch a time clock, and she put in lots of extra hours long after the regular workday ended and on weekends, just as her father had once done before her. But unlike her father, D. H. Lathrop, Joanna was consciously trying to create family time. These days she was home for dinner more often than she wasn't. And the thought of having some alone time with Butch—just the two of them—sounded heavenly, even if pushing a cart around Costco or tracking down a lingerie bag at Alice-Rae's Intimate Apparel wasn't her idea of a great time.

"Why not?" Joanna said. "Sounds like fun. I'll call into the office and make sure everything's under control. If it is, you've got yourself a date."

"Where are you now?" Butch asked.

"Just coming through Elfrida," Joanna said. "I'll stop by the house and change clothes—"

"No," Butch said. "Don't do that. I'll pick you up at the Justice Center. We can leave from there."

That seemed like an odd idea since Joanna would have to drive right by High Lonesome Road to get back to her office, but for a change she didn't debate the issue.

"Sure thing," she said. "See you there."

Once Butch was off the line, Joanna dialed her direct number, counting on her secretary, Kristin Gregovich, to pick up the phone.

"How are things?" Joanna asked when Kristin answered.

"As far as I can tell, everything's under control."

"How about next month's shift schedule?"

"I helped Chief Deputy Hadlock clean up a couple of items," Kristin told her. "But it's posted now. I think it's fine."

"Glad to hear it," Joanna said. Maybe Tom Hadlock was starting to get the hang of things after all. "Anything else I should know about?"

"Not that I can think of," Kristin said.

"Good. I think I'm going to take the rest of the afternoon off and go to Tucson with Butch."

"I hope you have a great time," Kristin said, which seemed like an odd response.

"I doubt it," Joanna said. "Shopping has never been my long suit."

When she pulled up into her reserved parking place behind the building, she was surprised to see Butch already waiting there. As she stopped her Crown Victoria, she caught him glancing at his watch. Rather than going into the building, she simply transferred her briefcase and purse into the backseat of his Subaru. Then she let herself into the passenger seat and buckled up.

"What time does Costco close?" she asked.

"Around six," he said.

"Good, then," Joanna replied. "We have plenty of time."

She sat back in the seat and closed her eyes, relishing the idea that Butch would be doing the driving.

"So what have you really been up to all day?" he asked.

Which meant that the understated "Fine" she had given him earlier hadn't done the trick. "I've been at a crime scene," she told him.

He knew without asking that this meant a homicide crime scene. In the course of the next two hours, as they drove the hundred miles between Bisbee and Tucson, she told him about it. At least she told him what she could. He was interested as her husband, but Butch was also interested in what she had to say because he was a mystery writer. Occasionally what she told him about real cases got run through his mental blender and emerged through his fingers transformed into fiction.

After that, they talked about plans for Frank Montoya's bachelor party. Since the bride was an ER physician and since most of the attendees would be police officers, the party would be tame by bachelor-party standards—no stripper and no booze—with the Texas Hold'Em proceeds and winnings going to the local Jail Ministry.

"We have enough tables and chairs now?" Joanna asked.

"Plenty," Butch told her.

"What's on the menu other than steak?"

"Don't worry your pretty little head about that," Butch said with a grin. "Carol and I have that covered."

Lost in talking, Joanna didn't pay attention to the exit signs and was surprised when they turned off on Kino. "Isn't this the long way around to get to Costco?" she asked. By then, if six o'clock really was the deadline, they were coming right up on the witching hour. Butch seemed unperturbed.

"No problem," he said. "We're fine."

When he turned off on Elm rather than Grant, Joanna was really surprised. "If we're going to go down side streets, we're never going to make it on time."

"Yes, we will," he said, pulling to a stop outside the valet stand at the Arizona Inn. "Our dinner reservation isn't until seven."

"Dinner here?" Joanna asked. "In this?" She looked down at a her uniform, which, after spending most of the day at a dusty desert crime scene, was much the worse for wear.

A bellman, pushing a luggage cart, came over to Butch's side of the car. "Checking in, sir?" he asked through the window.

Butch nodded and punched the button to open the gate to the Subaru's luggage compartment, then he turned to Joanna and grinned. "Happy anniversary," he said.

"But wait," Joanna objected. "Our anniversary is over a week away."

"I know," Butch said. "You're a very tough woman to surprise. I figured jumping the gun was the only way to make it work. If I had told you in advance, you'd have ended up finding a dozen reasons why we couldn't or shouldn't do it."

Right then, Joanna was a whole lot more than merely surprised. She was astonished, and not in the least because she herself had completely forgotten about their upcoming anniversary.

"But I don't even have a card for you," she objected. "And what about going to Costco?"

"Shopping is scheduled for tomorrow," Butch declared firmly.

"But by the time they open, I should be back at work."

"Didn't I tell you? Tomorrow you're taking a vacation day. With all the excitement of Frank's wedding festivities, I figured our own anniversary would get lost in the shuffle. So tonight it's just the two of us. We have the whole evening to ourselves—dinner with no kids, no dogs, no chores, and no telephones, either," he added. "Our cell phones are switched off for the duration as of now. If there's some problem at home or at the department overnight, they're going to have to figure it out without us."

By then the bellman had emptied the back compartment and closed the door. Joanna was relieved to see that there were two suitcases on the cart—one for Butch and one for her. "Just leave the keys," the bellman said. "I'll park it over there." He pointed to a graveled parking lot across the street.

Years earlier, the first time Joanna had stumbled across the Arizona Inn, it hadn't been as a paying guest. She had fled University Hospital, trying to escape the appalling news from the doctor that Andy was unlikely to survive, that his bullet wounds would most likely prove fatal. She had ended up at the grand old hotel tucked into a seemingly residential neighborhood entirely by accident. She had been surprised by its improbably pink walls and lush, lovingly manicured grounds. She had hidden out there, weeping in one of those Alice-in-Wonderland-looking blue-and-white-striped chairs and trying to grapple with the fact that she was about to become a widow. Now, though, walking into the shadowy lobby of the old hotel and up to the desk with Butch beside her, she felt entirely different. That had been one life; this was another.

When they reached their spacious room—a casita, really—there were two chilled glasses of champagne waiting. Joanna's suitcase, sitting on the luggage holder in the walk-in closet, was loaded with one dinner-suitable little black dress and with suitable underwear as well. There were panty hose and—even without the lingerie laundry bag—a black bra and matching panties that dated from their honeymoon. Packed in with the clothing was a pair of black sling-back heels and enough toiletries and makeup to make showering a welcome possibility.

"How did you pull this all together?" she asked.

"I had some help," Butch told her. "Jenny packed your bag, Kristin cleared your calendar, and Tom Hadlock said he'll hold down the fort."

"Thank you," she said. "You're really thoughtful."

He grinned. "And you're lovely," he returned. "I'm really lucky."

"We both are."

"Would you care to go to dinner?"

"Yes," she said. "Let's."

By the time I made it back to North Bend, it was late afternoon, and the snow had turned to rain—not the usual steady drizzle we're accustomed to in Seattle but a kind of torrential downpour that can melt snow too fast and send rivers pouring up and over their banks. I went to the address I had jotted down for Ken Leggett, the guy who had found the body.

North Bend has a bucolic sound to it, but it's a burg that seems more than a little schizophrenic. There's the "new" North Bend, which is essentially a cluster of outlet stores and fast-food joints, and the "old" North Bend, which is . . . well . . . old. Ken Leggett lived on a potholed excuse for a street in a neighborhood of mostly down-at-the-heels bungalows that had probably been built in the twenties or thirties—back in the old days when logging was king. Between then and now, no one had done much about routine maintenance.

Leggett's place was far and away the worst of the lot. It looked as though someone had painted it white with a cheery kind of red trim once, but most of the paint had either peeled or faded away, take your pick. The roof had far more moss showing than shingles. A tiny covered front porch sagged to one side, suggesting that it wouldn't take much to knock it down. At the end of a rutted drive, an older-model Toyota Tundra sat huddled under the roof of a carport, which, like the porch, didn't look like it was long for this world.

There were no lights or signs of movement showing from inside the place, but I parked out front and started up the short walkway, getting drenched in the process. As I stepped onto the crumbling front porch, the planking groaned beneath my feet, but it didn't give way.

As I raised my hand to knock, someone spoke to me. "He's not home."

The male voice came from the house next door, one on the far side of Leggett's driveway. There, under a similarly decrepit carport, stood another equally dilapidated pickup truck—an old Dodge Ram. The hood was open and a guy with a single Trouble Light dangling over his shoulder was actually working on it. Shade-tree mechanics may be a thing of the past in downtown Seattle, but not at the low-priced end of North Bend. Just looking at the scene I understood that the man wasn't working on his aging truck because he was spiffing it up for some antique car show.

The vehicle was what he counted on for wheels, and he was keeping it running with do-it-yourself know-how and probably, given the truck's age, mostly junkyard parts.

"Any idea where I could find Mr. Leggett?" I asked.

The man straightened up, pushed a pair of reading glasses up onto the top of his head, and stared at me. "It's early," the man advised, wiping his hands on a pair of grimy coveralls. "If I was you, I'd try his home away from home."

"Where would that be?" I asked.

The man jerked his head, gesturing back the way I had come. "Back thataway," he said. "Two blocks over and two blocks up. The Beaver Bar. You can walk it, but I'd advise driving. These here are what we call 'long blocks.' "

I took his advice. I went back to the Mercedes and drove. The Beaver Bar didn't look promising. The neon sign over the door had evidently burned out. In the window was another neon sign that said OPEN, along with a single blue neon cocktail glass complete with a green neon olive.

I had never set foot in the Beaver Bar. Even so, it was entirely familiar. I spent far too much of my life with my butt planted on bar stools in similarly seedy places. The place smelled of too much beer and not enough cleaning. Washington's bars have been "smoke-free" for years now, but not long enough for the smoke to have leached out of the wallboard and the torn and worn red-and-black faux-leather banquettes that lined the walls.

As I said, I'd never been inside the place, but the bartender made me for a cop the moment I stepped through the door. He gave me a careful once-over and probably decided I was liquor control.

"Evening, Officer," he said. "What can I do for you?"

"I'm looking for Kenneth Leggett."

"Over there," he said. "In the booth on the far side of the pool table. He's been eighty-sixed, by the way. He's had nothing but coffee for the last hour or so. We're waiting for him to sober up enough that he can get himself home."

Yes, I thought. The barkeep definitely thinks I'm liquor control.

The guys playing pool kept a close eye on me as I walked around them and stopped next to a booth where a big balding man sat staring down into a mostly empty coffee cup.

"Mr. Leggett?" I said.

He looked up at me, bleary-eyed and belligerent. "Who the hell are you?"

"My name's Beaumont," I said. "I'm with the Attorney General's Special Homicide Investigation Team. Mind if I sit down?"

I expected a fight. I expected an argument. You never can tell with drunks. They can go one way or the other. Instead, Ken Leggett pushed his empty coffee cup aside, buried his head in his hands, and bawled like a baby. I thought maybe I was going to come away with an impromptu confession. And I did, but not the one I was looking for.

"I didn't mean to do it," he said.

"You didn't mean to do what, kill her?" I asked.

He looked up at me with tears still streaming down his face. "I didn't mean to piss on her head," he said. "Nobody deserves that."

I've detected plenty of lies over the years, but this wasn't one of them. Detective Caldwell was right. Ken Leggett wasn't our killer by any stretch of the imagination.

"Come on, fella," I said to him. "It's raining outside. How about I give you a lift home."

Chapter 7

Having spent the better part of the day dealing with murder and mayhem in Ellensburg, it was difficult to remember that I had started the day in, as they like to say in Disneyland, "the happiest place on earth." I've always been under the impression that jet lag happens when you fly east or west across time zones rather than north and south. I also think I read somewhere that men are less likely to be affected by jet lag than women are. It turns out I was wrong—on both counts.

When I got home to Seattle that night, I was bushed, and I chose to blame it on jet lag rather than anything else. I barely managed to finish telling Mel about my adventures east of the mountains when I conked out, sound asleep in my recliner. Sometime after the news and Jay Leno, Mel woke me up long enough to herd me into bed.

When I woke up the next morning and stumbled out of the shower and into the kitchen for coffee, I could tell from the clock that I had overslept and most likely would be late getting into the office. "Why didn't you wake me up?" I asked.

Mel was up and her usual perky, bright-eyed and bushy-tailed self. To my surprise, however, she wasn't dressed for work.

"Good morning to you, too, Mr. Grumbly Bear," she told me, reaching out to hand me a computer printout. "Maybe you should go back into hibernation."

Of course she said it with a smile. The robe and gown she was wearing made a very fetching concoction—enough to make me wish that I hadn't gotten dressed quite so fast. When I made a tentative suggestion in that direction, she shook her head and returned her attention to the laptop on her lap. With my coffee cup in one hand and the paper in the other, I squinted at the impossibly vague printing on the page. Finding my arms far too short, I wondered where the hell I'd left my reading glasses.

"What's this?" I asked.

"A missing persons report," she said. "From November twelfth of last year. I think she's your victim."

One of the tasks Ross Connors had handed over to his Special Homicide Investigation Team was keeping track of missing persons investigations from all over the state. Someone reported missing in Vancouver, for example, wasn't likely to be noticed if he or she turned up in Bellingham either living or dead. By focusing on those cases and compiling all the information from various jurisdictions and agencies together in one spot, including dental records wherever possible, S.H.I.T. had already managed to solve several previously unsolvable cases. Among those were cases from several different people who, for one reason or another, had gone missing deliberately and wanted to stay that way. Mel's fine eye for detail made her a natural as point man, if you'll pardon the expression, on the AG's missing persons effort.

It was useless to stand around grousing about my missing glasses. As a general rule, Mel doesn't like grousing. Instead, muttering something about jet lag, I stomped back into the bedroom and did a thorough search. I finally found my glasses hidden away in the inside pocket of yesterday's still slightly damp sport jacket.

Thank you, North Bend, I thought.

I returned to the living room with my glasses perched on my nose and busied myself with reading the report. The missing woman's name was Marina

Aguirre, age twenty-nine. She was reported to be five feet five inches tall and was estimated to weigh 130 pounds. She had been reported missing from the City of SeaTac by her fiancé, a truck driver named Mason Waters.

Mel was still on the phone. I sat down next to her on the window seat, which happens to be Mel's favorite perch in our penthouse condo. The view is downright spectacular. I bought into Belltown Terrace long before I met Mel. The purchase had come during a real estate downturn in Seattle in the early eighties, and I bought it with some of the money I had inherited after my second wife's death. In recent years, condo living in downtown Seattle had come of age. Now, a space that had once been a real estate white elephant had turned into a real estate gem—at least that's how it looks when it comes time to pay the tax bill they send out from the King County Assessor's Office.

In the intervening years, other high-rise buildings had sprung up all over the Denny Regrade area, but none of them were tall enough to impinge on the panoramic view from our window seat. At night and to the south, we saw the myriad lights of downtown Seattle. Occasionally during the day and even farther to the south, we had a view of snow-topped Mount Rainier, but that was only on those rare but beautifully sunny

Pacific Northwest days when, as we say around here, "the mountains are out." Off to the west, rain or shine, daylight or not, we saw the wide expanse of blue or gray or black Elliott Bay and Puget Sound with their busy shipping lanes and motoring ferries. In other words, Mel isn't the only one who likes the view from the window seat.

Toward the end of the call she turned to me. "Jot down this number," she said, and reeled off a phone number which she simultaneously typed into her computer. Women can do that—talk on the phone, talk to someone in person, and work on a laptop all at once. But I did as she told me and wrote the number down on the only piece of paper available to me at the time—the one that happened to be in my hand. Strangely enough, that turned out to be a good choice.

"That's the phone number for the fiancé, the guy who filed the missing persons report," Mel said. "He's a long-haul trucker. According to his dispatcher, he'll be back in Federal Way early this afternoon. Maybe we can go talk to him after lunch."

"Excuse me for mentioning this," I said, "but if you're going to go to lunch, shouldn't you start by getting dressed to go to work?"

"I'm working from home this morning," she explained. "I'm due to show up at noon and bring the food with me. It's Harry's birthday, remember? I volunteered to handle the food for the party. And don't mention it to Harry when you get in," she added. "It's supposed to be a surprise."

Now, having had it pointed out, I did remember. Squad B's fearless leader, Harry Ignatius Ball, is now and always has been a sucker for barbecue. When Mel first moved across the water from the east side of Lake Washington to the west side, I had introduced her to several of my favorite hangouts. She had really fallen for one of them, the Pecos Pit Barbecue, and was now a die-hard fan. Any excuse is good enough for her, and the fact that Harry I. Ball adores barbecue made this a perfect match.

Pecos Pit Barbecue is located down in . . . Wait a minute. I'm dating myself again. I started to say "Sodo," which used to be Seattle-speak for "South of the King Dome," but the King Dome is gone now, so forget that.

Pecos Pit is in a born-again gas station on First Avenue South. Five days a week, the people who own it cook in the mornings, serve lunches until the food is gone, and then they go home. Customers stand in lines outside, rain or shine, and then eat outside on picnic tables, rain or shine as well. Don't expect to use your credit card. Don't expect to get moved to the head of the line. Restaurants wanting to discourage table hogging sometimes post signs that say, "Eat, Pay, and Go." For Pecos Pit, you walk up to the window, place your order, pay, and go eat somewhere else. In this case, the food would be coming across Lake Washington in individual paper bags, destined for Squad B's break room.

"Maybe I could go in late, too," I offered. To be honest, I wasn't really thinking about work per se. "After all, I put in a very long day yesterday."

Mel saw right through that lame excuse. "Go to work," she said. "Keep your mind on the job and leave me alone." Again, she smiled so brightly when she told me to shove off that it was hard to take it personally.

"But later . . ." I said, not exactly whining but close to it.

She nodded and smiled. "Later," she agreed.

I knew walking away that was a promise, not a put-off.

Joanna and Butch ate a leisurely breakfast in the heated cabana out by the pool. It was easy to spot the tourists. Escapees from the Midwest's perpetual winter were decked out in shorts or bathing suits and gave the propane heaters a wide berth. Thin-blooded locals, on the other hand, still wore long pants, sweaters, and the occasional corduroy jacket.

After checking out of the hotel, they stopped to pick up washer-saving laundry bags from Eleanor Lathrop Winfield's favorite lingerie shop, Alice-Rae. After that, they spent an hour trudging through Costco. It turned out there were lots more things on Butch's shopping list than just the steaks for Thursday night's party.

Once the boxes of groceries were loaded into the car, it was time to head back for Bisbee. As they drove south, Joanna reflexively reached for her phone. She took it out, looked at it, and put it away.

"No phone," she reminded herself. "It's a vacation day."

"Yes," Butch said with a grin. "I know it's a difficult concept for you to master, but at least you're trying."

"And you're right," she agreed. "If you hadn't taken the bull by the horns, our anniversary would have gotten lost in the shuffle."

"If you want to stop off at the department for a little while when we go by to pick up your car . . ." Butch offered.

Joanna shook her head. "Nope, you were right the first time. We'll just pick up the car and go. I won't even poke my head inside. Taking a whole day off now and then is the right thing to do."

The guy who came up with that saying about the war's not won until the paperwork is done was probably a cop in his other life. I believe most law enforcement officers would agree with me when I say that paperwork is the bane of our existence. The fact that it's done mostly on computers these days as opposed to on paper may be good for saving trees, but it's still a pain in the neck and takes inordinate amounts of time. As far as Team B is concerned, since Harry hates computers, everything has to be printed out for him, which means that the poor trees lose anyway, but at least we don't have to make quite as many copies.

So once I got to the office . . . yes, even later than I expected because traffic was hell . . . once I got there, I spent the rest of the morning working on a report that recounted everything I had seen and heard the previous day on my trek back and forth to Ellensburg.

After Harry had had a chance to read it, he strolled into my tiny office staring down at his hard copy through his own pair of Bartell Drugs "special" reading glasses. I found it comforting to know that I wasn't the only person around who'd had to eat crow and succumb to the indignity of needing them. I've said it before and I'll say it again. Getting older is hell.

"So do you think this doer is the same guy?" he asked.

"Maybe, maybe not," I hedged. "But one way or another, I think our burned girls are all connected. Once we figure out who they all are, maybe we can put the rest of it together."

"But this one still had her teeth?" he asked.

I nodded.

"And do you think yesterday's victim will turn out to be this Marina Aguirre, the missing person case Mel turned up?" Harry asked.

"Could be," I told him. "The dates work. We'll know more after Mel and I meet with Ms. Aguirre's fiancé later this afternoon."

"Speaking of Mel," he said, "where is she? Don't you two usually ride in together?"

I'm always at a loss when it comes time to spin a plausible fib. My limited ability to keep my face looking honest in the process is one of the reasons I don't play poker. At all.

"She's busy doing something," I said. "You should check with Barbara. She'll know."

Barbara Galvin is Squad B's indispensable clerk/typist, receptionist, ace coffeemaker, and all-around girl Friday. I knew that if anyone could pull the wool over Harry's eyes, she was it.

"Want to go have lunch later?" Harry asked. "I thought I'd run over to that tandoori place in Eastgate."

I felt sorry for the guy. It was his birthday, after all, and he was looking for a little company. "No, thanks," I said. "Indian food doesn't sound all that good to me today."

He moped off to his office. Minutes later, Mel arrived. With Barbara's help, she smuggled the barbecue as well as a decorated birthday cake into the break room. Usually we all cycle in and out of the break room in ones and twos. By the time six investigators and Barbara were gathered inside, it was crowded. Finally Mel called Harry to come join us. When he stepped inside, it was that much more crowded.

The party was fun. It was messy. Barbecued meat leaks out of those sandwiches with wild abandon. There were eight bags in all—seven Ms for mild and one H for not-mild. That one went to Harry, who was in his glory, chowing down while little beads of sweat broke out all over his nose and forehead. When someone spotted a tear or two, he claimed it was because of the hot food. I wondered if they didn't have more to do with the fact that we hadn't forgotten his birthday.

When the sandwiches were history and so was the cake, Mel and I took our leave and headed south on

I-405. In bumper-to-bumper traffic. That's the thing about the Seattle area—too many cars and not enough roadways. With two of us in the vehicle, we were able to use the express lanes, which helped some. Mel had opted to drive her Cayman. She's the kind of intimidating driver who doesn't need lights or a siren in order to encourage people to get out of her way. When she drives, we make good time, but it's not easy on hapless passengers dumb enough to join her—namely me.

"So," she said casually as she darted across three lanes of traffic, zipping us into the express lanes in front of a very annoyed solo driver in a red Volvo station wagon who used his horn to let us know what he thought about the maneuver. "Do you want to know what I found out?"

Of course I wanted to know. What kind of question was that? "What?" I asked.

"Whoever they've got in the morgue over in Ellensburg isn't Marina Aguirre," she said.

"You already know that for sure?"

Mel nodded.

"Why are we on our way to see the boyfriend then?" I asked. "Why bother?"

"Because the poor dope may think he was engaged to Marina Aguirre, but it turns out the real Marina Aguirre, at least the one whose Social Security number matches the one on the missing persons report, died in 1986. When she was eight. Of a ruptured appendix."

"How come nobody figured this out a long time ago?"

"Because nobody bothered to look," Mel said.

And I knew why. Missing persons reports are usually low on the list of law enforcement priorities. True, someone from another agency could have discovered this the same way Mel had, by investing a couple of hours in doing actual work. And it's the reality of that low priority accorded to missing persons cases that has caused Ross Connors to look into them.

To be realistic if not necessarily fair, Ross Connors is the attorney general. Other jurisdictions may be short on money or personnel, but they're also lacking in one other vital ingredient—political savvy. Ross is a good old boy who drinks too much and knows too much. He has political pull in spades, but he's also smart enough to let us do our jobs even when investigations step on high-profile toes. That's also why voters are smart enough to reelect him time after time.

"So maybe this is identity theft then?" I asked, going back to the situation of the two Marinas.

"At the very least," Mel said. "Maybe our victim is an illegal immigrant posing as someone else. What

I'm wondering is whether or not the fiancé knows about it."

I was wondering the same thing. "Me, too," I said.

People who talk about perpetually rainy Seattle forget about one important mitigating factor—afternoons. Around here, even in the winter, things tend to dry out a little during the day, but they hardly ever do that until after the morning rush hour. This was only early afternoon, closing in on two. As we turned off I-5 at Federal Way, one of Seattle's ex-burbs, the rain stopped, the skies cleared, the pavement turned into a shining strip of sunlight.

Mel had located an address for Mason Waters, and the Cayman's slick nav system led us there without a hitch. We drove to the end of a house-lined cul-de-sac. There, on one of the pie-shaped end lots, sat a neat little fifties rambler that had been painted a garish maroon. A hulking maroon-colored Kenworth was parked next to the carport. Inside the carport and dwarfed by its oversize neighbor sat a maroon Honda sedan.

"Looks like Mr. Waters is home," Mel said as she put the Cayman in park. "And maroon seems to be his favorite color."

I remembered that Mel had said Mason Waters was a long-haul trucker and that he'd been out on the road on a trip, but that afternoon the oversize tractor-trailer literally sparkled in the sunshine. There wasn't a dead bug to be seen anywhere. It had obviously just had a thorough detailing. On the driver's door, stenciled in gold letters, were the words: WATERS TRUCKING, INC. FEDERAL WAY, WA. DRIVE SAFE. ARRIVE ALIVE.

Stepping out of a vehicle driven by the death-defying Mel Soames, I couldn't help but notice those last few words—and take them personally. Someday a state patroller with more nerve than I have will give her a ticket and slow her down. In the meantime, as her husband, I find it works best if I keep my mouth shut, my eyes closed, and my seat belt securely fastened.

Mel led the way down the short walkway and onto a small covered porch. As she stepped onto it, the front door and screen door slammed open and a huge man wearing a wild-patterned green and yellow Hawaiian shirt barreled out onto the porch.

"Oh my God!" he exclaimed as both Mel and I leaned back in alarm. "Are you cops? Did you find Marina? Where is she? Is she all right? Please tell me she's all right."

That kind of anguish can be faked, but not at the drop of a hat. Even on stage, actors have to have some time before they can psych themselves up for a performance like that. My first impression was that Mr. Waters was the real deal. Mel appeared to agree.

"Yes, we're police officers," she answered, producing her ID and badge. "We need to ask you a few questions."

Mason Waters had no trouble connecting the dots. "Nobody's bothered to come see me about this, not once, not since I filed the missing person's report. I've talked to people at the police department on the phone, but no one has shown up in person. That means only one thing. She's dead, isn't she!"

It was a statement not a question, and when Mel responded, she didn't agree or disagree. "Please, Mr. Waters," she said. "If we could just step inside for a moment . . ."

The man looked close to tears, but he straightened his broad shoulders, nodded, and held the door open to let us enter. Nothing about Mason Waters was small—not his body or his well-used chair, a recliner that looked even older than mine, not even his TV set, a fifty-two-inch wall-mounted flat-screen that rested on the mantel of a redbrick fireplace. All of that looked overly large and out of place in the otherwise smallish fifties-era house. The living room walls were covered with dark-wood wall paneling punctuated here and there with large decorative brass plates that dated from the fifties as well.

Other than the television set, the living room resembled a time capsule. The sofa was old-fashioned leather, cracking in spots. At one end of the couch sat a set of nesting end tables, just like the ones my grandmother once had. An old-fashioned rocker that didn't look strong enough to support Mason's weight, or mine, completed the sparse furnishings. On the far side of the living room and through a framed archway we could see a small but formal dining room with an oak buffet and a matching pedestal table. Above it hung an aged chandelier. The place may have been dated, but it was also clean and neat. I had the feeling someone, Mr. Waters's parents, perhaps, had lived in the house for a very long time, and he was making every effort to maintain it to some kind of stringent standard.

Waters dropped into the recliner with enough force that I was afraid it might tip over backward. While he reached for the remote to switch off ESPN, Mel and I headed for the sofa. Once we were seated, Mel made a show of digging a notebook and pencil out of her purse. That's a signal we've developed between us—sort of like a secret handshake. Whoever gets out the notebook first takes the lead asking questions.

"Tell us about Marina," she said.

Mason's eyes misted over. For a long time he stared up at the black face of the television screen without saying anything. "She's the most wonderful person in the world," he declared. "We were engaged to be married. Next month."

The last broke off in a strangled sob.

"How long have you known her?" Mel asked.

"I met her in September," Waters replied. "September the twelfth, at twenty minutes past seven in the morning. I thought I was having a bad day. My car blew up. The radiator, not the whole car. The tow truck dragged it into a garage on 320th. It was one of my days off and I was mad that I was having to spend it hassling with car repairs. So I left the car and walked up the street to Denny's—the one on 320th—to have breakfast. I always order their Grand Slam, and there was Marina, working the counter. The moment I saw her, as soon as she poured me that first cup of coffee, that was it. I knew she was the one. You may not believe me. I mean, people laugh when I say it was love at first sight, but it was."

I wasn't laughing. I know that drill because that's what happened to me with Anne Corley. The moment I saw her, I knew. Since I'm married to Mel now, though, and since our relationship had developed on a more traditional trajectory, it seemed best not to mention it.

"She was a waitress then?" Mel asked.

Mason nodded. "I hated to see her having to work so hard, being on her feet all day. It's hard on the legs, you see. I told her I'd take her away from all that. I even offered to pay her way through driver's school so she could get a CDL and go on the road with me. She didn't seem to like that idea very much," he added.

I'll bet not, I thought. The faux Marina might have been able to walk her fake ID past whoever hired her at Denny's, but it probably wouldn't have stood up to someone who actually went to the trouble of examining her driving record.

"Did she have a regular driver's license?" I asked.

Mason shrugged. "I guess," he said.

"But you never saw it."

"No, but she did have a car. The missing persons guy I talked to on the phone told me he tried checking her driving record with the DMV just after she disappeared. He said she didn't exist, that she must have been working under an assumed name and that she probably disappeared because she wanted to disappear and because she was trying to get away from me. So there I was looking for help, and all he does is tell me Marina's a liar. I wanted to belt him one. If I'd been in the same room with him, I might've done just that," Mason Waters added forcefully—as though he still wanted to punch someone's lights out.

The trouble is, Mel and I had come to the house intending to give him much the same information—that the love of his life was a liar and a fraud. I looked again at Mason Waters's bull-like torso and formidable fists. If he decided to light into one of us or even both of us together, I wasn't sure we could handle him.

"What kind of car did Marina have?" Mel asked.

"A white 4-Runner," Waters said. "With Arizona plates. That's where she was from, someplace in Arizona. She told me she had to leave there in a hurry. Her ex-boyfriend was after her. He's the violent type, if you know what I mean. Abusive. She said if she hadn't gotten away from him right then, he probably would have killed her."

"Do you happen to remember the plate number?" I asked.

Mason shook his head mournfully. "I'm dyslexic," he said. "I'm no good at remembering numbers. I couldn't even tell you the numbers on my own license plates. I have to keep them written down on a piece of paper in my wallet."

"Let's go back to Marina for a moment," Mel said. "You met her that morning in Denny's. Then what happened?"

"I paid for my breakfast and left. They fixed my car, and I went on my next trip, but as soon as I got back, the first thing I did was go to Denny's for breakfast again. There she was, just as beautiful as ever, with long dark hair and brown eyes. So I say to her,

'Hey, gorgeous. You still here?' She gives me that look of hers and says right back, 'And are you still having the Grand Slam?' I was already head over heels, but that sealed the deal for me. She remembered me; remembered what I ordered. That never happened to me before. Usually waitresses see me and couldn't care less, even if I've seen 'em a dozen times before. But not Marina. Just that one time and she remembered."

Mel smiled and nodded. "So tell us about Marina," she said. "Is she from Arizona originally then?" Her tone was conversational rather than confrontational. She looked interested, and her use of the present tense belied our suspicion that Marina Aguirre was dead. Poor Mason. He lunged for the bait like a starving fish. He had been waiting for months for someone to show an interest in his missing fiancée, and now the details came flooding out of him.

"Yes," he said. "From somewhere down there. When she wasn't in her uniform from Denny's, she liked to dress like a cowgirl, you know, in boots and jeans and stuff."

Yes, I thought, remembering the charred Tony Lama boot in the evidence bag.

"She never told me exactly where in Arizona," Mason continued. "She said the less I knew about it the better, because if her boyfriend came looking for her, he might come after me as well. I told her I could handle myself, but I don't think she believed me."

"Did you ever meet any members of her family?"

He shook his head. "Never. She told me she had a son, but that she had left him back home, that he was staying with relatives where she knew he'd be safe until she got on her feet again."

"The son's name?"

"Louis."

"Age?"

"I don't think she ever said exactly how old."

"What about friends here?" Mel asked. "Did you meet any of those?"

"No."

"Doctors, dentists?"

Mason shook his head. "If she was sick, she never mentioned it to me."

"Where did she live?"

"In a mobile home court north of here, just this side of I-5, but I never went there until after she was gone. In fact, I didn't find it until long after she disappeared. By then, it was too late."

"What do you mean, you found it?" I asked while Mel jotted down the address details.

Mason gave me a pained look. "We always met somewhere else—at the mall or the movies or something. I thought she was ashamed to show me where she lived. I tried to tell her that didn't matter, not to me. By the middle of December, when I could see the cops weren't lifting a finger to find her, I hired a private detective. He's the one who found out about the mobile home park. He talked to the lady who worked in the office there. She told him Marina's rent was due on the fifteenth. When she didn't come back or pay up by the first of December, the landlady sent in a crew to clean out her trailer. They bagged up everything in it and sent it to Goodwill or the landfill."

Skipping town when the rent's about to come due is the oldest trick in the book. The local cops might have uncovered that detail themselves without bothering to pass it along to Mr. Waters. It would also go a long way toward explaining why they had determined Marina had left of her own free will.

"When they cleaned out her place, did they find anything of value?" Mel asked.

Mason shrugged. "If they did, I never heard anything about it, not from the cops and not from my PI, either."

"Did Marina wear any distinctive jewelry?"

"The ring I gave her," he said. "A pretty little diamond engagement ring that we bought from the Fred Meyer store in the mall. Picked it out together. We had just gotten it sized and on her finger when she disappeared. And that's what the missing persons guy told me. He claimed the ring was all she was looking for, and that once she had what she wanted, she took off. But you've got to believe me. Marina wasn't like that, not at all."

"Any other jewelry that you remember?" Mel asked.

I thought he'd mention the toe ring. Instead, Mason Waters heaved himself out of the recliner and then left the room for a moment. He returned carrying a small square box which he handed over to Mel before dropping back into the recliner. "When we were looking for the ring, I saw she was looking at this and that she liked it. I was planning on giving it to her for Christmas."

Mel opened the box, glanced at the contents, and then wordlessly handed the box over to me. Inside was a lady's watch—a Seiko with a gold band.

"The one she had was an old Timex. This new one is so much prettier that I could hardly wait to give it to her. In fact," Mason added, "I probably wouldn't have held out all the way to Christmas. I'm a sucker that way. I mean, if you want to give someone a present, why wait?"

Hearing the word Timex along with the cowgirl stuff pretty well sealed the deal for me. Mason's beloved Marina wasn't ever going to wear that watch.

But I wasn't ready to tell him that straight out and neither was Mel, not until we had actual proof about the identity of those charred remains in the morgue at Ellensburg. All the same, our physical presence in Mason Waters's humble Federal Way living room was a warning shot across his bow. It told him something was up, and it gave him a chance to prepare himself for what was coming. Truth be told, I think he already knew.

"Can you think of anything else?"

Mason shook his head. Mel closed her notebook and put it away, then she and I both stood up. Mason stayed where he was. "You'll let me know?" he said. "If you find out anything, I mean."

"Yes," Mel said. "If we learn anything at all, you'll be the first to know."

"How's your nose?" I asked as we crossed the porch and started down the walkway.

She touched her nose. "Why? Is something the matter with it?"

"Any minute now, it's going to start to grow," I told her. "Just like Pinocchio's."

Chapter 8

When we got back in the car, the clock on the dash said 3:30 P.M. With rush-hour traffic already settling in, I was ready to call it a day. While I fastened my seat belt, however, Mel went to work programming an address into the GPS. Clearly she didn't need to do that if we were headed straight home.

"Where are we going?"

"I thought we could just as well stop by Marina's trailer court," Mel said. "It's already rush hour. Even if we leave right now, we'll still be stuck in traffic. Let's work a little longer and wait it out."

That made sense, and traffic was already bad enough that it took us the better part of an hour to make our way north to the Silver Pines Mobile Home Park. I confess that while we drove I formed a pretty bleak mental picture of what we'd most likely find there. I expected to see a few run-down moldering mobile homes, weeds, dead cars, stray garbage cans, and plenty of stray dogs and cats as well. What we actually found was quite a bit different.

For one thing, Silver Pines was much larger than I had expected. For another, there was a remotely operated entry gate with a phone and a sign that said, GATE CLOSES AT 10:00 P.M. CALL MANAGER FOR ADMITTANCE. NO EXCEPTIONS. At that time of day, however, the gate stood open.

Inside the park we found what I estimated at first glance to be seventy-five to a hundred mobile homes parked next to a winding but smoothly paved street. Some of the mobiles were clearly older models, but they all seemed to be in decent repair. A few of them boasted awnings and many of them had patio furniture stationed on the concrete slabs outside their doors. The only visible vehicles appeared to be in running order. What grass there was showed signs of having been recently mowed.

Mel stopped outside the trailer marked MANAGER with a NO VACANCY sign posted just below that. As soon as we opened the car door, however, our ears were assaulted with the roar of traffic from the freeway just a few hundred feet away. The noise alone probably made the property less attractive and explained why, in the midst of a real estate boom, this mobile home park hadn't been bought up and turned into tract housing.

We entered a tiny, dingy office that was bisected by a Formica-covered counter. Beyond the counter sat a woman with her eyes glued on a television soap opera. Without rising to greet us, she pointed to the NO VACANCY sign.

"We're all booked up," she said. "Can't you read? The sign says 'No Vacancy' plain as day."

I'm used to being dissed by clerks and receptionists everywhere I go. It's the story of my life. Mel is not used to it at all. She's usually able to get around people by being both good-looking and gracious—a killer combination. The woman behind the counter had a hard edge to her—the kind of edge that comes with years of living on the streets and usually includes a natural aversion to cops of all kinds. In this case, the woman's hard edge struck Mel's hard edge the wrong way. The resulting clash sent sparks flying in all directions.

"We're homicide investigators," Mel said, slapping her ID badge down on the chipped gray counter. "With the Washington State Attorney General's Office."

"So?" the woman returned. She was still far more interested in what was happening on the screen than in the ID packet Mel had placed within her reach.

"We're here to speak to whoever was working this desk last fall—September, October, November," I added helpfully.

Mel seemed to regard my intervention as unwarranted. She turned her blue eyes on me and gave me a glacial stare that would have brought a lesser man to his knees. Then she turned back to the clerk. Between us, Mel and I had finally managed to get the woman's attention. She stood up and took a long careful look at Mel's badge. Then, blanching visibly, she flopped back down into her chair.

"It says homicide," the clerk managed. "Does that mean someone's dead?"

Homicide usually means murder, so it was clear the woman wasn't exactly the sharpest knife in the drawer.

"Yes," Mel said. "Someone is dead, and it's our job to investigate it. Now what about last fall? Were you working here then or not?"

Instead of answering, the woman reached for the phone and began to dial. "I'm not allowed to talk to anyone without talking to Mama first," she said.

Mel pushed down the button on the desk-based phone and ended the call before anyone could pick up. "It seems to me you could answer a few questions without having to consult with your mother," she said.

"I have no idea who was working the desk back then because I wasn't here," the clerk said pointedly. "And

Mama Rose Brotsky is definitely not my mother," she added. "She's my boss. She's the owner. And she most especially doesn't like anyone from here talking to cops."

For some reason that name, Mama Rose Brotsky, rang a bell, but right then, standing in front of the counter of that grim little office, I couldn't make the connection.

"What's Ms. Brotsky's number?" I asked. Passing my own ID across the counter, I stepped into the middle of the melee, notebook in hand. "And where can we find her?" I added.

"She lives somewhere over by Black Diamond," the clerk said. "Her number's unlisted. I'm not allowed to give it out."

Mel reached across the counter, picked up the telephone receiver, and punched the redial button. A moment later she read off a number while I copied it down. "That's the right one, isn't it?" Mel asked. "Mama Rose's number?"

Nodding, the clerk glared at Mel. "Yes, it is," she said. "But she isn't going to like it if you call."

"Too bad," Mel returned. "If you happen to talk to her in the next little while, you might pass along our names and let her know we'll be dropping by, if not later today, then certainly tomorrow."

There was, of course, no "if" about that phone call being made. Mel and I both knew that the clerk would be dialing Mama Rose's number the moment our backs were turned. And by the time we showed up at her place, she'd probably have an attorney or two in attendance. I had a suspicion that despite the fact that Silver Pines looked squeaky clean, some of the residents maybe weren't exactly upstanding citizens, and that probably meant Mama Rose wasn't one, either. Birds of a feather and all that jazz.

"Does the name Marina Aguirre ring a bell?" I asked.

"No," the clerk said. "Should it? Is that the person who's dead?"

"When did you move in?"

"January," she answered.

"And your name?"

"Donita," she answered. "Donita Mack, but I don't have any warrants. I swear."

I hadn't asked about warrants. In my experience, people who spontaneously swear they don't have them usually do. But Donita Mack wasn't our problem. Marina Aguirre was, and since she had disappeared in early November, if she really was our victim, Donita's arrival in January was two months too late for our purposes.

Looking across the counter, I noticed for the first time that something was missing. The only pieces of electronic equipment in the office were the telephone and the droning television set. There was no computer in attendance. Zero. None.

I had already estimated that the trailer park contained a hundred or so mobile homes. At probably a low-ball rental figure of seven hundred and fifty to a thousand dollars a month, that meant someone was collecting a whole lot of money—close to a hundred thousand a month. It also meant that Donita Mack wasn't the one doing the collecting.

"What's your job here exactly?" I asked.

She shrugged. "I answer the phone and sign for packages. I let repairmen in and out of mobiles. When there are vacancies, I show people what's available and give them the application forms. It doesn't pay much, but I don't have to type and that's a good thing because I don't know how."

"How much does it pay?" I asked.

"Some," she said. "But Mama Rose takes it off my rent. I'm not the only one. She does the same thing for some of the other girls as well. That way the office is covered around the clock."

"Is she the one who collects the rent?" I asked.

Donita nodded. "Cash only. Twice a month, on the first and the fifteenth. Some people only pay for two weeks at a time. Mama Rose's driver brings her down and waits while people bring her their envelopes."

Cash only? Mel and I exchanged glances as both of us arrived at a similar conclusion. That meant a great deal of cash, and it opened the door to a lot of other things as well, none of them good.

"Tell me about her driver," I suggested.

"Maybe he's more than a driver," Donita allowed.

"So you're saying the driver is actually her bodyguard?" Mel asked.

Donita nodded again. "That and maybe her boyfriend. I don't think they're married, but he carries a gun, and he acts like he knows how to use it. I think he used to be a cop," she added, "but I don't know where."

I didn't ask how she knew that. In the wild, crooks recognize cops. Cops recognize crooks. It's part of the natural order of things—a variation on a theme of survival of the fittest.

"Does the driver have a name?" Mel asked.

Donita shrugged. "Tommy something or other. I don't think I've ever heard his last name, and I don't pay that much attention to him. After all, I've only seen him a few times when they've come by to pick up the rent."

"How many residents live here?" Mel asked.

"One hundred and ten," Donita answered.

"Are all the units occupied?"

"Yes. Like I said before. No vacancy."

"How do you keep track of that many people?"

Donita reached in a drawer and pulled out a clipboard. On it was a computer-generated printout several pages long, with names and unit numbers. Once again my distant-reading skills gave me a distinct advantage. From the far side of the counter I could read the printout plain as day. Every name was followed by two numbers. The one on the left, running in consecutive order, was evidently the unit number. The second number was far more random. It didn't take long to guess that one would turn out to be an abbreviated form of the tenant's arrival date. One was 20305. Another was 20406.

The computer printout told us something else as well. Mama Rose might be dealing in cash, but somewhere there was a computer that was keeping careful records of all moneys coming in and going out. Once we talked to the person behind the computer, we'd be able to find out exactly when Marina had moved in and when she had disappeared. We'd also be able to track down some of her near neighbors to see if they had seen anything out of the ordinary—any loud arguments or stray people coming and going at odd hours.

"Anything else you can think of?" I asked Mel.

When she shook her head, Donita looked enormously relieved.

"We'd better head out then," I suggested. "It's starting to get dark, and I don't know my way around Black Diamond very well." This was not entirely true on two counts. For one thing, I had spent some time in Black Diamond years earlier. For another, the GPS navigation system knows its way around, regardless of whether it happens to be day or night.

Mel gave me an exasperated look, but she restrained herself from giving me the full verbal blast until we were safely inside the Cayman and well out of Donita Mack's earshot.

"What the hell were you thinking?" Mel asked as she waited on the phone to see what could be learned about Mama Rose's address. "If this Brotsky woman has anything to hide, once Donita lets her know we're on our way there, she'll probably be lawyered up before we can drive from here to there."

"Exactly," I said. " And if she does, we'll know for sure she has something to hide."

Shaking her head, Mel fed some address information into the navigation system and handed the phone over to me. "Call Records," she added. "Mama Rose sounds like a piece of work."

That turned out to be something of an understatement. Mama Rose Brotsky had what could only be referred to as a colorful past. Her record included more than a dozen arrests for prostitution and drug dealing in the late eighties. But all activity on her rap sheet stopped in 1990, with the exception of a speeding ticket in 1992.

When prostitutes go out of business, it's seldom due to old age. They usually wind up on drugs first, followed by jail and/or death. The speeding ticket—fifty-five in a thirty-five-mile-an-hour zone—meant she was alive and out of the slammer two years after she had supposedly started walking the straight and narrow.

"Maybe she wised up and stopped getting caught," Mel said as she weaved her way onto I-5. "Or maybe she found something more profitable."

"I'll say," I agreed, thinking that drug dealing was Mama Rose's most likely post-hooking career choice. "As far as I can see, dealing drugs would be the shortest distance between walking the mean streets in Tacoma twenty years ago and owning that much prime property along I-5 right now."

"It's not prime property," Mel reminded me. "It's a trailer park."

"It's a trailer park where everybody pays their rent in cash," I countered. "She may not be dodging the

Vice Squad anymore, but I'd be willing to bet she's cheating on her income taxes."

"Great," Mel said. "If I were Mama Rose, I'd prefer duking it out with the Vice Squad to tangling with the IRS."

After that we didn't talk much. Mel was driving. I kept quiet and let the woman's voice from the nav system do all the talking.

Now that Mel and I are married, I find it works better that way.

That afternoon, by the time Butch and Joanna got home from Tucson and had the groceries unpacked and put away, it was almost time for dinner. Fortunately, Carol had that end of things handled. The food—meat loaf and baked potatoes—was cooked. All they had to do was put it on the table. Once dinner was over, Joanna moved on to overseeing Dennis's bath. She had just rinsed the shampoo out of his hair when Butch came into the bathroom holding the telephone.

"You'd better take this," he said. "It's Tica."

Tica Romero was Joanna's nighttime dispatcher. Leaving Butch in charge of Dennis, Joanna stepped out of the bathroom. "What's up?" she asked.

"We've got a missing person," Tica said. "A ninety-three-year-old woman, Philippa Brinson, walked away from her assisted living home, a place called Caring Friends out in Palominas, earlier this afternoon."

"How long has she been gone?"

"Since three o'clock," Tica said. "There was a communications error of some kind. No one figured out she was missing until dinnertime, and they didn't call us right away even after they realized she was gone. I've dispatched a deputy and the K-9 unit to the scene along with Chief Deputy Hadlock. He's the one who wanted me to call you. He also asked for a homicide detective. Howell is on call."

Hadlock's request for a homicide detective was worrisome, but he was showing initiative here, so Joanna let that pass. "Patch him through," she said. "What's going on, Tom?" she asked once Hadlock was on the line.

"I'm sorry to interrupt your day off, but there's this missing person . . ." he began.

"Yes. Ms. Brinson. Tica told me. She said there was some kind of communication problem at the facility where she was staying."

"It's not much of a facility, if you ask me," Tom answered. "A private house that's been converted into a group home for Alzheimer's patients. The daytime nurse took the day off. As near as I can tell, the attendant who was supposed to be on duty until four left around two, and the one who was supposed to arrive at four had car trouble and didn't get there until five. The place is a mess. I think it should be shut down. If my mother or father were living here, that's what I'd do—call in the health department and have them pull the plug. But I'm just the chief deputy, Sheriff Brady. And the way things stand between Ms. Whitehead and me, you're the one who should make that call."

Peggy Whitehead was the head of the Cochise County Health Department. Joanna gave Tom high marks for understanding that what should have been a simple interdepartmental transaction could blow up into something far more complicated.

Peggy had long been jealous of Joanna's position in the county's administrative hierarchy. The sheriff's department had far more personnel than hers did, which meant that Joanna controlled a larger piece of the annual budget.

In the past year or so, Peggy had used her inspectors to keep the jail's kitchen facilities and even the department's break room under constant scrutiny. Tom, in his former position as jail commander, had borne the brunt of the criticism. The minor infractions that had been found there had little to do with inmate or employee health and well-being and everything to do with Peggy's being able to put Joanna in her place. Well-placed notices in the *Bisbee Bee* that had focused on jail-kitchen health department infractions had served to turn the feud between two competing heads of departments into public fodder.

There was the potential for the same kind of drama playing out here as well. Unless Joanna proceeded carefully, the situation might turn into yet another political football. Rather than simply shutting down an underperforming facility and protecting vulnerable patients, Peggy Whitehead was liable to keep it open just to spite Joanna.

"You were right to call me," Joanna assured Tom. "I'm the one who needs to make the call, and I can't do that without assessing the situation firsthand. I'll be there as soon as I can. In the meantime, what are we doing to find Ms. Brinson? Do we know exactly what time she left?"

"Not really," Tom said. "Like I said, she disappeared while the place was unsupervised, sometime between when the one attendant left and when the other one arrived."

"No surveillance cameras?"

"None. Deputy Gregovich and Spike got here just a few minutes ago. I'm hoping they'll be able to track her."

Terry Gregovich and his German shepherd constituted Joanna's K-9 unit.

"I'll get the address and directions from Tica once I'm on the way," Joanna said. "How far is the house from the highway?"

"Half a mile at least."

"And how cold is it supposed to get tonight?"

"Upper thirties," Tom replied grimly. "Which is pretty cold if you're in your nineties and out wandering around with nothing more than a sweater on."

"That's all she's wearing—a sweater?"

"We don't know that for sure, but it's likely. Sylvia Cameron, the nurse who was supposed to be here all day, finally turned up a little while ago. Someone must have called her. When she got here, she smelled like a brewery."

"You mean she's drunk?"

"Seems like it to me," Tom answered. "Anyway, she claims Ms. Brinson only had a sweater here at the home, not a coat, and the sweater's not here now."

"But it's been cold these past few months," Joanna objected. "Why wouldn't she have a coat?"

Tom paused a moment before he answered. "You need to see this place for yourself, boss," he said. "It reminds me of what they used to say in that old commercial about the roach motel: They check in but they don't check out."

"Have you spoken to any of Ms. Brinson's family members?"

"We have a phone number for a grandniece who lives in the Phoenix area. We're trying to reach her. So far that's a no-go."

"I'm on my way then, Tom. Thanks for the call."

As she closed the phone, Butch came out of the bathroom carrying Dennis. His hair was still damp. When Joanna leaned over to kiss him good-bye, he smelled of baby shampoo.

"Bye-bye," she said. "Mommy has to go to work."

Dennis smiled and waved.

"Be careful, Joey," Butch said, leaning across Dennis to kiss Joanna as well.

"I will," she told him. "But don't worry. It's just a missing persons case."

"I always worry," Butch said, and Joanna knew that was true.

"I know," she said. "So do I."

"You are arriving at your destination on the right," the computer-generated female voice of the GPS told us.

"On our right where?" I asked the question of Mel as much as the disembodied voice emanating from the dashboard.

As far as I was concerned, we were in the middle of nowhere on the Maple Valley/Black Diamond Highway. It was well after dark by then and raining again.

On either side of the road, Douglas fir and lodgepole pines loomed like towering black shadows against a slightly lighter sky where the undersides of lowering clouds were lit by reflected light from the megalopolis behind us.

"Right here, I guess," Mel said. She turned onto an almost invisible dirt track that led off into the woods. From my point of view, it didn't look promising. There was no gate, and no visible sign of security. If Mama Rose was running an all-cash business, I wondered about that.

"Why would a slumlord live out here in the sticks like this?" I asked.

"Slumlady," Mel reminded me. "And maybe because she can."

Several hundred yards into the forest, the trees disappeared. Before us, set on a slight rise in the middle of a clearing, stood an eye-popping, brightly lit two-story house with an illuminated fountain spouting water in the middle of a circular driveway. The lower level of the house was lined with a series of French doors that opened out onto a long veranda.

"I'm guessing Mama Rose doesn't spend a lot of money fussing around with eco-green fluorescent lights," Mel muttered.

Just as she said that, all around the house several blindingly bright motion-activated lights flashed on.

Although we hadn't passed through a gate, we had obviously just encountered Mama Roses's first line of homeland security. The second one appeared a moment later, when an immense dog, a German shepherd, came careening out of the darkness, barking fiercely and charging at the car as if wanting to take a bite out of it.

Mel stopped at once. The dog didn't. Instead of backing off, the dog threw himself at her window, where he rose up on his hind legs, still barking and snapping. If the window hadn't been shut, he might have bounded straight through it. Then suddenly, in response to something Mel and I couldn't hear or see, the dog stopped barking. Dropping to all fours, he turned and trotted off toward a spot at the side of the house where yet another light had just switched on.

Hoping the dog was gone for good, I risked cracking open my window. "Hello," I called. "Anybody here?"

"Beaumont?" a man's voice said as a figure materialized next to what seemed to be a garage. "Is that you? It's Tom."

His reply told me two things. Just as Mel had thought, Donita had called Mama Rose the minute we left the trailer park to let her know we were on our way. The fact that the speaker used my name that way—with no Mr. and no J.P., either—told me this was someone who knew me, and probably someone I knew as well.

"Tom?" I said tentatively, meaning "Tom who?" But as he walked toward us I added, "I'm Beaumont. My partner, Mel Soames, is here as well."

"Tom Wojeck," the man said. "Don't worry about the dog. Regis is back in his run."

I breathed a sigh of relief when I recognized a voice and name out of the past: Thomas Wojeck—Detective Thomas Wojeck. He had to be at least ten years older than I was. He had been a homicide detective for Seattle PD while I was still working Patrol. We had never actually worked together, although I seemed to remember that at one time, before my appearance on the scene, he had been partnered with Big Al Lindstrom, one of my former partners. Wojeck had left the department to go work somewhere else shortly after I was promoted to Homicide. After that, as far as I knew, he had pretty much disappeared from view.

I wondered if Donita was right and if he was more than just Mama Rose's driver. If he was the boyfriend or even the man of the house, I had to admit it was one hell of a house, verging on palatial. Tom had either moved up or married up. In landing in such very posh digs, Tom Wojeck, like me with Anne Corley, had done all right for himself.

"Hey, Tommy," I said. Taking his word as far as the dog was concerned, I opened the door, stepped out of the car, and walked to meet him with my hand extended in greeting. "Long time no see. How the hell are you? Some place you have here," I added.

"Not bad," he said. "We like it."

His comment did nothing to clarify his exact position in this universe, and I was well mannered enough not to ask.

Mel climbed out of the Cayman and came around to where we were standing. "This is my partner, Mel Soames," I told him. And by way of keeping things even, I didn't explain the true nature of our partnership, either.

"Mel, this is an old colleague of mine from Seattle PD, Tom Wojeck."

"Glad to meet you, Mr. Wojeck," she said.

Wojeck smiled and pumped her hand. "Forget the mister stuff," he said. "Most people call me Tommy. It's what my mother called me, and I've never gotten over it. Let's go inside before you're soaked. I hope you don't mind coming in through the garage. The front entry is a lot nicer, but getting to that door is a bit of a wrangle in the dark."

The well-lit four-car garage was impressive on its own. So were its occupants. Parked side by side were a looming black Hummer, a shiny black Lincoln Town Car, a deep maroon Mercedes S550, and a bright red Dodge Grand Caravan.

"Quite a collection of rolling stock," I said.

"We mostly use the minivan for taking Regis for rides," he said. "Rosie insists that everything else is a dog-hair free zone, including the house."

"Good call," Mel said.

"Don't worry about him being stuck outside in the cold, though," Tommy added. "For a guard dog, Regis has it pretty good. His doghouse is fully climate controlled. It has radiant heating and cooling in the floor. Cool, don't you think?"

I nodded my agreement, but what I was thinking was that no expense had been spared here. Money—or at least the lack of same—was not a problem for Mama Rose Brotsky.

"Right this way," Tommy said.

He took us into the house itself through a massive kitchen, a catering kitchen, really, that had double everything, from sinks and ovens to dishwashers, warming drawers, and microwaves. The appliances were top-of-the-line stainless steel. The countertops were a gorgeous tawny granite and I suspected the cabinets were solid cherry. The materials that had been used here were way upscale compared to the grim and gray

Formica on the counter at the manager's office back at the Silver Pines, but that's how come they're called slumlords and ladies.

"This is some kitchen!" Mel enthused. Since I happen to know she barely cooks a lick, I understood this to be another blatant case of her playing good cop/bad cop. No need to specify which one of us was which.

"You should have seen it when we bought it," Tommy said, smiling at her. "It was framed in, but that was it. No windows and hardly any interior walls. It was a mess. The guy who was building it lost his shirt and his money in the big dot-com bust. Rose bought it for a song. I think most people thought she'd just bulldoze the house and start over, but Rosie's idea was to finish it and turn it into a showstopper. We've been working on it for years. I think she did very well."

So did I.

Tommy led us first through a breakfast kind of area, then a huge dining room with a boardroom-style table that would easily seat a dozen or so guests. Beyond that was a spacious window-lined living room followed by a much smaller, more intimate room. In the old days it might have been called a sitting room, or maybe it had been intended for use as a library or a study. A flat-screen TV hung on the wall over a cheerfully burning gas-log fireplace. Ranged in front of it were four comfortable easy chairs. Seated in one of them was one of the most stunningly beautiful women I had ever seen. She lifted the clicker and turned off the television set as soon as we entered the room.

I think I may have mentioned before that Ross Connors encourages us to use our own vehicles rather than company cars. That means we don't drive around with the kind of communications capability that's now routine in patrol cars. Yes, we have a high-end nav system, but we don't have a computer that can deliver Records information to us on the road. The clerk I had spoken to had given me a rundown of Rose Marie (Mama Rose) Brotsky's rap sheet. But from the name, I expected a little Polish woman, short and a bit wide, with a face and body that showed some hard miles.

The records clerk hadn't hinted that although her father may have been Polish, Mama Rose was at least a quarter and maybe even half African-American. She was stately; she was serene. When she held out her rail-thin arms in welcome, I noticed that her hands were beautifully manicured. When she smiled at me, her face was transformed. She was simply gorgeous.

I noticed that right off. So did Mel.

"Why, Mr. Beaumont," Mama Rose said. "That is correct, isn't it—Mr.—since you're no longer a detective? Welcome. Tommy says he knew you back in the day. And this is?"

"My partner," I said. "Melissa Soames."

Mel stepped forward to accept her own handshake. "People call me Mel," she said.

"I hope you'll forgive me for not standing up to greet you," Mama Rose said. "I have MS." She reached out and patted a walker that was stationed strategically on the far side of the chair. "When they told me years ago that I was HIV-positive, I thought that was a death sentence. And, without all the progress they've made in AIDS treatment, it could have been, but it turns out that dealing with MS has been much more debilitating. Won't you please have a seat?"

Mel and I sat. "Can I get you something?" Tommy asked. "Beer, a soda, coffee, tea. We have pretty much everything."

"We're working," I said, which was easier than saying the truth, which would have been to say that I'm off the sauce and have been for years.

"Coffee," Mel said decisively. She can drink coffee at any hour of the day and sleep like a baby. I used to be able to do the same thing. Now I can't do that, either.

"Nothing for me," I said. "I'm fine."

Tommy disappeared, but instead of going back toward the kitchen the way we had come, he continued on through a swinging door just to the left of the fireplace. I suspected that it most likely led into a small butler's pantry.

"You have a lovely home," Mel said. The compliment may have sounded phony and ingratiating, but it was absolutely true. Mama Rose knew her home was spectacular, and she accepted the comment with good grace.

"It's easy to have nice things when money's no object," Mama Rose said with a small shrug. "When I first got the HIV diagnosis and didn't have insurance or a place to live or enough money to pay for the medicine, that was scary. Now, whatever the prescriptions cost, I just pay it. Or, rather, Tommy does. It's no big deal."

And that's when it came back to me. I remembered how, years ago, I had encountered the improbable rags-to-riches story of a young homeless woman (the word "prostitute" had been discreetly edited out of the newspaper account) who, within months of being diagnosed with HIV, had been one of the first-ever Powerball Winners in Washington State.

"I remember now," I said. "Aren't you the person who had one of the first winning Powerball tickets around here?"

She smiled at me. "Thank you for not saying 'Weren't you the whore who won . . .' Believe me, I've heard that more than once. But yes, that's true. Mine wasn't 'one of the first' winning tickets in Washington

State. It was the first winning ticket. And you're right—it was a big one—sixty-seven million after taxes!"

Mel was living back east at the time. I doubted she knew any of the story. "Whoa!" she exclaimed. "That's a lot of money."

"Yes, it is," Mama Rose agreed.

"So why do you even bother with something like the Silver Pines?" Mel asked. "Isn't that more trouble than it's worth?"

"It is a lot of trouble on occasion," Mama Rose admitted. "But it's made it possible for me to help a lot of people over the years. And that feels good, of course. Giving back always feels good. But do you want to know the real reason I keep Silver Pines in business?"

Mel bit. "Why?" she asked.

Mama Rose smiled her serene smile. "Because I can," she said. "It's my way of slipping it to those bastards at Planning and Zoning."

Chapter 9

Tommy returned to the room through the swinging door beside the fireplace. He was carrying a tray with three cups and one of those French press coffeepots where you have to lower a screened plunger through the hot water and squeeze the coffee grounds at the bottom of the pot. I prefer Mr. Coffee any day.

"Oh, no," he said. "Not Planning and Zoning again. It's a very long story. You're not going to tell them that whole thing, are you?"

"My house, my rules," Mama Rose said.

"Whatever you say," Tommy said with a certain amount of resignation. He finished pressing the coffee. He poured a cup for Mel and handed it her, then turned to me. "Are you sure you won't change your mind?"

"Why not?" I said. "The night is young."

And so, knowing I'd live to regret it later, I took the cup of that very strong coffee and sat back to listen.

Tommy turned to Mama Rose. "What about you, my dear? Would you care for anything at all?"

"No, thanks," she said. "I'm fine." Her next comment was addressed to Mel. "So I take it you know nothing of my history?"

"Only what I've heard here just now," Mel said.

"Back in the eighties, the idea of safe sex was a joke, especially to those of us who were working the streets. Oh, we heard about HIV and AIDS, but we were young. We thought we were immortal and those awful things only happened to other people. But then it happened to me. Once I had my diagnosis, I quit working cold turkey. I quit and never went back. I may have been a whore, but giving some poor unsuspecting john HIV wasn't something I could or would do. Just because someone gave it to me didn't mean I had to pass it along to someone else. The problem was, I didn't know how to do anything else. I'd never had a regular job and didn't know how to find one. Do you have any idea how many jobs there are for ex-hookers with no education and no other marketable skills? I couldn't even type."

I thought about Donita back at Silver Pines. Hadn't she said something about the receptionist job being one she could do without knowing how to type?

"I suppose I could have sold drugs," Mama Rose continued. "I had all the contacts in the world to do that, but I knew firsthand what drugs do to people. And I wouldn't do that, either, so when I was well enough to work, I cleaned other people's houses, the same way my grandmother did. I didn't have enough money to get an apartment. I couldn't squeeze out enough money to pay for my treatment and pull together enough for the first and last months' rent at the same time. One of my clients—one of my old clients—helped me find a room to rent over a friend's garage. And for my birthday that year, he gave me a card with a Powerball ticket in it."

"The winning ticket," Mel breathed.

"Exactly. When I won, I offered to split it with him fifty-fifty, but he turned me down. I still remember what he said to me, 'Honey lamb, if you do that, I'll never in this world be able to explain it to my wife. So you just go out and do what you want, and whenever you do something good for someone else, do it for me, too.'

"I couldn't get his words out of my head," Mama Rose continued. "I found an investment counselor and put the money to work to earn more, but then I tried to think what else I should do. It was a big responsibility. I asked people for advice about that, including the guy who gave me the ticket—who's still my friend, by the way. 'Work with the people you know best,' he said. 'Someone gave you a chance to get out of that mess. Maybe you can do the same thing for someone else.'

"That made sense to me, but I don't think he meant that I should give them a free ride. He meant I should help them help themselves, just like he had with me. The problem is, when you're trying to get out of that kind of mess, either drugs or prostitution, no one really trusts you. No one wants to give you a job. You have no place to live except maybe some rat-infested subsidized housing."

I had seen plenty of those in my time, and I'm sure Mel had, too.

"I came up with the idea of buying some property and starting a shelter," Mama Rose continued. "I wanted to create a group-home situation, someplace safe where women from the street could live while they made the transition back into real life. The Silver Pines was for sale at the time, and I made an offer to buy it. The place was affordable and I thought it would be a good place to put my shelter. Except, after I bought it,

Planning and Zoning turned my plans down cold. They told me they didn't want 'that kind of place' or 'those kinds of people' inside their precious city limits."

"So you went around them and built your shelter anyway," Mel said.

Mama Rose smiled again and nodded. "I certainly did. I already owned the park itself. As the people who rented the spaces moved on or died, I bought up their mobile homes one by one. I was always fair. I always paid at least the asking price and sometimes even more because I wanted to own them all. And now I do. I own every single unit in the park, and I rent them to people who would have trouble renting otherwise, and it's all still inside the city limits."

"And sometimes you let them work off the rent," I said.

"Occasionally," Mama Rose said. "Not all the rent, only some of it. They have to have real jobs as well. But if they can't earn enough to keep a roof over their heads, I let them work for me. Some people do office work. Some work outside doing maintenance—yard work and painting. It's on-the-job training for people who have never used a lawn mower or a paintbrush. By helping with upkeep, residents can take pride in where they live, but they all know they have to live by my rules—by Mama Rose's rules. That means no hooking and no drugs, no exceptions. I believe some people call it zero tolerance."

To me, it sounded a lot more like tough love.

"I believe Donita mentioned that when it comes to collecting the rent, you only take cash," Mel said.

"That's right," Mama Rose replied.

"How come?"

Mama Rose shrugged. "People who have been living on the street, who don't have jobs and have never touched a lawn mower or a paintbrush have never opened a checking account, either. Besides, checks bounce. Cash never does."

The story was starting to make me smile. The city had objected to the idea of Mama Rose's charitable intention to open a shelter, but she had outfoxed them and done it anyway. In the process, she had outmaneuvered the naysayers by marching over or around their roadblocks. And how had she done it? By using the oldest ploy in the book—plain old garden-variety capitalism.

"I'm guessing the local city fathers would still like to put you out of business?" I asked.

"They certainly would," Mama Rose agreed. "Probably some of the city mothers as well, but it turns out I have something they don't have."

"What's that?" Mel asked.

"Better lawyers." Mama Rose beamed. "I happen to have the big bucks here," she added. "I've got plenty of money, and I'm not afraid to use it."

It was nearly eight-thirty when Joanna finally arrived at Caring Friends, the privately run Alzheimer's group home in Palominas. On the drive out, she had called Peggy Whitehead's home phone and left a message for the head of the county health department, letting her know about a possible problem at the facility. When she arrived, she had to wait while three separate ambulances drove out of the yard and toward the highway with their lights flashing. Tom Hadlock hurried forward to bring her up to speed.

"Those were for the other residents?" Joanna asked, nodding toward the disappearing aid cars.

"Yes," Tom said. "We couldn't very well leave them here. According to the EMTs, they're all dehydrated. At least one is severely malnourished, and another one has bedsores."

"How many patients in all?"

"There are six rooms altogether. One is apparently unoccupied at the moment. One belongs to the woman who's gone missing. The other four patients, all women, are being transported to area hospitals. The most serious one has been airlifted to Tucson Medical Center."

"Do we know who's in charge and where he or she is?"

"She," Tom replied. "Her name's Alma DeLong. She evidently lives in Tucson. We've tried contacting her. Left a message on her machine."

Tom handed Joanna a piece of paper. She leaned back inside her Crown Victoria and switched on the reading light. The paper was a three-fold full-color brochure about Caring Friends. It showed several silver-haired women, smiling and neatly dressed. One showed them eating at a table in a tastefully decorated dining room. Another showed two women seated on chairs on a sun-drenched front porch. A third showed a woman standing in the shade of a huge cottonwood tree while looking into the far distance.

At the bottom of the back page of the brochure was a photo of Alma DeLong. She was an attractive-looking woman, probably somewhere in her fifties at the time the picture was taken. According to the brief bio under the photo, she had spent years working in the area of health-care administration before taking on the management of Caring Friends.

"What about the attendants?" she asked.

"The one who was here at the time and called in the missing persons report has no papers, no ID, and no driver's license. She's been taken into custody by ICE."

"At least she called in the report," Joanna said.

Tom nodded. "But if there are charges to be filed, by the time we finish our investigation and get around to doing that, Immigration will probably have put her on a bus and shipped her back to Mexico."

"What about the other attendant?"

"Same deal. I sent a deputy to the address where she supposedly lives. He says it looks like she's skipped town."

"And the nurse?" Joanna asked.

Tom Hadlock nodded in the direction of a tow truck that was hooking on to an older-model Toyota sedan. "Her name is Sylvia Cameron. She was supposed to be on duty today but called in sick. She showed up tonight about the same time we did. She stepped out of her vehicle smelling like a brewery and couldn't walk a straight line. If somebody looks like she's drunk and smells like she's drunk, she probably is drunk. We administered a Breathalyzer."

"How'd she do?" Joanna asked.

"She blew a .20," Tom replied. "She's on her way to jail right now. She already has two other DUI convictions."

"No wonder she called in sick," Joanna said. "Once she sobers up, maybe we'll have a chance to talk to her about what's really going on here."

"Exactly," Tom agreed. "As it says in the brochure, Caring Friends is supposed to provide 'skilled nursing care.' It looks to me like the care in question was being provided mostly by unskilled illegal immigrants supervised by somebody too drunk to talk or walk, to say nothing of drive."

"What about our missing person?" Joanna asked. "Any word on Ms. Brinson?"

"Not so far," her chief deputy told her. "The K-9 unit was able to follow her trail all the way out to the highway and across to the other side. Terry says that after that he lost her."

"So someone may have picked her up and given her a ride into town."

"Yes," Tom agreed. "Most likely someone headed eastbound, toward Bisbee."

"Have we located her next of kin?"

"Not yet. The niece in Phoenix still hasn't returned our calls."

"Whether she's been notified or not, we still need to get the word out on this," Joanna said. "It's going to be cold tonight. We need to find her."

Tom nodded in agreement. Joanne knew that if the missing patient died of exposure, Tom's summoning a homicide detective was a good call.

"While I go inside to check things out, how about if you talk to the news producers for the Tucson TV outlets and see if you can get them to make an announcement on the ten o'clock news. We're probably too late to make the broadcast that comes on at nine."

Tom Hadlock was still so new in his dual positions as Joanna's chief deputy as well as her media relations officer that he had yet to establish the kind of rapport Frank Montoya had enjoyed with some of the local newsfolk.

"I'll do my best," he agreed. "All their contact information is on the computer in my Crown Victoria, but before you go inside, you'd best prepare yourself. It's pretty bad."

The brochure photos may have looked lovely, but the conditions inside Caring Friends weren't just bad; they were appalling. Detective Howell met Joanna at the door to give her the tour.

Stepping inside one room, Joanna found her nostrils assailed by a sour, all-pervading odor. "What's that awful smell?" she asked.

Debra nodded toward the bed, where a tangled mess of soiled bedclothes indicated someone had been left lying in her own filth. "This is the one with the bedsores," the detective added grimly. "As far as I'm concerned, this seems way more serious than simple neglect," she said. "More like reckless endangerment. Animal Control takes better care of the stray animals they have locked up in the pound."

And it was true. There were six rooms in all. Each contained a bed, a single chair, and a small bedside dresser. The bedding in the other occupied rooms was also disgustingly filthy. The bed in the empty room was clean and made up and awaiting the arrival of another resident.

Another victim, Joanna thought.

In one of the rooms a set of cut-through Flex Cuffs lay near the legs of a chair. Whoever had been bound to the chair had been left there long enough that she had soiled herself.

"The woman in this room was still confined to her chair when deputies arrived," Debra said. "The EMTs cut her loose. Ms. Brinson was evidently in a chair, too, but she somehow managed to walk it over to the dresser and found a nail clipper. That's what she used to cut her own restraints."

"Smart lady," Joanna said.

Deb nodded. "Smarter than they thought."

"We'll need to document all of this."

The detective nodded again. "I know," she said. "I've already put in a call for Dave Hollicker to come here and bring his camera."

"Good," Joanna said. "Have him inventory and photograph everything."

"What the hell's going on?" someone demanded behind them.

Standing in the narrow hallway, Joanna turned in time to see a tall dark-haired woman in a turquoise-colored brushed-silk pantsuit come storming toward them. She was clearly angry. Only when she reached them did Joanna recognize the woman from her photo on the brochure. This had to be Alma DeLong.

"Who the hell are you?" she asked, looking from Joanna to Debra and then back again. "This is private property. What do you think you're doing here?" She was spoiling for a fight.

Trying to defuse the situation, Joanna stepped forward and identified herself. "I'm Sheriff Joanna Brady, Ms. DeLong," she said, holding out her hand. "Please calm down. My people and I are here in response to a missing persons report. One of the patients here has gone missing."

Ignoring the proffered handshake, Alma continued her tirade. "I have no intention of calming down!" she replied. "I happen to own this place, every inch of it. Now, where are my residents? What have you done with them? You can't come waltzing in here without a search warrant."

Alma's right hand strayed toward the pocket of her jacket, and Joanna's heart skipped a beat. The previous summer, one of her newer deputies, Dan Sloan, had been shot to death with his own weapon while trying to apprehend a homicide suspect. That life-ending tragedy had set Joanna off on a one-woman campaign to arm her officers—herself included—with effective but nonlethal Tasers. It hadn't been easy to make that kind of department-wide change in the face of falling revenues. Buying new equipment and making sure she and her officers knew how to use it had been an expensive proposition, but Joanna had managed to convince the Board of Supervisors that using Tasers was a cost-effective alternative to handguns or batons in many combat situations.

Her biggest selling point had been the proposition that Tasers would improve the bottom line when it came to preventing line-of-duty deaths and injuries. Officers sometimes hesitated before deploying a lethal weapon, and it was often that single moment of hesitation—those bare seconds when a cop asks himself whether or not he should pull the trigger—that proved fatal. And if the criminal managed to get control of the officer's weapon—as had happened in Danny Sloan's case—the officer might well end up on the ground after being Tased, but at least he or she wouldn't be dead.

Tasers were now Joanna's officers' first line of defense. That was the case for Joanna as well. She still carried her Glock, but she also wore a Taser X26 along with her Kevlar vest. She didn't leave home without them, not even tonight on what had seemed to be nothing more than a simple missing persons call-out. That's what happened when you were a cop. You could never tell in advance what might happen. Better to be safe than sorry. And she drew her Taser now, but before she could fire it, Alma's hand emerged from her pocket holding a cell phone rather than a weapon.

Focused solely on her cell phone, Alma seemed oblivious to what had just happened. Instead, she flipped open the phone. Then, turning her back on both Joanna and Deb Howell, she punched in a series of numbers. "I'm calling my attorney, by the way," she announced over her shoulder. "Believe me, Don Foster will be happy to set you straight."

"You'll have to talk to him outside," Joanna said as she prepared to return her Taser to its holster. "Get her out of here, Detective Howell. Let's secure the scene."

The truth was, Tom Hadlock should have handled that. Joanna was disappointed that he hadn't.

Obeying Joanna's order, Debra approached the woman. "Excuse me, Ms. DeLong," she said calmly. "If you wouldn't mind coming with me—"

"I most certainly would mind." Alma's answer was close to a snarl. "I already told you. I own this place, and I'm not leaving. You're the ones who need to step outside. If you know what's good for you, you'd better have a properly drawn search warrant. You can't come charging onto my property without one of those."

Joanna was in no mood for a lecture on police procedures from someone like Alma DeLong. "We don't need a search warrant when lives are at stake," she explained. "Several of your 'residents,' as you call them, appear to be in dire need of adequate medical care. They have all been transported to hospitals for treatment, except for the one who apparently walked away from this facility on her own earlier today."

"Someone walked away?" Alma echoed. "That's not possible. Our residents aren't allowed outside unaccompanied."

"I'm sure they're not," Joanna replied.

But Alma didn't appear to be listening. Since there was evidently no answer at the first number, she immediately ended that call and punched in the numbers for another one.

"I believe the incident occurred late this afternoon," Joanna continued. "At a time when your facility was left unstaffed for several hours."

"Unstaffed?" Alma repeated in disbelief, holding the phone at arm's length without punching the "send" button. "That's utterly preposterous! There's supposed to be someone here at all times. If my people weren't here when they were scheduled to be, I'll fire every single one of them. As for you, get out."

"You don't seem to understand," Joanna said. "This is a crime scene now, and it's a serious matter. You're welcome to make your phone calls, but please do as Detective Howell suggested. Make them from outside."

Defiantly, Alma pressed "send." "And as I already told you, I'm not leaving. Crime scene or not, this is my property, and you can't force me to leave."

"Yes, we can," Deb Howell insisted firmly. "Come along now, Ms. DeLong. Let's go."

Furious, Alma snatched her arm away from Debra, then spoke into the phone. "Don, it's Alma. Please call me as soon as you get this message. You're not going to believe what's happened. Some moron cops have taken over one of my homes, the one down in Palominas. They've invaded it! It's utterly outrageous, and they've taken my clients away—kidnapped them. You've got to do something about this."

"I said, 'Let's go,'" Deb repeated. "As Sheriff Brady said, you can finish your phone calls outside."

"Don't you understand?" Alma raged. "I'm talking to my lawyer. Now get your hands off me, you stupid bitch!"

Brandishing her phone, she took a single swipe at Deb's face. It was an ineffectual blow which the detective easily dodged. For a long moment the two women stood staring at each other.

"That's enough now, Ms. DeLong," Joanna warned. "Either you go with Detective Howell or you risk being booked for disorderly conduct."

"Disorderly conduct?" Alma retorted. "She was trying to manhandle me, and now you're threatening me with arrest? No way! It's not going to happen. I haven't done anything wrong."

"For starters, you're interfering with officers of the law, to say nothing of criminal assault. If Ms. DeLong refuses to go willingly, Detective Howell, cuff her and read her her rights."

With a nod, Debbie produced a pair of handcuffs. At the sight of them, Alma went wild. She began backing away, as if preparing to make a run for it, but by then Tom Hadlock had appeared at the far end of the hall. When Alma saw him and realized she had lost that avenue of escape, she evidently decided to take her chances with Debra. First she flung her phone full in the detective's face, then sprang after it. For a moment the two women grappled there in the hallway. Before Joanna could join the fray, Tom waded into the fight. In a matter of moments the two officers wrestled Alma DeLong to the floor. Once they had her down, Debra snapped the cuffs in place.

"My outfit!" Alma screeched as they hauled her back to her feet. "Look what you've done to my outfit. You've ruined it. That floor is filthy."

"Maybe you should have had someone clean it," Joanna suggested.

Deputy Matt Raymond appeared just then to offer his assistance. Taking over from Tom, he and Detective Howell headed back down the hall, holding the still-struggling woman between them.

"What got into her?" Tom asked.

"She's upset," Joanna said. "She should never have been allowed inside here."

Tom nodded. He had been charged with securing the scene, and he hadn't done so. "I know," he said. "Sorry about that. I was talking to a reporter from Tucson when a car drove up and stopped behind me. Before I had a chance to stop her, she hopped out of her car and came racing in here."

"It's okay," Joanna told him. "Don't worry about it. For right now, we're charging her with interfering and assault. Those will do for starters."

Just then Peggy Whitehead of health department fame arrived on the scene. Dealing with another irate woman was pretty much the last thing Joanna needed.

"What's going on here?" Peggy demanded. "If this is a health-related issue, my department has jurisdiction. You've got no reason—"

"I have every reason in the world," Joanna interrupted. "This is now a criminal matter, Peggy. It's also a crime scene. If you'd been doing your job, maybe it wouldn't be. Get her out of here, Chief Deputy Hadlock. Now."

Joanna realized immediately that she should have been more diplomatic. As she was still shaken from the confrontation with Alma DeLong, however, diplomacy wasn't high on Joanna's list. And once the words were out of her mouth, it was too late.

Tom Hadlock didn't come right out and say, "With pleasure!" but the slow smile of satisfaction that spread across his face spoke volumes. Peggy Whitehead had done everything in her power to make his life miserable. Now Joanna had handed him an opportunity to return the favor.

"Right this way, please, Ms. Whitehead," he said politely.

Peggy hesitated for a moment, then turned and strode away.

Good riddance, Joanna thought, watching her go. Good riddance to both you and Alma DeLong!

She stood there for a long time staring into yet another appalling room—a room with soiled and stinking bedclothes along with a handy supply of damning Flex Cuffs right there on the nightstand. She doubted Alma DeLong would spend more than a single night in jail before being bailed out, and she would be staying in far better conditions than the poor residents of her "care" facility. It was a shame Joanna couldn't have ordered her to be locked up in one of these very rooms. The same went for Peggy Whitehead. Wasn't she supposed to see to it that places like this didn't exist? To Joanna's way of thinking, the head of the health department deserved to be locked up as well.

Dave Hollicker, camera equipment in hand, came hurrying down the hallway behind Joanna. "Are you all right, boss?" he asked.

"I'm fine," she said, and she meant it. For one thing, her officers were all safe, and so was Alma DeLong. When their shifts ended that night, all of her people would be going home to their families, and so would she.

"I'll be a lot better than fine," she added, "once we locate Philippa Brinson."

By the time Mel and I finally left Black Diamond and headed back to downtown Seattle, it was much later. Traffic was no longer an issue, but believe me, we were a long way from those Pecos Pit sandwiches we'd had many hours earlier. It was almost ten. Late-night dining choices in downtown Seattle aren't what they used to be, but we stopped by the 13 Coins to grab a quick dinner. I had the steak salad. Mel had the buttermilk chicken salad.

"If she hadn't won that lottery, she'd be dead by now," Mel said thoughtfully as she cut into a chunk of crispy fried chicken. "Medicine can keep people alive, but not if they can't afford it."

"Yes," I said. "Mama Rose is a remarkable woman."

"A survivor," Mel added. "And I notice you liked the idea that she put what's essentially a homeless shelter where they didn't want a homeless shelter."

That made me grin. "I always like it when somebody manages to pull a fast one on over-reaching bureaucrats."

"Most people see us as bureaucrats, too," Mel reminded me.

"Yes," I said. "But we're the good guys."

"Mama Rose is a good guy," Mel added. "She's not helping people because she's naive. She knows these people—really knows them. She cares about them because she's been there."

I nodded. That had become clear the moment we mentioned the name Marina Aguirre. A troubled look had crossed Mama Rose's face and she sighed.

"Oh," she said. "That one. Marina really disappointed me. Most of the time I don't have unreasonable expectations, but Marina had that special something—the spark; the determination. I thought she was going to be a star."

"You remember her then?" Mel had asked.

Mama Rose laughed. "Who could forget her? For one thing, she still had her looks. Most people go to the consignment store or St. Vincent de Paul and come away looking like drudges. Marina came out looking like a rodeo queen, boots and all."

Mel and I exchanged looks. I had told her about that single singed boot I had seen in Ellensburg.

"She was smart," Mama Rose continued. "And she was determined. She told me she wanted her son back."

"How did she lose him?" Mel asked. "A custody fight?"

Mama Rose shrugged. "Could be. She didn't give any details. She was pretty closemouthed about where she came from, but that goes with the territory. Most of the girls don't want to let on to the folks back home that they're working the streets. When Marina walked out on Silver Pines, I assumed she'd decided she wanted to be back in the game and didn't want to tell me to my face. In a way, I don't blame her. Waiting tables at Denny's is very hard work, and it doesn't pay very well—not compared to what she was used to earning. I'm sure she could have done something else eventually, but to do that, she would have had to go back to school and get some training."

It crossed my mind that Marina might not have wanted to change jobs because she was using some long-dead girl's name and Social Security number. I didn't mention any of that to Mama Rose. Instead, I asked, "When Marina disappeared, who cleaned out her unit?"

Tom Wojeck raised his hand. "That would be me. It's pretty tough for Mama Rose to get around much these days. That means I'm the one stuck with doing the dirty work." He smiled fondly at Mama Rose when he said it, as though it was a point of regular teasing between them.

"Did you find anything?"

Tom shrugged. "As I recall, the place was a mess. Worse than usual, especially considering she'd only been in the mobile for a matter of months. But we brought in our cleaning crew, mucked it out, and had it rented again within a matter of days."

"Who's on the cleaning crew?" Mel asked. "Some of the residents?"

Tom nodded. "But as far as I know, nothing of value was found."

"And nothing that would have told you who she was or where she was from?"

"No," he answered.

"What about her vehicle?"

"A 4-Runner, I think. I remember it had Arizona plates. I told her that once she had a job she would need to reregister it and get Washington plates. I don't think she ever got around to doing it."

"After she left, did you do any skip-chasing?" I asked.

"Look," Tom said. "She had paid her rent up until the middle of November. When she wasn't there to pay up on the fifteenth, we packed up her junk and got rid of it. It's not like she owed months of back rent. She was gone, her rent wasn't being paid, we moved her stuff out, and moved someone else in. End of story."

"Her fiancé, a guy by the name of Mason Waters, filed a missing persons report," I said. "I don't think the local cop shop expended much effort on the case."

"Waters," Mama Rose said. "Isn't that the name of the guy whose private eye came around asking questions about Marina a couple of months ago?"

Tom Wojeck nodded. "I think that's the right name, but by the time the detective showed up at Silver Pines, Marina's stuff was long gone."

And so was she, I thought.

With me mentally going over that previous conversation, Mel and I had been silent for quite some time. Finally I noticed that she was only picking at her chicken, which meant she was probably doing the same thing.

"What?" I asked.

Mel shook her head. "So chances are, the young woman in the morgue over in Ellensburg is the woman who claimed to be Marina Aguirre, but we have no idea who she really was. I wonder if we'll ever figure it out."

I wondered that myself.

"And what about Tom Wojeck and Mama Rose?" Mel asked. "They weren't wearing rings."

Being a man, I had somehow missed that small detail altogether.

"I wonder how long they've been together," Mel continued. "I don't think they're married, but they seem to have a good working relationship."

"They're probably as close to being married as you can get," I told her, "especially when one member of the team is HIV-positive."

"Wake up," Butch said. He sat down on the edge of the bed and bounced up and down until Joanna opened her eyes. "Here's some coffee. Time to rise and shine."

"What time is it?" Joanna mumbled groggily.

"Ten to eight," Butch answered. "I already called in and told Kristin you'd be late."

Joanna took a sip of the coffee. "Thank you. But it was a great night. We were working a missing persons case. An old lady named Philippa Brinson walked away from an Alzheimer's home out in Palominas."

"Did you find her?" Butch asked.

"We certainly did," Joanna answered. "They took her to the Copper Queen Hospital for observation, but I think she's okay. Her niece was coming down from Phoenix. Once Ms. Brinson is released from the hospital here, she'll go to Phoenix with her grandniece."

"How about you tell me the rest of it over breakfast," Butch said. "Otherwise you're going to be even later."

Showered and dressed, Joanna went out to the kitchen, where she had to weave her way through a scatter of boy, toys, and dogs to make it to the kitchen table. Dennis, as at home with the three dogs as he was with people, lay contentedly on the floor with his head propped on Lucky's back while he chewed on the ear of a teddy bear that had originally been a dog toy.

While Butch whipped out two eggs over easy with bacon and toast, Joanna told him about the previous evening's adventures. She edited out some parts of the story, focusing less on the appallingly filthy conditions inside Caring Friends. She failed to mention that on Alma DeLong's watch, residents there were treated more like prisoners than patients, or how vulnerable and frail people had been left unsupervised and helpless for hours on end. Instead, Joanna told Butch about how they had successfully tracked down Philippa Brinson.

"Tom Hadlock managed to get an announcement about her being missing on the ten o'clock news from Tucson," Joanna said. "Before the news broadcast ended, we had a tip from a man who called in and who said he had found an old woman standing beside the road in Palominas yesterday afternoon. He had stopped and asked if she needed help. She said she needed a ride to Bisbee, that she had to get back to her office."

"Office?" Butch said. "Isn't she in her nineties?"

"Ninety-three," Joanna said. "But remember, she's an Alzheimer's patient. Things that happened a long time ago are far more real to her than something that happened this morning. She thought she was going back to her office after a noon meeting out at Sierra Vista, and she was clear enough that she convinced the driver she was okay and should be dropped off. The problem is, she left that office for the last time over thirty years ago. Even so, that's where we found her. Up by the old high school. She retired as the county superintendent of schools in 1973."

"So why was she at the high school?"

Dennis abandoned the teddy bear in favor of climbing into his mother's lap to freeload on some of Joanna's toast.

"That's where her office was when she was superintendent, but she had worked there even earlier than that. Back when the old high school was still in operation, she was the school librarian. She wanted to be a principal, but women didn't become high school principals back in the forties and fifties, so she became a school librarian. Then she pole-vaulted over the principal job and became the county superintendent of schools instead."

"Sounds like somebody else I know," Butch said with a smile as he refilled Joanna's coffee cup. "She's okay then?"

"I think so. She was cold, of course. We took her down to the hospital so the ER doctors could check her out and wrap her in warm blankets. By the time we knew she was okay, her grandniece was on her way from Phoenix. The grandniece is hoping to find a facility closer to her home so she'll be able to keep better track of Ms. Brinson's care and caretakers."

"That makes sense," Butch said. "Why didn't she do that to begin with?"

"Philippa Brinson lived in the San Pedro Valley all her life and she didn't want to leave it. She was born there. That's where she and her husband lived after they married, and it's where she wanted to stay. Bad idea. Caring Friends is a joke. The only thing Alma DeLong cares about is her bottom line. And if I can figure out a way to charge her with reckless endangerment, I will."

"You go, girl," Butch said. "So what's on the program today, aside from the bachelor party, that is?"

"A homicide investigation," Joanna said, gulping the last of her coffee. "And I'd better head out, or they'll start the briefing without me."

Chapter 10

In actual fact, most of the players were already assembled in the conference room by the time Joanna arrived. In the old days, Frank would have started without her. Tom Hadlock kept everyone waiting.

"Sorry about my slow start this morning," she apologized, settling into her usual chair. "It was a short night without much sleep, but it was a successful one. Good work, guys, and good work on the media contacts, Tom," she added, addressing her chief deputy. "Without your making that ten o'clock news slot, we might have had an entirely different outcome on Philippa Brinson."

Hadlock accepted the praise with a self-conscious nod. "Marliss Shackleford isn't too thrilled about it," he said with a mirthless chuckle. "She just called to give me an earful about giving a scoop to the Tucson media while ignoring the locals."

Marliss, a reporter for the local paper the *Bisbee Bee,* had long been a fly in Joanna's ointment. In that regard, however, she had recently learned that she wasn't alone. It turned out Marliss was every bit as much of a pain for Alvin Bernard, Bisbee's chief of police. Now, as Tom Hadlock learned the ropes as media spokesman for Joanna's department, Marliss was becoming Tom's problem as well. He would have to learn how to handle her.

"Don't let Marliss get to you," Joanna advised. "She's always on someone's case. If she mentions it again, you might point out to her that the so-called locals don't have a ten o'clock news broadcast. If we'd had to wait until this morning's paper to put out our missing persons announcement, Philippa Brinson might well have succumbed to hypothermia. In that case Alma DeLong would be sitting in jail and facing a possible homicide charge."

"She may be anyway," Deb Howell said. "I just got off the phone with a woman named Candace Welton. She's the daughter of a woman who was a patient at Caring Friends. Her mother, Inez Fletcher, developed a severe infection that turned into sepsis. When she died, the physician who works with the facility listed the cause of death as natural causes, but the daughter thinks the infection started as a result of an untreated bedsore. Her older brother, Bob, was evidently in charge of making the mother's final arrangements. The daughter didn't ask for an autopsy at the time. She was told that because her mother's death was due to natural causes, she'd have to pay for an autopsy herself. She didn't have one done because she didn't have the money. But she's heard about the Brinson situation, and she's asking for one now."

"She's willing to have her mother's body exhumed?"

Deb nodded. "That's what she said."

"If the brother was in charge of arrangements, we'll probably have to clear the exhumation with him as well," Joanna said. "In the meantime, I'll talk to Dr. Machett about it and see what he has to say."

Joanna had no doubt that if George Winfield were still in charge, the investigation would be given an immediate go-ahead. With Guy Machett at the helm, she wasn't so sure.

"What else?" Joanna asked, looking around the table. Jaime Carbajal raised his hand. "I have an appointment with Chuck Savage later on this morning. He's bringing me a copy of the surveillance tape from the Lester Attwood homicide."

"From the camera by the gate?"

Jaime nodded. "According to Chuck, he and his brother installed that camera just recently—only a week or so ago. He also said that when Mr. Attwood found out about it, he was upset. He claimed that if they were putting in a camera, it must be because they didn't trust him, and Chuck Savage told me confidentially that was true. They didn't want to hurt their stepmother's feelings, so they hadn't let on about it to her, but they had heard Attwood was back in the chips—that he seemed to have more money than he should have had. They decided to check up on him.

"They set up the system so there was a video recorder and monitor in Attwood's trailer. The tape from that is missing. Luckily for us, they also created a feed to a second off-site recorder, one Mr. Attwood knew nothing about. That's the one we'll be getting a copy of later today."

"Great. What about the crime scene?" Joanna looked around the table and realized her crime scene investigator, Dave Hollicker, wasn't there. "Where's Dave?" she asked.

"His wife called in and said he didn't get home from photographing the Caring Friends scene until after five this morning," Tom replied. "I told her to let him sleep until he woke up."

"So we don't have photos from either scene?" Joanna asked.

"Not yet. We'll have to take a look at those later, but he did tell me that he found a spot at the far corner of the Action Trail property where it looked like somebody did some pretty heavy loading and unloading. At least three vehicles were involved, along with lots of movement going back and forth."

"A drug-smuggling operation, maybe?" Joanna asked.

"Maybe," Jaime said. "We'll know more once we see the tape."

Without much more to discuss on the homicide situation, the detectives went on their way, leaving Joanna and Tom Hadlock to go over more routine matters. They had finished and were about to leave the conference room when Tom added one parting comment.

"When we were on the phone, Marliss Shackleford asked about Frank's party tonight," he said. "I told her no comment."

"That's correct," Joanna said. "It's a private party. No comment is the right answer."

It was close to midnight before we finally got back home after our side trip to Black Diamond and our late-night dinner. Mel fell into bed and was out like a light. I love the woman dearly, but the truth is, she snores. Most of the time it doesn't bother me, but it did that night, mostly because Tom Wojeck's hairy-chested coffee, combined with indigestion from our late-night dinner, left me tossing and turning. Finally I gave up on sleeping altogether. I climbed out of bed and went into the room that's now our combination family room/office.

I spend a lot of time there now that my recliner has been permanently banished from the living room. I don't blame Mel for insisting that if I refused to opt for a new one, the old one would have to disappear from the living room. The furniture she bought for the living room is stylish and surprisingly comfortable. And, much as I hate to admit it, the recliner no longer measures up.

For one thing, the poor old thing lists badly to one side these days. I had it recovered with leather a long time ago, but even good leather doesn't last forever. It's developed a certain sway to the cushions. And the last time the kids were here, I caught Kayla jumping on it. By the time the grandkids went back home, the recliner had lost the benefit of full motion. It no longer goes all the way up or all the way down. In other words, the recliner is a bit like me—a little butt-sprung and with a hitch in its get-along.

I sat there for a while looking at the city lights playing off the low-lying clouds and thinking about Mama Rose. Finally I picked up my laptop and logged onto the Internet, put in my LexisNexis password, and went looking for Rose Marie Brotsky. And found plenty. Her recent history wasn't nearly as colorful as her earlier history, but as the owner of the Silver Pines Mobile Home Park, she was in the news. A lot.

Somewhere along the way, Mama Rose had missed the memo about not fighting city hall. Just as she had told us earlier that evening, she and her lawyers had taken on the local city council and city manager and had won one round after another. The city had tried to shut down Silver Pines based on the fact that the place harbored registered sex offenders—although, for the most part, former hookers are sex offenders in only the broadest sense of the word. The city next claimed that the mobile home park was too close to a local elementary school, even though the school had been built long before Mama Rose became the owner of the property. But that hadn't worked either. A new survey, conducted at Mama Rose's expense and using modern GPS technology, had determined her property was 2.3 inches to the good. After that, the city had tried to condemn the trailer park under eminent domain so they could sell it to a developer. Her lawyers had succeeded in stopping that one in its tracks as well. In the process, Mama Rose had become something of an idol to property-rights-minded people everywhere.

But if articles about Mama Rose were in abundance, I found no mention of Tom Wojeck, Thomas Wojeck, or even Tommy Wojeck. It seemed he had left Seattle PD and fallen into a hole of utter obscurity. If he had taken up with Mama Rose, a lady of ill repute, it was possible there was more to his quiet exit from the force than anyone had ever let on, and that left me with one option.

When you work partners with a guy, you pretty much have to know everything about him—good, bad, and indifferent. It's the only way you can be sure that when push comes to shove, he'll have your back covered. Or not. And if not turns out to be the case, your very life may be at risk. It seemed reasonable to me that if Tommy Wojeck had left the department with some kind of blemish on his record, Big Al Lindstrom would know all about it. He'd also know where the bodies, if any, were buried.

In order to find out for sure, I'd have to go see Big Al in person and ask him. The big question in my mind that morning was whether or not I'd have nerve enough to do it.

Al Lindstrom had turned in his badge, pulled the plug, and retired from Seattle PD shortly after being shot in the gut while trying to protect an endangered homicide witness, a little five-year-old boy named Benjamin Harrison Weston. Ben Weston Senior, little Ben's daddy, had also worked for the department. Senior had been about to unmask a whole gang of crooked cops when someone had broken into the family home in Rainier Valley and slaughtered the whole family—every one of them except for little Benjamin. He had fallen asleep in a closet during a long-drawn-out game of hide-and-seek. That was the only reason he was still alive—the only reason little Benjy hadn't died that night along with the rest of his family.

Big Al Lindstrom and Ben Senior had been friends, and Big Al took those senseless murders very personally. In trying to protect Ben Junior, he had also taken a bullet. He had recovered from his wounds enough to come back to work for a while, but something had changed for him. His heart was no longer in the job. He told me he had put in his time and now he needed to spend some time with his family. I have to confess that, once he was gone, I more or less forgot about him. Out of sight; out of mind.

I suspect I'm not alone there. Women seem to hang on to their friends with real tenacity. Men don't. I've heard it claimed that's due to our being so egotistical that we don't care about anyone but ourselves. I still keep up with Ron Peters and Ralph Ames on a regular basis, but other than those two, most of my male friendships, which were usually job-related, have fallen by the wayside.

When it came to Big Al Lindstrom, I didn't even know if he was still around. It was possible that he and his wife, Molly, might well have sold out and turned into snowbirds. I doubted he had corked off. If that had happened, I'm sure someone from Seattle PD would have let me know. I remembered hearing that he'd gone in for quadruple bypass surgery a while earlier—was it a year or so ago, or maybe longer?—and I'd even sent a get-well card, but I had been too caught up with my own life—with my new job and my new relationship with Mel—to pay much attention to anyone else. Now I felt guilty because I hadn't made time to go see him—not while he was in the hospital and not later, after he got out.

Wrestling with the question of whether or not I was a worthy friend, I finally drifted off to sleep—with the laptop on my lap. I awakened to find Mel standing over me, shaking her head in disgust. She was up, dressed, ready to go to work, and holding a cup of coffee in her hand.

"You spent the whole night in that chair?" she demanded, passing me the cup. "Are you nuts? Just you wait. By tonight your back will be killing you."

The truth was, now that I was awake, my back was already killing me, but I wasn't about to admit it, not to her.

"Don't worry," I said. "I'll be fine."

She rolled her eyes and then held up her cell phone. "I just got off the phone with Harry," she said. "I told him what we learned last night. He wants all hands on deck and in Federal Way ASAP. Everyone else will be canvassing Silver Pines. I'm supposed to start with Denny's, since that's where Marina was supposedly working at the time of her disappearance. Care to join me?"

It was a fair question. And it shouldn't have been hard to answer, but it was. During our dinner at the 13 Coins, I somehow hadn't mentioned that Tom Wojeck and I had once shared a partner. I can see being squeamish about talking about former spouses or girlfriends with new spouses or girlfriends, but the truth was Big Al was a part of my old life, and I wasn't sure I wanted to bring him into my new one.

"I've got something I want to check out first," I told her. "I'll come down in my own car."

She gave me one of her freeze-your-balls blue-eyed stares. "Okeydokey," she said cheerily, "but do me a favor. Don't leave home without taking some Aleve."

In the old days, if Karen had said those same words, I probably would have regarded them as nagging. Now

I recognized them for what they are—one person looking out for another.

"Thanks," I said. "I will. And once I get there, shall we do lunch?" I added.

She gave me a brushing kiss on her way past. "You tell me. Call me later."

Forty-five minutes after that, I headed for Big Al's place in Ballard's Blue Ridge neighborhood. Despite two cups of coffee, two Aleve, a very long shower, my back was in a world of hurt.

Big Al and Molly Lindstrom's Craftsman bungalow still looked much the same as it had back when he and I were partners, including that awful night when I had come here straight from a crime scene to tell Molly that her seriously wounded husband had been transported to Harborview Hospital. The small front yard was pristine, without a weed in sight. The azaleas on either side of a small wooden porch were awash in bright pink blossoms. They looked far more cheerful than I felt. Since I hadn't called in advance to let Molly and Big Al know I was coming, I wasn't sure of how I'd be received. But I put my misgivings aside and rang the bell. What was the worst that could happen? I'd either find out Big Al had died while my back was turned or he'd be so disgusted when I finally showed my face that he'd bodily throw me out of the house.

Big Al himself came to the door. Having heard about the bypass situation, I expected him to look frail and gray. He didn't. He looked as rosy-cheeked and hearty as ever, but he was leaning on a cane. He gave my face a dubious once-over. I remember seeing that wary look a thousand times when I was out selling Fuller Brush. It means: Who the hell are you and what are you doing ringing my bell? But then he recognized me, and his scowl transformed into a wide grin.

"I'll be damned!" he exclaimed, reaching out to pump my hand. "Look what the cat dragged in. You'll never guess who's here, Molly," he called over his shoulder. "It's J.P."

"As in J. P. Beaumont?" a woman's voice inquired from somewhere inside the house. "After all this time? You've got to be kidding."

Molly Lindstrom appeared then, with her face wreathed in smiles and looking the way I remembered her, apron and all. Her hair was grayer—whiter, really—but other than that she seemed just the same. She grabbed me and hugged me. "Boy," she said. "If you aren't a sight for sore eyes."

I glanced at Big Al, with particular emphasis on the cane. "What's that all about?"

Big Al held it up and looked at it as if he weren't sure what it was. "This old thing? Hopefully I won't have to use it much longer. I kept griping to Molly about how much my knees hurt. She asked me if I was going to complain about it all my life or have them fixed. Now I've got two bionic knees. This is the second one. No telling what Homeland Security will say the next time I try to get on a plane." With that he turned and limped back into their cozy living room. "Come on in," he said to me. "Mol, do you mind getting us some coffee?"

Molly left without a word. Big Al took a seat in an easy chair with tall arms and then set his cane down next to him, carefully making sure it was within easy reach. "So what's this all about?" he asked. "To what do I owe the honor of this visit?"

"You know I've gone to work for S.H.I.T.?" I asked.

Big Al nodded. "For the Attorney General's Special Homicide Investigation Team. I heard you're working with that wild and crazy guy from up in Bellingham. What's his name again?"

"Harry I. Ball," I said.

"That's right. Good old Harry. People used to complain about him . . ."

"They still do," I said with a smile.

". . . but as far as I could tell, he always struck me as a pretty squared-away guy."

"He is," I said.

Big Al straightened in his chair. "It's been a long time, Beau," he said. "So what's up? What brings you here?"

It was a fair question that deserved a fair answer.

"Tom Wojeck," I said. "I seem to remember the two of you were partners at one time. What can you tell me about him?"

"You mean to tell me he's still alive?" Big Al asked, looking surprised. "I thought he died a long time ago."

"No," I said. "He's still around. As a matter of fact, I saw him just last night. He seems to have done very well for himself. Lives in a mansion out by Black Diamond with a woman named Mama Rose Brotsky."

Molly came into the room carrying two mugs of coffee. "Who's still around?" she asked.

"Tommy," Big Al told her. "Tommy Wojeck."

"And he's got a girlfriend?" Molly asked. "That figures."

Molly Lindstrom's disapproval was obvious, but I had to ask. "What do you mean?"

"He was married at one time," she said, "but that never kept him from fooling around."

Big Al nodded. "Tommy liked to walk the wild side."

"I'll say," Molly agreed. "Believe you me, he didn't do that poor wife of his any favors." With that, she turned on her heel and left the room.

"How so?" I asked.

Big Al sighed. "He got himself involved with a gentlemen's club down in Tacoma."

"You mean a strip club?"

"Yes. That's what it was really. Word about Tommy's extracurricular activities got back to the department up here. Internal Affairs was gearing up to do an investigation, but he quit before they had a chance. Not quit exactly. In the middle of all that, he got sick. The powers that be decided they'd be better off medically retiring him rather than putting on a dog-and-pony show and airing all that departmental dirty laundry in public. So they sent Tommy down the road with a one-hundred-percent disability. No muss, no fuss. Besides, they all probably thought he'd be dead and gone within a matter of months. But then he fooled them," Big Al added with a shrug. "When he didn't die on schedule the way he was supposed to, there wasn't a whole lot they could do about it."

I thought about the man I had seen in Black Diamond the night before. He hadn't looked like someone who needed to be on one-hundred-percent disability.

"That's medical science for you," Big Al continued. "What they did to fix my knees wasn't remotely possible not all that long ago. It's the same thing with AIDS. People still come down with it, I'm sure, but not as many are dying of it now as there were when it first showed up back in the eighties. Or maybe they're just not dying as fast—at least not in this country."

"You're telling me Tom Wojeck has AIDS?"

"Sure," Big Al said. "Didn't you know that?"

"No," I said. "I had no idea."

But I did now.

When it came time to leave Big Al's house a little while later, he walked me as far as the door. On a table in the front entry sat a framed photo of a handsome young black man. The suit and tie meant it was probably a senior photo. Big Al caught me studying it.

"That's Benjy," he said in answer to my unasked question. "His daddy would be so proud of him. He's going to Gonzaga in the fall on a full basketball scholarship."

I felt a lump in my throat, remembering a very different little boy, in the aftermath of a horrific home invasion that had left the rest of his family dead. I could still picture him in the pulsing lights of emergency vehicles, clutching a Teddy Bear Patrol teddy bear. That plush bear had been his only source of comfort on what was and would always be the worst night of his life. I was thrilled to know that he was all right now; that he had grown up and was moving forward.

"I'm glad he stays in touch," I said.

Big Al nodded. "Me, too," he said.

As I headed south on I-5, some things about Tom Wojeck that hadn't been clear to me before made sense now. I suspected that Mama Rose Brotsky had used her lottery megamillion windfall to keep herself alive and to keep Tom Wojeck alive as well. They were probably both walking medical miracles. But they were also both connected to a murder victim who had died while pretending to be someone she wasn't. Tom Wojeck had told us he had cleaned out Marina Aguirre's apartment. I had a feeling there might be a few telling details that he had left out of that story, however, and I wanted to find out what they were.

After being out of the office for a day and a half, Joanna was behind the eight ball when it came to paperwork. Shuffling through it to get an idea of what was lurking there, she came across Lester Attwood's preliminary autopsy report. She scanned through it and learned that the victim's body had shown signs of multiple contusions and abrasions as well as numerous broken bones, all of which were consistent with having been struck several times by several different moving vehicles. None of those were fatal wounds. What had actually killed him was being left facedown and unconscious in the sand. Cause of death was suffocation.

When Joanna reached the line with Dr. Machett's florid signature, she picked up her phone. The M.E. answered, but he wasn't happy to hear from her. "I can't believe how much damage that crazy old battle-ax did to the van when she pulled me out of the sand. It's at least a thousand bucks' worth of body work."

And you think that's my fault? Joanna thought. That's what you get for not waiting for a regular tow truck!

"Sorry to hear it," she said, hoping she sounded more sympathetic than she felt. She went on to give Guy Machett an overview of the problems at the Caring Friends facility, ending with the fact that the body of another possible victim might need to be exhumed.

"Why wasn't an autopsy done at the time?" Machett wanted to know. "That's how it's supposed to work, you know."

Joanna ignored the man's condescending sarcasm. "From what Detective Howell told me," she said, "the woman was supposedly under a doctor's care at the time she died. Family members were informed that, since she had died of natural causes, if they wanted an autopsy it would have to be done at their expense. They couldn't afford it. Now that there's a possibility of wrongdoing on the caregiver's part, however, all bets are off."

“All right,” Machett agreed reluctantly. “I’ll see what I can do.”

“Good,” Joanna said. “We’ll put Detective Howell in charge of this case since she’s already had some interaction with the family. I’ll have her contact you to work out the details—necessary court orders and so forth. In the meantime, Detective Carbajal will be doing some of the Caring Friends interviewing and helping Ernie Carpenter with the Attwood homicide.”

Joanna knew that at that very moment Ernie was on his way to interview Lester Attwood’s former girlfriend in Benson. While Jaime awaited the arrival of the backup security tape from Action Trail Adventures, he was hoping to interview Alma DeLong and Sylvia Cameron, who, as far as Joanna knew, were still being held in the Cochise County Jail.

With only three detectives in her department, dealing with two cases at once meant that her investigative unit was acting at full capacity. And so was she. Once she finished with the phone call to Machett, she turned to her daily deluge of paperwork.

During her years as sheriff, Joanna had learned to love the investigative part of the work—bringing down bad guys and putting them away. The administrative part of the job? Not so much.

An hour later, she had pretty much cleared the decks when, with a tap on her door, Jaime let himself into her office.

"We've got the backup file from the security company at Action Trails," he said. "I loaded it onto a disc. Want to take a look?"

"Sure," Joanna said. "Let's see it."

He popped the disc into Joanna's computer. Several moments later, her screen came to life with a series of ghostly nighttime images. Clearly the security camera was set to record only when there was activity in its field of focus. While Joanna watched, three vehicles came through the gate and past the camera. Two were 4-by-4 trucks with ATVs loaded in the back. The third was a hulking van of some kind. All three vehicles came through the gate one after the other, starting at 12:58 A.M., according to the time stamp in the corner of the screen. Immediately after they entered the property, the gate closed. The vehicles turned to the right and drove off past the point where Joanna had parked her Crown Victoria when Ernie had given her a ride out to the crime scene.

On the recording the next scene appeared immediately, but the time stamp said 1:10 A.M. In this scene the gate was still closed. Instead, an ATV erupted from somewhere offscreen—most likely from somewhere near Lester Attwood's trailer. The vehicle crossed the camera's limited line of vision and then disappeared.

"Is that Lester Attwood's ATV?" Joanna asked.

Jaime nodded. "That's what Mr. Savage said—that the one on the screen now belongs to our victim. The way I see it, the three vehicles arrive from outside about one A.M. and enter the property. A few minutes later, Mr. Attwood goes rushing off in the same direction. Now watch this."

Joanna stared at the screen. A pair of headlights pulled into the camera's field of focus and stopped. A door opened. A shadowy figure emerged from the vehicle and quickly walked out of the frame. A moment later, Joanna's screen went blank and returned to her desktop directory.

"That's it?" she asked. "That's when they wrecked the camera?"

Jaime nodded again.

"So the people in the three arriving vehicles were up to no good and wanted to destroy the evidence," Joanna said thoughtfully.

"That's how it looks to me."

"Can we go back and replay the videos slowly enough to get license plate numbers?"

"Not from this," Jaime said. "The resolution isn't good enough. In order to do that, we'll have to enhance what's here. We can try. It probably won't be easy because we don't have the right equipment. I've got a call into the Department of Public Safety crime lab up in Tucson to see if they can help."

"If you were going to get a security camera, doesn't it stand to reason that you'd get one where the resolution would actually tell you what you need to know?" Joanna asked.

Jaime shrugged. "There's that old saying: You can have good, cheap, or quick. Pick any two. I'm guessing the Savage brothers opted for cheap and quick."

"Let's hope the DPS video guys can ride to the rescue on this," Joanna said as she removed the disc from her computer and handed it back to Jaime. "And what about Alma DeLong? Did you talk to her?"

Jaime shook his head. "Nope. She lawyered up. I'm guessing, when she goes before the judge, he'll let her post bail on the assault charge."

"That's probably just as well," Joanna said. "We can leave her on the loose until we have a better idea about whether we can charge her with anything else. What about the patients?" Joanna added. "How are they?"

"The two in the hospital at Sierra Vista and the one in Bisbee are all in satisfactory condition. Philippa Brinson has been released. The patient who was transported to Tucson is in the ICU at Tucson Medical Center. She's listed as critical and may not make it."

"What about the nurse?"

"She's still in the jail. This is her third DUI in as many years. She's asking for a public defender."

On the one hand, Jaime was just giving her information, but there was something in his guarded tone that warned Joanna something was wrong—something that had nothing to do with what had happened at Caring Friends or at Action Trail Adventures.

"What is it?" she asked. "What's going on?"

Rubbing his forehead with one hand, Jaime sank back into his chair. For a long moment after that, he stared out the window, disconsolately examining the limestone cliffs that crowned the steep hillsides behind the Cochise County Justice Center.

"What?" Joanna asked again. Then she remembered the previous day's difficulty with Jaime's nephew. "Is this about Luis?"

Jaime nodded. "I went to the high school late yesterday afternoon and spoke to the principal."

"Debra Highsmith isn't one of my favorites," Joanna said.

"Mine, either," Jaime said. "But she came through this time. The office keeps a comprehensive list of all the padlocks on the lockers—a list of who has which locker and what the combination is. The students and the parents sign a contract at the beginning of the year. If the lock on any given locker isn't on the official list or on the right locker, the administration has the right to cut it off."

"You're saying you went through Luis's locker?" Joanna asked.

Jaime nodded bleakly, and Joanna's heart sank. She knew a lot of bad stuff had a way of turning up in high school lockers these days, everything from illicit drugs to illicit weapons.

"I take it you found something?"

"It's a letter," Jaime said. "A letter Luis wrote to his father in prison, asking if he knew where his mother was."

"That's hardly surprising," Joanna said. "In fact, under the circumstances, I'd be surprised if he didn't try to find her. Luis could have had lots worse things in his locker."

"The letter hadn't been opened until I opened it," Jaime continued. "Someone at the prison had sent the envelope back to Luis with the word D-E-C-E-A-S-E-D written across the address in big red letters."

Joanna was appalled. "Luis's father is dead and that's how the poor kid found out about it?"

Jaime nodded. "Whoever crossed out the address had no idea who Luis was. The return address is to a PO box in Bisbee—a PO box Luis rented in his mother's name and without my knowledge, by the way. He evidently forged his mother's name to make it work, and he was using the address to try to find her—to find Marcella. I guess he didn't want Delcia and me to know what he was up to."

"How long ago did the letter come?"

"A month ago," Jaime said. "Which is about the time things started going downhill with him at school. Before that he had been doing fine. After this came, he fell apart."

"And when did his father die?" Joanna asked. "Were you able to find that out?"

"I called California first thing this morning and spoke to the warden's office," Jaime said. "Marco Andrade died the last week in October. On October 31. Someone shanked him in the shower. According to the corrections officer I spoke to, they have no idea who's responsible. It was a medium security facility with more drug dealers than anything else."

"Why wasn't Luis notified?" Joanna asked.

"That's what I wanted to know as well," Jaime said. "Marcella is listed on Marco's prison records as his next of kin, but the address he gave was her old one.

When she and Luis moved down here from Tucson, she didn't tell anyone where she was going and she didn't leave a forwarding address, either."

"Because she didn't want to be found," Joanna added.

Jaime nodded. "Because she and Marco had evidently ripped off money from one of their fellow drug dealers or maybe from one of their drug suppliers. I don't know which. At any rate, according to the warden's office, they did attempt to notify the family about Marco's death."

"But they didn't try very hard," Joanna added.

"Exactly," Jaime agreed. "But if whoever did this was able to get to Marco inside the walls of the prison, what if they decide to come after Luis? Any bad guy who gets a look at Marcella's missing persons report will know everything he needs to know. If she was reported missing from here, this is the logical place to find her son. Bisbee's a small town. If somebody comes here looking for Luis, they won't have much trouble finding him."

"In hopes he might still have the missing money," Joanna said.

Jaime nodded again.

"Did you tell the warden's office that Luis is your nephew?"

"I didn't even mention Luis," Jaime replied.

"I seem to remember your telling me about one of Marco's drug-dealing pals in particular . . ." Joanna began.

"That's right," Jaime said. "His name is Juan Francisco Castro. His street name is Paco. He used to live in Tucson and was a minor player for the Cervantes gang out of Cananea. Supposedly he's the one Marco and Marcella ripped off."

"Where's Paco now?" Joanna asked.

"He seems to have disappeared. I have some pals inside Tucson PD, and I've made some discreet inquiries. No one seems to have any idea where Paco is at the moment. For all I know, he could be dead or he may have gone back to Mexico."

"Is there a chance he landed in the same prison where Marco died?" Joanna asked.

Jaime shook his head. "Nope. I already asked. That would have been too easy." For several long moments they sat in silence. Finally Jaime continued. "So what do I do about Luis?" he asked glumly. "How do I handle this?"

"We," Joanna said, emphasizing the pronoun. "We handle it by protecting him. We do everything in our power to protect him, including, if necessary, sending him to live someplace else until we find out who was responsible for his father's death."

If need be, we'll send your whole family somewhere else, Joanna thought.

"But what do I tell him?" Jaime insisted.

"You tell him exactly what you told me," Joanna replied. "That you're afraid whoever killed his father might come looking for him next."

"There's a problem with that."

"What problem?"

"I wouldn't have known Marco was dead if I hadn't broken into Luis's locker. How's he ever going to trust me again when he finds out about that? He probably already knows, because there was a new lock on his locker when he got to school this morning."

"Look," Joanna said, "you broke into his locker because you love him. Tell him you knew something was bothering him and you were trying to find out what it was."

"I suppose I could lie to him," Jaime said. "What if I told him I found out about Marco through work?"

Joanna stood up. She came around the desk and sat down next to Jaime. "Don't do that," she urged, placing a hand on his knee. "A lie takes constant maintenance. One thing leads to another until it screws up your life. You know that. It's what you do in interview rooms—you catch crooks in the little lies so you can nail them on the big ones.

"Considering the kinds of stunts your sister pulled over the years, don't you think your nephew has been lied to enough? Even if Marco was a bad father, he was still Luis's father. Tell him the truth about how you found out and then be there for him when he needs you to be. It takes time to grieve. That poor kid has been doing it all on his own. No wonder he's been a problem at school."

Jaime Carbajal thought about that for a moment. Finally he nodded. "You're right, boss," he said softly. "Luis Andrade has been lied to long enough."

Chapter 11

I caught up with Mel in Federal Way in time to buy her lunch at Marie Callender's. She had spent the morning at Denny's talking to the people who worked there, and she was sick of it. She wanted to eat somewhere else.

"So what did you find out?" I asked over steaming potato soup with a side of corn bread.

Mel shook her head. "It's one of those places with enough employee turnover that there's zero corporate memory. Well, maybe not quite zero. One of the cooks thought he maybe remembered someone named Marina, but he wasn't sure. They evidently had the manager from hell for a while and everyone who could walk away did so. In that regard, Marina was no different from anyone else. She left without telling anyone and without bothering to pick up her final paycheck. That was sent in the mail."

"To Silver Pines?"

"That's the address they had," Mel told me. "That's the only address they had."

"Was it ever cashed?" I asked.

"Nope. It came back."

"But no one bothered to mention that she had disappeared."

"No one from work. What did you find out?"

"I went to see an old buddy of mine from Seattle PD." I was going to let it go at that, but then I remembered that Mel and I are married now. And that bit about "the truth, the whole truth, and nothing but the truth" is a good idea if you want to stay that way. "Al Lindstrom and I used to be partners," I added. "He used to work with Tom Wojeck, too. Big Al claims Tom Wojeck left under a cloud. And that he has AIDS—has had for years."

"Big Al," Mel mused, latching on to the part of what I'd said that I would have preferred her to skip. "How big is he?"

"Not that big," I told her. "There were two Als in his class at the academy. He came out Big Al, the other one came out Little Al."

"What happened to Little Al?"

"He quit right after graduation. Went to work for State Farm or Farmers selling car insurance."

"But the Big Al part stuck?" Mel asked.

"Pretty much," I said.

As far as the partnership deal was concerned, I thought I had gotten off relatively easy. What I failed to understand is that God has a sense of humor about these things, and He was about to show me an ex-partner problem that was a whole lot more complicated than Big Al Lindstrom.

"Anyway," I continued, "from what Big Al told me, Tom Wojeck had a dark side that caused him to leave Seattle PD in a hell of a hurry. They were about to launch an Internal Affairs investigation. Then he was diagnosed with AIDS before I.A. got around to him."

Looking thoughtful, Mel said, "And Tom Wojeck just happens to be the same guy who cleaned out Marina's apartment where there might have been some stray drug-dealing money."

Sometimes Mel's uncanny ability to put things together makes me feel like she's reading my mind, but don't get me wrong. I love it when she does that.

"Yes, ma'am," I told her. "Want to do a ride-along and go see him?"

"What do you think?" she returned.

So back we went to Black Diamond. This time I drove. When we cleared the trees on the driveway to Mama Rose's house, I wondered at first if we had somehow made a wrong turn.

The night before, the house with all its lit windows had been our main focus. In the daylight it was even more impressive. It was a sprawling two-story home with a standing-seam steel roof in a gleaming copper color—a choice that made sense in a house that was in the middle of nowhere with forest all around. The outside walls were covered with neat gray siding. The many windows were trimmed out in impeccable white, and an expansive veranda covered the entire front of the house. What hadn't been apparent on our previous visit was that this was clearly a work in progress.

Last night we had been the only visible vehicle. This time, however, when we broke through the trees it looked as though we had landed in a subdivision-in-progress. The place teemed with machinery, trucks, and workers. A dump truck was unloading an avalanche of man-sized boulders. A jigsaw puzzle of white PVC pipes was laid out in a complicated pattern indicating that a comprehensive irrigation system was being installed. There were workers everywhere. A whole group of them was laying down a flagstone walkway that led from the edge of the veranda down to where another group of workers was installing a metal trellis over a big water feature of some kind. That, too, was under construction.

Tom Wojeck, wearing muddied work boots and denim coveralls, seemed to be overseeing much of the action. He left a huddle of workmen and came over to where Mel and I were climbing out of the car.

"Patrol cars seemed to have come up in the world since I quit the force," he said, casting an approving glance in the direction of my S550 Mercedes, which, except for the color, was very much like the one in Tommy and Mama Rose's garage.

"It's mine," I said. "They let us use our own rides these days. I bought it used and got a great deal on it."

Mel doesn't have a lot of patience with boy/car small talk. She likes driving fast cars fast; she doesn't like standing around discussing them.

"What's all this?" she asked, waving toward the beehive of activity.

Wojeck shrugged. "If Mama Rose wants a rose garden, we build a rose garden. Like that old song 'Whatever Rosie wants; Rosie gets.' I designed it myself, with a little help from a landscape architect. We've got a hundred and eighty varieties of roses that should be arriving in the course of the next week or so. That's why we're doing a full-court construction press right now."

"That's a lot of roses," I said. "Who's going to take care of them?"

"We have a full-time gardener who'll be doing that," Tom said. "And you'll notice that we've regraded the entire area so the walkway is wheelchair accessible coming and going."

He was clearly proud of his project, and I couldn't blame him for that, but we weren't here as building inspectors. "So which is worse?" I asked. "AIDS or MS?"

Tom gave me a sharp look. "So you know about that?"

I nodded. "I talked to Big Al. And to Molly."

"I suppose Molly is still pissed at me?" he asked.

"That's a reasonable assumption."

"She was good friends with Abbie, my ex. Did you know we were neighbors at one time? Big Al and I used to carpool to work."

I hadn't known that, but it stood to reason.

"I didn't give it to her, thank God," he went on. "We'd been fighting a lot, which isn't exactly conducive to rolling in the hay. As soon as I got the diagnosis, I moved out. She took the kids and moved to Spokane, where she ended up marrying another cop. I would have thought she'd have learned her lesson after marrying me, but her second husband is more of a team player than I ever was. I believe he's moved up to being an assistant chief."

"Was Mama Rose one of your girls?" Mel asked.

"She wasn't," Tom said. "We met at a support group, several months after Abbie and I split. We were the only heterosexuals in the group, so we sort of bonded. At the time, we were both down on our luck. Rosie wasn't doing very well, and neither was I. It was looking like we were both going to be short-timers, but that's when Mama Rose won her Powerball prize. That changed everything—for both of us. It turns out there are things money can buy. We found doctors who got us into clinical trials. And here we are."

"You're married?" Mel asked.

Tom shook his head. "No point," he said. "We're registered domestic partners. Her AIDS strain is different from mine. If I happened to give mine to her or if she gave hers to me, it could be fatal. Actually, long-term, with all the medications we take, it's probably fatal anyway. If the disease doesn't get us, side effects will. If she dies first, I'm set for life. If I die first, the folks from the AIDS Partnership will dance on my grave."

"Why's that?" Mel asked.

"Because a big chunk of whatever I don't get will go to them. Overnight, they'll turn into the city's eight-hundred-pound charitable gorilla. But somehow I don't think you came all this way to ask about Rosie's and my health or the state of our domestic tranquillity."

"We had a few more questions about Marina Aguirre," I said.

Just then one of the French doors opened, and Mama Rose wheeled her walker out onto the veranda. It was a chilly spring day, with temperatures still in the fifties. She was wrapped in a heavy-duty sweater over a maroon-and-gray Cougar sweatshirt. It made me wonder what connections a former prostitute and her best boy might have with Washington State University.

"What's going on?" she called down to us.

"We're just asking a few more questions," Mel told her.

"Well, come inside to ask them," Mama Rose ordered. "I've asked the cook to make more coffee. It's cold out, Tom. If you just stand around talking, you'll end up with pneumonia."

With that she turned around and tottered back into the house. I was surprised Tom didn't object to that summary summons—at least he didn't voice an objection aloud to her. I suppose if you're already walking around with AIDS, coming down with pneumonia isn't a good idea. I could see that Mama Rose's calling Tom inside was a lot like Mel telling me to take my Aleve. Only more so.

"I don't want to discuss this in front of her," Tom said urgently. "Ask me now and then get the hell out of here before you make things worse."

"I take it Marina is a sore spot?" Mel asked.

Tom nodded. "But not the way you think. I never touched her. Rosie loved that girl; thought she walked on water. I think she saw a lot of herself in Marina, and she really wanted her to succeed in getting out of the life. I've never told her what really happened."

"And what was that?"

"Look," he said impatiently. "I never would have done it if I hadn't thought Rosie's life was in danger. She means the world to me, understand?"

"What happened?" I insisted.

"Some guy showed up out here—right here in the yard. A tough guy—a Hispanic tough guy. I don't know how he found us but he did. He said Marina had ripped off a friend of his. He said he knew Marina had taken off again, but he thought she might have left the money in her trailer at Silver Pines or else with us."

"When was this?" Mel asked. She was already taking notes.

"Sometime in early November," Tom said. "I know it was before her rent was due. The guy knew Marina lived at Silver Pines, but he didn't know which unit. He wanted me to go into her place and look for it."

"Did you?" I asked.

"Yes, I did. I checked it out."

"Why?"

"Because he made it pretty clear that if I didn't, something bad would happen to me or to Rosie."

"Did you find anything?" I asked.

"Yes, I did," he answered shamefacedly. "It was there in the freezer compartment of her fridge—several Ziploc bags filled with cash. Not a very original hiding place, if you ask me."

"How much was there?" Mel asked.

"I didn't count it all. It looked to be fifty thou or so. Maybe more. Tell me this. Where does a girl who's waiting tables at Denny's come up with that much moolah? I figured she was either dealing drugs or else she stole it, both of which are against Mama Rose's rules. So I gathered it up, hauled it out of the house in a brown paper bag and gave it back to the guy who came looking for it."

"Are you kidding?" Mel asked. "You gave away that much money just like that—because some asshole claimed it belonged to a friend of his?"

"It had to," Tom said. "Who else's would it have been, and how would they have known about it? Besides, in the larger scheme of things, it wasn't that much money. Choosing between giving it back and protecting Mama Rose or calling in the long arm of the law wasn't a big contest."

I couldn't help wondering if Tom was telling us the truth or if he was conning us. His cell phone rang just then. "I'm coming," he said without bothering with a hello. "I'll be right there." Then, after a pause, he added, "It'll just be the two of us. They won't be staying."

"And you didn't tell Mama Rose about any of this because . . . ?" I asked when he ended the call.

"Because Marina was supposed to be one of Mama Rose's rising stars. She had a job and a boyfriend. The boyfriend was legitimate, as far as I can tell. I don't think he had anything to do with the drug money. I was planning on finding a way to bring it out in the open the next time we went to collect Marina's rent, but it turned out there never was a next time. The guy who came here was right. Marina had already taken off for good. She must have realized the bad guys were closing in on her. She bailed in such a hurry that she left the money behind."

Mel stood with her pen poised over the paper. "Any idea about the ID of the crook who threatened you?"

Tom shook his head. "No idea. I did some checking at the time. Like I said, we're not too popular with the city administration in town, but out here in the boonies, Mama Rose is something of a folk hero. When the guy came back to pick up the money . . ."

"He came here?" I asked.

"Yes. I already told you. He knew where we live. But when I handed off the money, I made a mental note of the vehicle license. You know how it goes. Once a cop, always a cop. You're trained to remember those kinds of details, and that training never goes away. But then, just to be sure, as he was leaving, I went one step beyond that and managed to take a photo of his license plate. Later I checked with one of our local deputies. The vehicle turned out to be stolen—no surprise there. What was left of it wound up in a chop shop down in Tacoma a few days later."

"So you don't know who the guy was," Mel said again.

"No, I don't. And I've got to go now. Otherwise Rosie is going to start asking questions."

My impression was that he was playing it straight, so I gave him one of my cards. "If you think of anything else, call us."

"Right," he said. "I will."

He walked away, heading inside for his coffee. Mel and I got back into the Mercedes. Mel looked unhappy.

"What's wrong?" I asked.

"I think he was gaming us," she told me. "I think he's the kind of guy who could look you straight in the eye and lie through his teeth."

Which only goes to show that we're not always on the same wavelength.

"We were gaming him," I pointed out. "We didn't tell him we're pretty sure she's dead."

"So?" Mel asked.

I sighed. "Where to now?" I asked.

She picked up her phone. "I'll call into the office and see if Barbara has any marching orders for us. And it's Lola, by the way," she added, waiting for Barbara Galvin to pick up.

All of a sudden I was lost. I had no idea what we were talking about.

"It's 'Whatever Lola wants, Lola gets . . .' Not Rosie. It's a song from *Damn Yankees. The Year the Yankees Lost the Pennant.*"

It annoyed me to think that Mel felt it necessary to repeat the title like that. I mean, I understood *Damn Yankees* the first time. And I didn't understand why, just because Tom had misquoted a song lyric, that somehow made him more suspect than he was before.

As we drove back toward Federal Way, I couldn't help wondering how Mel and I had ended up being mad at each other. How had that happened? But then I remembered another very useful quote: "Men are from Mars; women are from Venus."

Based on my slim experience with the opposite sex, that's a good rule of thumb. Right that minute, however, Mel was looking and sounding a lot like Mars.

Because Joanna had spent so much time out of the office the previous two days and because she knew she'd be leaving early that afternoon to help get ready for the bachelor party, she had brought along a sandwich for lunch. She ate it at her desk, accompanied by some coffee Kristin brought in from the break room. She had just tossed the wrapper in the wastebasket and was about to go back to work when Ernie Carpenter stalked into the office.

"What the hell's going on with Jaime?" he wanted to know, dropping heavily into one of Joanna's chairs. "I stopped by the bull pen on the way in. I was about to tell him what I'd found out in Benson. He about took my head off. I know his nephew's been giving him all kinds of hell, but still . . ."

The "bull pen" was home to Joanna's homicide unit. It had been crowded when only two investigating officers, the Double C's, as Ernie Carpenter and Jaime Carbajal were called, had been the occupants. Now that there were three detectives, including one female, the bull pen was not only misnamed, it was also beyond overcrowded. Joanna's suggestion that they steal some space from Patrol had met with adamant resistance. Her best bet in this situation was to try to placate Ernie.

"You're right," Joanna said. "I'm sure Jaime has his hands full of family issues at the moment."

"Don't we all?" Ernie asked.

"Tell me what you found out."

Shaking his head, Ernie pulled out a notebook and opened it. He leaned back in the chair, crossed his legs, and scanned a page covered with cursive writing that was tiny when you considered it came from a man of his size and girth.

"Deb was on the money when she said we should track down the girlfriend. Believe me, LaVerne Hartley is a piece of work."

"From what Margie Savage told us," Joanna replied, "I thought LaVerne was Lester's ex-girlfriend."

"She was ex up until a month or so ago, but once the guy had some spending money again, she was ready to let bygones be bygones. They were back to being an item before he turned up dead."

"He ended up with money?" Joanna asked. "How much money?"

Ernie nodded. "Enough that he was able to buy her a slick little turquoise ring. To hear her tell it, they were practically engaged."

Joanna realized that squared with what Lester Attwood's sister had told them at the crime scene—that LaVerne was a good-time girl. According to her, if Lester had no money, there was no LaVerne.

"So where was Lester getting all this extra cash?" Joanna asked.

"That's what I'd like to know," Ernie agreed. "Whatever it was, LaVerne claimed that she had no knowledge of anything out of line. He claimed the Savages had given him a raise."

"Not according to Margie Savage," Joanna put in.

Ernie nodded. "That didn't seem too likely to me, either. As for Jaime, he was good enough to tell me what was on the security tapes. Too bad we didn't get better visuals, but what about this for an idea? What if drug traffickers were routinely using Action Trail Adventures as a rendezvous point? And what if Lester was in on it?"

"Good point," Joanna said thoughtfully. "Action Trails is a long way from anywhere, but it comes with a clear reason to have traffic coming and going on a regular basis. It would give dealers a relatively private place to make their load transfers without anyone being the wiser. Lester probably saw the wisdom of letting them do it. All he had to do was keep quiet to earn a little extra cash on the side. Everything was peachy-keen until the Savage brothers came up with the bright idea of installing video surveillance."

"Right. And if the traffickers were about to be caught, so was Lester," Ernie said. "I think that's what happened the night of the murder. Lester went out to warn them. First they took him out, and then they came back to do away with the recording equipment without realizing that the Savages had a backup system running somewhere off site."

"There were ATVs on two of the trucks in the video," Joanna said. "Dave's analysis suggests that there were three vehicles used in the attack on Lester. If they're using the ATVs as camouflage—as a ticket to come and go from out-of-the-way places with no questions asked—what are the chances that they've pulled the same stunt at other spots as well—other places where ATV enthusiasts hang out? We need to find a way to enhance those videos."

Ernie nodded and stood up to go. "Jaime told me he was working on the enhancement situation. In the meantime, I'll start checking to see if I can find any other locations they might have used. Maybe we'll get lucky and find someone who bought better surveillance equipment."

Ernie left then, and Joanna went back to work. She had promised Butch that she'd leave by three to help out with party preparations.

Debra Howell came by just as Joanna was clearing her desk. She was furious. "Machett turned us down," she said. "He says that Inez Fletcher's son refuses to allow her remains to be exhumed regardless of what his sister says."

"Did you get a look at the death certificate?"

"Better yet, I have a copy of it."

"Who signed it?"

"Someone named Dr. Clay Forrest."

"Never heard of him," Joanna said.

"He's from Tucson," Debra replied.

"Which means he's probably a close personal friend of Alma DeLong," Joanna said. "See what you can find out about him."

Debra nodded and headed for the door. "By the way, have fun at the party tonight," she added on her way out.

"I don't understand why I couldn't invite everyone," Joanna said. "I mean, we've all worked together for years."

She had been upset when she had learned that Dr. LuAnn Marcowitz's bridal shower was scheduled for the same evening and time as the bachelor party.

"Don't give it another thought," Deb said. "I spend more than enough time with these clowns. I'm happy to be going to a ladies-only event."

"I'd be glad to trade places."

"Too bad, boss." Deb Howell grinned. "No way. Hosting the bachelor party goes with the best-man territory. I hear you're playing poker?"

"That's right," Joanna said. "Texas Hold'Em."

"Is Dr. Machett coming?"

"He may," Joanna said. "We invited him because we pretty much had to, since George Winfield will be there, too. After all, Machett will be working with Frank's department as well as ours. I don't know for sure if he sent back an RSVP."

"If he shows up, then," Deb Howell said, "do me a favor and clean his clock."

Joanna nodded. "I'll do my best."

When I returned from my musings, Mel was still on the phone. She had dragged her notebook out of her purse and was taking notes with a kind of indecipherable shorthand that is beyond my capability.

"Okay," she said finally to Barbara. "Thanks for the good news. Sounds like we're making progress."

"What progress?" I asked when she closed her phone.

With any other woman, it would have been different, but Mel doesn't carry a grudge. We may have spats from time to time, but when the fight is over, it's really over, as this latest one evidently was.

"Brad may have found Marina's vehicle," she said.

Brad was Brad Norton, one of our colleagues and a fellow investigator for S.H.I.T.'s Squad B.

"Stolen?" I asked.

"Not exactly," Mel said. "Brad was checking statewide for any 4-Runners that showed up in police reports around the time Marina disappeared. He found one with Arizona plates that had been parked with the hazard lights on and the keys still inside at an abandoned weigh station on I-90 east of Issaquah."

That sounded about right to me. "When was it found?" I asked.

"In the early morning hours of November 9."

"That would fit," I said. "That's right in line with the time Marina disappeared."

Mel nodded in agreement. "When the vehicle was found it was in good running order," she continued. "The keys were in it and it still had gas in the tank. When a Washington State Patrol officer ran the plates, he found out that the registered owner was a woman named Frances Dennison, who lives in Tucson. She told him that the previous summer she had decided that the 4-Runner was getting to be too much for her. She wanted something smaller, but since the dealer wouldn't give her what she thought her vehicle was worth in trade, she had sold it herself."

"When was this ?"

"Back in July. She listed it in something called the *Nifty Nickel* and sold it to a young woman—a young Hispanic woman—who paid her thirty-five hundred in cash and promised that she would go straight to the vehicle licensing office to change the title."

"Which, of course, she didn't do."

"Right."

"Does the woman in Tucson have a bill of sale?"

"Yes," Mel answered. "Brad asked her to look at it, and she did. Evidently the buyer's signature is an illegible scribble."

"Why am I not surprised?" I asked. "What happened to the car?"

"Brad says there was no sign of foul play in the car. No blood; no nothing, including no fingerprints. The steering wheel and door handles had all been wiped clean, which was suspicious, but since Frances was still the registered owner of the vehicle, they returned it to her. Her grandson flew up, paid the impound fees, and drove it back to Tucson."

"Is the grandson still driving it?" I asked.

"As far as we know."

"There might still be forensic evidence inside," I said.

"Right," Mel said. "Brad's already working on that."

That's one of the good things about working for S.H.I.T. We're all on the same team and usually on the same page, and we all pull in the same direction. I don't get the feeling that there's someone waiting in the woods to undermine me. Ross Connors is the state attorney general, but he's someone who engenders a lot of personal loyalty. Yes, he's a politician who has a bit of a problem with demon rum, but he's also the best boss I've ever had. He's a straight shooter who doesn't stand on ceremony. He always backs up his people, and he gets as good as he gives.

Nursing a case of pre-party jitters, Joanna came home to find what they had come to call the "Gang of Four"—Jenny and Dennis and Carol Sunderson's two grandsons, Rick and Danny—playing in the side yard, where she and Butch had installed a redwood kiddie gym set, complete with a minifort, slide, teeter-totter, and swing.

It was a busy scene. Dennis was strapped into the toddler seat on the swing, with Danny, Carol's younger grandson, pushing him to what Joanna considered breathtaking heights. Rick, the older boy, was practicing pitching tennis balls into the far distance, with three of their collection of dogs—Jenny's Tigger and Lucky along with the Sundersons' sheltie, Scamp—racing to retrieve them. Joanna's more dignified Australian shepherd, Lady, was content to look on from the sidelines while Jenny practiced her lassoing technique on the handle of the teeter-totter.

Joanna parked in the garage. Not ready to face the house, she left her briefcase on the car seat and went to see the kids.

Over the months, she had found plenty of reasons to be grateful for the tragedy that had brought Carol and her two boys into the picture. After a fierce trailer fire left Carol's husband dead and her and the two boys homeless, it had been Joanna's mother, Eleanor, who had come up with the idea of letting Carol and the grandsons live in Joanna's old house on High Lonesome Ranch in exchange for helping manage Joanna and Butch's sometimes chaotic household. The arrangement gave Carol a job that came with a stable place for her and the children to live. Within weeks of Carol's arrival on the scene neither Butch nor Joanna could imagine how they had functioned without her.

The Gang of Four was a natural outgrowth of that arrangement. Over the months the four kids had become pretty much inseparable. Despite the age differences, they seemed to get along fine. Jenny had taken it upon herself to teach Rick and Danny both how to ride her sorrel quarter horse, Kiddo. And all three of the older kids were tremendously patient with Dennis, whom they regarded alternately as either an annoying pest or else a beloved mascot.

Hearing Dennis's gleeful squawk, Joanna realized this had to be one of the mascot days.

"Hey, Mom," Jenny said. She caught the handlebar with her rope, shook it off, and then recoiled it to throw it again. "Butch and Carol threw us out. They're setting up for the party and said no kids or dogs allowed."

All of which made good sense.

"But we get to have pizza for dinner," Danny added. "Pepperoni. Wanna come?"

"She can't," Jenny told him. "She's got to go to the party."

Joanna had grown up as an only child. She had been an adult when she finally met her older brother, who had been given up for adoption long before her parents married. Jenny, too, had spent most of her young life as an only child. With that kind of background, Joanna had been amazed to see how the four kids managed to cope with one another. Sometimes the four were all the best of friends; sometimes they weren't. Joanna often found herself wondering if that wasn't how real sisters and brothers functioned.

There was a redwood picnic table next to the gym, and Joanna eased herself onto one of the benches. "I think I'd rather have pizza," she said.

Jenny gave her mother a questioning look and then came over to sit down beside her. Jenny was about to turn fifteen, but she was already a good five inches taller than her mother and still growing.

"What's wrong, Mom?" Jenny asked. "Are you okay?"

"The best man seems to be having a case of nerves," Joanna admitted. "I've never been to a bachelor party, much less hosted one."

"I don't know why you're worried about it," Jenny told her. "You should be used to doing weird things by now. You'll be fine."

Joanna couldn't help laughing at that bit of reassurance. That one word—weird—pretty well said it all. In Jenny's book, having her mother be sheriff or "best man" was pretty much one and the same.

Danny let Dennis out of the swing and he came racing toward Joanna at a toddler's broken-field dead run. "Mommy, Mommy, Mommy," he squealed gleefully, hurtling himself into her lap. "Denny swing! Denny swing."

"I saw you," she said, gathering him into her arms. "What a big boy you are."

She hung out with the kids for a while, but before long Carol emerged from the house. "All right, kids," she said. "Time to gather up and head out. We'll keep the dogs at our house tonight. Except for Lady, of course."

Scamp and the kids piled into Carol's station wagon and she drove away, with Lucky and Tigger trailing behind. Meanwhile Lady shadowed Joanna as she closed the garage door, collected her briefcase, and went inside.

"What can I do to help?" she asked.

Glancing at his watch, Butch came over to kiss her hello. "Not a thing," he said. "Carol and I have it all under control. The rented card tables and chairs are all set up, the food and drinks are in the fridge, chips and dips are out. All you need to do is get dressed. And you'd better hurry. People will be here soon."

Joanna disappeared into the bedroom and stripped out of her uniform. She had bought a bright green blouse to wear with her jeans that night, along with a pair of boots that she had inherited from Jenny when her daughter outgrew them. As for Jenny appropriating some of her mother's clothing? Jenny's last sustained growth spurt made that no longer an issue.

With her hair combed and her makeup retouched, Joanna headed out to the living room to play hostess just as the first guest arrived. In terms of food, Butch and Carol had clearly outdone themselves. They had assembled an inspiring array of chips and dips and salsas to serve as ice-breaking snacks. Knowing that most of the guests would have a law enforcement background, Frank had insisted that his bachelor party would be a booze-free zone. Since Frank was now joining Joanna in a media fishbowl, she had applauded the decision. Neither she nor Frank could afford to have any of their officers picked up and charged with post-party drunk driving.

Frank had also made his wishes clear when it came to proposed party entertainment. He placed an absolute embargo on the idea of strippers. Period. He and Butch had settled instead, on the idea of a roast augmented by a charitable poker party, with all proceeds from Texas Hold'Em going to Frank's charity of choice, the Jail Ministry. Since this would be considered social gambling, there had been no need to purchase any kind of gaming license, but just to be sure, Butch had checked out the applicable statutes with the county attorney well in advance of the party. His inquiry to Arlee Jones's office had given Butch the information he needed, but it had also backfired and generated a minor tempest all its own due to the fact that Arlee—also at Frank's behest—hadn't been invited to the party.

The guests arrived one and two at a time. With the exception of a couple of relatives, most of the guests came from Frank Montoya's world of work. Some were old colleagues and some new colleagues. To begin with, the two sets of folks seemed to stalk around one another, stiff-legged and suspicious, until Butch's smooth program of hospitality began to work its magic. Before long, people were laughing and talking and settling in to have fun.

In advance of dinner being served, Ted Chapman, the Jail Ministry's executive director, circulated among the snack-munching guests hawking poker chips. "Best of luck to you," he said with a smile each time he managed to extract a twenty- or thirty-buck donation from someone's pocket. "And don't worry. There are plenty more where these came from. God does provide, you know," he sometimes added with a wink.

Joanna's mother and stepfather had delayed their planned springtime departure for Minnesota long enough to enjoy the festivities. That meant George Winfield was there on his own. As M.E. emeritus, he seemed to be enjoying himself immensely. To Joanna's considerable relief, Guy Machett was a welcome no-show. The last guest to arrive was Frank's older brother

Thomas, who had driven down from Phoenix. When Joanna opened the door and found him on the porch, she felt more than a little guilty. By rights, Thomas Montoya should have been Frank's top choice for best man, but he didn't seem the least bit offended by the oversight. He greeted Joanna warmly, first with a handshake and then, after a moment's consideration, with a hug as well.

"Now where's that little brother of mine?" he asked as Joanna ushered him into the house. And with that, Thomas Montoya went wandering off in search of the groom.

Chapter 12

About the time Butch stepped outside to grill the steaks, Frank's ritual roasting began in dead earnest, and for the most part it was good clean fun. Old and new colleagues alike teased him about trading in one short red-haired woman for another, taller model. (Frank's fiancée, LuAnn Marcowitz, was a good six inches taller than Joanna, and her hair—a wild tangle of bright red curls—was a good six inches longer than Joanna's hairdo as well.) Joanna was glad no one mentioned that both she and the bride tended to be bossy at times.

People pulled Frank's leg about his going for an "older woman." LuAnn was four years older than Frank, and there were plenty of people who were ready to assure him, jokingly or not, that, as a longtime bachelor, he would soon regret stepping into the middle of a ready-made family.

That thought had occurred to Joanna as well. Frank was used to the peace and quiet of living by himself. She wondered how he'd manage with a new wife, two teenage stepchildren, and a mother-in-law, all living under the same roof. On the other hand, Joanna knew he'd been lonely for a long time. Even so, a sudden dose of that much togetherness, combined with a stressful new job, might be challenging for anyone to handle.

But Tom Montoya had the final word on the family situation. "My mother had given up on Frank's ever having children a long time ago," he told them. "I can tell you she's thrilled to have a new set of grandchildren, no matter how she gets them."

For the time being, his comment carried the day.

A while later, Butch enlisted Tom's help in bringing the steaks back into the house. They brought in separate platters loaded with mouthwatering grilled rib eyes on Fiesta Ware platters. Steaks on the red platter were rare. The ones on the peacock-blue platter were medium, and the few scrawny steaks on the black platter were well done.

Before Carol left, she had set out stacks of plates, silverware, and napkins that would make serving easy. The platters of cooked steak took the place of honor at the top end of the counter, next to the plates and cutlery, but they were soon joined by the rest of the abundant feast: a huge bowl of mixed-greens salad; two kinds of potato salad, hot and cold; a steaming crock of cowboy beans accompanied by a vat of fiery jalapeño-dotted salsa. At the far end of the counter was the bread-and-butter station, which boasted two loaves of freshly baked and sliced sourdough bread and several pie plates of corn bread.

Joanna waited until the guests had loaded their plates before she filled her own. Then she wandered into the family room and took one of the few remaining spots at one of the tables—a chair that happened to be next to Jaime Carbajal's. He had come to the party because he had said he would be there, and he was clearly having to make an effort to be part of the festivities.

"How's it going?" Joanna asked.

He shrugged. "Okay, I guess," he said.

"You don't sound very convincing," Joanna told him. "Did you talk to Luis about his father and about the locker situation?"

"Yes," Jaime said.

"How did it go?"

Jaime shrugged. "He was pretty mad at first and stormed off into the bedroom. But I think you're right. He'll get over it and come around eventually. It'll take time. He and Pepe were still in their room talking when I left to come here. I could hear their voices, but I couldn't hear what they were saying."

Pepe, Jaime's son, was only a few months younger than his cousin.

"I suppose Luis had already told Pepe about what had happened to his father." Joanna's comment was more a statement than it was a question, and Jaime shot her a sidelong glance.

"How did you know that?" he asked.

"You've told me before that Pepe and Luis are close, more like brothers than cousins. Since they're also kids, it stands to reason that if Luis had confided in anyone, it would have been Pepe. That's a good thing, Jaime. Give Luis some credit. He was smart enough to realize he couldn't deal with this crisis by himself. We should all be thankful that he had someone to go to with his troubles. We should also be glad that he was smart enough to go looking for help."

"You're right," Jaime agreed. "I am glad about that, but what about Pepe? My son knew all about this for a long time, but he never let on to me. That hurts, boss. It really hurts. Pepe and I have always been close. I don't like finding out that he's been keeping secrets."

"Of course he's keeping secrets," Joanna told him. "Why wouldn't he? Pepe may be your son, but he's also a teenager. Keeping secrets goes with the territory."

Even as she said the words, Joanna couldn't help wondering what secrets her almost-fifteen-year-old daughter might be keeping from her. On the surface, Jenny was a joy. She helped around the house, adored her little brother, and had a part-time job helping out at a local veterinary office. She was also within months of having her learner's permit. Joanna knew only too well the kinds of secrets she had kept from her own mother at that age. The possibility that Jenny might be doing the same thing and pulling the same stunts was disturbing. Joanna didn't want to go there. On the other hand, it turned out that at the time Joanna's mother had been keeping quite a few secrets of her own.

"The boys will be all right," Joanna assured him. "Both of them."

"I hope so," Jaime said.

Joanna waited for a moment before she went on. "With all the turmoil at home, I don't suppose you had much time to work on the Action Adventures video enhancement problem."

"I made some calls," Jaime said. "I've got an appointment at the DPS crime lab in Tucson tomorrow morning. I'll hand over what we've got and see what they can do with it."

I dropped Mel off at the restaurant parking lot where she'd left the Cayman, and we drove back into town in the throes of afternoon traffic. I know, I'm always griping about the traffic here, but I can't help it. There are too many cars and not enough roads, and when I see one of those signs that say construction is coming and drivers should find alternate routes, I know it's a joke. For a lot of roads around here there are no alternate routes.

Once back at Belltown Terrace, Mel went out for her daily run while I worked my way through several crossword puzzles. After that, we set out on foot to find some dinner. Even on rainy days, the late afternoons and early evenings are often clear and warm. And that was the case as we walked down Second Avenue.

When I first moved to the Denny Regrade, the streets had been lined with tiny sticks of newly planted trees. Now they're fully grown, complete with root systems that play havoc with the smooth surface of the sidewalks. Still, I enjoyed our walk along beautiful, tree-lined Second Avenue with bright green leaves softening the hard-scape lines of surrounding buildings.

We walked as far as Mama's Mexican Kitchen, where we managed to score an outside table. That gave us a chance to watch the varied denizens of the Regrade—from the homeless people wheeling their possession-laden grocery carts to the high-flying BMW drivers jockeying for free parking spaces.

But we also talked shop. While Mel sipped her Dos Equis and downed a combination plate and I nursed a root beer along with my order of taquitos, we picked apart everything we had learned about the timeline of Marina Aguirre's disappearance and death. I had just popped the last bit of taquito in my mouth when the phone rang.

"Bingo," someone said in my ear.

I didn't recognize the voice, and I didn't recognize the phone number, either. For a moment I thought maybe it was one of those annoying solicitation calls where the Knights of Something or Other want me to buy a ticket to their annual charitable auction.

"I beg your pardon," I said. "Who's calling, please?"

"It's Lucy," she said. "Detective Lucy Caldwell from Ellensburg. This is my cell. I thought you'd want to know that we've IDed our victim. I just got the notice from Bob Craft over in the M.E.'s office. They entered her dental X rays in the national dental records database and got a hit. Her real name is Marcella Andrade. She was reported missing on July 16 of last year."

I had pulled my notebook and pencil from my pocket, and tipped my head in order to hold the phone to my ear while I took notes.

"Marcella Andrade," I wrote. "Disappeared July 16. From where?"

"From Arizona," Lucy answered. "The missing persons report was written by someone named Detective Jaime Carbajal. He's with the Cochise County Sheriff's Department," she added. "He's also listed as the next of kin because he's the victim's brother. Dr. Hopewell and I thought that since this goes across state lines and since the attorney general's office is involved, it might be best if the next-of-kin notification came from you instead of from one of us."

That's what I mean about God having a sense of humor. I had been reluctant to blab to Mel about my partnership with Big Al Lindstrom, but that was nothing compared to this!

You see, I happen to know the sheriff of Cochise County. Her name is Joanna Brady. She's a cute little redhead—make that a feisty little red-haired fireball. The two of us had worked a case together a couple of years ago. In the aftermath of a dramatic shoot-out where either one of us might have been killed, Joanna and I had shared a powerful but momentary attraction.

And that's all it was—momentary. Admittedly it was a hug that could have turned into much more, but Joanna Brady was married, even if I wasn't at the time, and neither one of us was prepared to play that game. So I came back home to Seattle, she stayed on in Bisbee, and life went on as usual. Until now.

"What?" Mel wanted to know.

I ignored her. "How do you spell that last name again?" I asked.

Lucy read off the letters. "It's Hispanic," she explained. "I believe the *j*'s are pronounced like *h*'s."

I remembered meeting Detective Jaime Carbajal. The *j*'s were most definitely *h*'s.

"What's going on?" Mel asked.

"They've identified our victim," I told her.

"Where's she from?"

"Arizona," I told her. "Bisbee, Arizona."

But, of course, Lucy hadn't said a word about Bisbee. I had supplied that little detail on my own.

"Obviously you know Cochise County," Lucy said. She sounded relieved. "I hope that means you'll be willing to handle the next-of-kin notification. I've only done one or two of those, and I'm not very good at them. I'm always afraid I'll fall apart and make a fool of myself."

"Right," I agreed. "We'll take care of the next-of-kin notification. Can you give me the contact information?"

So she did. She dictated all the gory details—the phone numbers and addresses that would make it possible for me to mess up Detective Carbajal's life with the terrible news that his sister had been murdered. And just because he was a cop wouldn't make it easier.

In a way it made it worse, but diligently writing it all down gave me a chance to put off having to tell Mel what she was waiting to hear. It was a useless diversion, however. It didn't work, not at all.

Mel was still gunning for me when I got off the phone. "Something's the matter," she said accusingly. "I saw the look on your face. It was like you had seen a ghost. What's going on?"

The waiter came by. "Can I get you anything?" he asked.

He had people standing outside, waiting for tables. The question was a polite way of saying how about getting moving, but I didn't take the hint. Instead, I ordered another beer for Mel and another root beer for me. Then I told Mel everything. I told her all about my encounter with Sheriff Joanna Brady; about how the two of us had chased a bad guy down a dry riverbed and how we had survived a shoot-out that left the bad guy dead. As for us? We were very much alive and grateful to be so.

"But nothing happened," I said as I finished. "Nothing at all."

There was a long disturbing moment when Mel said nothing. Finally she nodded. "All right then," she said, making up her mind to accept what I'd told her at face value. "You should call Sheriff Brady. If the victim's brother works for her, she's the one who should tell him. It'll be better coming from her rather than from a complete stranger over the phone. And we shouldn't make that kind of call from here."

Mel looked around the sidewalk patio and caught the waiter's eye. "Check, please," she said. "We need to go."

We started back toward Belltown Terrace walking hand in hand.

"Did I ever tell you about Big Al Lindstrom?" I asked.

"Not really," Mel said. "Other than what you told me today. Why?"

"He's a great guy," I told her. "I worked with him for a couple of years—up until he got himself shot."

"Oh, boy," she said. "Don't tell me this is another one of those J. P. Beaumont missing partners stories, is it?"

"Pretty much," I said.

"You'd better tell me then," she said. "I need to know."

So I told her about that, too. Thinking about it now, I can see exactly what I was doing—stalling. The longer it took us to get back to Belltown Terrace, the longer I could put off making the call to Sheriff Brady and ultimately to Jaime Carbajal.

No matter how long I do this job, making those tough calls never gets any easier.

Once dinner was over, people began sorting themselves into tables for the poker games. Joanna had learned to play poker at her father's knee. D. H. Lathrop had taught her well, and her skill at the game was well known both within the department and beyond. As a consequence, her table was the last one to fill up.

The other tables had already started playing and Joanna was about to cut the cards for hers when the landline phone rang in the kitchen. For several years after Joanna's first election, she had served as county sheriff while still keeping her residential phone number listed in the phone book. In the course of a rancorous reelection campaign, however, she'd been the target of so many crank calls that she and Butch had finally been forced to move to an unlisted number. Now when calls came in on the landline, they were usually for Jenny.

When the phone rang, Joanna assumed that would be the case this time as well. Instead, a moment later Butch appeared in the doorway between the rooms, holding the kitchen's portable receiver in one hand and motioning for her to come answer it with the other. Joanna tried shaking her head, hoping he'd take the hint and tell whoever was calling that she wasn't available. Her head shake seemed to make Butch's motions that much more insistent.

What now? she wondered irritably. Can't Tom Hadlock handle anything on his own?

With a resigned sigh and without dealing the cards, she passed the deck to the guy sitting next to her—Bisbee's chief of police, Alvin Bernard. Then she excused herself and went to the kitchen to take the call.

"Sheriff Brady?" an unfamiliar male voice said when Butch handed her the phone.

"Yes," she said. "Who is this? I'm really busy at the moment. I have guests. If you'll excuse me—"

"It's Beaumont," the man said urgently. "J. P. Beaumont. Remember me?"

The words stunned her. Beaumont? She remembered—all too well. Hearing both the voice and the name, she was reminded of that one moment in particular. To her dismay she found herself blushing from the top of her collar to the roots of her hair.

Even though their encounter was years in the past, she remembered it as if it had been yesterday. She and the Washington State investigator had found themselves conducting a joint investigation, one that had ended with a life-threatening encounter with a dangerous killer. In the aftermath of that, Joanna and the visiting detective had been caught up in a moment of emotional heat that could easily have gotten out of control.

There was no question that the attraction had been mutual. They had both felt the momentary magnetism. What shamed Joanna now was knowing she had been the instigator in that situation, the one who had made the first move. She might well have gone on to moves two and three as well if Beaumont hadn't called a halt by summoning her back to reality. She was, after all, a married woman. And once Joanna came to her senses, she agreed wholeheartedly.

As the blush subsided, Joanna stepped into the doorway of her home office to continue the call.

"Of course I remember," she said. "How nice to hear from you again."

That was an outright lie. Hearing from him again was anything but nice. With Butch back in the kitchen cleaning up after the party and with a houseful of company, this was not a good time to be reminded of things past. It wasn't that Joanna had been unfaithful to her husband—it was that she might have been.

"How are you doing?" she asked. "And how did you get my number?"

It seemed unlikely to her that Beaumont would have kept her old phone number or had access to her new one.

"I called your office and spoke to your chief deputy," Beaumont told her. "A Mr. Hadlock, I believe. When I told him why I was calling, he said I should probably speak to you directly."

Joanna's heart gave a little squeeze—a premonition that something was seriously out of whack. Everyone in the department, including Tom Hadlock, knew that handing out her unlisted number to anyone was a big no-no. This had to be important.

"Why?" she asked. "Is something wrong?"

"Actually, there is," Beau replied. "I'm calling about one of your cases—a missing persons case from last year, a young woman named Marcella Maria Andrade."

Jaime's sister! Joanna thought at once. "Marcella," she repeated. "Have you found her?"

"Yes," he said. "I'm afraid we have."

Right at that moment Joanna was unable to recall the name of Beau's agency, but she understood that he worked homicide and the tone of his voice told her what she didn't want to hear—Marcella's story wouldn't have a happy ending.

"She's dead, then?" Joanna asked.

"Yes," Beaumont responded. "I'm afraid so. It turns out she has been for several months. The partial remains of an unidentified female homicide victim were found near a town called North Bend, Washington, late last week. It took until today for the M.E. over in Kittitas County to get around to entering the victim's dental X rays into a national missing persons database. Notification of the hit came back to her office late this evening. When the local homicide dick called to tell me about it, I felt I should make the call."

During the course of the evening, Jaime had gradually loosened up. For the first time in months, Joanna had actually heard him laugh. The previous summer, Jaime's life had been slammed with two separate disasters. First had come the line-of-duty death of his young protégé, Deputy Dan Sloan. At about the same time, Jaime's sister, Marcella, had abandoned her son and disappeared. Since then, Jaime had walked around with a black cloud over his head. Peering around the doorjamb, Joanna looked into the family room, where she spotted Jaime chatting amiably and sharing a joke with Frank Montoya's new second in command.

Joanna wished she could preserve that precious moment of lighthearted banter, but she couldn't. It would be gone the moment Jaime heard the bad news.

"Her next of kin is listed as her brother," Beaumont continued. "A man named Jaime Carbajal. I think we met when I was there in Bisbee."

As he spoke, Joanna could find no discernible subtext in Beau's Joe Friday, "just the facts, ma'am" delivery. Maybe she was the only one who actually remembered that moment.

"Yes," Joanna replied. "That's correct. Jaime is one of my homicide detectives."

"In view of that, I was hoping I could ask you to let the family know."

"Of course," she said at once. "Absolutely. You don't even have to ask. I'll handle that right away."

The moment I get off the phone with you, she thought.

"The information I have also makes mention of the victim having a son," Beau continued. "Is there a chance he could provide us with any information about his mother?"

Joanna suspected that might be true. It seemed likely that Luis had known more about his mother's lifestyle and her unsavory friends and associates than he had ever admitted to anyone, including his uncle or his cousin. Joanna also understood that's what homicide investigators do—they backtrack through the victim's circle of family and friends trying to find clues about what happened and why, but Joanna's first instinct was to protect Luis Andrade from everyone, including J. P. Beaumont.

"He might be able to help you," Joanna conceded, "but not right now. First he learns his father is dead, and now his mother—"

"Wait a minute," Beau interrupted, pouncing on that bit of information. "You're saying his father is dead, too? What happened to him?"

"Luis's father, Marco Andrade, was a small-time drug dealer. Detective Carbajal learned this morning that Andrade was murdered in prison several months ago."

"I'll need the details on that as well," Beau said. "The two cases could be related."

"Yes, they could," Joanna agreed. "And I'll have Jaime be in touch with you about that as soon as I can. I'll have him call you, but not until after the family is notified."

"Of course. Do you need my number?"

"No, thanks. If this is the right number, I can get it off caller ID. But tell me about what happened to Marcella, and why you are involved."

"My agency is investigating a series of homicides that all have the same MO," Beau said.

"Which is?"

"It's ugly," he said. "We have a total of six young female victims. We suspect that some or all of them may have had connections to prostitution, although Marcella had evidently been making some effort to get out of the business. All of them were bound and gagged, wrapped in construction tarps, and then set on fire."

"While they were still alive?" Joanna asked.

Beaumont sighed before he answered. "Possibly," he said. "And in every case but Marcella's the victims' teeth were forcibly removed at the time they were killed."

"In order to make identification more difficult?" Joanna asked.

"Exactly."

Joanna was appalled. And she hated hearing about these horrifying details. What she hated even more was knowing they would have to be passed along to Jaime so that he in turn could give the devastating information to his parents and to Marcella's son, Luis.

Joanna retreated into her office far enough to collect a piece of paper and a pen. "When did all this happen?" Joanna asked. "And where?"

"We haven't established a definite time of death. At the time she disappeared, Ms. Andrade was living in Federal Way, Washington, under an assumed name. She had evidently appropriated the ID of one Marina Aguirre, who died as a child. She was waiting tables in a local Denny's. As I said before, I think she was trying to put her past behind her."

That may be a comfort, Joanna thought. But not much.

"Any idea when the body will be released?" she asked.

"We're not talking about a body," Beau cautioned. "Skeletal remains only. Her family needs to be prepared for that. As far as a schedule for releasing the remains, her family will need to discuss that with the medical examiner over in Ellensburg."

He gave her the names and applicable phone numbers.

"And where exactly is Ellensburg?"

"A couple of hours east of Seattle on I-90."

"All right," Joanna said after writing it all down. "I'll talk to Jaime, and then I'll have him call you."

When the call ended, Joanna stood in the quiet of her office for a moment, gathering herself. Out in the living room she heard the sound of easy laughter, but she had moved far away from the world of bachelor party fun and playing poker. She went back to the kitchen looking for Butch, who was grabbing a fresh set of sodas. He took one look at her face and got it.

"What's wrong?" he asked.

"How are you at Texas Hold'Em?" she asked.

"I stink. Why?"

"Because Jaime and I are leaving," she said. "I just found out that his sister's been murdered. I have to go tell him."

Joanna went back into the family room and beckoned for Jaime to come with her. He put down his cards and followed her into the hallway. "What's up?" he asked.

"It's Marcella, Jaime," Joanna said with a catch in her throat. "I've just received a call from a homicide detective in Washington State."

"A homicide detective." He repeated the words aloud and in the process seemed to come to an understanding of what they meant, even if he didn't want to. "She's dead, then?" he asked.

Joanna nodded. "Murdered."

The naked shock on Jaime's face left Joanna momentarily unable to speak. She knew that look from the inside out as well as all the hurt that went with it. She had been there herself on the day Andy died.

After a few moments, though, Jaime's cop mind switched on. "Where?" he asked. "When? What happened?"

"I don't know the details, but she's evidently been dead for several months," Joanna replied. "Her skeletal remains were positively identified through dental records late this afternoon."

"I'd better go," Jaime said. "I need to tell Luis and my parents."

He made as if to turn away, but Joanna caught his arm. "Wait," she said. "Let me change my clothes. I'll go with you."

"You don't need to . . ."

"Yes, I do," she insisted. "Please."

She handed him the piece of paper with her scribbled notes. Jaime studied it for a moment. Before he could say anything more, she pressed her cell phone into his hand.

"Use this to call the detective," she said. "I put his number in this. All you have to do is hit 'send' twice. That should take you straight to Mr. Beaumont. I'll be right back."

Joanna hurried into the bedroom, where she stripped off her jeans and the bright green top. Next-of-kin notifications were tough, but this one in particular required a certain protocol and decorum. One of the grieving family members happened to be a teenager who was about to lose his second parent. Such an occasion called for nothing less than a full-dress uniform.

As Joanna went about putting on her uniform, it seemed to her as though she was also putting on the job. She had zipped up the pants, had fastened the Kevlar vest, and was buttoning her shirt when the name she had been searching for finally came through.

"S.H.I.T.!" she muttered aloud, just as Butch came through the bedroom door and closed it behind him.

"What's wrong?" he asked. "If you've lost a button, change shirts. Cussing about it isn't going to help."

"I wasn't cussing," she said. "I just remembered. S.H.I.T. is the name of the outfit in Washington, the one J. P. Beaumont works for. It's called the Special Homicide Investigation Team."

"Oh," Butch said. "I see. Beaumont. Isn't that the same guy you worked with a couple of years ago?"

Joanna nodded and hoped to hell she wouldn't blush again. Fortunately she didn't.

Butch walked over and waited patiently for her to finish with her shirt. Once she had fastened the last button and tucked in the tail, he gathered her into his arms for a long hug.

"I know you have to go," he said. "I came in to kiss you good-bye and tell you to be careful."

"Thank you," she said, kissing him back. "I will be."

I always am.

Once I hung up, it seemed like only a few minutes had passed before the phone rang again. Mel had gone into the bedroom and slipped into "something comfortable," as they say. It was a slick enough outfit that, as soon as I saw her again, I started having amorous ideas. The ringing phone, however, effectively put an end to any considerations other than work.

"Beaumont here."

"My name's Jaime Carbajal." The man's voice cracked as he spoke.

I hadn't expected to hear back from him quite that soon. "I'm so sorry for your loss," I told him.

If Jaime heard my expression of sympathy, he didn't mention it. Instead, he asked a question I didn't expect. "Did you find the money?"

I paused for a moment, taking stock. Was Carbajal referring to the same money Tom Wojeck had mentioned? And if so, how did Marcella's brother know about it? Maybe he was involved somehow, and if he was, he wouldn't be the first cop who had been enticed over to the dark side by the siren song of easy money.

"What money?" I asked aloud. If you don't know what the hell you're talking about, answering a question with a question is usually a good strategy.

"When my sister left here, she had a sum of money in her possession."

"How much?" I asked.

"I have no idea how much," he returned. "I didn't see it. Her son, Luis, did. He said it was quite a lot."

So we need to speak to the son after all, I thought. "Do you have any idea where the money came from?" I said aloud.

"We believe it was money Marcella's husband had stolen from a drug dealer down here in Arizona. But now the husband is dead, too. He was murdered in prison in California several months ago. Somebody shanked him. I'm guessing that whoever killed him may also be responsible for killing Marcella."

"Do you have any idea who?" I asked.

"I've only been able to pull up one name, Juan Francisco Castro," Jaime said. "His street name is Paco. He's a drug dealer who moves back and forth between Arizona and Mexico, and probably California as well."

I wrote down the name.

"Do you have any idea where Paco might be right now?"

"Not really. I've had feelers out all along. So far nothing's turned up."

In the background I heard Joanna Brady's voice. "Ready?" she asked.

"I have to go now," Carbajal said. "We've got to go talk to my nephew, Marcella's son."

That wasn't a job I envied.

"You go ahead," I said. "But keep me posted. If you learn anything on your end, let us know. We'll do the same."

"What?" Mel asked.

I handed her the piece of paper I had used to jot down Juan Francisco Castro's name. "Let's look into this guy," I told her. "He may be the one."

Without another word, we both reached for our respective laptops.

When they stepped out of the house, Joanna took one look at the yard. The garage door was blocked by several parked cars. The only way to retrieve her Crown Victoria would have meant going back inside and asking several guests to abandon their poker hands long enough to come move their vehicles. When Jaime wasn't at work, he drove a Toyota Camry. As a latecomer to the party, no one had blocked him in.

"It's all right," Joanna said. "I'll ride with you."

"Why don't you just stay here—" Jaime began.

Joanna cut him off in mid-sentence. "I'm coming," she said determinedly. "When we finish, if I need to, I'll get one of the night-shift deputies to bring me home."

Once buckled into Jaime's car, they were silent as he maneuvered down the bumpy dirt track that led from the house back down to High Lonesome Road. As they bounced across the cattle guard at the end of the of the ranch's private road, Joanna caught sight of a vehicle tucked in close to the fence line and the stand of mesquite trees behind it. Caught up in his own thoughts, Jaime seemed not to notice and started to drive past.

After registering the vehicle's presence, it took only a moment for Joanna to identify it. The snub-nosed Toyota RAV-4 sitting just beyond Joanna's mailbox belonged to none other than reporter Marliss Shackleford.

"Stop, please," Joanna said. "Go back."

Jaime pulled a U-turn. The Camry's wheels had barely stopped moving when Joanna hopped out of the passenger seat. She charged over to the parked SUV and rapped sharply on the window, which Marliss eventually opened.

"What are you doing?" Joanna demanded. She asked the question, but she already knew the answer. Marliss was here hoping to dredge up some dirt on someone; whose dirt it was hardly mattered.

"It's a party," Marliss said.

"Yes, it is," Joanna agreed. "And I'm quite sure you weren't invited. As I said before, what are you doing here?"

"I wanted to see who all came."

You wanted to see if anyone had too much to drink before they left, Joanna thought. "Now would be a good time for you to leave," she said.

"This is a county road," Marliss objected. "You can't order me off it. I have every right to be here."

"She's right, boss," Jaime called from behind her. "Leave her be. Let's go."

"Where are you going?" Marliss asked. "What's so important that you're leaving in the middle of your own party?"

Joanna definitely didn't want Marliss trailing along behind them. Taking a deep breath, Joanna suddenly found herself remembering Marianne Maculyea's sermon from the previous Sunday. It had been all about turning the other cheek, along with the verse from Proverbs about a soft answer turning away wrath. Maybe, in this situation, giving a soft answer was the only solution.

"When we left, Butch was about to serve dessert," Joanna said. "I'm sure there's plenty to go around. Why don't you mosey on up to the house and see for yourself who all's there?"

Joanna saw at once that her invitation left Marliss torn. She wanted to know all the details about who had come to the party and what was going on. She was also curious about where Joanna was going. In the end, curiosity about the party won out.

"Are you sure it'll be all right?" she asked, turning the key in the ignition.

"Absolutely," Joanna said. "Tell Butch I sent you."

Joanna stood there and waited while Marliss turned her RAV-4 around and headed up the road toward the house. As soon as she got back in Jaime's car, he put it into gear.

"Thanks for getting rid of her," he said. "I don't think I would have been that nice."

Chapter 13

When the next-of-kin notifications had been made, Joanna asked Deputy Raymond to drop her off at home. By then the bachelor party was long since over. She fell into bed and into a sound sleep. When she staggered into the kitchen the next morning with Lady at her heels, Joanna was amazed to see that the place was clean as a whistle and unnaturally quiet. Dennis and the three other dogs were evidently still at Carol's place. Butch had made use of the child- and dog-free time to haul the rented tables and chairs out of the family room and to return pieces of furniture to their customary positions.

"How was it?" Butch asked, studying her face as he handed her a cup of coffee.

"Pretty rough," she admitted, stroking Lady's long smooth fur.

"Pretty rough" was an understatement. It had been more than rough. Joanna would never forget how fifteen-year-old Luis had heard the awful news of his mother's murder in stoic silence. Only when Jaime finished had the boy's narrow shoulders slumped. He had turned away and tried to bolt from the room, but Jaime had caught him on the way past. Engulfed in a smothering embrace, the boy had sobbed brokenly into his uncle's chest.

Eventually, leaving the boy in the care of Jaime's wife, Delcia, Joanna and Jaime had gone on to take the bad news to Jaime's parents' house. The moment Elena Carbajal answered the bell and saw who was standing on her doorstep, she knew why they were there. She had burst into a keening wail of grief before either Jaime or Joanna said a word. The gut-wrenching sound had prompted Jaime's father to burst into the living room. He had emerged from the bedroom wearing slippers and pajamas.

"What is it, Elena?" Conrad Carbajal, Jaime's father, had asked. "What's going on?"

Jaime, as he had done with Luis, was the one who gave his parents the bad news.

"Naturally the parents blame themselves for what happened to their daughter," Joanna told Butch over coffee. "But parents always do. Marcella was evidently a headstrong, out-of-control teenager. She ran off at age seventeen without ever completing high school. Her parents disapproved of her friends and her life-style, but they were thankful when she and Luis moved back here a year or so ago. At least that gave them a chance to look out for Luis."

"How's Jaime doing?" Butch asked.

"He's on bereavement leave as of this morning," Joanna answered. "Naturally he's devastated."

"Why wouldn't he be?" Butch replied. "When someone dies, the people who are left behind assume that they're somehow the root cause—that the tragedy happened because of something they did or didn't do at some critical juncture."

Joanna nodded. "You've got that right," she said. "On our way uptown Jaime told me about a family Easter-egg hunt when he and Marcella were little. He was three years older than she was. She was running. She tripped and spilled her basket. Jaime tried to find all the missing eggs and put them back. He traded some of his own good eggs for some of her broken ones."

Butch looked puzzled. "What does that have to do with the price of tea in China?"

"I think that was probably the first time Jaime tried to smooth things over for his little sister, but I think he's been doing the same thing all his life."

"Except this one can't be smoothed," he said.

Just then Carol Sunderson bustled in through the back door with a bright-eyed Dennis parked on her hip and with the three boisterous dogs trailing behind. None of them seemed any worse for wear for having spent the night away from home. For the next several minutes the kitchen was a chaotic circus of dogs and boy as Dennis did his best to relate everything that had gone on the evening before. Eventually, though, Dennis trotted off, taking the dogs with him. In the sudden quiet, Butch turned to Joanna.

"How about some breakfast?" he asked.

"Toast, maybe," Joanna said. "I'm not very hungry."

While Butch set about fixing it, Joanna leaned back, rested her head against the wall behind her, and closed her eyes.

"So what's the plan?" Butch asked.

Joanna looked at her watch. "It's supposed to be a light day," she said. "The daily briefing first and then the Board of Supervisors meeting. After that, you and I are supposed to have our farewell lunch with my mother and George, followed by a haircut and a wedding rehearsal."

The plate Butch set in front of Joanna contained a piece of buttered toast along with a hunk of leftover steak. "Have some protein," he advised. "Even the

Energizer Bunny needs to refuel sometime. Oh, and about that lunch," he added.

George and Eleanor Winfield were about to embark on their second snowbird season, driving back to George's Minnesota cabin in their motor home. They had delayed their spring departure in order to attend Frank Montoya's wedding. Now they were due to leave on Sunday morning. Hence the scheduled get-together today.

"What about it?" Joanna asked.

"I may not make it," Butch said. "My editor sent me an e-mail early this morning. They want to have a telephone conference later on today so we can get the next book tour organized. If the call is over in time, I'll come. If not . . ."

"That sounds a little lame," Joanna said.

Butch grinned. "I know," he said. "But it's a good excuse. Besides, she's your mother."

Based on Jaime Carbajal's phone call, Mel and I had stayed up until the wee hours tracking down information on Paco Castro—no relation to Fidel and Raul, by the way. It didn't seem likely that a tip from a grieving relative would lead us straight to a killer. That hardly ever happens. But what our research did do was show us that Paco Castro had an extensive rap sheet dating back to juvenile days. If he was representative of the caliber of Marco and Marcella Andrade's friends, they had run with a pretty tough crowd.

The next morning, Mel and I filled our traveler's cups with java, got in our two separate vehicles, and headed across the water to our office in Bellevue's Eastgate neighborhood. It's a fifteen-mile commute that, under good traffic conditions, can take as little as twenty minutes. As I've mentioned before, during rush hour in Seattle, there are no good traffic conditions. That day the drive took over an hour door-to-door in wall-to-wall rain. Once inside the building, we settled into our tiny but nonetheless private offices. My job that morning was to go nosing around in the world of a now-deceased two-bit thug named Marco Andrade.

From the multiple offenses listed on Marco Andrade's rap sheet, everything from aggravated assault to attempted murder, I was mystified as to why he would have been transferred from a maximum security facility near Lancaster in southern California to a medium-security lockup called Wild Horse Mesa Prison near Redding. While doing time in Lancaster, Marco had been tagged with numerous infractions, including fighting and being noncooperative. If it had been up to me, I would have left him where he was instead of transferring him to something less severe.

Anyone who has ever tried to outwit a recalcitrant two-year-old will be happy to tell you, chapter and verse, why it's never a good idea to reward bad behavior.

Once again, however, I was grateful to be working for Ross Connors. When I'm initiating contact with folks in other jurisdictions, it always gives me a big leg up on the credibility ladder when I'm able to drop the name of Washington State Attorney General into the mix. If I need to go to the top, using his name makes it possible for me to take the express elevator, so to speak. It was a lot tougher back in the old days when I was a grunt working for Seattle PD.

In this instance, the top turned out to be a guy named Donald Willison, the warden of Wild Horse Mesa Prison. When his secretary put me through to him at ten past nine, Willison sounded surly and argumentative, but then again, if I had to spend every day and hour of my working life locked up inside an institution right along with a bunch of convicted criminals, maybe I'd be surly, too.

"Who are you?" he demanded. "And what do you want?"

I told him who I was and that I was calling about Marco Andrade.

Willison sighed. "Oh, crap," he said. "Him again? You and everybody else. I knew that mope was going to be trouble the minute they dropped him off in my sally port. And once I got a look at his paperwork, I was even more convinced. I could see right off that he was going to be a problem and had no business being here. Sure enough. As soon as he got in a pissing match with one of my guards, I started trying to send him back where he came from, but reversing transfers is a lot like trying to push a rope uphill."

That's the way it works in bureaucracies. It may be possible to undo whatever's been done, but you can count on it taking lots of time and extraordinary amounts of effort.

"And now that he's dead," Willison continued, "things will probably get worse. I expect that a whole army of grieving relatives will come crawling out of the woodwork in time to file a bunch of wrongful death lawsuits against me and the state of California. As a matter of fact, I've already heard from one. He called on the pretext of working a missing persons case on Andrade's wife, but I checked the paperwork. Surprise. That so-called detective also happens to be Andrade's brother-in-law. He said nobody had told his family that Marco was dead. God knows we tried. But it turns out Marco's wife—this detective's sister—seems to have gone to ground. If he can't find her, why the hell does he think we should be able to?"

"What happened to Marco?" I asked.

"I already told you. He's dead."

"I mean, what happened to his body?"

Willison sighed. "We buried him."

"On site?"

"Not exactly," Willison said. "We've got a little plot just outside the gate that's dedicated as a cemetery. When guys die in prison, it often happens that no one's willing to step up and take responsibility for the body or for final arrangements. We do it here, but we bury them outside the fence, not inside. I'm of the opinion that a life sentence shouldn't turn into more than that." He paused and then added, "But you still haven't explained why the Washington State Attorney General is interested in one of my dead inmates."

"We've been investigating a series of homicides up here in Washington. In the course of the last year and a half, we've had six women with known or suspected connections to prostitution who have been murdered and dumped. As of yesterday, Marco Andrade's wife, Marcella, was positively identified as one of our six."

"And you're wondering if what happened to Marco had anything to do with what happened to his wife."

"Exactly," I told him.

"Hang on just a minute," Willison said. "Let me get his file. I had it pulled after I heard from the alleged brother-in-law so I'd be able to know what I'm talking about."

I heard paper rustling somewhere in the background. I found it reassuring to know that paper files still exist somewhere in the world. I've met a few wardens in my time, and they're not often likable, but behind Willison's gruff delivery I glimpsed a guy who sounded a lot like me—like someone determined to do a tough job to the best of his ability and someone who doesn't need everything in life boiled down into bare-bones computerese.

"Here it is," he said at last. "Name is Marco Javier Andrade. Age thirty-four. Died as a result of homicidal violence at four forty-six P.M. on October 31 of last year. He was doing five to ten for drug dealing and for attempted homicide. What else do you want to know?"

It interested me to hear that Marco Andrade had been murdered within two weeks of the time his wife had disappeared from her new home in Federal Way. That seemed like more than a mere coincidence.

"Halloween," I said. "Not my idea of trick or treat. Do you know who killed him or why?"

"There's an ongoing investigation into that incident," Willison said.

That's CYA-speak for "I don't know squat." I waited long enough. Finally Willison continued just to fill up the dead air.

"Andrade's throat was slit with what started out as a toothbrush with a handle that got turned into a deadly weapon. Twelve guys went into the showers; eleven came out. He bled out right there on the shower floor."

"What about surveillance cameras?"

Willison paused again. "Funny you should ask," he said with some reluctance. "It turns out we just happened to be having a facility-wide problem with our surveillance equipment at that very same time. We have no tape of what happened in that shower and no way of knowing who was responsible."

How convenient, I thought, but I could hear what he left unsaid. Willison didn't know who had murdered Marco Andrade, and he also didn't know who had sabotaged his surveillance equipment. It seemed to me, and most likely to Warden Willison as well, that Marco Andrade had attracted the unwelcome attention of someone with a lot of deadly horsepower.

"I suppose your investigators have talked to all the inmates who were in the shower at the time."

"My investigators haven't talked to anyone!" Willison retorted. Outrage was clearly audible in his voice. "Because of the surveillance camera screw-up, I was ordered to hand the investigation over to someone else—to the local guys, in this case—in order to avoid 'any further appearance of impropriety.' "

In other words, Willison had been disciplined for both the death of his inmate and the breach of the prison security cameras. That gave me an even better idea of why the warden wasn't happy to be discussing Marco Andrade.

"And none of the guys in the showers have come forward to volunteer any information?" I asked.

Willison hooted aloud at that one, but I don't think he thought it the least bit funny. "You could say that," he said. "And why would they? If there was even the slightest suspicion one of them had turned snitch, he'd probably be next on the hit list."

"What about the surveillance cameras? Did you ever find out what happened to them?"

"I've been told that someone from outside hacked into our supposedly 'super-secure' system and that the breach has been handled, that it's a done deal," Willison said. "Super-secure, my ass! Just for the record, I'm not at all sure this whole thing, Marco's death included, wasn't an inside job, but that's strictly between you and me. And just because I've been told something is a done deal doesn't mean it is a done deal."

In other words, Donald Willison does not play well with others, I thought. And he's still following up on this even though he's been told not to.

"Who's handling the homicide investigation then?" I asked.

"Shasta County Sheriff's Department," he said. "A homicide detective named Gerald Lowell. He seems to be a pretty squared-away, conscientious guy, but I don't think he's made a whole lot of progress. For one thing, he's on the outside and his potential eyewitnesses aren't. Not only that, Lowell is having to work against the grain inside his own department."

"Which is?"

"If one punk knocks off another one inside, it's considered good riddance. They're doing society a favor and saving the taxpayers' money. Who cares? Nobody gives a rat's ass!"

But I could tell by the way Donald Willison said it that he did give a rat's ass. He was mightily offended that one of his inmates had been murdered on his watch. That was a major blow to his own job record. Willison was further offended because the powers that be were tying his hands when it came to finding out who, why, and how.

"Who do you think did it?" I asked.

"I know who did it," he echoed. "The killer is either one of my inmates or one of my guards. There's no way to tell which, and I'm mad as hell about that. This is a medium-security facility. We're not supposed to be harboring killers. We're supposed to focus on rehab and on getting people ready to go back outside and live in the real world. Now I'm faced with the possibility that one of those eleven guys, two of whom are supposed to be released in the next several weeks, is a cold-blooded killer. For the time being, I've put a moratorium on releases for all of them, but I won't be able to keep them here forever. I need to know which one did it before I'm forced to let him back on the streets."

I noticed it was easier for him to focus his anger on the inmates than it was to consider the idea that one of his guards might have switched sides.

"How long was Marco Andrade at Wild Horse Mesa?" I asked.

"He arrived here on October first," Willison said. "Like I told you before, I knew the guy was trouble as soon as I saw his paperwork, even before he took a swing at one of my guards."

"And the guard in question?" I asked.

The question was a natural follow-up, and Willison answered it without hesitation. "He wasn't here. He was on medical leave from October 6 to November 15."

It wasn't difficult to look at all the machinations and see the same thing Warden Willison was seeing. Whoever was behind this had worked in the background, pulling strings and manipulating the system so that

Andrade could be shipped from a facility where he wasn't touchable to one where he was. In this case he was better off when he was doing hard time than when he was pressing the easy button. Maybe not better off, really, but safer.

"Were any of Andrade's known associates in that set of showers at the time?"

"No," Willison answered. "Not as far as I've been able to ascertain. What I do know is that this was a hit—as much as anything the Mafia does—and every bit as deadly."

I heard the frustration in his voice, and I didn't blame him for being pissed.

"I'll talk to Detective Lowell then," I said. "I assume he has all Andrade's personal effects?"

"Yes. He's got everything. By the way, what's your name again?"

"Beaumont," I said. "With the Washington State Attorney General's Special Homicide Investigation Team."

"Lowell can't very well talk to me about what's going on," Willison said. "But he might talk to you. If someone who works here is a crook, I want to know about it. Understand?"

I understood completely.

"You bet," I said. "If he comes up with a name, I'll be happy to pass it along."

By the time the morning briefing started, everyone had already heard about the situation with Jaime's sister, so it was a subdued group of officers who gathered in the conference room as Joanna brought them up-to-date. With Jaime out on bereavement leave, Joanna was gratified to see how eagerly her remaining officers were to pick up the slack. Ernie Carpenter volunteered to take charge of the DPS photo enhancement project while Debra Howell agreed to take the lead on the situation with Caring Friends.

The briefing was almost over and people were preparing to leave when they heard the sound of raised voices on the other side of the closed door. Hearing the disturbance, Ernie reached over and opened the door. From Joanna's place at the head of the table she saw a mountain of a man standing in front of Kristin's desk in the small lobby outside Joanna's private office.

"I don't care what she's doing!" he exclaimed. "I need to see Sheriff Brady now! Understand?"

With that, he slammed his fist into Kristin's desktop. There was enough force behind the blow that Kristin's crystal paperweight went skittering off the desk and onto the carpeted floor. Fortunately it didn't break. Every officer in the conference room was ready to leap to Kristin's defense, but Joanna beat them to it.

"Excuse me," she said calmly, walking up behind the man. "What seems to be the problem?"

The man-mountain spun around, whirling to face her. He was six-six if he was an inch, portly and slightly balding. He could have been in his late sixties or early seventies. He was also mad as hell.

"Problem?" he repeated. "You're damned right there's a problem. You people want to dig up my mother, and it's not gonna happen. Understand?"

"That would make you Mr. Fletcher?" Joanna asked. Walking toward him, Joanna paused long enough to retrieve the fallen paperweight and return it to Kristin's desk. In the meantime her officers emerged from the conference room one by one and edged into the room. Their very presence made it plain that they were all ready and willing to provide backup in case things got out of hand.

"Yes," the man said. "That's right. Robert Fletcher. Bobby."

"Very well, Bobby," Joanna said. "Let's go into my office and discuss this. And if you don't mind, I'd like to invite Detective Howell here to join us. She's the detective who is most familiar with the situation out at Caring Friends. Would you care for a cup of coffee?"

The man seemed surprised and disarmed by her unexpected kindness. "Yes," he said quietly. "Thank you. That would be very nice."

"How do you take it?"

"Black. Just black."

Joanna glanced in Kristin's direction. Taking a cue from her boss, Kristin marched off to get coffee. Meanwhile Joanna ushered Fletcher into her office and motioned him into one of the captain's chairs, where he very nearly didn't fit. Deb took a seat in the other one.

"I'm sorry for your loss," Joanna said.

To her surprise, Bobby's eyes filled with tears. Nodding, he used a meaty paw to wipe them away. "Thank you," he murmured.

"How long ago did you lose your mother?" Joanna asked.

"Six months," he said. "Two months shy of her ninety-second birthday. Of course, mentally she's been gone much longer than that. Alzheimer's, you know."

The office door opened. Kristin came in carrying a cup of coffee. With a wary look in Bobby's direction, she placed the cup on the desk and then hurried back out as if worried that the man's temper might flare up once more.

He took a sip of his coffee and cleared his throat. "Why?" he asked. "Why do you want to dig her up? Hasn't she suffered enough? Can't you leave well enough alone?"

"Some serious deficiencies have come to light at Caring Friends in the last few days," Joanna explained.

"I know," he said. "I heard about that. Philippa Brinson took off. I never met her. She must have arrived after Mother . . ."

The remainder of the sentence drifted away unfinished.

"There were problems with some of the other patients as well," Joanna continued. "Serious health issues. Helpless patients were left alone and unsupervised. We need to see that the people who did this accept responsibility for their actions."

"My sister started it, didn't she," Bobby declared. "Is Candace the one who came up with the bright idea that you should dig Mother up?"

Joanna glanced in Deb's direction. Her detective gave a small nod.

"Yes," Joanna said.

"It figures."

"So you and your sister aren't close?"

"You could say that," Bobby replied, crossing his arms over his chest.

Joanna waited to see if he would say anything more. Finally he did. "Look," Bobby said, "I admit it. I was stupid when I was young—really stupid. I ran with some bad people and did some really bad things. I ended up doing time. When I got out, I had nothing. I had no job, no education and nowhere to go, so I came home, carrying all my worldly possessions in a single duffel bag. My mother was still living in the little house on Black Knob where Candace and I grew up. She was living there on Social Security and her widow's pension from PD."

That meant Bobby's father had probably been a miner—underground or open-pit—for Phelps Dodge.

"I'll never forget the look on her face when she opened the door and saw me there. She just beamed. She was so happy to see me. She called me her baby. 'Come in, come in,' she said. 'I've been praying every day that you'd come home and here you are.' And so I stayed. Like I said, I didn't have much of an education and I wasn't really qualified to do anything other than make license plates—I was pretty good at that. But Mother helped me get odd jobs here and there—carrying out groceries at Safeway, cleaning people's yards and garages, detailing their cars. That way I was able to help with the bills, and we got along fine. For a while. For quite a while."

He paused for a moment, as if he wasn't ready to go on with the story. Finally he did. "Then Mother started slipping," he said. "At first it was just little things, like putting her purse in the freezer or not being able to remember whether or not she'd eaten lunch. Then, one night, I came home and found her in the living room cussing like a sailor and breaking up the furniture. That's when I knew I couldn't handle it any longer."

"And that's when you went looking for Caring Friends?"

Bobby shook his head. "Actually, no. Mother had already found it on her own. She had been looking for places to go if she ever needed to. She wanted something that wouldn't break the bank, a place she could pay for out of her Social Security and her pension. And Caring Friends was it. She was already signed up and on their wait-list. Once they had an opening, they admitted her."

"That was when?"

"Three years ago."

"Your mother's death certificate says she died of sepsis," Deb Howell said. "Your sister claims she had bedsores."

"How would Candace know anything about it? Was she there every day, holding Mother's hand and feeding her lunch? No, ma'am, she was not, but I was. I went there every single day and I didn't see any sores. This is all sour grapes, you know. That's why Candace is doing this. She wanted me to take Mother home. When Caring Friends started going downhill, Candace said keeping Mother there was just a waste of money, but Mother liked it. The place was familiar. Besides,

Candace doesn't understand what Alzheimer's does to people. You have to watch them like a hawk. They're like little kids, you know. They get into everything."

"So you knew the people running Caring Friends sometimes used restraints?"

"They had to," Bobby said with a shrug. "Otherwise the patients would just run away—like that Brinson woman did the other night."

"You said Caring Friends started going downhill," Deb put in quietly. "Does that mean it used to be better than it is now?"

"Lots better," Bobby said. "Then the new people took over. They started letting people go—you know, the workers—the aides and the cleaning ladies and the cooks. After they took over, the food wasn't as good as it was before and the place wasn't as clean. But Mother didn't want to leave. And since Mother had put me in charge of her affairs, there wasn't a thing Candace could do about it. Then when she found out about the house—"

"What about the house?" Joanna asked.

"Two days after mother died. We hadn't even had the funeral yet, and Candace sent a real estate lady over to see about listing the house. I told her to take a short hike. You see, Mother had set up something that gave me a lifetime . . ." He paused, searching for the word.

"A lifetime tenancy, maybe?" Joanna offered.

Bobby nodded. "Yes," he said. "That's it—a lifetime tenancy. It means I can live in the house until I die. Then it gets sold and the proceeds are divided up among the remaining heirs."

"And Candace thought this was a bad idea?" Joanna said.

Bobby half smiled. "I'll say," he said.

"Do you remember anything about your sister requesting an autopsy at the time?" Joanna asked.

Bobby shook his head. "Not a word. All she wanted was to get Mother buried as fast as humanly possible."

Joanna glanced at her watch. The Board of Supervisors meeting would be starting in a matter of minutes.

"I'm afraid I'm going to have to go soon, Mr. Fletcher," Joanna said. "I have another appointment."

The man lumbered to his feet. "You do understand, don't you?" he asked. "I just want my mother to be left in peace."

"I think I do," Joanna said.

He let himself out. "He's a lot different from what I expected," Debra said, once the door closed behind him.

"You mean he's a lot different from what his sister led you to believe."

Debra nodded.

"Do you have the sister's address?" Joanna asked.

"Sure," Deb said. "It's right here in my notebook."

"Read it to me." Joanna said, pulling her computer closer. "Let's see what Zillow has to say."

When Deb found the address and read it, Joanna typed it into a Web site. A few minutes later she nodded. "Interesting," she said. "Look at this. The home at that address is currently valued at $784,000." She did a few more clicks. "And here's the photo from Google Earth. Foothills location. Swimming pool. This lady has way more money than her poor brother does, but she's ready to sell the house out from under him."

"If she has enough money to live in a house like that, how come she claimed she couldn't afford to have an autopsy at the time of her mother's death?"

"Because she didn't really care that much back then," Joanna answered. "But now she's got a chance to get that autopsy on our nickel."

"But why?" Deb asked.

"My guess is that once Caring Friends hit the news, Candace saw a chance to make some money out of the deal. She's hoping we'll help her make a case for a wrongful death suit. And she probably figures she won't have to go to court—that just threatening to do so will be enough to get Alma DeLong to send some money Candace's way just to get her to shut up. And I'm guessing if we scratch Candace's surface, we won't have to go very deep to find a personal injury lawyer."

"No wonder Bobby Fletcher is pissed," Deb said. "I would be, too."

Joanna stood up and grabbed her purse from the credenza behind her. "Gotta run," she said. "I'm off to do my weekly song and dance with the Board of Supervisors."

As I put down the phone, Mel came into the room, sat down beside my desk, and crossed one shapely stocking-clad leg over the other.

"I just spoke to Marcella's brother, Mr. Carbajal. The family is eager to make funeral arrangements. He's planning on coming up later today to collect the remains. I told him to send us his flight time and number—that one or both of us would be glad to pick him up and drive him to Ellensburg."

"Picking his brain all the while."

Mel grinned. "Sure," she said.

We both know that it's often easier to elicit information in a casual setting than in a more formal one.

"Any luck locating Paco Castro?" I asked.

Mel shook her head. "None so far," she said.

Just then Brad Norton poked his head into my tiny office. "Is it safe to come in?" he asked. "No office hanky-panky, right?"

Being the only newlyweds on the S.H.I.T. squad leaves Mel and me open to a lot of good-natured teasing from our associates.

"None whatsoever," I said. "What's up?"

"I just had a call from Frances Dennison, the woman who's the registered owner of that abandoned 4--Runner. She said when her grandson brought it down to Tucson, it was a mess—full of trash and garbage. She said when they cleaned it out, she found a man's wallet. She didn't tell me about it when I first talked to her because she had put it away somewhere and wasn't sure she could find it again. Now that she has, she wanted to know if she should open it and tell me what's inside. I told her to leave it be, that opening it or handling it might destroy possible evidence. I also told her that I'd send someone by her place to pick it up and log it into evidence. Here's the address. She lives on East Helen Street in Tucson."

"Tucson?" Mel repeated. "How far is that from where your friend Joanna Brady is? Maybe she could go by and pick it up."

I could have gone into a whole song and dance about Joanna Brady being a colleague rather than a friend.

After all, I had already come clean with Mel about Joanna Brady. But then I remembered that old line "Methinks she doth protest too much." I certainly didn't want to make that mistake. Instead, I picked up the phone and dialed.

My spotty remembrance of Arizona geography told me that the state is a lot like Washington in that it's bigger than you think. And it's a lot farther from Tucson to Bisbee than it appears when you're looking at it in your handy *AAA Road Atlas.*

Joanna answered on the second ring. She sounded stressed and not the least bit happy to hear from me, which may have been because (a) she really was busy; or (b) she wasn't particularly interested in hearing from me ever again.

"Hey, Joanna," I said cheerfully. "We've got a situation here. We're hoping you can give us a hand."

"All right," she said after I explained what I needed. "I'm on my way to a meeting right now. I have a detective who's currently on his way to Tucson on another matter. His name is Ernie Carpenter. I'll have him give you a call."

Chapter 14

Joanna placed the call to Ernie while pulling into a parking place in the county government complex on Melody Lane. It was only after she got out of the car and was walking toward the building that she noticed Marliss Shackleford's RAV-4 parked three spots away from her Crown Victoria.

That in itself seemed odd. Marliss seldom attended "Board of Stupidvisors" meetings, as she sometimes playfully referred to them in her column. Had Joanna been more on her game, she might have sensed a trap, but she'd had a very complex past several days.

The meeting was already well under way when she stepped into the room and slipped into the last row of chairs reserved for heads of departments. Her arrival, however, didn't go unnoticed. The door had made a slight swishing sound as it closed. Several people looked up and glanced in her direction. Marliss, seated in the second row, gave her a smile and a tiny wave. The smile especially should have been ample warning, but it wasn't.

When the chairman announced it was time for new business, Peggy Whitehead surged to her feet and walked briskly over to the speaker's podium, unfolding a piece of paper as she stepped in front of the microphone.

"I'm here today to lodge an official complaint against Sheriff Joanna Brady," she announced, reading from a prepared text. "Her actions this past week and those of her officers have deliberately undermined my department as well as my ability to do my job. As head of the county health department I've been hired by this board to look out for the health and well-being of our citizenry. This is an important endeavor and a complicated one. Sheriff Brady seems to be under the impression that her job is the only one of any importance. As an elected county official she seems to be under the mistaken impression that she's won some kind of popularity contest, one that gives her the right to be rude and disrespectful to the rest of us.

"Two nights ago, at Caring Friends, a fully licensed Alzheimer's care facility in Palominas, her people, supervised by an inexperienced chief deputy, grievously overstepped their authority. Without consulting anyone other than Sheriff Brady—without consulting medical personnel or family members, I might add—they moved several frail and at-risk patients to other facilities. When the owner of the facility attempted to object to those precipitous actions, she was verbally attacked by Sheriff Brady and physically assaulted by several of Sheriff Brady's senior officers. They went so far as to jail her overnight.

"Caring Friends is a health-care facility and it falls in my area of responsibility. It may be that there are and were serious deficiencies at Caring Friends, but it's impossible for me or my people to do a proper investigation with Sheriff Brady and her officers running roughshod over the premises. I don't get in the way of how Sheriff Brady does her job, and I respectfully request that she stay away from mine.

"I am placing my words in the minutes of this meeting as a way of expressing my dismay about the manner in which this was handled and to officially serve notice to the board that I expect you to properly supervise Sheriff Brady and her officers in the future. Thank you."

Stunned to momentary silence, Joanna was about to stand up and respond to Peggy Whitehead's charges when Claire Newmark, the chairman of the board, unexpectedly came to Joanna's defense.

"It's my understanding that the sheriff's department was summoned to Caring Friends the other night on a missing persons call. Is that correct?"

Peggy had been about to sit down. Now she returned to the podium. "Yes," she said. "That's right. One of the patients had walked away from the facility."

"How did that happen?" Claire asked.

"I understand there was a staffing problem," Peggy answered.

"And was this patient found safely?"

"Yes, but—"

"As for those patients who were moved. Where were they taken?"

"Two of them were admitted to the hospital in Sierra Vista, one went to the Copper Queen Hospital in Bisbee, and one to Tucson, Tucson Medical Center, I believe."

"And did Sheriff Brady's deputies drag those unfortunate people out of their beds and force them into patrol cars in order to transport them?"

A titter of laughter went through the room. This wasn't going the way Peggy had intended, and she flushed angrily. "No," she said. "Of course not! They were transported in ambulances."

"Presumably ambulances accompanied by EMTs," Claire added drily. "Which means that there was some agreement on their part that the patients in question required further medical assistance. And isn't it true that what you refer to as a 'staffing problem' was actually a situation where the patients were left entirely on their own for a number of hours? And weren't the conditions found there something less than sanitary?"

"Yes, it was unstaffed," Peggy admitted. "But when the nurse on duty arrived and tried to intervene, she, too, was waylaid and manhandled by Sheriff Brady's overzealous deputies."

That nurse was drunk, Joanna wanted to say. But she didn't have to.

"Thank you, Ms. Whitehead," Claire Newmark said, dismissing her. "That will be all. Now, is there any other new business?"

A few minutes after getting off the phone with Joanna Brady, I was speaking to Detective Gerald Lowell with the Shasta County Sheriff's Department. When I identified myself, he didn't sound any happier to hear from me than Joanna Brady had been. My lack of popularity was almost enough to give me a complex.

"Warden Willison told me you'd be calling, but there's not much I can tell you. Marco Andrade's dead and so is my investigation."

"But—"

"I was ordered to back off," Lowell told me, "and I have."

"Who told you to back off?" I asked.

"My boss," Lowell said. "That's who. When he said drop it, I did."

"Does Warden Willison know you've dropped it?"

"For all I know, Willison may be part of the problem. So, no, I haven't told him, and I'd be much obliged if you didn't mention it either."

"Part of the problem—" I began.

"Look," Lowell interrupted. "This is evidently a much bigger deal than some worthless punk getting his on a shower-stall floor. At least that's what I was told by the people who took over."

"What people?" I asked.

Lowell sighed impatiently, as though I were a complete idiot. "How do you spell F-E-D-S?" he asked.

"You're saying the feds have taken over?"

"Yes, they have—lock, stock, and barrel."

"What about Marco Andrade's personal effects?"

"Gone;" Lowell said. "I already told you. They took everything I had. I was told this is all part of a much larger investigation into one of those new Mexican drug cartels. The DEA doesn't want any of us local guys getting in the way of something they've been working on for months."

"Did they give you any names?" I asked.

Lowell laughed outright at that. "You've got to be joking. They didn't tell me anything—not a single damned thing. They told me that the case operates on a need-to-know basis only. I must have come up short in that department because so far they've given me nothing. So what's your interest in all this? If the DEA finds out you're asking questions, my guess is that they'll send you your very own personal cease-and-desist order."

For the next few minutes I told Gerald Lowell how I had run across Marco Andrade while working a series of Washington State homicides. I was telling him about Marcella Andrade's murder when he interrupted me.

"Wait a minute," he said. "What's her name again?"

"Marcella," I said.

"And where did you say she was from?"

"A town called Federal Way," I told him.

"Just a sec," he said. "Hang on."

He was off the line for several long seconds. In my ear I heard what sounded like someone paging through pieces of paper. Eventually he picked up the receiver again.

"Here it is," he said triumphantly. "I thought Federal Way sounded familiar."

"What?" I asked.

"When the feds showed up here with a warrant, they went away with Marco Andrade's personal effects, the evidence we had gathered, including the murder book. They're planning to make a federal case of it, but they didn't bother taking my trusty everyday notebook. You say her name was Marcella?"

"Yes."

"In with Marco's personal effects was a note from Marcella telling him she had met someone else and that she wanted a divorce."

"Was there a return address?"

"There was no envelope," Lowell answered. "Right, here's what I was looking for. You might want to make a note of it. The address is in Federal Way." He read off a street address complete with a zip code.

"Whose address is that?" I asked. I knew for a fact that it wasn't anywhere near Silver Pines.

"Beats me," Lowell said. "But it was important enough that Marco Andrade had it tattooed on the inside of his left arm. The M.E. found it during the autopsy. It's a crude homemade job, just barely legible. My guess is that he did it himself. Before I got ordered off the job, I tracked it down through the reverse directory."

"And?"

"Turned out to be a Denny's restaurant. I spoke to the manager. He claimed he didn't know anybody there named Marcella Andrade."

Of course he didn't, I realized. Because Marcella Andrade had worked there under an assumed name.

"Boy howdy," Lowell said. "That would be a kick, wouldn't it?"

"What would be a kick?" I asked.

"If that big federal case turned out to be nothing more than a little old romantic triangle. Marco wouldn't give Marcella a divorce, so the boyfriend put out a hit."

I signed off the call. I thought Lowell was barking up a wrong tree. I had met Mason Waters, Marina Aguirre's grieving fiancé. He didn't seem like the type to put out a hit on anyone, most especially not a complicated in-prison hit. Besides, Marina hadn't let on to Mason Waters that she was still married. She had claimed to be dodging an ex-boyfriend, not a current husband.

Knowing these background details caused a lot of other things to start making sense. Marcella had stayed in touch with her soon-to-be-ex-husband by using her work address instead of her home address. Worried about being found, she hadn't told many people where she lived, including Mason. Once she disappeared, the poor guy had been reduced to hiring a private eye to find out where his missing fiancée had once lived.

It occurred to me that if Marcella's killer or killers had snatched her from her workplace, that would help explain why the man who had come to Tom Wojeck in search of Marcella's missing money had no idea where she lived, either. He might have uncovered the Silver Pines part, but he couldn't risk breaking into one trailer after the other until he finally hit on the right one.

The conversation with Lowell brought me up against another realization—one I didn't like. In all the busy hubbub—in finding out Marina's real name and notifying Marcella Andrade's family—I had forgotten all about Mason Waters. Down in Federal Way, Marcella had left behind one additional survivor, a not-quite-family member who had not yet been notified. My heart went out to the poor guy who still cherished the Seiko watch he had purchased as a Christmas gift for his missing fiancée. Somebody needed to go see him and let him know that the Christmas morning he had in mind was never going to come.

I picked up my car keys and headed for Mel's office. She was on the phone. When she saw me standing there waiting, she signed off. "That was Detective Carpenter on the phone," she said. "He went by that house in Tucson and picked up the wallet. The name on the driver's license is Tomas Eduardo Rivera. He lives on North Wright Avenue in Cle Elum. There was money in the wallet—five twenty-dollar bills and six ones. Carpenter said that tucked in among the ones and written in pencil on what appeared to be the corner of a paper napkin was the name Miguel, along with a phone number that listed a 360 prefix. There were also school pictures of two dark-haired boys. I told Carpenter that I'd see what I can do to track Rivera down, find out where he works, et cetera, as well as what his connection might be to Marina."

"Great," I told her. "In the meantime, someone needs to have a talk with Mason Waters and tell him what we've learned."

Mel doesn't like doing next-of-kin notifications any more than I do, and she was happy to pass the buck. "Good thinking," she said. "And since you're going to be so close to the airport, maybe you could stop by and pick up Jaime Carbajal. His plane's due in at two-thirty."

I glanced at my watch. It was just past noon. "It should work," I told her. She gave me the flight information and I headed out.

When Joanna arrived at Daisy's Café, she was surprised to find Daisy herself standing by the cash wrap. "Where's Junior?" Joanna asked.

Junior Dowdle was a middle-aged developmentally disabled man who had been abandoned by his caregivers and who had been taken in by Daisy Maxwell and her husband Moe. For several years now, Junior had been a constant presence at Daisy's—greeting arriving customers, handing out menus, and busing tables. In the past few months, Joanna had noticed that his smile wasn't as ready as it had once been and that he sometimes seemed confused.

Daisy's face clouded. "He's a little under the weather today," she said, leading Joanna to the booth where Eleanor was already seated. "He's at home with his dad."

"I'm sorry to miss him," Joanna said.

Daisy nodded. "Thank you," she said.

Joanna slid into the booth.

"At least you're here," Eleanor said. "I thought you were going to stand me up, too. George is working on his baby. Packing. Everything has to be in just the right place. I swear, sometimes I think he loves that RV of his more than he loves me. He wants to be under way at the crack of dawn Sunday morning."

George's "baby" was a hulking Newell motor home that they had bought used and would be traveling in on their jaunts back and forth between their two homes, one in Arizona and the other in Minnesota. Joanna was disappointed to learn that George wouldn't be there for lunch. She had wanted to talk to her stepfather about the situation concerning Inez Fletcher's possible autopsy and the poor woman's two feuding offspring.

"He had a great time at the party last night," Eleanor added. "Where's Butch? He's late, too. Still cleaning up after the bachelor party?"

"No," Joanna said. "The cleanup is pretty much done. His publisher scheduled a surprise conference call for sometime today. He didn't know if he'd be able to make it or not."

Eleanor clicked her tongue. "Men," she said disapprovingly. "You can't live with 'em and you can't live without 'em." But Joanna noticed Eleanor smiled when she said the words. From Joanna's perspective, it seemed as though the last year or so, since George had retired, her mother seemed truly happy for the first time in her life.

Now, peering across the top of her menu at Joanna's face, Eleanor's smile was suddenly replaced by a frown. "You look upset," she said. "Don't be. The two of us are perfectly capable of having lunch on our own."

It was Joanna's turn to smile. "It's not that," she said. "I just came from the Board of Supervisors meeting. Peggy Whitehead would like to have my head on a platter. Marliss was there. I'm sure you'll be able to read all about it in one of her upcoming columns."

The fact that Marliss Shackleford and her mother continued to be good friends was something that had bugged Joanna for years.

"The two of you are a lot alike," Eleanor said now. "Both of you are ambitious. Both of you are determined to make a mark in your hometown. Both of you have nontraditional jobs. I've never understood why you couldn't be friends, the same way you and Marianne Maculyea are friends."

Because Marianne doesn't come after me with knives drawn, Joanna thought as Daisy came to take their order. The daily special was two shredded beef tacos and a cheese enchilada. Joanna and Eleanor both ordered that.

"So how's the best man this morning?" Eleanor asked, changing the subject.

Eleanor had been more than disapproving when she had first heard Joanna would be standing up with Frank Montoya, but when it came to planning the details, Eleanor was also the one who had tracked down a suitable outfit—a gray silk ankle-length skirt topped by a matching boxy jacket studded with rhinestone buttons. The material was a close match to Frank's tux, and Joanna was relieved that she wouldn't have to walk down the aisle in a tuxedo.

"Fine," Joanna said.

"And you're going to Helene's this afternoon?" Eleanor asked.

"For a cut." Joanna nodded. "Right after lunch. It's the only time Helen could work me in." Helen Barco had added an *e* to her name in hopes of lending Helene's Salon of Hair and Beauty a little class. But Helen was still Helen.

"You might ask her if she could put a bit of a color rinse on your hair," Eleanor suggested. "You may not have noticed, but you have some gray showing these days."

As soon as she said the words, Joanna knew her real mother was back. This sounded more like the Eleanor Joanna had known and loved all her life.

"Sure, Mom," she said. "I'll see what can be done."

Even as Joanna said the words, she knew she would do no such thing. Yes, relations between Joanna Brady and Eleanor Lathrop Winfield had changed some. Things had improved but not that much. If Eleanor didn't like the fringe of gray that was showing up on her daughter's otherwise red head, too bad.

I'll wear that gray proudly, she thought ruefully to herself. Like a red and gray badge of courage.

I could have called ahead, but I didn't. Mason Waters deserved more than a phone call. Tracking him down in person to give him the information he dreaded was the right thing to do. At least, it was the right thing for me to do.

I was relieved when I drove up the cul-de-sac and saw both the Kenworth and Mason Waters's Honda parked out front. That meant he was home. I found him out in his carport. Armed with a DustBuster vacuum, he was cleaning the front floorboards of the little maroon sedan.

When I walked up beside the car, he straightened up, looked at me, and said, "This is going to be bad news."

I nodded.

His eyes filled with tears. "You'd better come inside," he said, quickly brushing them away.

I followed Mason into his house. By the time he lowered himself into the recliner, he seemed to be under control. "Tell me," he said.

So I did, explaining that the woman he had known as Marina Aguirre was actually Marcella Andrade. I didn't spare any of the details. Eventually they'd end up being media fodder. I thought he was better off hearing them from me in the privacy of his own living room. He listened to it all, sitting in stark silence with his big hands folded in his lap. When I finished, he shook his head.

"How do you know it's her?" he asked. "How can you be sure Marina and this Marcella are one and the same?"

"Marcella was found through dental records. But she was wearing a Timex watch at the time of her death—a Timex watch, an engagement ring, and a toe ring. I believe you bought the engagement ring for her."

He nodded. "From Fred Meyer Jewelers, here in the mall."

I reminded myself to check with the jeweler. They might be able to identify the stone as the one Mason had purchased.

"And you think this is all about the money?" Waters said. "Some drug dealer's money. But I never saw her using drugs, and if Marina had the kind of money you say she had, why was she busting her butt working at Denny's? That makes no sense."

"My guess would be that she was trying to keep a low profile and trying to distance herself from her former associates. Can you remember anything at all unusual in the days before she disappeared?" I asked. "Did she seem worried or on edge?"

Waters shook his head. "No more than usual," he said. "She always seemed to be looking over her shoulder, but that was because of her ex-boyfriend. What about him? I know she was scared of him. Terrified, even. One way or another, I'll bet he's behind what happened."

Even though I had explained that Marco and Marcella Andrade were husband and wife and that Marco was already dead by the time Marina disappeared, Waters still clung stubbornly to the lies Marina Aguirre had told him. In a way, what he was doing was every bit as understandable as Warden Willison not wanting to consider that one of his people might be behind the security breach that had concealed Marco Andrade's killer.

"As I said, Marco couldn't have done it, because he was already dead," I told him. "But I have reason to believe that the two of them had maintained some kind of contact while she was involved with you."

Mason Waters shook his head. "No," he said. "She didn't."

I could have told him about Marcella's note to Marco, the one saying she wanted a divorce. But at that point Mason's mind was made up, and I didn't try changing it.

"So what's going to happen to her now?" he asked woodenly. "To her body, I mean."

"Her brother, Jaime Carbajal, is due in on a plane from Tucson later this afternoon. I'm supposed to pick him up at the airport a little more than an hour from now. Once the M.E. in Ellensburg releases the remains, he'll be taking the body back to Bisbee for burial."

"Bisbee," Mason mused. "That sounds familiar. I think I drove through there years ago, hauling a load of equipment down to Douglas. Do you think her family would mind if I came to her funeral?"

"I doubt they'd mind," I said. "When I see her brother, I'll mention you to him. I think her family would be glad to know that she had someone like you in her life."

"And what about her son?" Waters asked. "Louis. What's going to happen to him?"

Marina had told him that much of the truth—that she had a son, but Waters had only heard the name spoken. He hadn't seen it written down. "It's L-U-I-S," I corrected. "From what I've been able to learn, he's staying with his aunt and uncle on a temporary basis."

Which will probably become permanent, I thought.

I stood to leave. "I can show myself out," I said. "I'm sorry to have brought such bad news."

Waters nodded. "It's all right," he said. "I guess I've been expecting it all along, and knowing is better than not knowing."

"Is there anyone you can call?" I asked. "Someone who could come stay with you."

"No, thank you," he said. "I'll be all right. I've been alone with it all these months. I can be alone with it now."

I left him sitting there brokenhearted, and made my way back outside. I had turned off my phone when I went inside to speak to him. When I turned it back on, there was a missed call from Mel. I called her right back. "Detective Caldwell and I have been tracking on Mr. Rivera. It turns out he didn't show up at work today. Lucy's afraid he may have skipped. She's got an unmarked car stationed outside the suspect's house in Cle Elum. Rivera's truck isn't there at the moment, so apparently he's not home. She asked me if I wanted to be in on a sit-down with the suspect's wife. I'm on my way there now. Care to join us?"

"Give me the address. Once I pick up Jaime Carbajal, we'll come there, too."

"Is dragging him along a good idea?" she asked.

"I can only do so many things at a time," I told her. "If I'm coming there, he'll be with me."

She read off the address, and I loaded it into my GPS.

"Anything else?"

"We tried tracking down Miguel—the guy whose phone number was found on a scrap of paper in Rivera's wallet. The number turned out to be a throw-away cell phone that's no longer in service, so that's a dead end."

"Oh, well," I said. "You can't win 'em all. See you when I get there."

With that I headed for the airport. I suppose I could have muscled my way past security and made arrangements to meet Marcella's brother at the gate. Instead, I stood in a clutch of limo drivers waiting at the foot of the arriving passenger escalator. Like them, I carried a handwritten sign with the word CARBAJAL printed on it. Unexpectedly, the plane landed several minutes early. Soon after the loudspeaker announced the flight's arrival, a young Hispanic man riding down the escalator noted the sign, caught my eye, and nodded.

I held out my hand in greeting. "Luggage?" I asked.

"No," he said, hefting a small athletic bag. "Carry-on only."

Jaime may have been traveling light as far as luggage was concerned, but from the look in his red-rimmed eyes and the set of his mouth, he seemed to be carrying the weight of the world on his shoulders.

"Let's go, then," I said.

"Where to?" he said. "Ellensburg?"

"No, a place called Cle Elum. My partner is on her way there to interview a possible suspect. I thought you'd like to ride along."

"Yes," he said. "Yes, I would."

On the drive across the mountains I brought Jaime Carbajal up to speed on everything Mel and I had learned about Marcella/Marina. I told him about how the wallet left in Marcella's abandoned vehicle had led us to the guy in Cle Elum. I told him about Mason Waters, his sister's grieving fiancé, and I let him in on everything I had learned from Warden Willison and Detective Lowell about Marco Andrade's death.

"So the California homicide investigator claims the feds shut down his investigation into Marco's murder?" he asked. "Why?"

"I have no idea. I'm guessing Detective Lowell didn't tell me because he didn't know. But the one detail he gave me, the address tattooed on Marco's arm, is what links Marcella with the woman who was passing herself off as Marina."

"And the money?" Jaime asked. "The money Marcella's son claimed she had?"

"As far as I know, it's gone," I told him.

"Figures," Jaime said.

He fell silent after that. A few minutes later, I noticed he had nodded off. I let him sleep. From the looks of him, he needed it.

In the course of an hour-long hair appointment, Joanna had three separate phone calls. She apologized to Helen each time, but she needed to take them.

The first call was from Butch, apologizing (fingers crossed, Joanna suspected) for his having missed lunch and verifying that she would be coming home before the wedding rehearsal so they could ride to the church and rehearsal dinner together.

The second call was from Ernie. He reported that he had dropped off the Action Trails security DVD at the Department of Public Safety crime lab in Tucson. "They'll get to it eventually," Ernie said, "but don't hold your breath for a fast turnaround. It doesn't sound like this is a big priority for them. It's our homicide, not theirs."

"And the wallet?" Joanna asked.

"I picked it up," Ernie said. "I brought it down and checked it into our evidence room, but I also did what you told me and called the information to that detective up in Washington. There was some money, a couple of credit cards, and a Washington State driver's license."

"Good," Joanna said. "Anything else?"

"Nope, that's it for me," Ernie said. "See you tomorrow, then. At the wedding."

The third call was from Debra Howell.

"You called that shot," Deb said. "The lawyer one. Candace showed up with her smarmy Tucson lawyer firmly in tow."

"What happened when you told her Bobby said no dice?"

"She hit the roof," Deb answered. "Went absolutely ballistic. She told me that, if she had to, she'd go to court and have him declared incompetent."

"Bobby is not incompetent!" Joanna exclaimed.

"Right," Debra said. "I agree. He's mad as hell, but who can blame him? That sister of his is poison, and I suspect their mother knew it, too. I went to the courthouse and checked the probate records. Long before she got sick, Inez Fletcher went to a lot of trouble to see to it that Bobby had a roof over his head and that his interests would be protected."

Behind Joanna, Helen Barco heaved an exaggerated sigh and pointed at her watch.

"Good work, Deb," Joanna said. "I've gotta go. Talk with you later."

The Lady in the Dash, as Mel likes to call our GPS, mangled the word Cle Elum when she told me to take the next exit, but the sound of her voice was enough to rouse Jaime Carbajal. Once he was awake, I called Mel.

"Okay," I said. "We're just now coming into town. What's the deal?"

"Detective Caldwell and I have been gathering what information we can. Tomas Rivera works out in the woods. Under ordinary circumstances, he'd be home by now. But we found out from his crew chief that he didn't show up at work today. For as long as we've had the name and address, Lucy has kept a deputy in an unmarked patrol car parked on the street to keep an eye on the house, so we're fairly certain that he hasn't come or gone from there. He has an old Toyota pickup registered in his name. We've got people on the lookout for that, too."

"Does he have family?" I asked.

"A wife and two young sons. They came home from school a little while ago and went inside."

"So what's the plan?"

"Lucy thinks we should meet up at their house. She'll ride with me. We'll park a couple of blocks away. You do the same. That way we won't have a collection of unfamiliar cars sitting out front to warn him away."

Following directions, we parked on a side street two blocks away from the address on Front Street; then Jaime and I walked to a small frame house that reminded me a lot of Ken Leggett's place in North Bend. This house was of the same vintage and in much the same shape. We met up with Mel and Detective Caldwell on the rickety front porch, which creaked ominously beneath our combined weight. Detective Caldwell's partner was nowhere in evidence. Once we had dispensed with introductions, Lucy knocked on the door frame. The door was opened by a dark-haired, dark-eyed little boy who couldn't have been more than eight or nine.

"I'm Detective Caldwell," Lucy said, holding up her badge. "Is your father here? Or your mother?"

He simply stared at her and didn't answer. Finally he turned back into the house, letting go with a volley of rapid-fire Spanish. I picked out something that sounded like police, but that was about it. From inside a woman said something back to him in equally quick Spanish. The boy started to close the door, but Jaime Carbajal stepped forward. In the very best door-to-door salesman tradition, he put the toe of his shoe inside the door and spoke softly to the boy in what sounded like fluent Spanish. When Jaime finished, there was another long pause. At last the door was wrenched open, revealing a dark-haired young woman who shoved the boy aside and then barred our way herself.

"What do you want?" she asked, speaking slowly in heavily accented English.

"We'd like to talk to you," Lucy began. "To ask you some questions."

The woman shook her head. "No comprendo," she said vehemently, even though her English, although hesitant, had been entirely understandable. She was young, probably somewhere in her early thirties. She wore a sweatshirt and a pair of threadbare jeans. Not fashionably threadbare—really threadbare. She looked haggard and frightened. There were dark circles under her eyes, and it looked as though she might have been crying.

Jaime glanced questioningly at Lucy, who nodded imperceptibly, giving him the go-ahead to join in. Jaime spoke to the woman in Spanish once again. I picked out something that sounded like *esposo.* My foreign language skills are pretty limited. My Spanish comes from what I've gleaned from perusing menus in Mexican food joints like Mama's. Even so, I believe the word *esposo* means husband.

Jaime said something else. For a moment I thought she was going to slam the door shut in our faces despite Jaime's still intervening toe. But she didn't. Instead, relenting, she stepped aside, held the door open, and beckoned us into the house.

We trooped into a tiny but immaculately clean living room. In one corner sat a still-warm wood-burning stove, which I suspected was the house's only source of heat. On the wall next to it, a gold-framed picture of the Virgin Mary hung over a small table where a glass-encased candle burned. Other than the table, the only furniture consisted of a small couch, no bigger than a love seat, a single cushioned chair, and a hulking television set that looked as though it was a refugee from the eighties.

As we came into the room, a second boy, a year or so younger than the first one, hovered warily in the doorway of the next room. The woman barked an order, and the two kids scampered away, returning moments later with a mismatched pair of kitchen chairs. The woman took one of those and gestured the rest of us into the other seats while the boys sank down on the floor and huddled near their mother's knees. There was no disguising the anxious looks on their faces.

Under most circumstances, someone as close to the investigation as the victim's brother would never have been allowed into that kind of interview, but we needed a translator on the spot, and if it hadn't been for Jaime Carbajal's presence there on the front porch, I don't think we would have gotten anywhere near Lupe Rivera.

He mostly asked questions that were framed by Mel and Detective Caldwell, who had spent the afternoon gathering as much information as possible about Tomas Rivera. Once the suspect's wife answered, Jaime would translate what she said while both Mel and Lucy Caldwell took copious notes.

Where was her husband? Lupe didn't know. Was she aware he hadn't gone to work that day? Yes, she was.

Was he sick? That question produced a long thoughtful pause followed by a dubious maybe. Had she noticed anything unusual in her husband's behavior lately? Another maybe. It didn't surprise me that Mel and Lucy were deliberately beating around the bush, having Jaime Carbajal ask questions without giving away the bottom line—that Lupe's husband was now the prime suspect in a homicide investigation. Even so, each time Lupe answered she glanced at her children. It seemed to me that she was deciding how she should answer based on the fact that her sons were sitting there listening.

Jaime seemed to arrive at the same conclusion. He turned to me. "If you wouldn't mind taking the boys out of here . . ."

Before I could object, Mel and Lucy nodded in unison. I got the hint. It was more than a little embarrassing to be voted off homicide island by the woman of my dreams, but I set about doing what I'd been asked to do without complaint.

"I think I have a teddy bear out in the trunk of my car," I said, holding out my hand to the younger boy. His name was Tomas. He didn't look to be any older than six or seven. "Would you like to go see it?"

He nodded and scrambled to his feet.

"How about you?" I asked Alfonso.

"I'm too old for teddy bears," Alfonso declared, but he got to his feet and followed Tomas and me outside. It was a good thing Alfonso didn't want one, because the truth is, my vehicle was equipped with only one Teddy Bear Patrol teddy bear. Tomas's small face brightened as I handed it over. Then, with him cradling his bear, we walked back to the front porch and sat down on the top step.

We sat there in silence for a time while I struggled to find something reasonable to say.

Mel had passed me part of the paperwork. Tomas Rivera had a Social Security number, so he was most likely in the country legally. I doubted the same held true for his wife and sons. If they were illegal immigrants, having a collection of cops show up on their doorstep had to be scary for all concerned. From their point of view, the prospect of being busted by Immigration might seem catastrophic. But this was far more serious than that since we were investigating a homicide.

"How long have you lived here?" I asked.

Alfonso glared at me and shook his head, pretending he didn't understand when he was really refusing to answer. When Tomas started to, Alfonso elbowed him to shut up.

Another long period of silence passed. Then, because Tomas seemed the more approachable of the two, I addressed my next question to him. "What does your daddy do?" I asked.

"He works in the woods," Tomas answered with undisguised pride. "He cuts down big trees and saws them up so people can build houses."

Alfonso elbowed Tomas again. "Shut up," he said aloud.

I ignored him. So did Tomas.

"Your mom seemed real sad when we got here, like she'd been crying. How come?"

"Because of the picture," Tomas told me.

"What picture?"

He shrugged. "Just a picture," he said.

"Where is it?" I asked.

"In her pocket," he said.

I stood up. "Wait here," I told the boys. "I'll be right back."

Once inside, I spoke to Jaime. "Ask her about the picture."

"Picture?" he asked. "What picture?"

He turned back to Lupe and asked the question. Her face seemed to dissolve. For a long time she said nothing at all. Finally she reached into the pocket of her jeans. Slowly she removed a photo—a small wallet-size color photo, the kind of head shot that comes home each year with every school-age kid.

She held it out to me. I was about to reach for it, but Jaime Carbajal beat me to it. "Oh my God," he croaked, grabbing the picture out of her hand.

"It's Luis!" he exclaimed, staring at it. "That's my nephew. Where the hell did you get this?"

Where indeed!

Chapter 15

For several long seconds after Butch turned off the ignition, Joanna sat in the car staring up at the towering steeple of Saint Dominick's Catholic Church.

"What's wrong?" Butch asked.

"This is the first time I've been back at Saint Dom's since Deputy Sloan's funeral," she said. "I'm afraid that as soon as I step inside, that day will all come back to me." Even now, closing her eyes, she could see the uniformed police officers standing row on row and hear the bagpipes wailing. It was overwhelming.

"This is a wedding rehearsal," Butch reminded her. "You've got to let that other stuff go. Put it out of your mind."

Nodding, Joanna knew he was right, but it was easier said than done. Butch came around to the passenger side of the car and lifted Dennis out of his car seat. Then he opened Joanna's door and held out his free hand. "Come on," he said. "Let's go."

Just inside the double doors, Joanna was assailed by the screaming voices of two children. It turned out that the flower girl and the ring bearer, four-year-old fraternal twins, were in the throes of a total meltdown. The bride and the children's mother were ineffectively trying to broker a peace agreement between the two warring children. Finally Father Rowan, the rector of Saint Dominick's, stepped into the fray. With a calming word or two, he somehow put a stop to the battle.

The priest then turned to Joanna, smiled, and held out his hand. "How good to see you again, Sheriff Brady," he said. "You know what they say. If the dress rehearsal is a disaster, opening night should be great." He turned his attention to Dennis. "Is this your little boy?" he added. "With that red hair he clearly takes after his mother."

Just as the priest had somehow managed to settle the hash between the two battling four-year-olds, his kind words and unexcited manner calmed Joanna as well.

"And where's your lovely daughter this evening?" Father Rowan asked.

"Staying overnight with a friend," Butch said. "Somehow coming to a wedding rehearsal and dinner just didn't do it for her."

"No," the priest said with a smile. "I don't suppose it would."

Once the rehearsal started in earnest, Father Rowan walked the wedding party through their paces twice for good measure. The first time the recalcitrant flower girl was determined to go stand with her ring-bearer brother after her trip down the aisle and had to be convinced that her place was on the bride's side of the ceremony. The second time she raced down the aisle at a dead run and had to start over at a more decorous pace. Dennis, seeing that the other kids seemed to be allowed free rein at the front of the church, wanted desperately to join them. Besides, since his mother was standing right there in plain sight, why shouldn't he be up there, too?

It turned out that the ongoing uproar over the kids was good for Joanna's nerves, reminding her that this occasion was all about beginnings rather than endings. It helped immeasurably that Frank Montoya was nervous, too.

The rehearsal dinner was held in a private room at the clubhouse for Rob Roy Links, a golf club out near Palominas. They were driving there with Butch at the wheel when Joanna's phone rang. The caller was Jaime Carbajal.

"We have a suspect," he said.

"Who?"

"Tomas Rivera, the guy whose driver's license was left in Marcella's vehicle."

"Do they have him in custody?" Joanna asked.

"No, not yet, but at least we know who he is. His wife found Luis's school photo from last year hidden in her husband's underwear drawer. When she saw the picture, she thought her husband had been fooling around behind her back and that Luis was her husband's son with some other woman. I was able to tell her that wasn't true. Turns out he was doing a lot worse than screwing around."

"Does his wife know what he's done?"

"Not yet. The detectives running the interview were cagey about that. They didn't let on why we were there."

"Does that mean you were there, too?" Joanna asked. "For the interview? I thought you were just going to the morgue to make arrangements to bring Marcella's body home."

"It's a long story," Jaime said. "I happened to be there at the time and was able to help out. They needed someone to translate, and I was the only one who spoke Spanish. While we were just asking general questions, it didn't matter that much, but once we saw the picture, Detective Caldwell terminated my involvement. She took Lupe Rivera to her office and has an official translator helping with the next part of the interview. Beaumont dropped me off at the hotel."

"Has anyone been able to figure out Rivera's connection to Marcella?" Joanna asked.

"Not so far," Jaime said. "Once they take him into custody, I'm sure someone will ask. For right now, though, it looks like he may have taken off and left his wife and kids to manage on their own, which isn't going to be easy. The way I read the situation, he has a green card. She doesn't. Neither do the kids."

"How are you doing?" Joanna asked. "You sound tired."

"I am tired," Jaime admitted. "At this point, I'm not sure why I bothered coming. Delcia was on the phone with the M.E. while I was still on the plane. She helped my mother order a casket through Costco.com. They'll deliver it to the M.E.'s office here in Ellensburg sometime on Monday. They'll release the remains to me at that time and give me the necessary paperwork so I can fly home with the casket Monday evening. I've hired a hearse from a funeral home here to get the casket and me to the airport in Seattle. Norm Higgins from the funeral home in Bisbee will send a hearse to Tucson to meet the plane. He's cleared the funeral-home chapel schedule on Tuesday, so we can hold the service at our convenience. Since it's going to be private—family only and officiated by Father Rowan—we can be pretty flexible about timing."

It seemed to Joanna that Norm Higgins of Higgins and Sons Funeral Chapel wouldn't be thrilled to hear that a casket was coming his way from Costco.com. She herself never would have thought of ordering one online.

"Good," she said.

"And Delcia has spoken to the *Bisbee Bee*," Jaime continued. "Someone from there called to see if we would be posting a paid obituary. She told them to forget it—that the family doesn't want an obituary, paid or not. As you can well imagine, my parents don't want a lot of publicity about this. Thankfully, though, we don't have to worry about someone coming after Luis looking for the money Marcella and Marco stole. According to Beaumont, it's been returned."

"It has?"

"That's what he said. Someone came around to see Marcella's landlord and asked about it. The landlord went to Marcella's place, found the money where she'd hidden it, and gave it back to whoever came looking for it."

"That's a relief," Joanna said.

"I'll say. Beaumont also said that once Marcella got to Washington it seemed like she was trying to get herself straightened out. She was working at a regular job for the first time in her life—waiting tables in a restaurant—and staying out of trouble. She had asked Marco for a divorce so she could marry a new boyfriend—a nice one. According to Beaumont, the guy is a truck driver who had even given Marcella an engagement ring. He's hoping we'll let him come to her funeral."

"Will you?" Joanna asked.

"I don't know," Jaime said. "The idea that Marcella would ever hook up with someone decent sounds far-fetched, but Beaumont gave me his name and number. I thought I'd give the guy a call and check him out."

By then Butch had parked the car in the Rob Roy Links lot and had been waiting patiently for Joanna to finish the call. Meanwhile, most of the wedding party had walked into the restaurant. Finally Butch gestured at his watch. "We need to go in," he mouthed.

"I have to go," Joanna told Jaime. She didn't say she was going to the rehearsal dinner. The fact that Jaime was missing Frank Montoya's wedding was one detail that didn't bear repeating. "But if you need anything . . ." she added.

"Yes, boss," Jaime said. "I know who to call. Thanks."

People who aren't citizens of this country are at a distinct disadvantage in dealing with law enforcement.

They often come from places where cops have an inarguably upper hand. Lupe Rivera wasn't a suspect in Marcella's homicide and so far no one had mentioned that word in her presence. Her husband was the guy with the problem. Lupe would have been well within her rights to have refused to speak to us, but she didn't, mostly, I believe, because she was petrified.

While we were still at the house and still using Jaime Carbajal as her translator, Detective Caldwell managed to make it sound like going back to the sheriff's department in Ellensburg to continue the interview and record it was the most routine thing in the world.

Lupe made a small attempt at objection. "But what about the boys?" she asked.

"I'll look after them," Mel offered helpfully. "They can come with me. Maybe they'd like to go get something to eat."

It was another of those good cop/bad cop, divide-and-conquer routines that Mel Soames does so well, and in the end, that's how we did it. I drove Jaime Carbajal into Ellensburg and dropped him off at the Best Western. Then I drove back to the Log Jam Diner in Cle Elum where Mel had taken the two boys. Tomas was cheerfully mowing through a platter loaded with pancakes—the Log Jam is an all-day breakfast kind of place—while Alfonso sat staring out the window. His arms were folded stubbornly across his chest. He had refused Mel's offer of food. Even the glass of water in front of him remained untouched.

"Where's my mom?" he asked as I scooted into the booth next to Mel. "What did you do with her?"

"Your mother is fine," I said. "She's still with Detective Caldwell. She'll bring your mom back to your house as soon as they finish."

"You're lying," Alfonso insisted. "You won't bring her home. You're going to send us back to Mexico."

"I ordered a burger for you," Mel told me, then she turned to Alfonso. "You're wrong," she said. "We're not from Immigration. That's not our job."

"Why are you here, then?" Alfonso asked.

Mel took a long meditative bite of her hamburger and chewed it thoroughly before she swallowed and answered. "We're here because of your father. Has he seemed different lately?"

Done with talking, Alfonso shook his head and turned away. Tomas poured several more glugs of maple syrup onto a pancake that was already swimming in the stuff. Then he looked up at Mel.

"Papa has been mad," Tomas said. "At everybody."

Alfonso glowered at the younger boy and aimed an elbow in the direction of his little brother's rib cage, but Tomas neatly dodged the blow and went right on talking as though nothing had happened. "He's even mad at Mama," he added. "He hit her."

I've heard that kids learn new languages faster than older people can. Tomas's English was far better than his mother's, and better than his older brother's as well. Fueled by his sugar-high short stack, he seemed ready to tell all.

"He hit your mother?" Mel asked. "When did that happen?"

Tomas shrugged. "The other day. Sunday night, when they had a big fight. They thought we were asleep."

My burger came. It had obviously been sitting under a warming lamp for some time, and it wasn't anything to write home about. Not eating it gave me a chance to study Alfonso. He was biting his lip. I guessed Tomas wasn't the only one who knew about the fight.

"Why did your parents fight?" Mel asked.

"Mama was mad because Papa had been gone all weekend. She was yelling at him about that. That's when he hit her. He was drunk."

He said the words quietly and with no particular malice. That was simply how things were; how their lives were.

Then Mel sprang her trap. "Did you know your father lost his wallet?"

Alfonso shook his head.

"Just now?" Tomas asked.

"No," Mel said. "It happened a couple of months ago. Someone found it and returned it. We wanted to find him and tell him thank you. We think his name is Miguel."

Mel had mentioned the napkin fragment that had been found in Tomas Rivera's wallet—a torn napkin with the name "Miguel" written on it along with a no-longer-functioning cell-phone number. She brought it up innocently enough, but the reaction from both boys was nothing short of electric. Tomas dropped his fork into his plate, slopping a spatter of sticky syrup onto the table. Alfonso drew in his breath in a sharp gasp. The wary look that passed between them spoke volumes.

"Does your father have a friend named Miguel?" Mel asked.

Now neither boy answered aloud, so I stepped into the melee to give Mel a hand.

"Does he?" I asked.

After a long silence, the younger boy finally nodded his head. "We're not supposed to talk about him," Tomas muttered with a sideways glance in his brother's direction.

"Why not?" I asked. "Why aren't you supposed to talk about him?"

"Because . . ." Alfonso said. His eyes brimmed with sudden tears. I knew he was wavering, so I focused my attention totally on him.

"Well?" I persisted.

Even so, Tomas was the one who answered. "Papa told us never to say his name," the boy said. "He said Miguel is a bad man. That if we talk about him he might come here and kill us. Or else he'll tell Border Patrol about us and they'll send us back to Mexico."

"Have you met him?" I asked. "If you saw Miguel again, would you recognize him?"

"I would," Alfonso said. "He has a big scar on his face."

"When did you see him last?" I asked.

"This morning," Alfonso said. "Before we left for school. He came to the house looking for Papa. Mama told him he was too late, that Papa was already at work."

Tomas may have gone to work, I thought, but he didn't show up at work. Big difference.

"Did you hear what Miguel and your mother talked about?" I asked.

"He said that if Papa knew what was good for him, he'd keep his mouth shut."

"Keep his mouth shut about what?" Mel asked.

Alfonso shrugged. “I don’t know,” he said. “I don’t think Mama knew either, but after he left she was scared. And crying.”

And she was still crying this afternoon when we got there, I thought.

“Did you happen to notice what kind of a vehicle Miguel was driving?” Mel asked.

This time Tomas was the one who piped up. “One of those trucks like army guys drive.”

“A Hummer, you mean?” I asked.

Tomas nodded. “Except it wasn’t brown and tan,” he said. “It was yellow.”

“Washington plates?” I asked.

“Maybe,” Alfonso said. “I’m not sure.”

I signaled for the bill. “Time to go,” I said. “This is information Detective Caldwell needs to have ASAP.”

Joanna was polishing off the last of her crème brûlée and chatting with Frank Montoya’s mother when the waitress came up and whispered, “Sorry to interrupt, Sheriff Brady. There’s someone who would like to speak to you. His name is Norm Higgins, and he’s waiting in the bar.”

Shaking her head in exasperation, Joanna put down her napkin. She had thought Norm might object to

Jaime's using a store-bought coffin, but she was astonished that the man would track her down at a private function to hassle her about it. After all, the Carbajals were the ones making Marcella's funeral arrangements. Joanna had nothing to do with it. But then again, Higgins and Sons was a family-owned business. If their bread and butter was going away, Joanna supposed Norm had reason to be upset.

She walked into the bar and found Norm sitting in a booth at the back of the room. She didn't know him well, but she recognized him. He was nursing a beer and seemed engrossed in watching a televised basketball game.

"Hi, Norm," she said. "What seems to be the problem?"

"Thanks for stopping by, Sheriff Brady," he said. "Won't you have a seat?"

She didn't want to have a seat. Summoning her away from another function seemed incredibly rude. Not wanting to create a scene, however, she did as he asked and slipped onto the banquette across from him.

"Can I buy you a drink?" he asked.

"No, thanks," she said. "I'm due back in the other room."

That should have been enough of a hint, but Norm didn't take it. Instead he sampled another sip of beer.

"I knew your father," he said.

That was hardly surprising. In its copper-mining heyday, Bisbee's population had topped out at around sixteen thousand. Once the mining activity disappeared, so did half of the population. In a town of eight thousand people, everyone pretty well knew everyone else.

"Old D.H. was a good guy," Norm added. "Someone you could count on. I miss him."

It didn't seem likely that Norm had summoned Joanna into the bar to reminisce about her father.

"I miss him, too," she said.

"But you're a sheriff now, just like he was. DNA's odd that way," he added. "I studied to be a mortician and so did both my boys. Now it's my grandson. Third generation."

So? Joanna wanted to say, but she didn't. Norm was clearly working his way up to something. She needed to let him do it at his own speed.

"In this kind of a business climate, when you're trying to keep the wolf from the door—from the whole family's door—you sometimes do things you're not proud of," Norm said. "You do things you would never do under ordinary circumstances."

Joanna maintained her silence.

"Aren't you going to ask me what?" he asked.

"I don't need to," she said. "It's what you came here to tell me."

Norm nodded. "You've met Alma DeLong?"

For the first time Joanna understood that the conversation had nothing to do with Delcia's cut-rate arrangements for her sister-in-law's funeral.

"Yes," Joanna said noncommittally. "I've met her."

"Not a nice person."

"Not nice," Joanna agreed.

"Forceful, though," Norm said. "Very forceful, and a good saleswoman. Knows how to overcome objections."

"I wouldn't know about that," Joanna said.

"I do," Norm said mournfully. "That's how I got into this mess."

"What mess?"

"The group-sales agreement with Caring Friends. When clients check into her facility, they have a section of paperwork that deals with End of Life Arrangements. If the family doesn't have a personal preference, they can simply agree that Caring Friends will handle things, which means that, for a steep discount, we get the business."

"That may be goulish," Joanna said, "but it doesn't sound illegal."

"Have you ever met my grandson, Derek?" Norm asked.

"A few times," Joanna said. "Didn't he play basketball in high school?"

Norm nodded. "Won a basketball scholarship to ASU. He dropped out after his freshman year, though. Now he works in the family business. And that's why I'm here."

He reached into his shirt pocket, pulled out a camera memory card, and put it down on the table. He studied it in silence for a time before shoving it in Joanna's direction.

"What's this?" she asked.

"Last fall my boys . . ." He paused and then specified, "my sons and I went deep-sea fishing down at Guaymas."

He seemed to be wandering off on yet another tangent. Joanna wanted to grab him by the shirt, shake him, and say, "Get to the point!" Once again she kept still.

"We were gone for five days," Norm said. "Came home with a whole carload of red snapper. But it was the first time we left Derek on his own. Left him in charge."

"And?" Joanna prodded.

"While we were gone, he had a call from Caring Friends, from Alma DeLong. She said one of their clients—a woman named Faye Carter—had died. When Derek went to pick up the remains and bring them back to town, Ms. DeLong presented him with a signed death certificate, but she seemed quite anxious to have things handled in an expeditious fashion. She showed Derek paperwork that indicated it was the family's wish to have Faye cremated and that there was to be no service whatsoever. Ms. DeLong told him that she'd come pick up the cremains the next day. But when Derek brought the body back to the mortuary, this is what he found." Norm nodded grimly in the direction of the memory card.

"Derek took photos?" Joanna asked.

"They're pretty graphic," Norm said. "Of course, if you're accustomed to seeing autopsy photos . . ."

Joanna picked up the memory card and slipped it into her pocket.

"But Derek also knew Ms. DeLong was a good customer of ours. Since none of us was on hand for a consultation, he decided on his own to take the pictures, but he also did what she wanted him to do. Faye Carter was cremated the very next day. Her ashes were turned over to Caring Friends."

"And the photos?"

Norm shook his head. He seemed close to tears. "That's the bad part," Norm managed. "Derek gave them to me. I was shocked when I saw them. Appalled, even. With elderly bedridden patients, there are bound to be bedsores occasionally, but this was dreadful. Criminal."

"What did you do?" Joanna asked.

"I'm ashamed to say I did nothing," Norm said. "I took the photos from Derek. I told him I'd handle it and report it to the proper authorities, but I never did. I didn't want to rock the boat. Then I heard about Philippa Brinson. I knew Philippa Brinson from years ago, and I couldn't stand the thought that if she hadn't run away, Alma DeLong and her people might have done the same thing to her. It took a day or so for me to work up my courage to do something about it, but I did, and now you have them."

And if you had spoken up earlier, Inez Fletcher might not be dead right now, Joanna thought in sudden fury. But there was no need for her to say it aloud. Norm Higgins knew it all too well.

"Thanks for your help," Joanna said, getting to her feet. "We'll take it from here."

"Will this be enough to put her in jail?" Norm asked hopefully.

"I'm not so sure about jail," Joanna said. "That's best left up to a judge and jury, but if it's as bad as you say, it should be enough to shut her down."

"I hope so," Norm said plaintively.

So do I, Joanna thought.

I seem to remember that sometime in the not-too-distant past I hated computers. And there are times when I admire people like Warden Willison and Harry I. Ball, who prefer keeping records on paper; but from a law enforcement standpoint, computers are amazing. Databases are amazing. Search engines are amazing. Back at the sheriff's department, we went to the Records Department, where a clerk put in three separate fields in the Department of Licensing database—Hummer, yellow, and Miguel. Within seconds, out popped a name—Miguel Escalante Rios, with what turned out to be a waterfront address in Gig Harbor just up Highway 16 from Tacoma.

When we went looking for Mr. Rios's rap sheet, what we found was interesting. He had several convictions in his early twenties—grand theft auto, several drug-related offenses, and pimping, but those convictions were all nearly thirty years old. The most recent incident was a domestic-violence arrest three years ago, one in which charges were dropped when the wronged wife refused to take him to court. The mug shot from that arrest showed a handsome enough Hispanic man somewhere in his fifties. Only in profile could you see the vicious scar that ran down one side of his face where he was missing a good part of his right ear.

"So what's your guess?" Mel asked me, once we'd both had a chance to read through it. "Does it seem likely to you that this guy, just like Mama Rose, decided to straighten up and fly right?"

"No," I said. "I'm of the opinion that he just stopped getting caught."

The Records clerk, who had two sons of her own, happened to have an old GameBoy in the bottom drawer of her desk. She kept it around to use on those occasions when her kids dropped by to see her at work and she needed to keep them occupied. When we headed off to join Lupe Rivera, Detective Caldwell, and the translator in the interview room, Alfonso and Tomas were seated side by side in a worn armchair with their faces glued to the tiny screen.

Mel knocked on the door of the interview room, and Lucy Caldwell came out. "I hope you've got something for me," she said. "Either she knows nothing and she can't tell, or she knows plenty and she won't tell. Either way, I'm not making any progress."

"Let's try a reality check," I said. "How about we drop Mr. Rios's photo in front of her and see what happens?"

Lupe Rivera's reaction to seeing Miguel Rios's face was every bit as jarring as her sons' response to hearing the man's name. Her skin turned ashen; her jaw dropped. After a moment, she shook her head. "I've never seen him before," she said.

Not true!

"Look," I told her. "Up till now, you haven't been in any trouble. But if you start lying to us, you will be. You may not realize this, but if you don't tell the truth, we can put you in jail. Besides, we know you have seen this man before, just this morning, as a matter of fact. Alfonso says he came by the house today, looking for your husband. What did he want?"

As the translator delivered my words, Lupe buried her face in her hands and began to weep.

"Tell us," Mel urged. "We need to know what's going on. That's the only way we can help you."

Gradually, over the next hour or so, the story came out. Tomas had come to the country illegally and had arranged a green-card marriage. He had divorced the woman once he had his permanent residency, then had gone back down to Mexico and married his childhood sweetheart. Sometimes he came home and sometimes he sent money. Still not a citizen and wanting to have his family with him, he had made arrangements to smuggle Lupe and the boys into the country.

"And that's where Rios came in?" I asked.

Lupe nodded. "Not Miguel himself but people who work for him."

"Do these people have a name?"

"Tomas used the same people who brought him across the border years ago. Now it's more expensive. He had to save his money for a long time. Bringing us here cost him twenty thousand dollars in cash. We came across the border at a place called Agua Prieta and then rode north in a big Suburban with blacked-out windows. They dropped us off somewhere down around Tacoma. Tomas met us there and brought us here."

"When was this?" Lucy asked.

"Two years ago."

"And were you and your boys the only passengers on the trip north?"

"No. There were two men and some young girls—three of them—teenagers. They weren't much older than my boys, but they were traveling alone. They didn't have any money for food, so we shared what we could with them. On the second night, the driver asked one of the girls to have sex with him. She told him no. Later on I heard the driver and the two men joking about it. 'That's all right,' the driver said. 'She can tell me no now, but I'll have her later. After they get cleaned up, they'll smell a lot better.' "

I glanced at Mel and saw the tension in the muscles of her cheeks. She takes a very dim view of men who prey on young girls.

"In other words, the girls would be working off the price of their fares," she said. "As prostitutes."

Lupe nodded. "Sí," she said in a very small voice.

"Did the girls have any idea about what was in store for them?"

"No," Lupe said. "I don't think so."

"What did Miguel want when he came here this morning?"

"I know Tomas did things for Miguel sometimes, things he wouldn't talk about. This morning Miguel was very angry. He wanted to talk to Tomas, but my husband was already gone. Miguel said that I should give Tomas a message—that there were worse things than being dead."

"What do you think he meant by that?"

"I don't know."

"What happened then?"

"I called Tomas's boss at work, hoping to talk to him and let him know Miguel was looking for him, but my husband wasn't there. He hadn't shown up. And then I started thinking about what if Tomas was in some kind of trouble? What if he ran away and left us? That's when I went through his drawers and things. If he was supposed to keep his mouth shut, I thought maybe I might find something that would let me know what was wrong."

"And that's when you found the photo?" Mel asked.

Lupe nodded.

"The photo of the boy you thought might be your husband's child by another woman?"

Lupe didn't answer for a very long time. "If I tell you the truth now and if it's different from what I told you before, will you still put me in jail?"

"That depends," I said.

"The picture wasn't in Tomas's drawer," Lupe said. "It was in his Bible. Like he had been praying over it. And I thought . . ."

Tears spilled out of her eyes. She couldn't go on.

"You thought what?" I asked.

"I thought he was a . . ." She struggled for a moment before continuing. "A boy someone had used just like those men used those poor girls. And I thought Tomas knew about it and he couldn't stand it—that he was afraid the same thing could happen to Alfonso and Little Tomas. So when that other man told me the boy was his nephew and he was fine, I was very happy. But now that I know the boy's mother is dead, I'm afraid—afraid Tomas has done something awful. So afraid."

With good reason, I thought as she collapsed in tears once more. With very good reason.

Butch caught Joanna's eye as she returned to the table. "Is everything all right?" he asked.

She nodded. "Everything's fine," she said, even though everything wasn't fine. She found herself wondering how many times her own father and countless others like him had come home from work and told their families that everything was A-OK. She suspected it wasn't just a law enforcement subterfuge. Maybe it was a grown-up subterfuge. Maybe it was the kind of little white lie adults always tell the people they love.

Dennis was asleep within minutes of being belted into his car seat. On the way home, though, Joanna couldn't keep all the ugliness locked inside her, and so she told Butch all about the situation at Caring Friends because it was far too heavy a burden to bear alone. When they got home, Butch carried Dennis into his room and put him to bed while Joanna went into the office and inserted the memory card into her home computer.

Norm Higgins was right. The photos were appalling and as graphic as any autopsy photos Joanna had ever seen. Derek Higgins had used a ruler to document the seeping wounds on Faye Carter's back and buttocks. One of them was a full three and a half inches wide. Derek had also scanned a copy of the death certificate into the file. Joanna recognized the doctor's name. Dr. Clay Forrest was the same physician who had pronounced Inez Fletcher's death as due to natural causes. Sepsis. Again.

Scrolling through the photos, Joanna came face-to-face with the idea that now Inez Fletcher's remains would most likely need to be exhumed. The evidence in front of her was telling, but it wouldn't satisfy the requirements of a court of law. Derek's sworn statement wouldn't hold up to the demands of maintaining a chain of evidence. Only an official autopsy would do that.

A while later Butch came into her office and stood behind her, staring at the computer screen over her shoulder. Finally he heaved a sigh and walked away. By the time Joanna followed him into the bedroom, he was already in bed.

"I don't know how you do it," he said gruffly.

"Somebody has to," she said.

She undressed and then had to bound over Lady's prone sleeping body to make it into bed.

Butch reached over and wrapped his arms around her. "You'll probably have nightmares," he said. "I'll probably have nightmares."

It turned out Butch was wrong about Joanna having nightmares. She didn't. In actual fact, she put her head on her pillow, closed her eyes, drifted off immediately, and slept like a baby.

Lupe Rivera was still in the interview room when Mel and I went out into the lobby and placed a call to Ross Connors. Once he heard the background he was adamant. "Find 'em a hotel room," he said, "someplace with a restaurant. Put it on your company Amex. With this Rios character out gunning for them, you sure as hell can't take them home."

So that's what we did. It turned out that the same Best Western where Jaime Carbajal was staying was the only place that filled the bill as far as sleeping and eating were concerned. But it occurred to me that maybe that wasn't such a bad idea. At least Jaime would know what to do if things got rough.

By the time we took them to the hotel, there weren't any stores left open. "We'll come over tomorrow morning," Mel told Lupe. "We'll help you pack up clothing and so forth."

Or buy new, I thought. I found myself wondering how many times Lupe and her sons had actually worn clothing that wasn't secondhand.

Mel and I had driven over in separate cars, and we went back the same way. "See you at home," she said with a wave, and then set off out of the parking lot at something just under warp speed.

I took things a little slower, remembering the stenciled sign on Mason Waters's maroon Kenworth. DRIVE SAFE. ARRIVE ALIVE.

I was making my solitary way past North Bend when I remembered Ken Leggett, the heavy-equipment operator who had found Marcella Andrade's body months after her death. North Bend, Cle Elum, and Ellensburg are all little beads of towns strung on the necklace of I-90. Before today, we'd had only North Bend and Ellensburg. Now we had Cle Elum as well. On a whim, I turned off the freeway and made my way back to Ken Leggett's place with the Lady in the Dash telling me over and over in the firmest possible voice that I was "off route" and to "make a U-turn where possible."

No one answered the door at Ken Leggett's place, but that wasn't surprising. It was 10:00 P.M. on a Friday night. Without much worry about being wrong, I made my way to the Beaver Bar, and there he was—sloshed as can be and slouched in a corner booth.

As I came through the door, the bartender recognized me. "Don't worry," he said, nodding in Ken's direction. "I already cut him off. He's drinking straight coffee."

When I sat down opposite him, Ken gave me a bleary-eyed stare. "Who the hell are you?" he wanted to know. "And who said you can sit here? This booth is taken."

"I'm a cop, remember?" I said. "I'm the one who came to talk to you about that body you found in the woods."

He stiffened. "I don't wanna talk about it," he said.

"I don't blame you a bit," I said. "So let's talk about something else."

"What?"

"Who do you work for again?"

"Bowdin Timber. Why? What's it to you?"

My heart quickened as I heard the name. It was the same company that employed Tomas Rivera.

"Did you ever run into a guy by the name of Tomas Rivera?"

Ken squinted at me over the top of his coffee mug. "Sure," he said. "I know Tommy. I've known him for years. On the crew we all call him Tomba, Tomba, Tomba. Don't know why."

"Did you happen to see him today?" I asked.

"Do I look like somebody's attendance officer?" he said. "Maybe I did. Maybe I didn't."

"What does that mean?"

"I could have sworn I saw his red pickup parked outside my equipment shed as I was leaving, but I remember his crew chief complaining that he never showed up for work today."

If I could find Tomas's vehicle, maybe I could start to get a line on where he had gone.

"By your shed," I said eagerly. "Where's that? Can you tell me how to get there?"

"Hell, no," Ken said. "You'd be lost for years. Some elk hunter would find you dead in your car next winter. But I can show you."

He heaved himself out of the booth. "Come on," he said.

Ken staggered outside. There was no way I was letting him drive, but when I showed him my Mercedes, he hooted with laughter. "That thing'll high-center and we'll end up needing a tow."

In the end, we took his four-wheel-drive Toyota Tundra. I drove. He directed me down I-90 and off into the woods on roads that made no sense and where I began to believe he was right—that once we got in, we'd never get out. But eventually we rounded a corner and there, in front of us, was a massive metal shed with two sets of huge garage doors. And parked off to one side was a red Toyota pickup truck.

I suddenly felt nervous and wished I were wearing my Kevlar vest. I was there alone, except for Ken, but he was drunk and I knew he wouldn't be any help if push came to shove. I was going to tell him to stay put and let me go scout around. Before I had a chance, he swung open the door and half tumbled/half stumbled to the ground. Then he righted himself and started toward the shed, swearing under his breath.

I yelled at him to stop, but he ignored me. Instead, he set off in a staggering broken-field trot, lumbering toward the shed. I got out of the Tundra, too. Once I was on the ground, I heard what he had heard. Coming from inside the shed was the low-throated rumble of some kind of heavy equipment.

By the time I caught up with Ken, he had fumbled a set of keys out of his pocket and was opening a door that was set into the side wall of the shed. He reached inside and switched on a light. Then, after hitting a button that opened the garage doors, he came rolling back out of the shed coughing as a thick cloud of diesel smoke and carbon monoxide billowed behind him and rose skyward in a cloud through the open garage doors.

We waited for a few moments for the air to clear. When Leggett went back inside to turn off the bull-dozer, I followed behind. A man sat slumped at the wheel. I knew from the way he was sitting that Tomas Rivera was gone.

I pulled my cell phone out of my pocket. Amazed to see I had a signal, I called Mel.

"You'd better turn around at the next exit," I told her. "We have a problem."

Chapter 16

As best man, Joanna was due at the church for wedding photos at nine. By seven-thirty she knew she was having a bad hair day. After wetting her hair down completely and starting over, she managed to make the grade.

After the fuss Dennis had made during the rehearsal, she and Butch decided to run up the flag to see if Carol could keep him with her rather than having him mess up the ceremony. Jenny wouldn't be there, either, which meant it would just be Joanna and Butch. If kids did something to wreck the festivities, they would be someone else's kids and someone else's problem.

While getting dressed, Joanna had also decided that she would do nothing about the funeral-home photos until after the wedding. Most of the people who weren't on duty would be at the church.

People need to have a chance to enjoy themselves, she told herself as she sprayed her unruly hair into submission. Besides, since the victims in question had been dead for months, there was no point in putting in a lot of costly overtime to jump-start the investigations.

Butch whistled appreciatively when she finally emerged from the bedroom. "Most of the best men I've met aren't nearly this good-looking," he said.

They dropped Dennis off at Carol's place on the way. Once at the church, Joanna started inside for the formal wedding photo ordeal while Butch told her he would wait in the car until closer to the ceremony.

"You're just going to sit here?" she asked. "You didn't even bring along something to read."

"I'll be fine," he said. "I don't need anything to read. You'd be surprised how little time I have to just sit and think."

She made it through the photo session in good shape. The dove-gray silk ensemble her mother had found was a perfect complement for the tuxes worn by Frank and the ring bearer.

True to Father Rowan's words, the ceremony went off without a hitch. Well, mostly without a hitch. As the ring bearer, Joanna, and Frank filed into their places at the front of the church, Frank looked nervous and more than a little pale. Joanna worried that if Frank keeled over, she'd have a hard time holding him up. But then LuAnn Marcowitz, the bride, came walking down the aisle accompanied by both her son and daughter. The radiant smile she turned on Frank seemed to bolster him. He straightened his shoulders and a bit of color seeped back into his pallid cheeks.

When Father Rowan asked, "Who giveth away?" LuAnn's two kids gave a rousing "We do" and then sat down next to their grandmother, who, in true MOTB fashion, was weeping quietly in the second row. The ring bearer managed to drop the ring at precisely the wrong moment. When it rolled out of reach under the bride's dress, the ring bearer promptly scrambled under her skirt to retrieve it. He popped up again, holding it triumphantly in the air, and got a hearty round of applause from the assembled congregation. The bride's spoken vow of "I do" came through loud and clear. Frank's was a lot quieter.

When it was over and the newlyweds marched down the aisle to the joyous strains of the Wedding March, Joanna followed along behind, realizing as she went that she had made it through the entire ceremony without once thinking about Deputy Dan Sloan.

That was a good thing. It would have been very bad form for the best man to break down and cry, especially if she smeared her mascara.

By the time we left the suicide scene in the woods outside Cle Elum and made it back to Ellensburg, we were very thankful to find that the Best Western still had one room available, a room with two double beds. At home Mel and I sleep in a queen-size bed. Doubles don't fit us very well. When I woke up the next morning—at ten past eight—Mel was sound asleep in the other bed.

I went into the bathroom, showered with a tiny sliver of soap, and then got dressed in yesterday's underwear. My mother would not have been amused, and I couldn't help but wonder if that meant I was more or less likely to be in a car wreck that day.

By the time I came out of the bathroom, Mel was up. I know now what to expect when she hasn't had a chance to remove her makeup properly. So I gave her a clear shot at the bathroom and told her I was on my way to the restaurant. Fortunately, Detective Caldwell had volunteered to give Lupe and her children the bad news about Tomas Rivera's suicide. As I walked from our room to the restaurant through a chill and steady drizzle, I was grateful that I didn't have that next-of-kin sword hanging over my head.

Once inside the steamy restaurant, I looked around for Lupe and her kids. Fortunately, they were nowhere to be seen, but Jaime Carbajal was. Uninvited, I lowered myself onto the empty bench seat of his booth, motioning for the waitress to bring me coffee as I did so.

I told him what had happened after he left—how we had found Tomas dead, presumably of carbon monoxide poisoning, in a shed with a running bulldozer.

"If the place was locked, how did he get inside?" Jaime asked.

"Ken Leggett, the heavy-equipment operator, thinks maybe Tomas was hiding inside the building—maybe in the restroom—when Ken put the dozer away and locked up for the night. Once everyone left the job site, he hot-wired the dozer and that was it."

"Did he leave a note?"

"No."

I think Jaime was as disappointed as I was that Tomas Rivera had croaked out on us without telling us what we really needed to know. It's one thing to know who did something. I didn't have a doubt in the world that Tomas was our killer. What we didn't know was why he had done it or who was ultimately responsible.

"How does Miguel Rios fit into the picture?" Jaime asked.

"He started out as an ordinary street thug, but he's worked his way up to a waterfront home in a town called Gig Harbor. According to what Tomas told Lupe, he used to be hooked in with a group who smuggle people and goods across the border along with a lucrative side venture into prostitution."

A thoughtful look crossed Jaime's face. "Tell me about those smugglers," he said. "Did she mention any names?"

I hadn't listened to Lupe Rivera's entire second interview, but I had heard quite a bit of it. Removing my notebook from my pocket, I paged through the jumble of notes.

"Here it is," I said. "Cervantes."

Jaime Carbajal stiffened in his chair. "Cervantes?" he repeated.

I nodded. "When Lupe mentioned the name, I thought she was making a joke. I said, 'As in *Don Quixote*?' She said, 'No, definitely not *Don Quixote*.' "

"That fits!" Jaime exclaimed. He was already reaching for his cell phone.

"What do you mean, it fits?" I asked.

Holding the phone to his ear, he didn't answer. "Damn!" he said. "Went straight to voice mail." He glanced at his watch. "She's probably already gone to the wedding."

"What's going on?"

But Jaime was already dialing another number. When there was no answer on that one, either, he tried a third. "Ernie!" he exclaimed. "I'm glad I caught you. You're not going to believe it. We think the guy who murdered Marcella may have been hooked in with the Cervantes brothers from down in Cananea. I'm hoping you can call up the folks from the Border Task Force and see if they can tell us anything about what's going on with those guys at the moment." He paused, then added, "Sure, I understand. Have Tom give me a call. I don't have a computer with me, but he can fax whatever they send him to my hotel here in Ellensburg."

I waited until he finished the call. "How about putting me back in the loop?" I said. "Who are the Cervantes brothers?"

"Antonio and Jesus," he said. "Their father, Manuel, was a good man, a copper miner at Cananea, a mining town just south of the border in Sonora. He got dusted and died."

"Dusted?" I asked.

"Lung disease," Jaime told me. "Once he was gone, his two sons decided they didn't want the same thing to happen to them—and they were too lazy to work that hard. So they went into business for themselves—drug trafficking, running illegals across the border, you name it. As the bigger cartels started getting taken down, Antonio and Jesus moved in on their territories and in on their businesses, too. Prostitution, protection rackets, you name it."

The word "prostitution" made me think about Marcella Andrade and those other five murdered girls. She had been taken out because of the money. I wondered if maybe some of the other girls had objected when they'd found out the real price of admission for their ride across the border.

I said aloud to Jaime, "Sounds like the Mafia."

"It is the Mafia," he replied grimly. "Mafia Mexican style."

"But why would Miguel Rios of Gig Harbor, Washington, be dealing with people from—where was it again?"

"Cananea, Sonora," Jaime answered. "Maybe because they're all part of the global economy. Once I hear back from the Task Force, we may have an answer on that."

"We?" I asked. It seemed reasonable to point out to him that this was our case, not his.

"You," he corrected. "Obviously, if anything important turns up, I'll pass it along."

Mel came into the restaurant and made her way to the booth. Even in yesterday's clothes and with minimal makeup, she looked terrific.

"Morning, guys," she said, smiling at Jaime. "Mind if I join you?"

The reception was a catered affair in the basement of the Convention Center, a building that had once held the company store, Phelps Dodge Mercantile. The groceries, furniture, appliances, and dry goods were all gone now—had been for generations—but ghosts of the building's commercial past still lingered. There was a reasonably good restaurant along with several boutique shops on the main floor, while the basement was devoted to a single large meeting room.

Joanna and Butch walked down the worn terrazzo stairs and made their way through the reception line, greeting the smiling bride and groom and offering congratulations. A local and very enthusiastic mariachi band, Los Amigos, was playing in one corner of the room, next to a table stacked high with wedding presents. Emily Post may have decreed that gifts shouldn't be brought to wedding receptions, but Frank's and LuAnn's friends and relations hadn't gotten that memo.

Keeping the gifts and gift cards straight isn't my problem, Joanna thought gratefully. And neither are the kids.

True to form, the twins, still in their wedding-procession finery, were once again at each other's throats. Joanna knew that if she and Butch had brought

Denny along, he would have made a beeline for all the excitement and put his own toddler spin on the proceedings.

Along one wall was a buffet table laden with mountains of Mexican food provided by Chico Rodriguez of Chico's Taco Stand fame. The restaurant, in Bisbee's Don Luis neighborhood, was little more than a hole in the wall, but the spread here, pulled together by Chico and an assortment of his female relatives, was nothing less than splendid.

Painfully aware that her hairdo battle had left no time for breakfast, Joanna took her growling stomach and headed straight for the buffet table. She and Butch filled their plates with a delectable assortment of tacos, taquitos, enchiladas, and chips. After locating two seats together at the already crowded tables, Joanna looked after the plates and places while Butch went in search of punch.

Joanna was still waiting for him to return when Eleanor and George stopped in passing to say hello. George moved on to visit with someone else while Eleanor, eyeing Joanna's loaded plate, bent over and whispered in her ear.

"Try not to spill any salsa on that gray silk," she warned. "That stuff will never come out."

After imparting that bit of wisdom, Eleanor moved on.

"What did your mother want?" Butch asked when he returned a couple of minutes later.

"The usual," Joanna replied with a laugh. "She was giving me the benefit of her years of experience with silk suits."

For the next half hour or so, Joanna enjoyed herself immensely. It was fun to see her people—uniformed personnel and not; some active and some retired; sworn officers and not—enjoying themselves together. She knew that on this Saturday afternoon her department was functioning with only a skeleton crew, and she hoped nothing momentous would happen while they were all off having a good time.

A few minutes later, as the bride was gearing up to toss the bouquet, Joanna heard her cell phone's distinctive chirp. Joanna's outfit had no pockets and she wasn't carrying a purse. Butch pulled her phone out of his pocket and handed it over. Caller ID told her the number was unavailable.

"Hello," Joanna said.

Just then a cheer went up as Deb Howell, looking surprised, stood in the front row of onlookers holding LuAnn Montoya's bridal bouquet. The band swung into another number, and the accompanying din rendered Joanna's phone useless.

"Hang on a minute," Joanna said to her unidentified caller. "I can't hear a word. Let me go outside."

Pushing away from the table, she made her way through the crowd and up the stairs. Once she was on the ground floor, she spoke again.

"If this is Sheriff Brady, where the hell are you?" a man's voice asked. "In a bar somewhere?"

It wasn't a very pleasant way to start a conversation with a stranger. As far as Joanna was concerned, it was none of his business if she was at a wedding or raising hell in a local cantina.

"Who's calling, please," Joanna returned coldly.

"Agent in Charge Bruce Delahany," he replied brusquely. "What the hell do you people think you're doing down there? You're about to screw up fifteen months of work!"

In Joanna Brady's circle of acquaintance, Bruce Delahany of the Drug Enforcement Agency was a known but none-too-popular addition. Joanna's department had worked closely and successfully with several of Delahany's predecessors. In fact, until Delahany had taken charge, Joanna's department had hosted regular meetings of a DEA-sponsored coalition, the Border Task Force. Delahany preferred to have the meetings held closer to his own bailiwick, preferably at his offices in downtown Tucson.

Joanna had been forced to sit through any number of seminars and meetings where the square-jawed

Delahany, often with Arizona's newly elected governor at his side and with an absolute absence of humor, went on at tedious length (ATL, as Butch called it!) about the importance of interdepartmental cooperation. It wasn't lost on Joanna that Delahany talked the talk without ever walking the walk. He appeared to be far too focused on creating his own law enforcement fiefdom.

If Joanna's people had some kind of conflict brewing with the DEA, this was the first she'd heard anything about it.

"What seems to be the problem, Agent Delahany?" she asked.

"Problem? I'll tell you what the problem is," he shot back. "Your people are asking questions they shouldn't be asking. We're working on bringing down a major organization, one that has ties all over the West. We can't afford to have your ham-fisted people come barreling through and messing it up. For the time being, the Cervantes Cartel and everyone in it is absolutely off limits. Understand?"

Of course Joanna recognized the name. You couldn't be in law enforcement along the U.S./Mexican border and not know about Sonora's own home-grown drug cartel wunderkinder, Antonio and Jesus Cervantes. There was no danger of their ever crossing the U.S. border in person. Joanna understood that the two brothers lived in absolute luxury in specially built and well-fortified mansions next door to each other in an exclusive private compound south of Cananea. People who had dealings with the two came there to see them, and it was from that remote location that they ran a growing, murderous, and exceedingly profitable crime syndicate that had tentacles covering the entire western United States.

Right that minute, however, Joanna had no idea which of her officers might have expressed an interest in the Cervantes Cartel or why. She seemed to remember that Jaime Carbajal had mentioned the name in regard to his murdered sister. The exact details eluded her right then, and Joanna wasn't about to let Agent Delahany know about any of it, not until she understood the situation herself.

"We've been involved in this top-secret operation for months now," Delahany continued. "We've had assets in play, keeping an eye on things. And just when we're about to spring the trap on them . . ."

Joanna wondered if Delahany's outburst might have something to do with Ernie's checking into other ATV hangouts around the county. Was that what had gored Agent Delahany's ox?

"We're investigating a murder that took place at Action Trail Adventures near Bowie last weekend," she told him now. "If there happens to be some overlap between your investigation and ours, so be it."

"I don't believe you're hearing me," Delahany said, his voice rising. "I want you and your people to stand down. This is important. We need to bring these guys down all at once, not piecemeal, one dumb crook at a time."

"And I'm working on solving a homicide that happened inside my jurisdiction," Joanna said firmly. "And we're going to keep on working that homicide."

"I swear, if you mess up this operation . . ."

Joanna didn't wait long enough to hear the remainder of his threat. "This conversation is over, Agent Delahany. Have a nice day."

He was still blustering into the phone when she ended the call. When her phone chirped again a few seconds later, she didn't answer. Instead, she made her way back downstairs, where George had commandeered her seat and was talking with Butch.

When she said she needed to leave, Butch started to stand up. "Let's go then," he said.

"Stay here and have fun," she said. "Ernie or Deb can give me a ride."

George immediately grasped the transportation dilemma. "Give Joanna the car keys and let her drive herself," he said. "Ellie and I will be glad to take you home later."

Joanna plucked Ernie off the dance floor and Deb from the line of people waiting for punch. "Come on," she told them. "We have work to do."

One of the most unusual additions to Ross Connors's Special Homicide Investigation Team in recent years is a remarkable guy named Todd Hatcher, who originally hails from southern Arizona. In the course of a year, our department had made good use of Todd's geeky Ph.D. in forensic economics and his computer savvy.

In terms of background, I doubt anyone in his senior class at Benson High School would have voted him Most Likely to Succeed. Born the son of a convicted repeat bank robber and a waitress, Todd had grown up with a father who had ostensibly been imprisoned for life. He had been raised in a home where money was in short supply but library books were plentiful. He had turned into a serious student who had won a scholarship to the University of Arizona, where, with a combination of scholarships and summers spent working as a ranch hand, he had earned both a B.A. and master's degree in economics. Later on, a fellowship had brought him to the University of Washington to work on a Ph.D.

When Todd's father had developed early-onset Alzheimer's, the prison system had seen fit to turn him loose and make him his wife's problem rather than theirs. The strain of caring for her seriously ill husband until his death had been too much for Todd's mother. She had died within months of her husband. With that painful family history in his background, Todd had proposed doing his dissertation on the unfunded medical expenses caused by our country's aging and permanent prison population. The project had been nixed by his dissertation adviser, so Todd had completed the project on his own, turning out a modestly successful book in the process and turning my boss, Washington Attorney General Ross Connors, into a devoted fan who had brought Todd's talents to bear on any number of sticky projects.

Given Todd's considerable talents, I was pretty sure he'd be able to dig up plenty of information for us as well. Out in the car, I called Ross and asked him to put Todd on the case of Miguel Rios and the Cervantes brothers. Then I headed for Seattle.

Once again, because Mel had gone on ahead and because I was driving solo, my mind was running full speed ahead. Yes, people like Todd can use computers to put together amazing connections, but so can ordinary old-fashioned human beings. And just like the night before with North Bend and Ken Leggett, it was a road sign on the freeway that jarred me into making the connection out of the previous day's collection of word salad. It was the one for Highway 18, from I-90 to Tacoma.

Tacoma via Black Diamond and Mama Rose Brotsky. Mama Rose had known Marcella Carbajal Andrade as Marina Aguirre. Yesterday I had made time to let Mason Waters know the truth about what had happened to his missing fiancée. Now I needed to do Mama Rose the same unwelcome favor. Maybe learning about her protégée's death would be enough to cause her to remember some other helpful detail.

I immediately called Mel and popped the question, asking if she wanted to join me in a little side trip down to Black Diamond.

"Nope," she said without a moment's hesitation. "Not today. We worked until all hours last night. It's Saturday. I just got a reminder call from Gene Juarez about my three o'clock appointment for a much needed mani-pedi, and I'm not going to miss it. Too bad, buddy boy," she added. "This time you're on your own."

Joanna held a hurried strategy session with Deb and Ernie on the sidewalk outside the Convention Center, where she was surprised to learn that it had been a request for information from Jaime Carbajal rather than the ATV park inquiry that had set off Agent Delahany's temper tantrum.

"Jaime was looking for information regarding the Cervantes Cartel," Ernie said. "Since he was calling on his cell and since requests like that have to be sent through regular channels, I told Jaime I'd have Tom Hadlock look into it."

Joanna's temper flared. "There's a good reason reports are sent through regular channels," she said flatly. "Jaime's on leave right now. If that request has anything to do with his sister's homicide, he has no business sticking his nose in it."

"Sorry, boss," Ernie said. "He's my partner. He needed some help and I gave it to him."

Joanna shook her head in frustration. "I'm going home to change," she said. "We'll meet up at the office in half an hour and see where things stand."

On the way home Joanna called Tom Hadlock. "I understand Jaime Carbajal called in looking for some information on the Cervantes Cartel earlier this morning," she said. "What happened with that?"

"Nothing at all," Tom replied. "The duty officer for the DEA called back a little later and said they were having technical difficulties on their end—some kind of computer upgrade problem—and wouldn't be able to send anything out today."

What they really meant was wouldn't send, period, Joanna thought. Not wouldn't be able to send. Big difference. And that request for information was enough to send Agent in Charge Delahany into a spasm.

"I called Jaime to let him know I couldn't access the Cervantes records," Hadlock continued. "That's when he asked for a rap sheet on some guy named Miguel Rios. I found his records in the regular database and I faxed the information to Jaime's hotel room."

"How long ago?" Joanna asked.

"An hour or so, I suppose," Tom said. "Maybe longer."

"Do you have current address information on Rios?" Joanna asked.

"Sure," Tom said. "It's right here. He lives in a town in Washington called Gig Harbor."

Joanna felt her stomach knot. None of this was information Jaime Carbajal needed if all he was doing in Washington was retrieving his sister's remains.

"Do me another favor," Joanna said. "Look up the records on a guy named Juan Castro. I can't remember his middle name. Street name is Paco. If you can track him down, try to find out if he has any connections to the Cervantes organization."

"Done," Tom replied at once. "I've got Paco Castro's information right here in front of me, too. His full name is Juan Francisco Castro. Jaime had a file on him in his computer, and he wanted to pass the information along to the people investigating his sister's murder. He asked me to print it and fax that to him as well. I've still got the hard copy. Just a sec." The phone fell silent as Tom perused the file. "Yes, here it is," Tom said finally. "It says right here in Jaime's notes that Paco is suspected of being involved with the Cervantes Cartel, but so far nothing's been proved."

In other words, Jaime had been keeping a file on Paco that hadn't necessarily made it into the official records. Joanna had been holding her breath. Now she let it out.

"If Jaime calls in again, give him a message for me," she said vehemently. "Tell him he's to back off. That's a direct order!"

"Yes, ma'am," Tom Hadlock replied. "Will do."

The next number Joanna dialed was Jaime's. Not surprisingly, her call went straight to voice mail. "I'm unable to take your call right now."

"Detective Carbajal," Joanna said urgently. "Call me. Right away. You are on leave. You're to take no direct action, repeat N-O action, in regard to Marcella's homicide. She may be your sister, but it's not our jurisdiction and not our case. Understand?"

"Damn!" Joanna muttered as she ended the call. If Jaime wasn't answering his phone, he most likely wouldn't be picking up messages either.

By then she had arrived at High Lonesome Ranch. The dogs galloped in happy circles around Butch's Subaru, barking a joyous greeting but obviously puzzled that she wasn't getting out of the car. Instead, she redialed Tom Hadlock.

"Do you have the name of Jaime's hotel?"

"Yes," he answered. "And Jaime's room number. Do you want it?"

By the time Joanna called there, she was pretty sure what she would hear. "Mr. Carbajal isn't in at the moment," the desk clerk told her. "An Enterprise rental car was delivered here earlier this morning. He drove off in it a while ago."

Making up her mind, Joanna ended that call and then scrolled through her contact list until she found Bruce Delahany's number. Not surprisingly, he didn't answer, either, so she left him a message.

"Agent Delahany," she said. "Sheriff Brady here. This is a courtesy call to inform you that one of my officers may be about to pay a visit to a man named Miguel Rios in Washington State. It's my understanding that Rios may be connected in some way to the Cervantes Cartel. If you have any questions, you may want to give me a call."

After ending that call, she scrolled through her incoming calls list until she found the number she needed.

"Beau," she said when he answered, "I think we have a problem."

The early-morning drizzle had turned into a drenching downpour by the time I turned off the highway at Mama Rose's place. Even in the sodden weather, there was a crew of guys out planting what looked like nothing more than twigs in the muddy ground. Once again Regis came hurtling out of nowhere to greet me. I thought it interesting that, despite the fact that there was a whole army of workers out in the yard, the German shepherd decided I was the only real interloper. Once again, Tom Wojeck rescued me. He corralled the barking dog and then came back to see me, this time without a welcoming handshake.

"I was afraid you'd be back," he groused. "And I was right. Here you are. I guess it's a good thing I went ahead and told her."

"Told her what?" I asked.

"About Marina's money," he said. "About finding it and giving it back. We had a big fight about it, but it's settled now. I think she understands why I did it."

"And why was that?" I asked.

He gave me a scathing look. "You don't get it, do you?"

"Get what?" I asked.

"Self-preservation," he answered. "You may still be the guy you used to be, but I'm not. In the old days I wouldn't have thought twice about taking on a punk like the one who came here looking for Marina's money, but I can't do that anymore, Beau. I'm not that tough. My body isn't up to it. So that's what I did—I went along to get along. Giving him his money was the only thing I could do to protect Mama Rose and me, and that's what I did."

Unfortunately, I did understand because I'm in the same boat. I can't take punches the way I could back when I was a young Turk, and I can't deliver them the same way, either. And, unlike Tommy, I hadn't spent the last ten years or so of my life battling what would probably turn out to be a fatal disease. Right that minute, Tom Wojeck didn't look like he was at death's door, but he wasn't in the peak of health either.

"Why are you here?" he added. "What do you want?"

"Marina's dead," I told him. "We suspected as much when Mel and I came here earlier, but now we know for sure. We've made a positive identification. Her real name was Marcella Carbajal Andrade."

Tom sighed. "All right, then," he said. "Come on in. It'll break Mama Rose's heart, but she'll want to know."

This time we walked across the veranda and entered the house through the front door. We found Mama Rose Brotsky sitting on a sofa in the massive living room. She had been watching her rose-planting crew with avid interest, but when I walked into the room, her face hardened.

"It's about Marina," she said before I ever opened my mouth. "And it's bad news, isn't it?"

"Yes," I concurred. "I'm afraid it is."

Mama Rose wept as I related my news. I found it oddly comforting to realize that someone besides Marcella's immediate family mourned the young woman's passing. When I finished, Mama Rose dried her tears and squared her shoulders.

"How much money was that exactly?" she asked Tom.

"Right at forty-five thousand," he answered.

"We'll need to write a check for her son," Mama Rose said. "His name is Luis, right?" she asked me.

I nodded.

"No matter how Marina . . . Marcella . . . came by that money, it wasn't ours to give away. With her gone, it needs to go to the boy."

Nodding, Tom Wojeck left the room. He returned a short while later carrying a business-style checkbook. "What's his name again?" Tom asked.

"Luis," I told them. "Luis Andrade." I spelled it out for him.

"Go ahead and make it for a full fifty," Mama Rose said. "He'll need it."

When the check was written, Tom tore it out and handed it to Mama Rose. She examined it for a moment before passing it along to me.

"How old is Luis again?" Mama Rose asked.

"In high school," I said. "Fourteen or fifteen."

"If he wants to go on to college, that should help," she said.

"Yes, it should," I agreed. I folded the check and put it in my pocket. "But tell me this. According to her brother, Marcella didn't leave Arizona until sometime last summer. She couldn't have been here more than a few months before she died. How did you happen to meet her?"

"That's easy," Mama Rose said. "I'm the whole reason she came here in the first place. Working girls from all over the country know about me. When they're finally serious about getting off the streets and out of the business, Mama Rose Brotsky is often the only game in town—the only game in any town."

I would have asked more about that, but my phone rang just then. I was glad to hear Joanna Brady's voice until I heard what she had to say.

"What the hell do you mean, he's taken off from the hotel?" I demanded. "He doesn't have a car. Where would he go?"

"He rented a car," she said. "And I think he may be on his way to find someone named Miguel Rios who lives in a town called Gig Harbor."

"Crap," I said. "Why the hell would he pull a stupid stunt like that?"

But I already knew the answer. Jaime was on the trail of the man responsible for his sister's death, and he didn't give a damn about possible consequences. That's how young guys think—that they're invincible and that might makes right. With guys like Jaime, the painful lessons taught by the passing of time—the ones people like Tommy Wojeck and I have already learned—have yet to sink in.

"He isn't armed," I said. "He flew up with carry-on luggage only."

But after a moment's thought I knew that idea was bogus. The last time I saw Jaime Carbajal, he hadn't had a car, either. If he could get himself wheels, he could lay hands on a gun.

"Okay," I said. "I'm on my way. I'll need a description of his rental car along with license information."

"I don't have that right now," she told me. "But I'll have it by the time you call me back."

I called Mel as soon as I was out of the house. "You're going to have to cancel that mani-pedi after all," I said. "I need you to meet me in Gig Harbor."

"Why?"

"Because Jaime Carbajal has gone off the reservation," I said. "He's on the warpath and looking for Miguel Rios."

"He never should have been a part of that first interview," Mel said. "We both knew better. We should have put a stop to it."

That was true, of course. It was also too little too late.

Chapter 17

When Joanna changed clothes, her first wardrobe choice that early April afternoon would have been a pair of comfy jeans and a sweatshirt, but the way things seemed to be going, she settled instead for a freshly laundered uniform. On her way back out the door, she stopped in the office long enough to grab Derek Higgins's memory card out of her home computer.

She was backing her Crown Victoria out of the garage when Agent in Charge Bruce Delahany called her back.

"What the hell is going on down there?" he demanded. "I thought you told me a little while ago that you were working on a case over in Bowie. Now you say it's Washington State. Which is it?"

"Both," Joanna said. "The answer would be both."

"Who's going to see Rios? And why?"

"Jaime Carbajal is one of my homicide detectives. His sister, Marcella, was found murdered a little over a week ago. Jaime is under the impression that Rios may have been responsible for what happened."

Joanna's comment was followed by a long stark silence. It went on long enough that she began to wonder if she had lost the connection.

"Hello," she said. "Agent Delahany, are you there?"

"I'm here," Delahany said at last. "Are you telling me Marcella Andrade is dead?"

It wasn't the response Joanna had expected, and she didn't remember having mentioned Marcella's last name. That meant the agent in charge of the DEA's Tucson office was in on all this.

"When did it happen?" Delahany asked. "Where?"

"Somewhere outside Seattle," Joanna said. "In the mountains east of there. She had been dead for months with her body buried under the snow. They found her last week when the snow melted. The M.E. up there made the identification day before yesterday using computerized dental records."

"Damn," Delahany muttered. "I kept hoping like hell that she'd made it, but they got to her, too. Damn!"

"What do you mean, 'got to her, too'?" Joanna echoed. "And who is 'they'?"

"The cartel," Delahany said. "The Cervantes Cartel. Who do you think I meant? They apparently have people everywhere, including inside the California State prison system. That's why I pulled the task force out of the field and back into my office. I wanted to be able to control who had access to what we were doing and how. I didn't want people to know where we were getting our information."

"And where was that?" Joanna asked.

"Marco, of course," Delahany replied. "Who else? The intel he gave us was invaluable. We heard rumors that the cartel had wised up about his turning against them. Then we heard rumors that they were planning a hit on him down in Lancaster. That's why we moved him to Wild Horse Mesa."

"In hopes of taking him out of harm's way?"

"Yes," Delahany said. "You can see how well that worked out for us and for him. They still managed to get him. Marco had told us that he was worried about Marcella's safety, but by then she had already gone underground. Since we couldn't locate her, I didn't think they'd be able to find her, either."

Wrong again, Joanna thought. "I still find it difficult to believe that Marco Andrade was working with you."

"Well, he was," Delahany declared. "The information he gave us was just a starting point. We've been building on it and putting the pieces together for months now. We've been planning a major takedown. In the next few weeks we expect to hand down a series of indictments that will take key players out of the Cervantes organization all over the country. And that's what your detective—what's his name again?—may be putting at risk."

"Carbajal," Joanna said. "Jaime Carbajal."

"If he happens to spook one of them, he could spook them all. By the time we have our warrants in hand, the crooks will have disappeared."

"Is Miguel Rios part of all this?"

"Of course he's part of it," Delahany said impatiently. "Miguel Rios is a major player. From what we've been able to learn, he pretty much runs the cartel's prostitution interests in the Pacific Northwest. He also has the reputation of being the organization's chief enforcer. Never caught and never indicted—up till now."

Joanna thought about that. Wasn't that what Beau and his partner were investigating—a whole series of dead prostitutes in Washington State?

"What do you mean, enforcer?" she asked aloud. "I've heard that the Washington State Attorney

General's office is investigating a series of murders involving prostitutes. Might this Miguel Rios be involved in those?"

"If they were his girls and they stepped out of line? Absolutely," Delahany replied. "I'm telling you, Rios is a very dangerous guy and we're close to shutting him down, but we can't afford to have a Lone Ranger trying to take him out prematurely. Please, Sheriff Brady, talk to your detective. Ask him to back off. Beg him to back off. You can tell him from me that I swear we'll nail Rios and his pals eventually, but we need some time—a few more days. A week at the outside. But right now, today, we're not ready."

Delahany's words made sense, but Jaime Carbajal was already in motion. If he'd made up his mind to go after Rios, Joanna doubted there was anyone on the planet who could dissuade him.

"All right," she told Delahany at last. "I'm not making any promises, but I'll see what I can do. In the meantime, I need to make another call."

But Agent Delahany wasn't ready to hang up. "About Marcella," he said. "Where exactly is the body?"

"In Ellensburg, Washington," Joanna said. "In the morgue at the Kittitas County medical examiner's office. I believe the remains are due to be released on Monday."

"Will the family be bringing the body back to Arizona?" Delahany asked.

"Yes," Joanna answered. "That's why Jaime flew up there yesterday—to bring her home to Bisbee for burial. Why?"

"Regardless of what happens with the brother and Miguel Rios, please let the family know that my people and I deeply regret their loss. You can tell them from me that we'll help with bringing Marcella home. It's the least we can do."

Joanna was surprised to hear the sound of genuine regret in his voice.

"All right," she said. "I'll let them know."

"And one more thing," Delahany added. "About that homicide situation over in Bowie—the one your guys are working on?"

"The Lester Attwood case?" Joanna asked.

"Yes, that's the one," Delahany said. "Once the dust settles on all this other stuff, you can let your detectives know that I'm pretty sure we have some surveillance videos that will help you sort out what happened there."

"As in legible surveillance videos?" Joanna asked.

"Of course they're legible," Delahany declared. "Why wouldn't they be? It's my belief that it pays to buy the very best."

That's something the Savages have yet to learn, Joanna thought.

"All right," she said. "Detective Ernie Carpenter is my lead investigator on the Attwood case. I'll have him be in touch."

With that she ended the call.

I had awakened that morning in a strange bed in a Best Western in Ellensburg. If you had told me that a few hours later I'd be heading for Gig Harbor and chasing a fellow cop across the Tacoma Narrows Bridge, I would have said you were full of it.

By the way, I'm not exactly wild about the Tacoma Narrows Bridge, and my jaundiced opinion has nothing to do with the fact that it's now a toll bridge. My dislike goes all the way back to the time when I was a little kid growing up in Seattle. I was born only a few short years after the original Tacoma Narrows Bridge, otherwise known as Galloping Gertie, crashed into the drink. The bridge had been open for only a few months when it started swaying uncontrollably and then collapsed during a fierce windstorm during the winter of 1940. It took ten years to build a replacement. When that one opened in 1950, newsreels in theaters replayed the flapping demise of Galloping Gertie over and over. For me, seeing that film footage left a lasting impression.

These days and as someone who crosses Lake Washington's floating bridges on a daily basis, I'm well aware that they can sink, too—especially if you allow water to rush inside the hollow concrete pontoons, as a careless workman did on I-90 back in the early nineties. But at least if one of the floating bridges sinks, whoever happens to be on it at the time won't be hundreds of feet in the air when it goes down. If I had to choose, I'd rather swim than fall.

That's what I was thinking when my phone rang. I thought it would be Mel calling to let me know if she was ahead of me or behind me on the bridge. But the caller wasn't Mel.

"It's me again," Joanna Brady announced. "It turns out Marcella's husband, Marco Andrade, was a snitch. He was delivering the goods on some bad guys to the DEA."

"The Cervantes Cartel?" I asked. "Out of someplace in Mexico?"

"So you know about them?" Joanna asked.

"Only as much as Jaime Carbajal told me this morning."

"Anyway," Joanna continued, "it sounds like the cartel found out about Marco's participation and took him out. That probably explains why they came after Marcella, too."

"Jaime told me about the cartel," I said, "but I doubt he had a clue about Marco turning on them. Where did you hear that?"

"From Bruce Delahany, the DEA agent in charge in Tucson," she answered. "They've been putting together a massive takedown that's supposed to happen within the next few weeks. Unless . . ."

"Unless Jaime screws it up?" I asked.

"Exactly," Joanna replied. "Delahany is afraid that if Jaime spooks Rios prematurely, a lot of the other people involved will go to ground, but that's his concern. I'm a lot more worried about Jaime. I can't imagine him being pushed so far that he'd even think about going after Rios on his own."

"I can," I replied. "There are times when revenge sounds a whole lot better than whatever the justice system might get around to dishing out. Think about it. Jaime's sister is dead and, most likely, so is the triggerman, the guy who actually killed her. From Jaime's point of view it probably looks as though the guy who's ultimately responsible for his sister's death has a good chance of walking."

"But what about the other cases?" Joanna asked. "The ones you're working on, those other dead prostitutes? According to Delahany, Miguel Rios runs the cartel's prostitution interests in your part of the country. He's also supposedly the cartel's chief enforcer. So maybe if one of his girls doesn't toe the line, the next thing you know, she's gone."

I could see where this was going, and suddenly I felt like we were on to something. Maybe our dead prostitutes were actually Miguel Rios's dead prostitutes, and if they had been imported by the cartel—smuggled across the border and brought north, like the girls Lupe Rivera had told us about—no wonder no one in this country had ever bothered reporting them missing.

During my momentary lapse in attention, Joanna had gone right on talking. "With any kind of luck we'll be wrong," she was saying when I tuned back into the conversation. "You'll get there and Jaime won't be. But I did ask Tom Hadlock to check with the car rental agency. Jaime is driving a blue Chevy Cobalt with a GPS. Do you want the license number?"

"I can't write it down right now. If you could text it to me . . ." There was a buzz in my ear. "Sorry," I said. "Another call's coming in. Gotta go."

This time it was Mel on the phone. "I'm just coming up on the bridge."

"Good," I told her. "You're only a couple of minutes behind me."

"Wait for me at the Gig Harbor exit," she said. "I'll catch up with you there."

I stopped on the far side of the first gas station I saw. Then I got out, went around to the trunk, and dragged out my Kevlar vest. It was while I was putting it on that I noticed for the first time that it had stopped raining—completely. The sky was clearing. The sun was out. It had turned into a bright spring day.

A beautiful day, I thought. Too beautiful for someone to die.

Because if Jaime Carbajal had come to Gig Harbor bent on taking out Miguel Rios, it seemed likely to me that someone was bound to die. Maybe even me.

What if that one trip to Disneyland is all I'll ever have? I wondered. What if that's all Kayla remembers about me—that I took her to Disneyland once and got sick on the teacups?

Once inside the office, Joanna went straight to the bull pen, where she told Ernie he needed to be in touch with the folks from the DEA for information on the Lester Attwood homicide.

"They may try to put you off," she said, "but let them know that we're going to be dogging their heels until they give us what we need."

"What about me?" Deb asked as Ernie reached for his phone.

"For you I have another whole problem," Joanna said. "Take a look at what's on this and then we'll talk." She plucked the memory card out of her pocket and tossed it to her detective, who caught it in midair.

"Great catch, by the way," Joanna added. "Not just the memory card—the bridal bouquet, too."

Looking embarrassed, Deb shook her head. "Catching that bouquet was a freak accident," she said. "It was coming straight at me. If I hadn't caught it, it would have hit me full in the face. Trust me, I have zero intention of getting married again. I tried it once. I'm not very good at it."

Joanna disappeared into her office. The place was unnaturally quiet. There were no ringing telephones. No people talking. She wanted desperately to call Beau and find out what the hell was going on with Jaime, but she didn't dare interrupt. If he was caught up in a life-and-death situation, the last thing he needed was a ringing cell phone.

When Deb appeared in Joanna's doorway a few minutes later, her face was decidedly pale, and she was once again holding the memory card.

"These pictures are awful," she said. "Where did you get them?"

"From Norm Higgins," Joanna answered. "From the mortuary. They were taken by his grandson,

Derek. While Norm and his sons were out of town, Alma DeLong evidently showed up with another dead client and bullied him into cremating the remains in a hell of a hurry. Once you see the photos, it's no wonder she was in such a rush."

"What do we do now?" Deb asked.

"I want you to go see Bobby Fletcher," Joanna said. "Take your computer and that memory card with you so you can show Bobby the photos. It's one thing for him to put his foot down about exhuming his mother out of respect for her or even because he's at war with his bossy sister. But if Bobby realizes that exhuming his mother's body might prevent some other poor patient's suffering, I think he'll step up and give us the go-ahead."

"Dr. Machett isn't going to like it," Deb said.

"Too bad for Dr. Machett," Joanna answered. "That's why the county pays him the big bucks."

Mel pulled up and stopped. I waved at her, got back into the Mercedes and drove off with her tailing behind while I followed the confident turn-by-turn directions issued by the Lady in the Dash. Just as she told me my destination was one half mile ahead on the right, I caught sight of a bright blue Chevy Cobalt parked on the shoulder of the road overlooking a bluff.

It could have been a sightseer parked there to enjoy the view, but a quick glance at the text message on my phone told me otherwise. It was Jaime Carbajal's rental, all right, and it was empty.

"Bingo," I said aloud. It seemed likely that he had parked here and hiked the rest of the way down the hill to Miguel Rios's house.

"You are arriving at your destination," the Lady in the Dash announced.

Ignoring her, I drove another three hundred yards or so beyond the turnoff and pulled off onto a wide spot on the shoulder that was lined with mailboxes. That's where I parked and got out. Mel did the same. Once out of her car, she hurried up to me and handed me a windbreaker.

"Put this on over your vest," she said. "That way you won't look quite so much like a cop."

And a target, I thought.

I put on the jacket. Together we walked back toward the steep driveway that led down to Miguel Rios's waterfront home at the base of the bluff.

"You're sure you don't want me to come with you?" Mel asked.

We had already discussed the matter on the phone. The fact that there were no emergency vehicles in sight made me think that we might have arrived in time to avert disaster, but if it all went bad, it was important to have someone up at the top of the driveway to sound the alarm and call for reinforcements.

"I'm sure," I said. "Jaime's a cop."

"A cop who's bent on revenge," Mel said.

I couldn't disagree with that, and I didn't.

"Right," I said. "I get that. My job is to talk him out of it."

"What if talking doesn't work?"

"Then we drop back and punt."

It was a joke. Mel wasn't smiling. "Is your Bluetooth on?" she asked.

I nodded. I hate walking around with the damned thing in my ear. It makes me feel like I've turned into a pod person, but she was already dialing my number.

"I love you," she said into her phone. "But I'll be listening every step of the way. If anything goes wrong . . ."

I could hear her voice coming from two directions, through the phone and not through the phone. On my way by, I stepped close enough to give her a glancing kiss. If she had tried to talk me out of it right then, I might have relented, but she didn't. We both felt responsible for the part we had played in putting Jaime Carbajal in harm's way, and we both needed to extricate him.

"Be careful," she said.

"You, too," I told her.

With my heart pounding a warning tattoo in my chest, I started down a single-lane paved driveway that wound through a stand of windblown cedars. It was steeply pitched. Walking downhill hurt like hell. It felt like my knees were on fire.

Why does going down hurt so much more than going up? I wondered. But all the while I was walking, I was also listening—listening for the dreaded sound of a burst of gunfire or for a car passing by on the road above me. What I mostly heard, however, were the loud squawks of a massive flock of seagulls that wheeled back and forth in the air far overhead. Other than that, it was quiet—deathly quiet. Scarily quiet.

At last I emerged from the trees and could see Miguel Rios's place laid out below me. It was sprawled in a huge clearing at the base of the forested bluff. At first glance the house looked like a misplaced Mediterranean villa, complete with white stuccoed walls and a red tile roof. It was surrounded by an expanse of green lawn that ended in another steep drop-off where a series of wooden steps led down to a long dock that jutted out into the water. A big sailboat was moored next to the dock. Clearly Rios had done all right for himself. I also noted there was no sign of a yellow Hummer, although it might well have been parked behind one of the closed doors on the three-car garage.

"Do you see anyone?" Mel asked in my ear.

"Not yet," I told her.

But even as I said the words I spotted someone. On the far side of the yard, near the steps that led down to the dock, stood one of those new-style swing sets—not the kind of tire-on-a-rope affairs that were in vogue back when I was a kid. No, this one was built of cedar planks that formed a playhouse sort of fort. A slide led down from that. There were also a couple of swings and a teeter-totter. I could see the figure of a man resting his butt on one of the swings. Silhouetted against a bright blue sky, he was too far away to identify, but I was pretty sure it had to be Jaime Carbajal.

"I think I see him," I told Mel. "He's on a swing over by the dock."

"Maybe nobody's home," she said.

"Or maybe we're already too late," I replied.

Stepping closer, I waved at him. I could see that his carry-on bag lay open on the ground at his feet. I suspected he was armed, but I couldn't see a weapon, not from there.

"Hey, Jaime," I said. "How's it going?"

"Get out of here, Beaumont," he said. "This is none of your business."

I kept walking, moving closer all the time. "You're wrong," I said. "It is my business. I'm a homicide cop too, remember?"

"Tomas Rivera killed my sister." His voice was taut, a bowstring wound too tight. "Most likely he did it on Miguel Rios's orders, but do you think the law will ever hold him accountable? No way. I know how the system works. He's got money. He'll hire some hotshot attorney to get him off or else he'll negotiate a slap-on-the-wrist plea bargain. I'm here to make sure that doesn't happen. I'm going to get him to confess. Then I'm going to take him out."

"Right," I said sarcastically. "Sure you will. Let's see how the old eye-for-an-eye routine works for you. Maybe you'll end up wringing a confession out of the guy, but if you do it at gunpoint, without reading him his rights, you'll be winning the battle and losing the war. Nothing he says will stand up in court. He'll get off on a technicality."

"He won't get off because there won't be any technicality," Jaime said. "I'm a good shot."

I was close enough now that I could see the weapon. He was holding it at his side, pointed at the ground. I was glad it wasn't pointed at me. It looked like a .45 caliber Smith & Wesson. That's not the kind of handgun you use if you're intending to wing someone.

They call it a deadly weapon because that's what it is—deadly.

"I know you're doing this because of Marcella," I said. "But I'm here because there are five other victims, five victims who are all just as dead but whose names we don't know. I think there's a good chance that Miguel Rios killed them as well—that he's responsible for wrapping them in tarps and setting them on fire. But if you wreak your revenge on Rios for Marcella's death, you're taking away any hope of justice for those other families."

"I don't care about the other families," Jaime said. "I care about my family."

"Like hell you do," I told him. "You don't care about anyone but yourself. What you're planning right now is premeditated murder. What happens to Luis if you go through with this? His parents are gone. Who'll be left to take care of him? He'll be devastated."

Jaime wasn't persuaded. "He'll live," he said.

"And what about the people who didn't live?" I asked. "What about Marcella and Marco? Is your killing Miguel Rios going to bring them back?"

"Marco was scum," Jaime spat back. "He deserved to die."

"He didn't," I said. "He was working with the DEA."

"Marco was a snitch?" Jaime returned. "Don't make me laugh!"

"It's no joke. Sheriff Brady told me all about it a few minutes ago. Marco was spilling his guts, and the feds were listening."

"And they're claiming that's why he died?" Jaime scoffed. "I don't think so."

"But it's true," I said. "With Marco's help the feds have spent months putting together a program that should bring down the whole cartel. It's all supposed to happen in the next few weeks and it's going to work—at least it may work if you don't screw it up, that is. Because if you go through with this, Jaime, that's exactly what will happen. The Cervantes guys will know someone is closing in on them and everyone connected to the cartel will disappear like a puff of smoke. It'll take years to bring them back out into the open."

"You expect me to believe all this?"

"Call Sheriff Brady," I said. "Ask her."

"You're saying that's why they killed Marcella, too, because of Marco?"

"We think that's why, but we don't know for sure. Now give me the gun, Jaime. Let's get the hell out of here while there's still time. No one needs to know you've been here. No one needs to know what your intentions were. We just walk back up the hill, nice as you please, drive away, and let things take their course. The DEA says they're going to bring Rios in. Let's give them a chance to do just that."

I don't think Jaime heard a word I said.

"Miguel Rios had Tomas Rivera kill my sister," Jaime countered, going back to his original position. "For that he's going to die."

"Look," I explained. "The Cervantes Cartel is like a case of cancer. Miguel Rios is only one little tumor in a whole system of tumors. If you take him out, it's not going to make any difference, because the cancer has already spread—everywhere. With Marco's help, the feds have a plan and an opportunity to take out the whole mess. If you blow this and they don't succeed, then trust me, Jaime, you'll be responsible for a lot more dead people in lots more places, and every one of those unnecessary deaths will be your fault. And your sister and Marco Andrade will have died in vain."

"But Miguel Rios will be dead, too," Jaime insisted.

"And most likely so will you, you stupid bastard!" I growled at him. "Don't do this. Please don't do this."

Suddenly I was transported back in time and space. I was standing at the bottom of a waterfall trying to talk Anne Corley out of doing something stupid. And I hadn't been able to do it. Losing Anne had almost been the death of me. If I lost Jaime Carbajal, too . . .

The only thing left for me to do was beg. My voice cracked as I spoke. "Please, Jaime," I said again. "Please don't."

Finally I seemed to have his undivided attention and maybe I was getting through, but just then I heard Mel's voice shouting frantically in my ear.

"Yellow Hummer coming your way with a man and woman inside. I told them we're from Windermere Real Estate. That you heard he might be interested in selling the property and you came here in hopes of getting the listing."

But even though Mel was screaming at me, I didn't take my eyes off Jaime's face. I couldn't afford to.

"Someone's coming, Jaime," I said evenly. "Give me the gun. We can still walk away."

I don't know how long we stood staring at each other, me with my hand outstretched and him sitting casually on the seat of the swing. Behind me I could hear the low growl of the Hummer's engine as it wound down through the trees. Any moment it would burst into the open and it would all be over. It would be too late.

At last Jaime bent down, put the gun in the bag, and handed it over.

"All right," he said, "but if it turns out you're lying . . ."

The Hummer braked to a stop at the edge of the driveway. A man leaped out and came charging across the lawn. The woman stayed where she was.

"This is private property," the man yelled. "Who the hell do you think you are?"

"Sorry," I said. "Someone told me you were interested in selling."

"Whoever told you that was wrong. Now get the hell out of here!"

Jaime looked at him with unmistakable fury, then looked away. He had made his choice and he was abiding by it no matter what it cost him because Jaime Carbajal was a man of his word.

"Sure thing," I said to Rios, giving Jaime a slight shove in the direction of the driveway. "Sorry to bother you."

As we trudged back up the driveway, I may have been huffing like a steam engine, but to my astonishment, my knees didn't hurt.

Not at all.

By the time we reached the trees, Jaime Carbajal was sobbing. It could have been letdown or grief or even a little of both. At the top of the driveway, Mel was waiting in the Mercedes. She had the doors unlocked and the engine running.

"Get in," she urged. "Let's get out of here. We can come back for the other cars later."

And so Mel drove. Like a bat out of hell, of course. After fastening my seat belt, I handed Jaime my phone. "You'd better give Sheriff Brady a call," I said. "She's waiting to hear from you."

As Jaime took the phone, Mel glanced in my direction. "Are you all right?" she asked.

"I couldn't be better," I said. "The good guys won."

Chapter 18

I was surprised when Jaime Carbajal asked if I would serve as a pallbearer at Marcella's funeral, but given everything that had gone before, I could hardly turn the man down. Mel and I flew down to Tucson late Monday afternoon. Jaime had managed to catch an earlier flight. His sister's remains, transferred to a deep-blue casket, traveled in the cargo hold of that same aircraft.

Mel and I sucked it up and flew commercial. Going to Disneyland was one thing, but I couldn't see blowing thirty thousand bucks so we could go to the funeral on a private jet. Besides, once you've done that, flying first class seems downright affordable.

Mason Waters, looking miserable and uncomfortable in a rumpled sports jacket and a badly knotted tie, filed past us on his way to coach. He nodded in our direction, but he didn't say anything. I was glad Jaime had invited him to come, but I was sorry about it as well. He was grieving, and I couldn't help but wonder how he'd be received by Jaime's parents and the rest of Marcella's bereaved family.

I needn't have worried. Jaime had someone waiting at the airport to pick Waters up and drive him to Bisbee. Mel and I had made arrangements to rent a car, and we drove ourselves. The last time I had driven to Bisbee I had been in another rental, an underpowered Kia that barely made it over the mountain pass just outside of town. This time our new Caddy DTS had no such problem. We checked into the Copper Queen Hotel, where we were booked into the John Wayne Suite.

By the time we got to the funeral home on Tuesday afternoon, it seemed as though Mason had been taken into the bosom of the Carbajal family. He sat in the front row, between a woman who turned out to be Marcella's mother, Elena, and a scrawny teenaged boy who, I learned later, was Marcella's son, Luis. I wondered if Jaime had told Luis yet that he had a full-ride scholarship to the college of his choice.

When the priest spoke about Marcella as a troubled young woman who had been working to turn her life around, Mason broke down into shuddering sobs. It was Elena who put her arm around the man's heaving shoulders and gave him a comforting hug. That was when I noticed the watch on her wrist—a brand-new Seiko. It pleased me to know that Mason Waters had chosen to give Marcella's Christmas present watch to her mother.

I'm used to the well-manicured, perpetually green cemeteries we have in the Pacific Northwest. On that blustery April day, Bisbee's so-called Evergreen Cemetery was anything but green or well manicured. We gathered in a surprisingly small group of twenty or so as Marcella's Costco.com casket was lowered into the ground.

Mel and I were on our way back to the Caddy when someone called my name. I turned back to see Joanna Brady hurrying after us, followed by a man who, although he appeared to be somewhere in his early forties, was already completely bald.

"I couldn't let you get away without thanking you for what you did for Jaime," she said, taking my hand and pumping it. "What you both did," she added, turning to Mel. "I'm Sheriff Brady. This is my husband, Butch Dixon."

What might have been an awkward moment wasn't. As Mel and Butch chatted amiably, I turned my attention on Joanna. She seemed older than she had been back when we first met. There was that indefinable something in her eyes—a natural sadness that comes from having seen too much. And I detected a tiny patch of gray in her otherwise bright red hair.

"If you hadn't intervened . . ." Joanna continued.

"Look," I said. "For a while there, wanting to take revenge got the upper hand. What finally carried the day is that Jaime Carbajal is a good man. More than that, he's a good cop. If he had used that gun on Miguel Rios, Jaime would have been going against everything he believes in—everything we all believe in."

"Yes," Joanna said, looking up at me. "Sometimes walking away is the best thing you can do."

In the old days I would have taken that remark at face value and assumed she was still talking about Jaime Carbajal. But I'm smarter now, at least as far as women are concerned. She had changed the subject.

"And believe me," she added, "I really appreciate it."

Moments later, she took Butch's hand and the two of them did just that—they turned and walked away. I knew as they did so that whatever had happened or might have happened between Joanna Brady and J. P. Beaumont was over, completely over, once and for all. She had put it firmly in the past, and so had I.

"Come on, Mel," I said. "We've got a plane to catch. Let's go home."